Sonora Wind

By Florence Byham Weinberg

Maywood House
San Antonio, Texas

Table of Contents

List of Characters

Main Characters

*Fr. Ignaz (Ygnacio) Pfefferkorn, S.J., Missionary at Cucurpe and Opodepe
Beatriz Urrutia, Widow of Lieutenant Salinas
Fr. Wolfgang (Pío) Wegner, S.J., Assistant Missionary at Cuquiárachi
*Fr. Andreas (Andrés) Michel, S.J., Missionary at Ures
Nicolás Xavier Cuevas, Captain
Antonio Figueroa, Lieutenant Governor of Sonora (María Angélica, his deceased wife; Baltazar and Alicia, his children)
Fr. Luca Poncelli, S.J., Vice-Provincial
Mateo Salinas de los Herreros, Lieutenant, Deceased Husband of Beatriz Urrutia

Supporting Characters (Spanish and Indian)

Saúl Ayala, Corporal
Denzhoné, Apache Chief
Roberto (Berto) Durán, Beatriz' Butler
Miguel González, Corporal
Itza-chu, Apache Chief
Ricardo Morelos, Sergeant
Remedios Quijana, Beatriz' Maid
Qumara, Upper Pima (Tohono O'odham) Christian Wife of Itza-Chu

Supporting Characters (Jesuit)

*Fr. Jakob (Jacobo) Sedelmeyer, S.J., Missionary at Mátape College

*Fr. Carlos Rojas, S.J., Visitor General and missionary at Arizpe
Bendito Ortiz, S.J., Jesuit novice from Mátape
Enrique Ortuña, S.J., Jesuit scholastic from Mátape
*Fr. Bartolomé Saenz, S.J. Missionary at Cuquiárachi
Fr. Ramón Bernardo Zapata, S.J., young priest from Mátape

*Asterisks indicate that this person is historical.

<u>Supporting Characters (Indian)</u>

Diego, Eudebe Tribe, Gobernador at Cucurpe
Ernesto, Opata Tribe, Topil at Cucurpe
Pacheco, Eudebe Tribe, Alguacil at Cucurpe
Carlito, Eudebe boy at Cucurpe
Lorenzo, Pima Tribe, Factotum at Arizpe
Jevho, Upper Pima (Tohono O'Odham) Medicine Man, Guevavi
Jacinta, Upper Pima woman and nurse, Guevavi
Antonio, Pima, Gobernador at Mátape
Sebastian, Pedro, Pima boys at Mátape
Hernán, Pima, Gobernador at Ures
Felipe, Pima boy and Witness, Ures
Juanito, Pima boy at Ures
Rita, Pima Medicine Woman, Ures
Victor, Pima, Gobernador at Misión Banámichi
Victor's Father (Banámichi)
Lupe, Sister of Victor, living at Cucurpe

Acknowledgments

This book would never have been written if it were not for my good friend Dora Elizondo Guerra. At the time, as Special Collections Consultant at the Library of Our Lady of the Lake University in San Antonio, Texas, she brought Father Ignaz (Ygnacio) Pfefferkorn, an eighteenth-century Jesuit missionary, to my attention. Through his book, *A Description of the Province of Sonora*, I gained my first insight into the Indian tribes he knew, the landscape and geology of Sonora, its minerals and medicinal plants. It struck me after reading his work that Fr. Ygnacio, with the warm personality his work conveys, his keen powers of observation and his vivid and precise descriptions, would make a fine detective in a murder mystery.

My long-time friend and almost-family member, Professor Ralph Freedman, has been a constant help and support, for we were simultaneously writing novels. We began to read our works to each other, chapter by chapter, and to trade suggestions and encouragement. He gave me precious guidance in character-building and emotional fine-tuning, telling me where I was prolix or laconic or obscure.

The Daedalus Critique Group has been indispensable in critiquing sections of the book, letting me know where I have committed errors in point of view, verbal 'caterpillars,' and other stylistic blunders, while catching logical gaps or too detailed descriptions.

If it were not for my friend Father James L. Lambert, S.J., I would still be gnawing my fingernails wondering if my Jesuits are behaving in a believable way. He reassured me on that score, clarified matters of rank within the Society, filling me in on much historical data, and preventing errors in my portrayal of the Tridentine liturgy.

The magnificent landscape of Sonora, Mexico, its fauna and flora, became familiar through three tours, when I also inspected the sites of the eighteenth-century Jesuit missions, some now in ruins, others still active as parish churches. I felt the presence of those early padres who labored *ad maiorem Dei gloriam*, in the face of Apache raids, Pima revolts, diseases that swept the Indian population and other misfortunes, until their expulsion in 1767.

The Archive of Ethnohistory at the University of Arizona in Tucson has provided a rich source of unedited letters. These stemmed from both clerical and lay sources; for example, letters between the Jesuit Visitor General of Sonora, Carlos Rojas, and his superior, Francisco Zevallos (Ceballos) in Mexico City, between the Father Visitor, Miguel Aguirre, S.J., to the same superior, and from Governor Juan Claudio de Pineda to various missionaries.

Research for this book has been fun and has opened many new vistas, which I hope to share with my readers.

Ihs. Ignacio Keßerkorn

Chapter I
A Summons[1]

"Father! Father Ygnacio! There's a crazy man in the church! He's going through your vestments! Come quick!"

Carlito, the most talented pupil among my Eudebe and Opata converts and the best Spanish speaker, garbled his speech with native words. The situation must be serious. I lifted the skirts of my black Jesuit robe and dashed up the hill toward the mission church, leaping half-picked rows of frijol beans, detouring around the straggling squash vines, leaving the field where I'd been helping my converts with the harvest. I tore through the church door and skidded to a stop, panting. Holding my breath between gasps, I listened. Sure enough, noises of rummaging came from the sacristy and a voice speaking. I rushed to the back of the church and flung open the door. Two paces away, amid fallen chasubles and stoles, stood a wild-eyed young man, bareheaded, his dark hair standing up in peaks. Medium height, thin to emaciation and hatchet-faced, he wore a ragged Jesuit robe, gray with dirt and dust, and was holding my best alb against his body as if trying it for size. He'd been at our last annual meeting, hadn't he?

"What do you think you're doing? I don't recall your name and don't appreciate your pawing through my vestments."

He drew himself up and turned with regal deliberation, as though I'd intruded on an audience with the pope. He sniffed,

---

[1] In this novel, *México* refers to the capital city of present-day Mexico, which was then called *Nueva España* (New Spain). The action takes place between 1766 and 1769.

looking me up and down. "You don't *look* like a sybarite: tall, thin, hardened by manual labor, hawk-nosed, blond. German or Swiss, I'll bet. But you *are* a sybarite, Father. Just look at all this worldly finery! And don't try to tell *me* all this lace, these gold-trimmed satin stoles and chasubles are for the glory of God. This is *worldly* ostentation! You need to use your resources for your flock, not to glorify *yourself!*"

His rebuke tumbled out with utmost scorn and in excellent High German as if he could tell at a glance I would understand. In itself, that struck me as peculiar. We German Jesuits had learned, as soon as we arrived in Spain, that it was considered next to heretical to speak our native tongue. Whenever a Spanish brother caught us speaking it together, he would reprimand us. "*¡Habla cristiano!* Speak Christian," which meant, of course, Spanish. I answered my madman in German, nonetheless.

"My name is Ignaz. Ignaz Pfefferkorn. My official name in the Company is Ygnacio. And yours?"

"Wolfgang Wegner. The Company calls me something else, but I've forgotten it. Rejected it. Wolfgang was what I was christened, and Wolfgang I am."

"And your mission, Pater Wegner?" I used his German title.

"I was sent to assist Bartolomé Saenz at Cuquiárachi Mission, among the Upper Pimas. He and I don't see eye to eye. He tells me he's a Basque from Salvatierra in Áraba Province. Studied in Pamplona—that's Navarre." He nodded, as if that opaque statement clarified his situation. "I walked out. I've been wandering a bit. Suppose I'll go back one of these days, if he'll have me. He may have denounced me already to the Provincial." His eyes found mine again. "And you? Where are you from? How long have you been here?"

Wolfgang must have taken too much sun and was off his head. I needed to get him out of my sacristy.

"Why don't you sit with me over a cup of tea? I'll answer all your questions and we can discuss worldly goods, missions and such. Does that tempt you?"

He dropped the alb and stepped toward me. "The offer of something wet, something to drink, tempts me mightily, but tea? What necessary item for your flock have you sacrificed to buy such a luxury?"

"Not bought, gathered. I tried drying and steeping mesquite leaves. They're not a bad tea substitute. Once I found that out, I gathered them young and tender and now have quite a store laid by. My flock didn't suffer on account of my 'tea'."

He cocked his head on one side, fixing me with his intense stare. "How did you know it wasn't poison?"

"My Indians taught me. If they're not the bitter kind, mesquite beans are edible at any stage. It stood to reason the leaves would be, too."

He followed me out of the church. I waved reassurance at Carlito, whose mop of straight hair and one wary eye appeared around the corner, then led Wolfgang to my house and into the kitchen. The house was cool, with its walls of sun-dried and plastered adobe brick. I laid shredded bark and sticks of wood on the coals I kept live, blew it all into flame and hung my sooty water pot on the hook above the fire.

"The water will heat in a few minutes. Meanwhile, sit and we'll talk."

"I'll sit when you've answered my questions. In case you forget, I wanted to know where you're from and how long you've been here."

"Ah! That's easy. I'm from Mannheim-am-Neckar. I landed in Veracruz in 1755 but didn't get started in mission work until the following year. I've been here ten years now."

"Ha! I thought I heard a Rheinlander twang in your speech." He pulled out and settled on one of my chairs of peeled saplings and strips of rawhide, elbows on the primitive plank table. I set out two clay mugs and the teapot, fished a spoon from the covered basket on the trestle counter, and opened the old metal canister that held my mesquite tea leaves. I measured four spoonfuls into the pot and filled it with boiling water. My eccentric guest gave me a wild-eyed glance.

"Luther was right, of course."

I poured the tea. "What on earth are you getting at?"

He ran his hands through his wild hair, ruffling it further. "Faith, not works. *You* think we get to heaven on our own, by observing our rituals, working hard, doing good and such like. Pharisees! Luther knew that without the firmest faith—and most of all without God's grace—you get nowhere, no matter how hard you work. You and your ilk with your silks and prescribed liturgy, your teas and your fine decorations, you'll go to Hell anyway without the grace of God. *Sola fide*, Luther said. By faith alone. Alone!"

I looked at him in pity. Here was a man in deep crisis, a crisis that had driven him mad. I spoke gently. "My son, you're undergoing a severe trial of your own faith right now. Isn't it so?"

It seemed minutes before he raised his eyes, full of fury. "Who asked *you* to delve into the struggles of my soul? You hypocrite! You whited sepulcher!"

He leaped up, spilling his tea, and reached the door in two strides. "I'll try to make it at least part-way to Opodepe. Thank you for your *hospitality*." His last word dripped with sarcasm.

"Wait! If you're going to rush off, at least you can take a gourd of water, a bundle of cold tortillas and some frijoles. That'll see you through today and tonight. It won't take me a minute!"

I bundled the leftover tortillas, ten of them, packaged the frijoles, and two handfuls of piñón nuts and dried berries. A spare long-necked gourd and its stopper lay on the shelf. I took it to the well, where I pulled up the tightly woven *cora*, the basket of yucca fiber that served as my bucket. The water was cool and fresh, and I offered it to Father Wegner. He gulped huge swallows like a man dying in the desert, water dribbling from the sides of his mouth over his chest. When he handed it back, I poured a thin stream into the gourd, some of the water splashing back down seventy-five feet into the well. I took a drink of the cold liquid before lowering the basket into the darkness. Once I had replaced the wooden lid on the stone wall around the well, I turned to my guest.

"Don't expect to see Father Francisco Loaiza at Opodepe Mission. He died on New Year's Day last year. Until our Provincial, Father Zevallos, sends us a replacement, I'm serving as missionary down there. It's hard on the converts and on me, but there's no help for it as yet."

"I knew about that." He turned to leave, offering no thanks, no farewell. He patted the bundle of food and water. "Remember. Faith, not works!"

With that, he strode into the mesquite scrub with a long, loping gait, the bundle under his arm. I returned to the kitchen and mopped the spilt tea. Wolfgang and his madness moved me, and I began worrying about his immediate fate. Why had I let him go like that? He didn't even have a hat! The August sun was hot enough to give him sunstroke; a snake could bite him; a Seri poisoned arrow or an Apache lance could find him, or the gray wolves could ambush him in some lonely glade among the mesquite bushes, when the moon was high.

I wiped his mug and replaced it in the cupboard, pouring the contents of the teapot into mine. Scooping out the mesquite leaves, I scattered them around the pomegranate bush I was trying to raise near the front door. I took my mug full of tepid mesquite tea with me as I returned to the church. I first went to the altar and knelt, praying that God and the

Blessed Virgin watch over poor demented Wolfgang. I wondered what name our Society had imposed on him. Wolfgang, I vaguely recalled, was the name of a tenth-century German bishop, back when the Church sainted people easily. In his present state, 'Wolfgang'—wolf's lope or stride—suited him better than some well-known saint's name.

In the sacristy, my vestments lay crumpled and scattered. I shook the dust off, folded and placed them in their chests and on their pegs, busy for a while devising a new system for storing them.

Once night had fallen, I took refuge with my violin, faithful companion and unfailing consolation, hoping to relieve my guilt over Wolfgang. We were allowed our musical instruments, since the first Jesuit missionaries had discovered the natives' great love and talent for music. Around 1716, my grandfather bought the violin in Leipzig from its famous maker, Martin Hoffmann, as a present for my father. He treasured and played it until his death when I was eleven. Three years later, Mother gave it to me on her deathbed, that and the silver crucifix I wear night and day.

I tuned the violin and listened for the usual rustling outside my window. The converts gathered as close as possible whenever I played. Their own culture teaches them that music is also prayer to God. Tonight, I played a sad and dreamy air by Marin Marais, and then, for my neophytes' sake, ended with a simple lullaby. The melody worked its magic on me, too, for as soon as I finished my prayers, I fell into dreamless sleep.

ഇരു

Ten days and August was almost past when a messenger, a Seri convert, called me downstream to Nacameri, a village served by Opodepe Mission. He told me a woman was dying from ague, a disease the natives called 'repeating sickness.' Since the sudden death of Father Loaiza, Opodepe and its outlying villages had become satellites of Cucurpe, and I was struggling to keep the faith alive there. The sick woman was therefore my responsibility.

Word had gotten around that I had found a cure for the ague. There was truth in the rumor, since I had caught the disease—lately called malaria—when serving in my first mission, Atí, across the mountains west of Cucurpe. The Provincial moved me north in the nick of time to Los Santos Ángeles de Guevavi Mission, to escape the bad water at Atí. I was near death by the time I got to Guevavi, but a medicine man named Jevho saved my life by dosing me with the powdered bark of a certain tree from the land of the Incas. Since the Company of Jesus distributed and sent it back to the Old Countries as a cure for ague, it was now known as "Jesuits' powder." Thanks to divine mercy, to Jevho and to the bark that I kept with me always, I was now in good health.

I reviewed the tasks to be done during the next several days and packaged a generous quantity of Jesuits' powder. The mission would remain in the hands of my *gobernador* and my *alguacil*, Diego and Pacheco, converts who served as tribal officers under my authority. I went out to find them and saw Carlito instead.

"Find don Diego and don Pacheco for me as quick as you can! Run, now!" He dropped the rope he'd been weaving out of yucca fibers and darted away. I gave both men titles of nobility. If I showed respect for them, so would the tribe. Diego, the Eudebe *gobernador,* would continue and perhaps finish the harvest in my absence; Pacheco, also Eudebe, could see to normal discipline as the *alguacil* or sheriff. No Masses would be said while I was gone.

"If I'm not back by Sunday, lead the others singing in the church. Sing everything you know. The congregation shouldn't let a Sunday pass without praising God."

Diego nodded. "But you will be back, Father. I know."

"I'll try."

ɛɔ

After spending the first night in the mission rectory at
Opodepe, I continued south to Nacameri along the San
Miguel River, where water and shade were always near.
My tough little mare, Trina, carried me as she had on many
medical missions. I had earned a small reputation among Jesuit
missionaries for my herbal medicine, most of it learned from
Jevho at Guevavi and from my native nurse there, Jacinta,
but also from watching the women dosing their children,
dressing wounds, or tending victims of snake or spider bites.
Every native plant seemed to have its uses: it was edible or
medicinal, its fibers could be woven into baskets, or its wood
used for building.

I was eager to learn more from the natives. They were
healthy when left to themselves; they had few deformities,
were physically our superiors in strength and endurance, and,
unless they caught one of our European diseases, they lived
long lives. It seemed obvious that their knowledge of native
plants accounted for much of their good health.

The village of mud-and-branch huts was not impressive,
and the sick woman's hut was more dilapidated than most.
The late afternoon sun through the door revealed her lying
amid the buzz of flies on a filthy blanket, stinking of vomit
and feces. Revulsion and pity took my breath away. I stepped
back, looking for help. When I asked the villagers, they pointed to her sister and another nurse.

"They fear she has one of the plagues you white faces
brought when you came here. They don't want to die, too."

"The messenger told me it was ague, but I'll examine her
to find out." I beckoned to her supposed nurses. "Come with
me! I'll look at her, and if it's safe, we'll carry her into the fresh
air."

I made a quick examination while holding my breath, twice darting outside to fill my lungs. I saw no signs of pox or measles, and concluded that I'd been correctly informed. She had the ague. I spoke to her sister, using my calmest voice and manner.

"Your sister has the repeating sickness. It doesn't spread from one person to another. It's safe to touch her and carry her out. Please, help me." I turned to the other woman. "Stir up the fire and put on an olla. We need plenty of rags and warm water to wash her."

The two of us carried her outside, and after I bathed her face and upper body, I turned the task over to the women. While they worked, I boiled the water the tribe was drinking from the river, in case it carried some disease. Her slack skin told me she was dehydrated, so as soon as the water cooled enough, I spooned it into her mouth until she would take no more. She was conscious enough to give me a wan smile when I sponged her hot forehead with a cool, wet cloth. I smiled and nodded reassurance, relieved to see she was rational.

When it was clear her system had tolerated the water, I gave her a dose of powdered bark. I waited until twilight, then fed her spoonfuls of clear jerky soup, lightly salted, flavored with onion.

She survived the night, and I rejoiced.

I continued dosing her and on the third day, to my great relief could see a marked improvement: she could feed herself, leaning on one elbow. I knelt.

I humbly thank you, Lord, for saving her. I know she would have died without your mercy and her own strong constitution.

On the fourth morning, I packed to go home and gave instructions to her sister, who had kept an eye on me and my doings the whole time. As a thank offering, the village chief presented a handsome *tilma*, a cloak woven of yucca fiber.

I was grateful, since it would warm me at night and keep off the rain. I counted on being back at Cucurpe in time for Sunday Mass.

The sun was well above the horizon before I started. I mounted and touched Trina's sides with my heels, expecting her to break into her usual ground-eating trot. Instead, she hobbled a few steps and stopped. Alarmed, I dismounted and examined her hooves. Her feet were rock-hard, and I'd never had to shoe her, but I found a hairline crack in her right hind hoof that extended well up into the quick. I mounted again, leaned over, and saw that with my weight on her, the crack widened to a gap. I dismounted and removed the saddle and my other baggage. I'd have to find another way to get home. Trina needed attention, someone to fit a shoe to stabilize that foot, to give it a chance to grow out and heal. At Nacameri, no such help was available.

What in heaven's name can I do now? As if in answer, I heard the clop of hooves. The rider, leading a handsome dark bay horse, trotted straight to me. I was not surprised, since my black robe topped by a shock of blond hair made me the most conspicuous person in the village. Once he was close enough, I could see he was a corporal in the army of New Spain.

His mount shied at my approach, while the horse he was leading nickered and pulled on the rope, trying to jerk free. The corporal, suddenly in trouble, juggled lead rope and reins to keep from being hog tied on his own horse. I dropped Trina's reins, grabbed the lead rope, and found myself restraining a spirited Andalusian stallion, who eyed my mare and tugged to get to her, while the corporal quieted his horse. He removed his hat and fanned his face.

"Father! The missionary at Ures, Father Andrés, needs you! There's been a murder."

Chapter II
Investigation

I stepped backward, relieved. The murdered man was not my colleague, Father Andrés! But I was shocked at my insensitivity.

"Who? Who was killed?"

"My superior officer, Captain Cuevas. Night before last. Father Andrés is frightened because, the way the murder was done, it looks like *he* killed him. My sergeant thinks he did it. I don't. Oh, pardon me. Father Ygnacio, isn't it? I haven't introduced myself. I'm Corporal Miguel González at your service."

"Pleased to meet you. But how did you know to come here?"

I squinted at him against the sun. He was lanky, tall in the saddle, with a long torso but short legs that did not reach below his horse's belly. A *Sitzriese*—a sitting giant—as we Germans say. His deeply tanned face was northern Spanish, topped with a crop of unkempt brown curls, sweaty and flattened by the hatband, falling over a prematurely lined forehead.

His dark blue eyes fastened on mine. "Father Andrés was pretty sure you'd be over here. He said a Seri messenger came to Ures about a sick woman in Nacameri, and he sent the man up to you, since you're a healer. He said you've solved some crimes, too, and he called you levelheaded. He's hoping you can prove he didn't murder our captain."

"I may not be able to prove anything. But the whole idea is preposterous! Father Andrés could never kill anybody!"

"That's how *I* see it, but my sergeant doesn't agree. Still, we soldiers decided to give the padre every chance to prove he's innocent."

Andrés calling on me *to prove his innocence? This is topsy-turvy!* My colleague, Andrés Michel, a Bohemian Jesuit from around Prague, became missionary of Ures when Father Felipe Segesser died. He was senior to me, older and running a more established mission. Why had he called for my help first? I shook my head.

The stallion surged toward Trina, dragging me with him and breaking my train of thought. I towed him back to the corporal, restraining him with his bridle as well as the lead rope. I was panting. "Father Andrés… would do better to get in touch… with Father Sedelmeyer at the College at Mátape or… better still, an official in Horcasitas or Durango. He needs someone senior to him to plead his cause, not me. After all, he's my superior!"

González ignored my struggle with the stallion. "I don't think Father Andrés wants anyone to pull rank, not yet. What he needs first of all is someone to look over the situation—to examine the body and where it was found. See what you can figure out about how the murder hap—"

Now it was the corporal's turn. His horse began to dance, apparently eager to be on the road.

"Be quiet, Señor!" González gave the horse a light tap with his whip, then continued. "Father Andrés knows you're a sharp observer of details with a good mind to put them together. He told us how you solved that little mystery of the Father Visitor's lost ring when you last visited Ures. You'll be riding that stallion you're holding. Father Andrés wanted you to have a strong, fast mount."

I took my first good look at the stallion. He was tall enough for me, with good conformation. I stroked him under his long, wavy mane but he, unimpressed, pawed and shook his head.

"I'll come. But I fear Father Andrés has too much faith in my meager powers. Besides, Corporal González, Ures Mission is hours away. We'll get there well after dark; it's a good twenty leagues from here, probably more."

"We'll get there sooner if we start right away. I started out yesterday afternoon after Father Andrés decided what to do, and spent the night in a canyon. You're right, we'll get there after dark."

I left Trina behind in Nacameri with instructions for her care, hoping the villagers wouldn't eat her instead. The corporal and I headed south at a fast trot, the stallion under me reminding me of fine horses I'd ridden as a young man. The trail followed the river for a while, but when the San Miguel took a turn to the west, we continued south on a fainter trail that followed canyons and dry arroyos through broken foothills that rose sharply into higher mountain peaks. I moved the stallion closer to González.

"What makes you think Father Andrés is innocent?"

"Something strange, Father. Not far north of Durango, another corporal joined our group. Said he was on his way to Horcasitas and could he ride along with us."

"So what's strange about that?"

"Said his name was Saúl Ayala. Looked like a marrano to me—dark complected but not Indio, curly black hair, big nose…"

"Could be. Saúl is an Old Testament name, and Ayala may be marrano. What was his business?"

"He only said he was carrying a message for the governor, either bound for Horcacitas or Hermosillo."

"I still don't see…"

"He and the captain seemed to hate each other on sight. Can't say as I blame Ayala, though…"

"Why?"

"Two reasons. One I'd rather not talk about. It may be a military secret; I'm not sure. The other… well, the captain was a little too interested in the lady, and Ayala got between him and her. He acted like he was protecting her. The captain wasn't happy about that, no sir, not at all. Anyway, we got to Ures, and the captain did his business with Father Andrés.

"What lady? What business?"

"That's one fine lady! She's a friend of the lieutenant governor. He persuaded Captain Cuevas to take her along on this tour of duty. She's a widow; her husband was killed by the Apaches at Mátape Mission nearly seven months ago. She insisted on visiting his grave, so she's riding with us."

I set aside that curious information until later. More important was finding out what issue these soldiers had with my colleague. "So, you came up here escorting a woman. But your main purpose was to see Father Andrés. What business was that?"

"Inspecting his books. Seems the king's inspector, the Royal Visitor, José de Gálvez, suspects he's been engaging in illicit trade and not paying proper taxes to the crown."

"Andrés? Unbelievable!"

"Well, that's what we were sent up here for. Anyway, the captain finished the inspection yesterday and last night he was murdered."

"I see why Andrés is under suspicion. But what about Corporal Ayala?"

"He, his horses and all his gear were gone before dawn yesterday morning. I woke up and heard horses passing by the stable where I was bunked. Something on the harness jingled, so I knew it wasn't an Indian. I didn't get up, though, and no one else heard it."

"And then you found the captain murdered, so you think maybe he—"

"Yes. I'd bet it was that marrano, not Father Andrés. He might even have joined us with murder in mind. Just a word to the wise, Father."

We rode on, my mind teeming with questions. Did the murder have something to do with that 'military secret'?

∞∞∞

Ures Mission, established by Father Francisco Paris beside the Río Sonora in the 1630s or 40s, was blessed with a dependable water supply. Its church dominated the other buildings, Indian huts, a solid stable, and several new workshops. I followed Corporal González into the nave and to the altar. The captain's body lay in state amid a small forest of candles, incense competing with the unmistakable odor of decay rising from the corpse. It rested on a trestle of boards covered with a colorful but thinly-woven cotton serape. A crude pine box waited nearby, ready to receive the captain for burial.

Father Andrés had been kneeling at the altar, keeping vigil over the body. He rose to greet me, interrupting his rosary. He pumped my hand and clapped me on the back. "Father Ygnacio! Thank God!"

"Father Andrés! Yes, we finally got here."

"I was getting worried, afraid the corporal hadn't found you after all."

His shaking voice and drawn, white face revealed his fear. I gripped his arm. "Corporal González found me right where you thought I'd be."

"I knew you wouldn't leave someone dying of ague without trying to help, so it wasn't just a lucky guess."

"I'll stand by you, Father. I don't know how much good I can do, other than see you don't have to face this ordeal alone."

He glanced aside at the corpse. In profile, his abbreviated nose and square chin had always made me think of him as a younger man. But not now. The flickering candlelight revealed tired brown eyes above twin pouches, a face both haggard and pale, the lines from nose to the corners of his mouth deeply engraved, the jaw line beginning to sag. His hair, brown only a few months ago, glimmered mostly gray in the candlelight. He faced me again. "I'm afraid there's no doubt about it; it's a murder, and the way it was done points straight at me. I'm hoping you can help point the accusing finger elsewhere." He paused, swaying a little, his eyes closed. "God, I'm *so* tired…. I've been racking my brains to understand how such a thing could've happened."

"It's my turn to rack brains. You need to get some rest."

"You're my hope, Ygnacio, my friend. You're good at puzzles; you're observant and not easily misled. I've seen that in you."

"They've been trivial up to now… except for killings, like that murder at Guevavi."

"I heard about that. Well, if you're not too worn out from the ride, would you examine Captain Cuevas' body, please? Then we can compare notes on what we've seen."

"Of course, Father Andrés. Right away."

I moved to examine the dead man. An Indian boy sat in the shadows on the altar step; I hadn't seen him before. I handed him the nearest candle, and he raised it high as I looked at the captain, still dressed in the clothes he must have been wearing when killed.

I turned back to Andrés. "I'm glad you didn't have the body stripped and washed. Leaving him as he was when he was found was the best idea, if we're to understand what happened."

"I thought of that, thank God."

"I'll also need to see where he was killed, and how he was lying when he was discovered."

Andrés nodded and sat heavily on the altar step. I could see his strength was nearly gone. How to go about probing this man's death? I had no idea, God help me! I could only blunder ahead. Anything would be better than allowing my brother in Christ to be accused of murder—unless, of course, he had done it. The strain on Father Andrés was obvious; the rosary jittered in his shaking hand. His expression as he stared at the body seemed vacant, his jaw slack as if his soul were already far away. Was he preoccupied with his eventual fate, or wondering how on earth he could have committed such an act?

Captain Cuevas lay on his back. The left side of his coat bore a two-inch cut, clean and bloodless. I overcame my reluctance and touched him, unbuttoning the coat and shirt. The deep wound underneath had barely bled, probably from a knife that might even have penetrated the heart. It had left only a spot of wetness on the shirt. Odd. As I re-buttoned the coat, my knuckles brushed his neck.

"Boy, raise the candle, please." My voice echoed in the silent sanctuary. When the light struck the throat, it illuminated signs of strangulation. The rope or chain had left irregular marks, almost like serrations, with larger, roundish indentations at regular intervals. I took the candle and held it closer. It made no sense. Nothing I could think of would leave marks like that. I'd already seen that the captain's wavy black hair was matted with blood and dirt.

"Corporal González, come help me raise the captain's upper body."

"Yes, Father Ygnacio." He came to my side. Together we raised the body a little, stiff in rigor mortis after nearly forty-eight hours. Unused to handling corpses this way, I could not suppress a shudder. The base of the skull bore a deep indentation. I steeled myself, and parted strands of the matted hair with my fingers to see the wound clearly. He'd been struck from behind with something square and heavy.

"Let's lay him down," I said, wiping my fingers on a rag I kept in my pocket as a handkerchief. I looked further, but saw nothing else unusual on the front of his body.

"Now, Corporal, you and the boy here can turn him on his side. I need to see if there are any more injuries on his back."

While the two did as I had asked, Father Andrés looked on, growing increasingly pale and beginning to sweat. The back of Cuevas' coat and the seat of his breeches were white with dust, with a few pulled threads and one three-cornered tear from being dragged from his resting-place. A few grains of gravel clung to his clothing, but there were no further injuries. I glanced up at the windows, and saw only darkness, though there should be a moon. I would look at the murder scene anyway.

"Who can take me to the spot where he was found? We'll need several candles."

Father Andrés stammered. "I-I'll take you. He was in the mission garden. Juanito, take four more candles."

The three faces around me, lit from below in the wavering candlelight, looked equally sinister. I took two of the many candles, handing one to the corporal and the other to Father Andrés. We cupped our hands to shield the flames and followed him, Juanito bringing up the rear with the extra candles.

An extensive, well-cultivated garden lay, pale in the moonlight, between the church and the priest's house, enclosed on two sides by the buildings, and on the back by an adobe wall. A brush fence with a gate made of sticks woven together protected the front of the garden, where Father Andrés' thriving pomegranate bushes evoked a twinge of envy. Several small fig trees drooped, heavy with ripe fruit, and the remaining space was filled with orderly rows of vegetables, herbs and flowers.

Andrés held up his candle and pointed to the ground. "It was here." A large rosemary bush, broken and half crushed, was sticky with a dark substance, undoubtedly blood. I bent closer. The clotted mess had snared gnats and a small fly or two. More blood formed a congealed puddle on the ground nearby, already half carted away by ants and dung beetles. Elongated drag marks showed how the body was removed, and a muddle of footprints marred the area.

"Who found him?"

"I did. I was showing doña Beatriz my garden yesterday morning when we literally stumbled over him." Andrés' voice was hoarse.

"Doña Beatriz? Is she—?"

The corporal interrupted. "That's the lady I told you about, whose husband was killed by the Apaches. She came all the way from Durango with the captain and the rest of us to see the spot where her husband is buried, like I told you. We were headed there—to Mátape Mission—but we came this way first, since the captain had that business with Father Andrés."

Now I could find out more details. "How did she come? On horseback? Not riding astride, surely."

"No, Father, she's a proper lady. She rode sidesaddle."

I shook my head, eyes wide. "This must be an unusual woman!"

The corporal's expression became worshipful. "She's one in a thousand. In ten thousand!"

I left it at that and turned to Andrés. "Tell me, Father, why did the soldiers come here? What, precisely, is their business with you?"

He closed his eyes in infinite weariness. "Could we talk about this tomorrow morning? There are technicalities… accounts to show you. It's complicated, and I'm exhausted. Please, Ygnacio."

"Of course. That part will surely keep. But I need to know when you found him. Did you say day before yesterday? About what time?"

"Shortly after Mass."

His speech was slurred, but I couldn't resist another question. The captain was struck by something square, and I'd seen neither it nor the means of strangulation.

"He was hit on the head. What with?"

"The small statue of the Blessed Virgin, of all things! The one from the niche to the left of the altar. I found it beside the body and held it to the wound, just to see. Its base fits the indentation in the skull, and it had blood and the captain's black hair on it." Andrés leaned as if losing his balance, and I braced his elbow. He gave me a weary nod. "Thanks, Ygnacio. Now, I must get some rest. I haven't slept since we found him. Juanito, could you find Hernán for me? Someone must keep vigil over the body while I sleep."

The boy ran to obey the priest. All of us, especially the corporal, were close to dropping with fatigue. I mumbled, just to fill the silence, "We should all get some sleep, if we can. I'll find out more tomorrow, if there's anything more to find. Meanwhile, where—"

Andrés held up his hand and turned towards the gate. Juanito had returned with a short, broad-shouldered man in uniform.

"Father Ygnacio, this is Hernán, my *gobernador*. Hernán, Father Ygnacio is from Cucurpe Mission."

His skin and hair were dark, his eyes luminous and intelligent—a handsome Pima tribesman of around forty. His Spanish was heavily accented, otherwise correct and even stilted.

"Yes, Padre Ygnacio, I recall you clearly from years ago when you came with the other new priests. Your yellow hair and blue eyes made a lasting impression. Some of you padres have such unusual coloring, like the pictures you show us of the angels."

I shook my head. "We're far from angelic, Hernán! All too human!"

Andrés' tired voice brought us back to the present. "See that the vigil continues through the night, and if you don't watch the captain's body yourself, be sure it's someone trustworthy. And we need to dig a grave in the churchyard."

"Where, Padre Andrés?"

"Hmmm. I'd say… next to Eugenia. You remember, the woman the Apaches killed last year in that raid."

"I know the one. She was Juan Romero's cousin."

"That's right. The grave must be ready before Mass. We'll have the service for the captain and bury him right afterwards."

Andrés ushered me into his house with its comfortable combination living room, dining area and kitchen. He cocked his head toward two dining chairs. "Let's sit for a moment." He lowered himself with a groan.

I spoke first. "We're finally alone, Father Andrés. We need to compare notes about the murder. How do *you* think it was done?"

"How *I* think it was done, eh?... Well… he must have been hit in the head first. If he'd been strangled first, he'd have struggled and maybe saved himself. But he must have been stunned, not killed outright. Then the murderer strangled him."

"You're right. He must have been struck first from behind. That alone would have killed him in half an hour or less, I imagine."

"What makes you think so?"

"There must have been enough bleeding inside the skull to kill any man. The brain would have been injured, too. Then, I think you're right: the murderer, seeing he was still breathing, strangled him… but with what?"

"Strange marks around his neck. I can't imagine… but what do you think of that knife wound in the chest? How and when do you think it was made?"

"I'm pretty sure the knife wound was made later, quite a bit later. You know how a deer carcass won't bleed after it's been killed and you stick a knife in to gut it. It must be the same with human bodies. Once they're dead, they don't bleed. There was only the slightest ooze around that knife wound. Someone with a grudge against the captain struck him with a knife, as if for good measure."

"Well, we at least agree on all of that, but it still doesn't clear my name, does it?" He stifled a yawn. "Ah, well, let's sleep on it. We're too tired to think now anyway." He rose and I followed him.

The spare bedroom was bare of any decoration other than a crucifix above the door. As he turned to go, I repeated my unanswered question. "I assume no one found what he was strangled with?"

"No, no. They didn't find the knife, either. We looked, but found nothing. Forgive me, Ygnacio, but I really *must* lie down before I drop."

"Of course. May God grant you a night of deep, dreamless sleep."

I turned, staggering, to my bed, about to collapse with exhaustion. After I pulled off my shoes, I stood and blew out the lone candle. Through the darkened window of my bedroom, I could see the plaza in front of the church lit by creamy moonlight. A tall, willowy figure stood there, a woman in a white, filmy nightdress, her dark hair hanging to her waist, rippling gently in the breeze. She faced the church door, her head bowed slightly as if in prayer. Then she crossed herself and moved away, disappearing among shadows.

Chapter III
Beatriz

Did I love Mateo Salinas? Do I love him now? *Yes* to both... I think. But my love—my feelings—evolved a great deal over the years we were together. Since his death six months ago, I've had more than enough time to sit and think about such matters.

Mother's family was wealthy, descended from the Moors who came to Spain some time after 711. Angela was my mother's name, and she married a Basque merchant from the north, Martín Urrutia, who became a partner and then owner of the family business in Málaga. He specialized in importing silks of all kinds, from transparent gauze to heavy brocade. He made a fortune importing in bulk and selling to neighborhood gentry, and once he had enough gold laid by, he took our family and moved north as far as Toledo.

The city was past its prime by then, a little shabby, in need of colorful new ideas for interior decoration and clothing, and my father, the eternal optimist, believed we could re-establish our genteel business and be accepted as equals by the city's aristocracy. Even though he had married beneath his class, outside his race, he knew that 1492 was three centuries behind us, when those Moors who chose to stay in Spain converted to Christianity. He thought mother's good looks would win over the local nobility.

My mother was never so naïve.

"*Mija*, my daughter," she told me, "don't expect to find a husband among these *viejos cristianos*, these Old Christians. They want to keep their blood pure and only marry among themselves."

I was old enough to wed, perhaps a little too old at nineteen. My mother, still an attractive, elegant lady, had been considered a great beauty in her time, and father told me I even surpassed her, and yet there seemed to be no prospects among the nobility, and papa had so far discouraged those merchants' sons who'd approached him asking for my hand.

My father, though not successful at social climbing, was a clever businessman. His imported brocades were so lavish that no one in that severe central part of Spain, the *meseta*, had ever seen the like. Such colors: reds with flowers, birds and ferns in glowing gold embroidery, emerald or deep forest greens adorned with silver peacocks—and the great families couldn't resist. He upholstered their chairs and curtained their windows; he clothed their wives in the vivid colors of the Orient, and the dressmakers of Toledo blessed him.

I had no brothers, only younger sisters, so there was no one to follow my father in business, and I had always impressed him as very bright for a mere woman. Even though it is a strange thing to do, he took me as his assistant in the business. I had learned to read, more-or-less on my own, much earlier. I also learned to figure, to keep accounts, and on many occasions he sent me to remind the aristocratic clients of their unpaid bills. I was almost always successful because of my looks.

I met Mateo Salinas de Los Herreros in the home of one of those families. Because I was the merchant's daughter, not a flunky, Ana the dueña and I were admitted through the front door rather than the servants' entrance around back. But we were left standing in the tiled entryway under a massive chandelier, waiting for the good pleasure of the master of the house. I stood looking around. The heavy, wine-colored drapes separating the entrance hall from the private areas of the house were threadbare and faded, dirty where many hands over many years had pushed them aside. A pair of chairs flanked the entrance, and my practiced eye saw that their upholstery was in similar condition. They threatened rather than invited the visitor, both double-seated with cruelly carved backs ready to martyr anyone who ventured to sit on them. The tan and brown tile floor looked as if it had not been swept in over a week.

The curtains moved aside, and a handsome young man stood before me, his velvet jacket in a state very like the upholstery.

"Señorita Beatriz, please follow me, my father is waiting in the salon."

We stood for a moment staring at each other before I moved to follow him. I think I loved him from that moment. We walked together down the gloomy hall and into the sparsely furnished salon. Señor Antonio Salinas stood before me. To my surprise, his face wore a pleading expression.

"Yes, I know I owe your father quite a sum of money, Señorita Beatriz. Just how much do you calculate?"

I gave him the tally of brocade and silk we had delivered three months earlier, and the sum owing.

"I'll need a little more time. Could you ask your father to be patient for... for another two weeks, please?"

"I'll ask him, Señor Salinas. We'll see."

I took my leave as graciously as I could, and Mateo escorted me out. He seemed awkward, like a much younger boy. "Señorita... what do you do during the day?"

"I work for my father, as you see."

"And afterwards?"

"I sometimes run errands for my mother."

He nodded. "Good. The next time you leave your house for an errand, I will escort you."

I must have looked incredulous. I gave him a half smile and hurried away, not trusting myself to reply, Ana trailing behind.

Late on the second day, after a long stint of calculating accounts, I left the house to supervise our cook, Lucia, to make sure she bought the right bread and meat for dinner. As we passed the first cross street, Mateo appeared and walked by my side. He spoke in a rush, as if he feared he would be caught at any moment. "You are the most beautiful creature I've ever seen, doña Beatriz."

I halted so abruptly that he had to turn and walk back. Lucia, a few paces ahead, stopped and watched. I planted my fists on my hips.

"Whom are you trying to deceive, don Mateo? I'm perfectly aware that my family, Moors as you call us and merchants besides, are not worthy of your exalted attention, you who are an aristocrat descended all the way from Roman times, no doubt. And I certainly don't claim the title 'doña'. Go along now, before you get into trouble."

He blushed and twisted his hands. "I meant what I said. I can't eat or sleep, thinking of you. Please, Beatriz, tell me when and where we can meet."

I walked on toward the baker's, Mateo keeping pace with me, Lucia behind us. I eyed him from time to time under my eyelashes. There were ways to get out of our house unseen and unchaperoned. After my day's work was done, I'd tell papa I needed to rest in my room until dinnertime. My heart began to hammer at the prospect. "Well, Mateo... there's a courtyard beside the cathedral, with a stone bench."

"When?

"Tomorrow at dusk."

We met for more than a week, spending an hour together, careful to avoid being seen on Saturday and Sunday when evening Masses were being said. I made up fanciful excuses to dispel my parents' suspicions. We began to understand each other, he and I; we exchanged our life stories, our ambitions and our dreams. During the eighth tryst, someone clutched me by the arm, someone I'd not heard coming from behind. I leaped up with a little cry and twisted my arm out of the man's grasp. Mateo jumped up when I did, but he stood like a lamb, his arm still in his father's grip. Señor Salinas spoke to me.

"What do you think you're doing with my son, you little vixen?"

I felt my face turn to stone. "We were talking, Señor, nothing more."

He gave Mateo's arm a jerk. "Come with me, son. You and I will have a talk of a different kind!" Salinas dragged his boy away, but not before giving me a long, calculating look.

The offer of marriage came a week later. Mateo would marry me, if my father would provide a generous dowry and forgive all Salinas' debts. My parents, overjoyed at marrying their daughter into the aristocracy, however impoverished, agreed with only a passing consultation with me. Fortunately, I had become more than fond of Mateo. Thanks to my father's wealth, the ceremony was a lavish affair, celebrated in the cathedral.

Such an obvious marriage for money didn't sit well with Salinas de los Herreros' peers in the community. Mateo, who pined for adventure and an opportunity to make his mark somewhere other than in the close atmosphere of Toledo, opted for a military career, and to come to New Spain, where both adventure and opportunity seemed limitless. Surely, prejudices in the New World did not run so deep, and Mateo would be able to regain his social status.

With his commission as lieutenant in His Majesty's army, we sailed for Veracruz, traveled by coach to the capital, México, and Mateo was assigned to duty in Durango. We lived there for four years, in the heart of the city. My father's money allowed us to buy and furnish a lovely home with enough servants to keep us in comfort. Thanks to our wealth and Mateo's aristocratic lineage, we moved among high society. You'd think I would have been idyllically happy. But the same traits that attracted me to Mateo—his love of adventure and drive to make his mark—marred our happiness, that and my inability to have a child. I had two miscarriages, the second serious enough that I was ill for at least a month afterwards. And then there were Mateo's perpetual absences. He seemed to accept every assignment to ride out into the wilds to fight the Apaches or carry out other mysterious, no doubt dangerous, assignments.

I began to resent his eager acceptance of those assignments, to wonder how much he loved me, and, I must confess, how deeply I loved him.

And that left me open to the improper advances of the lieutenant governor, who fancies himself a ladies' man.

☙❧

Gray dawn came all too quickly. I awoke to rhythmic thuds of footsteps in the next room. It could only be Father Andrés, endlessly pacing. The cadence spoke of agony, of fear, possibly of guilt. If only I could somehow comfort him!

I poured chilly water into the blue clay basin on the nightstand from a matching chipped ewer, bathed my face and hands, pulled my robe over my head, and hurried out to take care of nature. On my return, I saw Andrés across from the priest's house at the church entryway, where he would ring the bell to announce Mass. Early morning light etched harsh lines in his haggard face, reddening his puffy eyelids. He had the far-away look of a man deep in thought. He startled when I spoke.

"Did you sleep at all last night, Father?"

"Not much. Some, or I wouldn't be standing here now. But let's get on with the day's work—heavy duties, my friend—the Requiem Mass. Please join me, if you wish, Ygnacio." He rang the bell.

Despite his obvious exhaustion, he celebrated the Mass with dignity. His homily struck me as eloquent for a man who did not know the captain, and whose dealings with him had been less than cordial:

> "The life of a soldier demands extraordinary sacrifices. Every soldier gives up time a normal working man could spend with his wife and children. He almost daily runs the risk of bodily harm and even the loss of his life. Captain Nicolás Xavier Cuevas was such a hero. A few months

ago, he and his men escorted our vice-provincial, Father Luca Poncelli, to Mátape Mission and its College. They crossed the wild lands safely, but were attacked by Apaches while at the mission. After a violent battle, Captain Cuevas drove off the attackers, but he suffered tragic losses: three fighting men and one gallant officer, Lieutenant Mateo Salinas de los Herreros, whose grieving widow is seated here before me now. Those heroic soldiers willingly traded their lives for the safety of the converts, students and clergy at the mission. All of them deserve our deepest respect and prayers for their souls…"

I sat near the altar during the homily, facing the congregation. The church was nearly full. Lined up in the front row were Corporal González and a sergeant, whose name, I'd just been told, was Ricardo Morelos. A burly man of about forty, he was a head shorter than the corporal. Straight dark hair cropped short revealed large ears that stood out from his skull like jug handles. His expression was severe, accusatory perhaps. Yes, it was clear, as González had told me, that the sergeant believed Father Andrés had killed his captain.

Beside him sat a woman dressed in a simple but elegant black dress, her head and face veiled in a gauzy black mantilla. She resembled the ethereal figure I'd seen last night, standing before the church. I tried not to stare. She sat still and erect, but as Father Andrés spoke of Lieutenant Salinas' death, she raised the mantilla to dab at her eyes. This had to be his widow, doña Beatriz. Andrés' final announcement brought my attention back to the homily: the burial would follow at once.

I inhaled a worried breath as Corporal González, the sergeant, Hernán and the *alguacil* grasped the corners of the threadbare serape under the captain and raised his body off the trestle. The cloth held despite my fears, and they placed him, cloth and all, into the open wooden box. Corporal González nailed down the coffin lid, and with solemn steps the four men bore the rough box out of the church to the open grave.

I followed Father Andrés to the graveside, regretting that I'd soon have to burden him further with questions about the captain's investigation. The native gravediggers shoveled clumps of soil over the wooden box. The burial could not have been simpler, plainer, with no attempt to disguise the finality, the harsh reality of death. What a contrast to the opulent European funerals I'd witnessed as a young man! Surely, God intended our flesh to melt away quickly to blend with the clay of which Adam was created.

The woman I assumed was doña Beatriz skirted the diminishing pile of dirt to speak to my fellow priest, raising her veil as she came.

"Father, thank you for a fine and meaningful service." She turned to me, her warm contralto voice like honey. "And thank you, too, Father Ygnacio. Your presence here lent dignity to the Mass."

I stood, wordless as an ox, amazed by her beauty. She seemed to be of mixed ancestry—perhaps North African—for her coal black hair and eyes were too dark to be typically Spanish. Yet, her skin was white, her cheeks rosy, her lips sensual, full and red—even though she used nothing artificial to heighten their color. That morning, her flowing hair was tamed, pulled back from her forehead and tied in a shining knot at the nape of her neck. She had a marked widow's peak, appropriate under the circumstances, and the severe arrangement revealed the lobes of delicate, shell-like ears, a small golden hoop in each. Her large eyes regarded me obliquely from under high, arched brows, exotic eyes, their corners a bit slanted by her high cheekbones. Her full breasts filled the severe bodice of her black dress, buttoned to the neck with a ruffle of white lace. Her waist was narrow, and the slightly flared skirt molded the shape of her perfectly rounded hips.

I gulped air, ashamed that a woman's physical beauty had stunned me so. I stammered an answer. "Wh-why th-that's nice of you… uh, thank you! How… how did you know my name?"

Her smile mocked me. "Don't you remember? Father Andrés introduced you at the beginning of the service."

"Oh. Oh, yes, yes. So he did. And you must be doña Beatriz?"

"Yes. Beatriz Urrutia. My husband was Lieutenant Mateo Salinas."

I reflected that Spanish married women retain their maiden names, whereas German women, although they include their maiden names, are generally called by their husband's surname. My mother was Frau Pfefferkorn.

Beatriz continued, "Where are you from, Father Ygnacio? You must be from northern Europe somewhere. "

"Yes, quite right. I'm from Mannheim, a city on the Rhine. My name is actually Ignaz Wilhelm Pfefferkorn, but the Society has given us all Spanish names. Are you a native of New Spain, Señora?"

"No, the old country. My mother was from Andalusia, of Moorish extraction; my father was born in Aragón. So, you see, I represent all of Spain in one person. I met my husband in Toledo."

"And how did you come to the New World and to this wild outpost, Señora?"

"My husband was an ambitious young officer who couldn't wait to find adventure in the New World. Soon after we were married, we sailed for Nueva España, and settled in Durango. We'd been happy there, as happy as a couple can be if the husband is a soldier, until he was ordered to accompany your vice-provincial, to inspect Mátape Mission."

Odd. I thought. *Juan Lorenzo Salgado is the Father Visitor, our official inspector, and his superior is Visitor General Carlos Rojas in Arizpe. It looks like the vice-provincial has taken Rojas' place and shoved Juan Lorenzo aside. Why? Why go to Mátape? Is Salgado ill? Is Rojas?*

I turned back to doña Beatriz. "And Mátape Mission, that's where…" I hesitated, searching for a tactful way to finish my question.

"Where Mateo was killed. Yes." She lowered her eyes from mine and turned her head away, but did not weep.

A tangle of emotions shook me: pity for her vulnerability, awareness of her beauty, and admiration for her strength and courage. "How long ago was your husband killed?"

"It's been nearly seven months. When I heard Captain Cuevas had been ordered to come to this mission, I persuaded the lieutenant governor, who persuaded the captain that I should come along. As a special favor, he asked Captain Cuevas to escort me all the way to Mátape."

"But why must you go through such hardships just to get to Mátape?"

"I know it's a bit mad, but I can't rest until I see my husband's grave and the site of the battle where he was killed. I need to pray there. That's why I'm riding with the captain and his men." She paused, and her speech, voice and posture became formal. "It is indeed a terrible blow that such a tragedy should have overtaken Captain Cuevas."

"Will you be able to go on to Mátape?" The anxiety in my voice surprised me.

"I don't know. If not, I'm afraid all my efforts will have been wasted. It took me weeks to convince the lieutenant governor—not just that I *should* go, but that I *could* go. I mean, he couldn't believe a woman could stand up to such a long ride—weeks—on horseback." She shook her head, smiled a rueful smile, and I was charmed.

"If there is anything I can do to get you to Mátape, just let me know, doña Beatriz."

"Thank you, Father Ygnacio, I'm truly grateful." She cast her eyes down with demure grace and turned away from the grave.

I looked for Father Andrés. He was now talking with Hernán in the plaza in front of the church, gesturing and pointing. I joined him. When he finished instructing the *gobernador*, he turned to me.

"You need to know what business these soldiers had with me. That's probably uppermost in your mind." His face had never regained the ruddy color I remembered from previous visits, but remained as gray and haggard as in the early morning light before Mass.

"I'm afraid so, Father. I need to know why they came here in the first place."

"Come with me, then. Let's get this over with." He drew a deep breath and exhaled an explosive sigh. I followed him through the church into the sacristy. An alcove held a battered desk, brought by oxcart from the capital city, México, flanked by two chairs and hand-hewn and planed shelves, loaded with books and papers. We sat facing the desk.

"They came to examine my accounts. The vice-provincial, when he came here acting as visitor, saw them nearly seven months ago and made an exhaustive report... but that was to our Society. The royal inspector, Visitor José de Gálvez, suspects—I've been denounced, it seems—that I've been trading our excess produce, cattle, horses, farm products, whatever, to the settlers in the neighborhood, and I've pocketed the profit for myself."

"Absurd—and vicious! Who denounced you, I wonder? He must have a grudge against you for some reason. That bears further investigation, Andrés, if we can get you out of this present mess. Something else bothers me. What was Poncelli doing, usurping Juan Salgado's job? He's been one of our best visitors. Father Rojas was getting too old and… uh, heavy, for a job that demanding, though he's as clever as a fox. Juan came in like a breath of fresh air and took over the strenuous traveling. What?—"

"I can only think that Francisco Zevallos, our Provincial, already had wind of the accusation and thought it serious enough that he sent his right-hand man to check on several missions, not just mine."

I shook my head. "They always suspect us missionaries of profiteering. I hear even the Franciscans are suspected of shady dealings. And they aren't allowed to touch money."

"Yes, of course, it's a variation on the usual theme. Captain Cuevas seemed suspicious—maybe already convinced he'd find proof of wrongdoing—when he demanded to see all my records. I showed them to him, and he found nothing irregular, not the least thing. Then he left me, and no one saw him alive again." He allowed his head to droop, his voice fading.

"I see. Then he was found bludgeoned and strangled, and no one will ever know whether he found incriminating evidence against you or not. But I need to see those records for myself."

With a grunt, he hauled a couple of leather-bound ledgers off the shelves and opened them on the desktop. To my eyes, at least, his system seemed supremely orderly, nothing left out, nothing that didn't add up. After half an hour spent poring over his records, I looked up. Andrés had been dozing in his chair, but started awake when I straightened and the chair creaked.

"Well?"

"Your records seem as clean as a peeled egg. But since Cuevas was killed before he could tell anyone else he'd discovered nothing, I can see what others are—or will be—thinking, and why you needed my help."

"The sergeant is convinced I did it."

"So Corporal González tells me. But if they accuse you of the murder, the court examiners will never believe these books haven't been doctored."

"Of course. I'll have had time to rewrite them, smudges and all."

"So, you see, Father, I'm not the miracle-worker you need."

"Odd you should say that… Wolfgang Wegner told me something similar on the day before the murder."

"He came to *my* mission less than two weeks ago. He must be traveling day and night. What was he doing here?"

"Preaching Luther, mostly. Good thing we're Jesuits and not Dominicans—he'd have been roasted at the stake long since."

"The young man's off his head. What did you do with him?"

"I took him in, fed him, and told him he could sleep in the hayloft. He told me I was in extreme danger, and I'd need a miracle worker to save me. He said he was not the man."

"His home mission is Cuquiárachi, isn't it? With Bartolomé Saenz?"

"He's *supposed* to be poor Bartolomé's assistant." Andrés grinned at me. "He told me some time ago Wolfgang had wandered off, and he considered it a blessing in disguise. He certainly wasn't sending out search parties to bring him back!"

"Does Wolfgang have a second name? More Christian? A little less primeval and pagan?"

"I think it's Pío." Andrés threw back his head and we laughed together for the first time since I'd come.

"Pío! The pious one! Well, it fits in a way. He's going around preaching piety, faith over works as our only means of salvation. Otherwise, he shows his piety in strange ways. But where is he? I haven't seen him since I got here."

"He was gone that morning—the morning we discovered Captain Cuevas' body, I mean. Didn't say goodbye or thank you, just vanished."

"Typical." I shook my head. "You don't suppose he had anything to do with the mur—"

An imperious rap on the sacristy door made us both jump, and Sergeant Morelos stepped inside uninvited, holding up a large but broken rosary. "Father Michel, does this belong to you?"

"It looks like mine, but it couldn't be. The only rosary like that is right here in my desk drawer…."

He opened the creaking central drawer and looked inside, then thrust his arm in and groped about, pulling out papers and tossing them helter-skelter on the desk.

"Let me see that!"

The sergeant held out the rosary so Andrés could see it, but not close enough for him to touch it. Some of the beads were dark with blood, and the leather thong they were strung on was broken. Several beads were missing.

Andrés covered his face, paled to the color of long-buried marble. "Oh, my God, my God… it *is* my rosary! Mary, Mother of God, preserve me!"

I stood and confronted the sergeant.

"Where did you find that?"

"In the priest's garden, in the corner near the rear of the church where the murderer tossed it. Now we know what was used to strangle my captain."

The strange pattern on the corpse's throat at last made sense. Ten Hail Mary beads and then an Our Father—all around his neck.

"Sergeant Morelos," I said, "I'd better get my colleague to his room. If you think it necessary, post Corporal González outside his door. But Father Michel has had so many blows, one after another—you can see as well as I that he needs time to rest and think."

The sergeant nodded. I helped Andrés off his chair, and supported him as he stumbled back to his house.

"Thanks, Ygnacio." His voice was faint. "You're right. I'm completely worn out but so much on edge I can't sleep. I must think, rest, *pray*. In any case, I must be alone for a while." He collapsed on his cot.

I tiptoed out, closed the door behind me, and returned to the garden with its bloody and broken rosemary bush. The loose, sandy earth around it might still reveal something useful. At first I saw nothing, but I persisted. Then as I stooped lower, I noticed a round object, half buried in the sand. A bead! I dropped to hands and knees, and brushed away sand and dirt. Another bead, then another, up to five. The captain had been strangled on that very spot, probably shortly after he was struck with the Virgin's statuette.

Before rising, I glanced around. The perspective was different at this level. Between me and the brush fence across the front of the garden I could see the drag marks and jumble of impressions left by many different feet, both barefoot and booted. A few small footprints must be from doña Beatriz's boots, although hardly anyone else's could be identified.

I turned to the rear of the garden. The soil seemed undisturbed… or was it? I leaned closer. Beside the rosemary bush, behind the area where I'd found the beads, the slanting light revealed a footprint. No boot, no bare foot had made it; this foot had worn a moccasin. I rose and began to look behind the rosemary bush. More moccasin prints.

Father Andrés' Pima converts and the aggressive and deadly Seris often preferred to go barefoot, and so far I'd seen no footgear on any of them since I'd been here except on Hernán, and he, like my own converts, wore sandals. All other identifiable prints in the garden, except for those from shoes, boots and sandals, were made by bare feet. These prints, judging from the size of them, were left by a grown man. A double circle of prints by this same man looped behind the bush, as if he'd circled the body twice.

Where had he come from? A crushed parsley plant and a partial print next to it pointed to the rear of the garden. I followed the tracks to the adobe wall, where they stopped. He'd gone over. This was his escape route, but he must have come in another way. Who was he? Not a mission Indian, but perhaps an Apache warrior, since the Apaches wore moccasins. Had he murdered the captain? Or was he inspecting an already dead body?

Andrés must not have told everything he knew, and the Apaches were somehow mixed up in this murder. I needed to talk to him right away. His life might depend upon his telling me the whole truth.

He needed rest and prayer, but my discovery drove me to disturb his solitude. I knocked, noting that Sergeant Morelos had not, after all, posted a guard. "Father Andrés! It's Ygnacio!" I wanted him to know it was not a soldier who'd come for him.

He opened the door after a moment, tousled hair and bleary eyes showing he'd fallen asleep in the short time I'd been gone. "Forgive me, Ygnacio. I must have dropped off for a moment."

"Please, Andrés!" I used his given name for the first time without a title. "It's I who must apologize for disturbing you. But look! I found two things when I examined the rosemary bush—*that* rosemary bush. First, I found five beads from the rosary. More important, I found a double set of moccasin prints around one side of that bush. Andrés, I think there was an Apache out there. Can you tell me anything about that?"

He stood, eyes wide, wordless. I spoke again, more urgently. "Are the Apaches mixed up in this? Tell me, Andrés, please! Your answer may clear up what really happened. It may even clear your name."

He stretched out a hand and touched the beads without taking them, then his hand went to his neck. "I feel that rosary—*my rosary*—around my throat. May God have mercy on me—the noose is already in place!" He stumbled to his cot and sat, covering his face again. His words came out in a near whisper.

"My own Indians, my Pimas, know what I'm about to say, but my superiors do not. I've been interested… passionate… about converting the Apaches."

"Andrés! You too? I knew the Franciscans were trying that. But I had no idea any of the Jesuit—"

"You're right. The Society isn't willing to back the effort, not now. They think the Apache cause is too risky, when our missions are overextended already. But I got to know an Apache chief, Denzhoné, after a raid two years ago. He'd been shot by a guard, and fell from his horse."

"And you saved him?"

"I found him while I was searching for our own dead and wounded. I doctored him and bound his wounds. The bullet grazed a rib and tore a chest muscle. It bled a lot but hadn't broken anything. I brought him to this very house. No one saw us because it was already after dark, and two nights later when he felt strong enough, I gave him my horse to get back to his tribe and told my people it had been stolen."

I shook my head in mock disapproval. "Go on."

"I spoke just enough Apache—and he just enough Spanish—to understand each other. He promised he'd try to forge a peace pact with the Jesuits. Our missions would be safe from raids by his people."

"That's quite a concession. What did you promise him?"

"I tried to persuade him to bring his tribe to our mission. We were still negotiating about that."

"Yes, but what do you know about the night of the murder?"

"Hernán said he saw him come over the wall two days ago—at twilight—and that night the captain was killed. But then the soldiers came. Denzhoné considers them deadly enemies."

"For God's sake, Andrés, why didn't you tell us about this? It makes all the difference."

"Ygnacio, I don't know if you or anyone can believe this in the face of such damning evidence. I swear in the name of Our Savior that I didn't murder the captain. I fear the chief killed him, not realizing he was putting me under suspicion. He may have been crouching in the sacristy, saw the captain, picked up the rosary and then the statue, and followed Cuevas into the garden. I pray God he didn't, but I fear that's the solution to the murder."

"Andrés—"

He held up his hand. "I can't betray my Apache friend to the authorities. In the name of the Blessed Virgin, Ygnacio, promise you won't repeat what I've told you!"

"But—"

"I'd rather be executed for the murder myself than allow an injustice. After all, he might *not* have done it. And you know how our secular authorities always believe the worst of the Apaches."

I bowed my head in obedience. "Very well, Andrés, I'll not repeat what you've told me. You're risking your life, though. The circumstances all point to you—except for those tracks."

"I forbid you to show them or to mention them to any one of the soldiers! I have only marginal authority over you, but we Jesuits are an army in Christ, and I *command* you to keep this secret from the civil authorities."

I raised my eyes to Andrés Michel's face, my respect for him increasing by the minute, a plan taking shape in my mind. I would go after Denzhoné, not to bring in a murderer but to find out the truth. Somehow, I would clear Father Andrés' name.

His strident voice struck me like a slap. "Ygnacio! Did you hear me?"

"Yes, Father, I will obey. I still say this may cost you your life."

"Well then, *Amen;* so be it. The overriding cause, ending the hostilities between the Apache tribes and the missions, outweighs the value of any one life." He paused while I waited for a final word.

"But… but to tell the truth, Ygnacio, I am mortally afraid."

Chapter IV
Two Ride to Mátape

My feelings have been in turmoil ever since I learned of Mateo's death. For weeks I was blinded by grief. Then, Corporal Ayala found me and told all he knew or deduced about what had happened. It was a relief to substitute rage for grief.

Ayala came to me after midnight. Remedios, my maid and guardian angel since Mateo died, let him into the house. I was half awake when she entered my room holding a candle high, and I sat up, pulling the sheets up to my neck.

"Who's there?"

"Señora, forgive me for waking you, but—"

"Remedios! You frightened me! What do you mean coming in here without knocking?"

"It's important, doña Beatriz, something you must know. A soldier's here. He was with Tenente Mateo when he died."

"What? Who? What are you talking about?" I was beginning to gather my wits. "Someone wants to tell me something about my husband?"

"Yes, doña Beatriz. He's here now, the soldier. He says he couldn't come in daylight."

I scrambled out of bed and pulled on my dressing gown, taming my hair with three or four quick strokes of a brush. "Take me to him, Remedios, but stay with us. I need a witness."

He was pacing the drawing room floor, a tall, thin man, sallow complected, with curly, black hair and a beak of a nose. He wore a uniform. "I am Corporal Saúl Ayala, doña Beatriz. Please forgive me, but I couldn't rest until talked to you. I knew your husband, you see."

"You knew Mateo! How?"

"I was in the escort that accompanied the Jesuit vice-provincial, Father Luca Poncelli, to inspect Mátape Mission in Sonora. That's where the Apaches attacked us, and your husband died defending... well, not exactly defending the mission, but..."

"You've come to tell me what happened. Your life must be in danger, too, else you wouldn't be here after midnight."

"I would have come sooner, but I was wounded in the battle that took your husband's life and am barely recovered. The authorities—some authorities—need to know what happened, but most of all, you, his widow, should know."

"Yes? Go on!"

"You knew that your husband was second in command of the squad of soldiers that escorted Vice-Provincial Poncelli to Mátape College in Sonora, yes?"

"Yes. And?"

"Something about that assignment smelled from the beginning. Jesuits, even prelates, usually travel light. But this time, other than Father Poncelli and his secretary, we were escorting a mule train loaded with what looked like bottles of oil."

"What for?"

"Apparently for sale. After we got there, a caravan of Dutch traders rode into the mission. Poncelli and his secretary met with them, then they left the next day loaded with that oil—if it *was* oil."

"The letter I received about my husband's death said there was an Apache attack."

"Yes, they attacked the Dutch. A wounded merchant made it back to Mátape to get help. Captain Cuevas sent your husband out with four men, including me. Four never came back."

"Five men to stop an Apache raiding party? You saw Mateo die. How?... How did you get away?"

"Your husband was a brave man. He fought on with several arrows in him. Apaches killed the horses under us and kept circling. Barely time to reload, then out of ammunition. One of them threw a lance and hit me in the chest. I was lucky. The lance struck my ribs, skidded and stuck in the muscles along my side. I fell, another man on top of me. Blood gushed from the artery in his neck. It soaked us both. I played dead. When the fighting was over—it didn't take long—the Apaches checked us and thought they'd killed us all. I crept from under the bodies once they were gone and walked back to Mátape. I still don't know why they didn't scalp us."

I dug my fingernails into my thighs through my nightdress so I wouldn't scream. Instead, I said, "Weren't you bleeding badly?"

"Bleeding, yes. Shocked. Suspicious. Why were we sent out like that to be killed?"

"You think it was deliberate?"

"I'm sure of it. Someone—your husband, maybe—found out something he shouldn't. I think we were sacrificed."

"What did you do?"

"I asked the converts if they had someone who knew herbal medicine. An old woman tended me. I didn't show myself to Father Jacobo until the vice-provincial and the caravan left after the funeral the next morning, then I asked for a bed for a few nights. Thanks to the herbs the Indian woman used on my wound, I didn't get infected. The infection started later, once our own doctors began treating me."

𐹠𐹣

That's what Saúl Ayala told me, and I laid plans to find the ones responsible and bring them to justice. I needed more details and wanted to see the site of my husband's slaughter first hand. But I could do nothing without help. I stooped so low as to encourage Lieutenant Governor Figueroa's attentions. The man has made overtures to me for a year or two—long before Mateo's death. He and Governor Claudio Pineda own large haciendas near Durango, and when the governor is at Sonora's capital, Horcasitas, the lieutenant governor takes care of paperwork and various diplomatic tasks in this city. Thanks to his influence, I was able to come on this expedition with a reliable horse—a hand-me-down from his superior, Governor Pineda. The little mare has perfect conformation, but is too small to carry either man. Señor Figueroa had her brought to me with a note:

> Doña Beatriz, I am pleased to present this fine little animal to you. She is gentle, well trained, and just the right size for a lady's mount. May she serve you well.
> Your Obedient Servant, (etc.), Antonio Figueroa

So far, the mare has served me very well indeed. The trip here to Ures took almost two weeks. On the second day, Corporal Ayala joined us with a message for the governor in Horcasitas, so he said. If he had not, Captain Cuevas might have forced himself upon me; he made his desires clear enough. But Ayala stuck by me like a dueña, and the captain left him—and me—alone. Cuevas surely knew that the corporal blamed him for sending my husband and the four men to be killed. He probably feared an attack on his life if he gave the corporal the slightest pretext.

But now Saúl Ayala, my protector, has disappeared and the captain is dead. What will happen to my crusade? How can I continue?

My task is to find out who gave Cuevas *his* order, and why. I'll try to pry information from these two priests, Andrés and

Ygnacio. I'm almost certain the Jesuits are responsible for my husband's murder.

৪৩৬৪

Andrés, Beatriz and I lingered at the table after our noon meal. I turned to the lady.

"Do you still intend to go on to Mátape? Are the soldiers willing to escort you?"

"Of course I want to go on! After the struggle to get this far, I'd be devastated if I couldn't. But Sergeant Morelos and Corporal González will certainly go back at once to report their captain's murder."

"You're right. Murder takes precedence over anything else, but I'll speak to the soldiers to see when they're leaving. They may have time to pass by Mátape. If not, there may be another way to get you there and back to Durango."

Beatriz flashed a hesitant smile. "Any help you can give me, Father, is much appreciated."

I found the two men in front of the stable, busy with their horses and tack. González finished paring a rough spot off his horse's left hind hoof and began to re-set the shoe, hammering nails through the toe, nipping off the sharp ends and pounding them flat. Morelos was hunched on a battered stool; his thighs spread wide, feet gripping its base. As I watched, he pulled a long needle loaded with heavy waxed thread through a leather saddle girth. He glanced up when my shadow dimmed his light.

"Blasted girth might've come apart in the middle of nowhere! Good thing Padre Andrés' tack room's well stocked. He's got everything—awls, thread, hammers, leather shears, spare leather—in good order, too. Can't see how a man like him would murder the captain; it doesn't figure. But he's the only one with a real reason."

I moved aside so he could see better. "At least you're giving him the benefit of the doubt. I can't imagine him murdering anybody in the first place, and if he did, he'd be clever enough to point the clues at an Indian, not at himself."

Corporal González stopped hammering and crinkled his lined forehead. "Unless he was crazy at the time."

I shook my head. "Crazed enough to forget everything? Pretty unlikely."

Unlikely, maybe, but I must keep an open mind. Andrés is still the man with the most to lose if the captain had lived to denounce him. Did he rewrite those records? Maybe in part? Did the captain find something incriminating?

I dismissed these thoughts and turned to the sergeant. "You know that doña Beatriz came with you to visit her husband's grave at Mátape. Will you have time to drop her off there?"

"Not a chance." Morelos shook his head. "We have to hustle to Horcasitas to report to the governor. Our first duty is to our murdered captain and to justice!"

Gonzales glanced at his sergeant. "That's right. Doña Beatriz can either stay here or come back with us. I'll check her mare for lameness or loose shoes, though. I'll go over her tack, too, for weak spots. At least we can do that much for her."

I found Beatriz waiting for me in Andrés' patio. Deep blue glazed pots stood against the adobe walls, bursting with bougainvilleas and hibiscus in full flower. Their cascades of multicolored blossoms framed the lady in black.

"You were right. The soldiers are about to start back."

"Did they leave me my mare, or am I stranded?"

"They're checking her and your tack right now. At least they have that much conscience."

I circled the patio with long strides, nervous, composing a little speech. I stopped in front of her and words tumbled out.

"Look. This might work. I come with you to Mátape and talk to Father Jacobo Sedelmeyer, the rector there, to get you an escort back to Durango, and then I'll be on my way to my mission at Cucurpe. I can't leave it abandoned to my gobernador. I've been away too long already. I may not be of much use to you on the trail. I couldn't protect you from Indian attacks, and that could happen any time. You probably know I'm not allowed to carry a weapon—none of us Jesuits are. But *you* could, if you knew how to use one. What do you think?"

Her eyes sparkled. "What I want most in this world is to ride to Mátape. Believe it or not, I have a pistol in my saddlebag, and I know how to use it—my husband taught me." Her glowing eyes lost focus as she remembered. After a moment, she gave a throaty laugh. "Your company would be wonderful, Father Ygnacio. Perfect! Traveling with you would be a pleasure."

Did I detect a bit of irony in her voice?

She continued. "Your conversation would surely be more enlightening than the soldiers'. I accept your offer!" She reached for my hand. Her handshake was cool and firm.

When I left her, I looked for Andrés and found him writing a letter in the alcove of the sacristy.

"Ygnacio, I'm requesting that the vice-provincial release his file on me to the viceroy and the royal visitor. There's no way I can get those two soldiers out there to understand the contents of my accounts—they're both illiterate. I'm hoping Poncelli's word will carry weight with Viceroy de Croix, but our Society is under suspicion everywhere, it seems."

"Here in New Spain, you mean, or in Europe?"

"Everywhere, Ygnacio. Remember our last Junta at Mátape? All that discussion about how the situation in Europe might affect us over here? King Joseph banned us from Portugal ten years back and Louis XV of France suppressed us two years ago because of that financial scandal in Martinique."

I sat facing Andrés. "To me, the new ideas are a bigger threat. Politics are driven by ideas, and Voltaire and that group around him have had enormous success. And Voltaire was trained in a Jesuit school. What irony! We teach him to think and he tries to destroy us."

"We're open to suspicion because we do sell our excess produce, Ygnacio. That leads to accusations that we've mounted a massive conspiracy to defraud the Crown of its money. The viceroy may well believe it, the royal inspector, José Gálvez, would like nothing better than to find evidence against us. I fear he'll think the vice-provincial is merely shielding me, and I'll be convicted of killing the captain to prevent the evidence of fraud from coming out."

"It may do no good, but I'll add my own letter attesting to the pristine state of your books. I'd better get out there and delay the soldiers until our letters are written. They can carry them back to Durango. Surely, they have enough good will to do that for us."

"Let's hope, Ygnacio. But what's next?"

"I have to get back to Cucurpe, Andrés—I can't stay away much longer; I had no time to make proper arrangements for the mission to run on its own before I came. But before going back, I intend to ride to Mátape. You know doña Beatriz wanted to visit her husband's grave and the site of the battle where he died. She wants to pray there. It's important to her. She seems to be a modest, pious woman, a grieving widow. Since the soldiers can't take her even though she's ridden all these leagues, I'll escort her and arrange for someone from Mátape to accompany her back to Durango."

Andrés raised one eyebrow, his head on one side. "I hope you aren't getting on *too* well with the lady, Ygnacio. I saw how she affected you yesterday at the graveside. I may be old, but I'm not blind to her attractions, myself. Beware the Devil's wiles, my friend! But how can you protect her, or yourself for that matter, in case the Seris or Apaches take a notion to kill you and take your horses?"

I rose and paced the room. "It's a problem, Andrés, I agree. But, in a way, she'll be protecting *me*. She's got a pistol, and I'm convinced she knows how to use it. Sometimes I think we're safer without military escort than with it—the Indians hate the soldiers, but many know we're trying to do some good."

"The lady wants to take the risk?"

"She more than wants it—she's eager for it. She should've been born a man."

"Well, Ygnacio, you're level-headed and mature. It would be a sin to frustrate her pious intent after she's come all the way from Durango. Just keep your distance! My blessings go with you, and my prayers for your safety—both of you."

I stopped pacing and faced him. "Andrés, I want to continue your work with the Apaches. I'll see if I can get one of the young priests from Mátape to hold the fort at Cucurpe while I'm gone again. I'll look for your Indian chief Denzhoné and find out if he'd be willing to complete the peace pact he began. That way, your work would not be in vain, even if you should be arrested for the murder."

I wasn't lying to Andrés. I would speak to Denzhoné about the peace pact if I found him. But my primary purpose would be to see if he'd killed the captain. I wouldn't try to capture or arrest the chief, only establish the truth. My word, my witness, the facts and further evidence I might gather at such great risk to myself would surely carry enough weight in court to save Andrés from the gallows. It surprised me that I cared enough to risk my life for him.

His eyes misted over as he listened to my offer, but he began at once to point out its hazards. "You know only too well what you'll be up against. You could get killed in so many absurd, trivial ways—by snakebite, for example. Or, you could be shot by one of Denzhoné's tribe or by the Seris—though they don't usually range up in the mountains where you'll be going."

It seemed to me that, despite his protests, Andrés was giving me tacit permission to try.

"Tell me, then, just where *will* I find Denzhoné and his tribe?"

"First you need to go to Bacoachi, the last settlement before you enter the pass through the Mababi Mountains to the east. That's Apache territory, so rough the troops from Fronteras Presidio haven't been able to root them out. Denzhoné's ranchería is up there somewhere."

"Who knows those mountains? How will I find the ranchería?"

"When you get to Mátape, tell Father Jacobo you need his help—he's been up in there exploring. I'll write him a note telling him you're going with my permission to pursue a peace pact with one of the Apache tribes."

"Thanks, Andrés."

"Give him as few details as possible, and by no means mention Denzhoné by name, or that he could be connected with the murder. But Ygnacio, my brother—I don't know why I'm even considering your crazy scheme. It's suicide!"

Andrés seemed to know my message to Denzhoné would not be limited to talk of a peace pact. I gripped his shoulder. "It may be our only chance—for peace between the Apaches and us."

⅐⅑

The soldiers waited until we finished our letters, surprised by my plan to escort doña Beatriz to Mátape. Corporal González gave me a keen, blue-eyed glance and a nod, while the sergeant stared, looking me over, head to foot. Clearly, they were assessing my worth as a man and not a 'mere' priest.

Morelos challenged me. "You sure you're up to the task, Padre? What about the Apaches? Who's going to protect you?"

My face grew hot. I was ashamed to tell them that doña Beatriz would be my protector. It would only confirm their opinion of priests. Corporal González broke in and saved me further embarrassment.

"Well, Father Ygnacio, I wish both of you the best of luck. ¡*Vayan con Dios*!" He shook my hand, brushed back his mop of curls, donned his hat and pulled it down over his forehead. He turned away and mounted, squirming to settle himself in the saddle. "By the way, the lady's little mare is sound, and we checked the tack. It's in good order." Morelos mounted, too, and without another word, turned his horse's head and gave me a final wave. I watched them ride away.

Father Andrés persuaded us to stay until the next morning, since it was already mid-afternoon. The three of us ate together that night in better spirits. Andrés bustled about, relieved to be free of the soldiers. He beat precious hen eggs seasoned just right with high quality salt from the region and even added crushed fresh rosemary leaves. The eggs cooked slowly in the battered frying pan, adding flavor as he folded them over a chopped jalapeño, thin slices of mild red onion and chunks of ripe, fresh tomatoes, all from his garden. Hearty cornbread, freshly baked in one of the outside ovens, accompanied slabs of ham he'd smoked. He filled our clay cups with red Parral wine from a town on the slopes of the Sierra Madre Occidental.

We continued speculating about Spain and Europe in general, and how politics over there were affecting the New World. Doña Beatriz spoke of Hermosillo, Horcasitas and Durango.

"Sonora's governor, don Juan Claudio de Pineda, seems to be a fair-minded man. He's a wealthy land-owner, owns several mansions and breeds fine cattle and horses. The mare I'm riding is from his ranch, half Andalusian, half Arabian—he was willing to part with her because he thought her too small for his own purposes. Lieutenant Governor Antonio Figueroa thought she'd be the right size for me and persuaded Governor Pineda to give her to me."

Andrés gave her an admiring glance. "Doña Beatriz, if you have that much influence with the lieutenant governor, ask him to put in a good word for us, please! Could you do that? There seems to be so much slander against the Jesuits these days, and his good opinion might help us."

She nodded with a thoughtful crease between her fine brows. "Yes… yes I think I could do that, Father Andrés. I'll see what I can do."

I remained puzzled. "Is it usual for a lieutenant and his wife to move in such exalted circles? I'm sure a lieutenant is important to a governor for his military skills, but socially?"

"You'd be quite right, Father Ygnacio, under normal circumstances. But my family is wealthy, you see. My money bought us a fashionable house near the central plaza in Durango, and I keep a personal maid and a manservant. Mateo was from an aristocratic family, so thanks to that and my money from the family business in Spain, we were accepted by members of Durango's high society. We… I mean, I… see the governor at social functions when he's in the city."

I thought of my own family and the influence it once had. Perhaps she really would speak to the lieutenant governor for us.

We left for Mátape after Mass the next morning. I embraced Andrés, once more promising to find Denzhoné. He handed me the note to Father Jacobo.

"God go with you, Ygnacio. May He guide you and shelter you under His wings."

Andrés supplied a food basket, and we packed enough hay for a night out in the wilds. I made sure the water skin held enough to keep all of us for two days.

Beatriz led her mare to a large cube of stone that served as a mounting block. Her practical skirts reached only to mid-calf, overlapping the tops of her black laced-up boots, but she still might have trouble getting into that sidesaddle. I went to help her mount.

I was a pace or two away when she placed her left foot in the stirrup and surged upward, twisting to land in the side-saddle. In a flash, the stirrup slid off her boot sole, she lost her grip on the saddle, and fell backwards. I leaped forward and caught her in midair. Without pausing, I mounted the block with her in my arms and placed her on the saddle.

I held her there while she withdrew the arm that had slipped around my shoulders, trailing the tips of her fingers across the back of my neck in an unconscious caress. Her touch and the lingering feel of her rounded, soft body pressed against my own thrilled me to the marrow. I stepped off the block, turning so she'd not notice my red face and my trembling. I was pushing forty, and had never in my life been so close to any woman other than my mother, who died when I was fourteen, and my sister Isabella. I remembered Andrés' reservations of the previous afternoon and his warning against the Devil's wiles. Without looking at her, I vaulted on my horse, tucked my skirts around my legs, and we set off at a smart trot with a wave to Andrés and Hernán.

I mulled over my few contacts with European women. Five years ago, I'd been transferred from Misión Atí on the Río Altar to Misión Guevavi, a few leagues south of San Xavier del Bac and the little village of Tucson. I arrived at Guevavi nearly dead of ague—malaria. Patricia O'Meara, daughter of a nearby rancher, acted as nurse and assistant to the Pima medicine man, Jevho. Her healing hands had soothed and comforted me, but her closeness was not like this.

I became aware that doña Beatriz' eyes were fixed on my face as we rode side by side. To relieve my discomfort, I broke the silence. "Do you have that pistol handy?"

"Oh, yes I do, Father Ygnacio. I was just admiring your strength. Not many men could have caught and lifted me the way you just did!"

I glanced her way. Her expression was serious, not flirtatious, but her next statement shook me. "You really are such a handsome man, Father. I'll say this only once and never broach the subject again—it's such a pity a man like you should waste himself on the priesthood."

Waste himself? I looked away, my face again burning, and choked out a reply. "Thank you, doña Beatriz. Yes, by all means, let's drop the subject."

Was she flirting? I couldn't tell. I felt betrayed. It should be obvious that I'd *chosen* to become a missionary priest because of the overwhelming need to save thousands of Indian souls from certain damnation if they were not brought to God. Such an enormous task, of such immense importance, far outweighed the fulfillment of any one man's bodily needs. My sacrifice was joyfully made. But to her, a woman who lived the secular life, my ideals, my purpose, must seem a pale abstraction. Or had I misjudged her? Appearances can be deceiving. Perhaps she led a deeply spiritual life as well, and if so, she would know in her heart why I'd become a priest.

An awkward silence fell again, broken when the two of us began to speak at the same time.

"I can't imagine how anyone could believe Father Andrés killed the cap—"

"Even if Father Andrés murdered the captain, to leav—"

Our spontaneous burst of laughter relaxed and bonded us, and at last a real conversation began.

I let doña Beatriz complete her sentence first. "… to leave so many clues pointing to himself would be the height of idiocy in a man who is anything but stupid. Perhaps someone framed him."

"I think circumstances just came together to make it seem he did it."

"Maybe, Father Ygnacio, but the authorities won't see it that way. They always arrest the obvious suspect. And what are *you* going to do? Just leave him to his fate like that?" She gave me an accusing look.

I had a strong urge to tell her about the moccasin tracks around the body and about Denzhoné, but my vow of obedience won the day. Since I wouldn't tell her that, I couldn't tell her what I'd be doing next.

"I must get back to my own mission, to Cucurpe, and set things to rights up there. After that, if anything can help Father Andrés, I'll do it."

"Do the missionaries in those far-flung spots like yours have any contacts with the settlers round about?"

"If they don't have a parish priest, the settlers often come to Mass at the missions and they may choose to bury their dead there. Oh, we trade our surplus garden or dairy products for some of theirs from time to time. Beyond that, not much contact."

"Have many foreigners come here to settle?"

"Not that I've seen. They're mostly Spanish and mestizo along with an occasional Irish or German family."

"What about gold and silver mines? Have there been any important discoveries in your area, Father?"

What is this, an interrogation? "Yes, mainly silver—not too far away. If the Apaches don't attack and kill them all, there's a rush of people coming in to profit, and we have to protect our converts from being kidnapped and worked to death as slaves in the mines. Then the vein of ore gives out and they keep digging until they've exhausted the profits they made at first. Greed won't let them go. They work on an exhausted mine until their slaves and they, too, drop dead, and then there's nothing left. It's the middlemen and probably the

Crown that make the profit—the miners, if they survive, are left destitute."

"And the missions? Have they profited in any way?" Her face showed mere innocent interest.

"Only by the occasional gift. For instance, one miner brought me a pair of heavy solid silver candlesticks for the altar. He'd had them cast as an offering to the Virgin of Guadalupe in thanks for his discovery. But I heard he was murdered not too long after that in an Apache raid."

"And what have you done with the candlesticks, Father?"

"They're still on the altar, doña Beatriz."

☙❧

When the sun stood directly overhead, we stopped in the filtered shadow of an organ pipe cactus and unpacked the food in Andrés' basket. We discovered tortillas, ham, pinole, two hard-boiled eggs, and two ripe tomatoes that miraculously had not been crushed, thanks to his clever packing. He had even included salt twisted in a snippet of old document. The water in our gourds, though tepid, tasted good, and the ripe tomatoes refreshed us, eaten like apples with a few grains of salt on each bite.

Mounting this time was not the sensual experience it had been that morning, although I came into direct contact with the lady to hoist her into her saddle. This time, she laid her slender gloved hand on my upper arm and gently squeezed the muscle as I lifted her, but true to her word, she made no remark.

The shimmering heat that afternoon hampered conversation, but we talked from time to time of the people I served at the mission.

"Tell me about your successes at Cucurpe."

"The best example is my choir. I have two soprano voices that are so clear, so bell-like, that they could match any singer in Vienna or Milan. I can't imagine any voice surpassing them."

"I'd love to hear them, Father. But tell me, do outsiders come to the mission to enjoy those Masses? For your spiritual guidance? For help? Other than the settlers, I mean."

This is truly an interrogation. I wonder why? "We've had one strange visitor lately, but no real foreigners."

"Who was that?"

I told her about Wolfgang 'Pío' Wegner, and she laughed her throaty laugh, mopping her face with a lace-edged handkerchief.

"Do you ever have visits from people from other countries like the Dutch or the English—or even the French?"

Aha! All three are enemies or rivals of Spain. She's thinking we're guilty of treason. Perhaps she's spying for the Royal Visitor, Gálvez.

"Seldom. Cucurpe is too far inland to attract outlanders like those. The French occasionally send exploring parties this far west, but I've only seen one such party, years ago. The missions on the Sea of Cortés receive more visitors. The occasional ship wanders up the gulf, anchors, and the men come ashore just to see some fellow Europeans. There's a grand celebration then—but it's not a matter of trade or politics."

We camped that night in a dry wash. I unloaded and hobbled the horses and the mule and let them roam at will. We built no fire for fear of drawing hostile attention to our presence.

Doña Beatriz rummaged in the food basket and laid out half the remaining food, jerky and tortillas, leaving tortillas and boiled eggs for breakfast. "When do you think we'll reach Mátape, Father?"

"When I come down from Cucurpe, it takes me… well… I'd estimate we'll get there by mid-afternoon tomorrow."

We ate in quiet companionship, the horses and mule munching their hay nearby. Doña Beatriz set up a comfortable sleeping place—she'd had many days' practice. She settled down, wrapping the blanket around her to keep out wandering insects as well as the cold of the desert night. As I made a similar bed, I thought about the snakes that might snuggle under us to enjoy the warmth of our bodies, but decided not to mention it.

Dawn woke us undisturbed. I thanked God that He, in His almighty power, had brought us in safety to this new day. We blessed our eggs and tortillas and ate in good spirits. As we laughed together, I was seized with a tug of longing. Was the married state something like this? I quickly rose to catch and tack the animals. We reloaded the pack mule as if we'd been a team for months, and the day passed in intermittent conversation.

"Besides converting the Indians to Christianity and teaching them to sing, what more do you offer them to wean them away from their ancestral way of life?"

It was a good question. "We try to teach them to speak and read Spanish, to write and figure. If they adopt our dress and know enough to read the Bible and understand our mathematics, they might be able to find paying jobs and defeat the slave hunters that prey on the illiterate and the ignorant. We want them to have skills enough to compete with the European settlers who are often themselves illiterate."

"How do your converts react? Are they willing to learn?"

"It varies. Some tribes may never accept our teachings."

"Then why do they stay at the missions, Father Ygnacio?"

"Because we feed them year 'round, doña Beatriz."

The sun dipped toward the horizon, and I began to worry. Had I missed my way? Shouldn't Mátape be coming in sight? Doña Beatriz, whose attention was not, like mine, concentrated on the land ahead of us, called out to me and pointed.

"Look, Father! Over there, on that hill to the west!"

Silhouetted against a sky glowing orange and pink, a pair of Indians on their horses stood watching us. By squinting, I made out that they wore their hair bobbed short above the shoulders, bound by a cloth around the forehead. Apaches! The two men lingered only a moment and then disappeared behind the rise.

"Apache scouts! They'll report what they saw first. Maybe that'll give us enough time to get to Mátape before they attack."

Chapter V
Forbidden Contact

Our horses were tired, but we forced them to canter. Any minute, a yelling band of warriors could erupt from the nearest hiding place. Half blinded by the setting sun, we skidded to a halt atop a knoll, surrounded by stands of organ pipe cactus and ocotillo. A valley opened below us with a cluster of adobe structures at the bottom. Mátape, an emerald amid the grays and duns of the desert, lay along a stream, with leafy shade trees and flowering gardens. The mission at last!

We plunged down the trail. Once on level ground, we trotted toward the church that dominated a number of whitewashed buildings. I recognized the priest's house, and we headed that way, slowing when two Indian boys joined us and ran alongside. The taller one took hold of my horse's rein.

"You come for Father Jacobo?"

"Yes! We saw Apache scouts back there! Warn him! Warn the mission!"

"Follow me, Father. I'll find him!" He spoke to me, but his eyes devoured doña Beatriz as if he'd never seen a Spanish lady before. Perhaps he hadn't. He tore his eyes away and turned to the younger, scruffier boy next to him, who was gawking with open mouth. "Pedro! Run! Find Father Jacobo! Tell him about the Apaches." The younger boy streaked away, and the taller boy spoke to me. "I'm Sebastián, Father."

"And I'm Father Ygnacio. This is doña Beatriz. Lead on—we're in a hurry."

We followed Sebastián into the heart of the mission compound.

Father Jacobo appeared at his door, a dinner napkin still tied around his neck. "Father Pfefferkorn! What's this I hear about Apaches?" He put an arm around Sebastián's shoulders, drawing Pedro against his other side. "These two young men say you saw Apache scouts. Are you sure?"

"We saw them silhouetted on a hill. When they turned away, I saw colors—war paint. Bows too. They watched us, then disappeared behind the ridge. They may attack any minute."

Jacobo spoke in urgent tones. "Sebastián, run, tell don Antonio! Pedro, ring the alarm signal! That'll alert the sentinels." He glanced up at me. "We can't take any chances after what happened here seven months ago."

The boys ran in two directions, and Sedelmeyer turned to us. "My *gobernador*, Antonio, commands my native militia, trained by the soldiers. He knows what he's doing. We'll have fair warning if the Apaches attack." He paused, filled his lungs with air and expelled it slowly. When he spoke again, his voice was normal, as if no emergency were looming.

"Tell me, who's this young lady?"

His calm voice soothed me, too. I swung down from the saddle. "May I present doña Beatriz Urrutia? I expect you met her husband, Lieutenant Mateo Salinas, when he came out with the vice-provincial. You may have preached his funeral Mass. She's here to find out more about her husband's death, to visit his grave, and to pray."

He stared up at Beatriz, his face solemn. "I'm so terribly sorry for your loss, doña Beatriz. Yes, I did conduct his funeral Mass. I'll tell you whatever I can and show you his grave and the battleground. I hope… I hope after all your travels that this visit will be of some small consolation to you."

"Thank you, Father Sedelmeyer. At last, I'll see the reality. I won't have to go on making false pictures in my mind— where he lies, where he died."

"But first—until those savages attack, if they ever do—we need to care for the living. Please join me for supper. While we eat, doña Beatriz, I'll tell you something about the battle, how your husband died, and then tomorrow I'll take you to his grave."

He waited as if he expected her to hop down from her horse as I had done, but I saw she needed help. I stepped to her side just as the bells began to ring out a peculiar pattern.

Father Jacobo nodded toward the church tower. "Our alarm signal."

"Yes, I thought so." I reached up to Beatriz. She placed her hands on my shoulders and slid her arms around my neck while I hoisted her off the sidesaddle. Our routine felt completely natural by now, that is, until I caught Father Jacobo's expression. I set Beatriz on the ground and she marched in a little circle, stamping her feet and swinging her shoulders, gripping my arm for support.

"Thank you, Father Ygnacio. My back had a stitch in it and I could barely feel my right leg."

My colleague continued watching us, his narrowed eyes darting back and forth. What was he thinking?

Pedro trotted back after ringing the bell. "What now, Father Jacobo?"

"See to the horses, my boy. Walk them till they're cool, give them water, plenty of hay and a good rubdown. Hang the saddles and bridles in the tack shed. Spread those saddle blankets somewhere where they can dry out. There's plenty of room in there. Then you'd better get to bed."

Pedro turned to our two mounts, standing with their heads hanging low, and led them away.

"I'll see what I can find for your supper," Father Jacobo said, "You'll probably want to freshen up before you come in, though. There's a pan over there on the washstand next to the rainwater barrel. I'll get you a fresh towel; that one's pretty damp from being used all day. The outhouse is out back. When you're finished, come in and relax."

Doña Beatriz washed her face and hands with dainty care and tossed her wash water on a large shrub nearby. I refilled the pan, washed my hands and sluiced water over my face. I dunked my hair, toweled it and raked it back with my fingers. The water cooled my sunburned cheeks, dripped off my hair and shivered down my collar. Then I, too, dumped the water on the shrub. No wonder the oleander was covered with pink blossoms!

I'd seen Father Jacobo at least once each year at our annual meetings. We held him in awe as a worthy successor to our remarkable—almost superhuman—founding father in Sonora, Father Eusebio Kino. Sedelmeyer had come to Sonora twenty years before me—two and a half decades after Kino's death—and now, in his sixties, he was still a vigorous man. He stood about six feet, my height, but brawnier. A typical Bavarian, he was blue-eyed and fair, though by now the Sonora sun had turned his skin brown and tough as the bark on an old oak tree. His blond hair was mingled with silver.

Like Father Kino, he was an eager pioneer and explorer. He had followed the Gila River to its confluence with the Colorado, exploring northward where Kino had not gone, returning with stories of the Moqui Indians who, he said, call themselves the Hopi. He had been wounded at Tubutama Mission by a poisoned arrow during the Pima revolt in 1751, but escaped during the night. Surviving such a wound was a miracle, a tribute to his tough constitution and perhaps to his knowledge of native medicine.

Two other missionaries were martyred in the revolt: Father Tomás Tello at Caborca Mission and Father Enrique Ruhen at Sonóita. When I first arrived there five years after the revolt, I found Ruhen's grave violated, his body exposed and reduced to his skull, ribcage, pelvis and leg bones amid tatters of black robe. I gave him a Christian reburial. It was a grim introduction to my missionary service. I took it as a bad omen, but so far my fortunes, though at times extremely trying, have proven me wrong.

Father Jacobo gestured toward the kitchen table, where his half-filled plate sat congealing. "Sit down, sit down! I have a couple of yams, plenty of bread, and enough roast rabbit and gravy to share with you. Sebastián caught the fellow nibbling off our carrot tops this morning."

He produced two red clay plates, shiny with a transparent glaze, spoons and knives. Forks, a luxury on the frontier, were absent. Each plate received a baked yam, tender grilled nopal pads and a generous portion of rabbit, with hot gravy over all. Two small clay bowls held the seasonings: ground rock salt from a nearby deposit and ground chile. He passed us a partial loaf of crusty bread along with the cutting board and knife.

"Here. Cut what you need."

He poured us each a cupful of red wine, topping off his own cup, and nodded in my direction. I said a quick grace. We crossed ourselves in unison, and I gave Father Jacobo a muffled thank you around my first bite of yam. Beatriz and I devoured our food with more appetite than manners, enjoying it despite the tension. I could tell that she, like me, was listening for the alarm bell.

Father Jacobo spoke first. "Yours is the second visit I've had since the vice-provincial and his group came. At least you're not ranting and telling me that all my good works will avail me nothing without faith."

I choked on my mouthful of rabbit. "Don't tell me Wolfgang Wegner has been here, too!"

"Yes. Pío Wegner. The man's quite mad. Told me a terrible sin had been committed here. Said the place reeked of it! He gave me quite a shock."

"He told me he was making the rounds of our missions," I said. "When he's not preaching Luther, he's been saying uncanny things—at least to me and Father Andrés at Ures, and now you're included. When was he here?"

"More than a week ago, I think, maybe two. But given the deadly attack on us during that strange inspection nearly seven months ago, what he said struck me as eerie."

Doña Beatriz leaned forward, her body rigid, the look of a hunting eagle on her face. "Father, tell me more about that—what happened back then. I've ridden all the way from Durango to find out how and why Mateo died. I came to Ures with Captain Cuevas and three soldiers, so I've heard the captain's version of the battle, but unfortunately, he was killed at Ures by… by… well, nobody knows who."

"What! Cuevas dead? Killed, you say? At Ures?"

I nodded. "Yes, hit in the back of the skull with a heavy little statue of the Blessed Virgin and strangled with Andrés' own rosary—a big one he kept in his desk drawer. Their Corporal Gonzalez doesn't think Andrés did it but their sergeant, Morelos, does. A third soldier disappeared before dawn shortly after Cuevas was murdered. Oh, yes, and Wolfgang Wegner was there too, but also vanished that same morning." I kept Father Andrés' secret and made no mention of the tracks left by Denzhoné, the Apache chief.

Jacobo frowned. "Doesn't sound a bit like Andrés, unless he was off his head. He hasn't taken to drinking now, has he?"

"No, Father Jacobo. Father Andrés is as sound in soul and body as you or I. He was cold sober the whole time we were there. Scared, too."

"I should think so! What will happen to him now?"

"The soldiers went back to Horcasitas to report the murder. Heaven only knows what will happen next. As doña Beatriz says, the authorities tend to prosecute the most obvious suspect. That's Father Andrés. He's in extreme danger. I think we German Jesuits are under greater suspicion because our own superiors—not to mention the king's royal visitor—are all Spaniards."

Father Jacobo propped his chin on his fist, his face darkening.

"Any way you look at it, this is grim news."

We sat in silence until our host turned to doña Beatriz. "How did you get your information about your husband's death, Señora?"

"From Corporal Ayala, one of the survivors of your battle. But I'd like to hear about it from you. Please."

Father Jacobo was about to begin when we heard a knock on the door, and a man I took to be Antonio poked his head through.

"We're ready if they come, Father. Adriano's stationed at the bell. If they attack he'll ring, and you'll take refuge with the other padres in the College."

"Well done, Antonio. We'll be listening." Father Jacobo turned back to us. "It began on a Tuesday, as I recall. Our vice-provincial, Luca Poncelli, came here acting as visitor, assisted by his secretary. He was inspecting the College along with an escort of twelve men, including Captain Cuevas and your husband. They came with pack mules loaded with bottles of something that looked like oil. Toward evening, a group of seven men arrived, also leading pack animals. They were Dutchmen who'd traveled overland from Guaymas, and—"

I interrupted. "Dutch! This far inland? What on earth were they doing here?"

Doña Beatriz' shot me a speculative glance, one eyebrow raised. She echoed, "Yes, just what *were* they doing here, Father Jacobo?"

"They said they were on their way to the gold mines in Soyopa and had missed their way, veered too far north. I suppose they followed the Mátape River northward instead of

the Yaqui. The mouths aren't that far apart down near Guaymas. Anyway, they asked me to lend them a guide to get
them to the mines by the shortest route. Of course, I couldn't
let them leave yet—it was too late in the day—so I invited
them to share our food and our beds. They were happy to
accept."

The Dutchmen could only be merchants, and their presence made a mockery of what I'd told doña Beatriz on the
trail. I spoke quickly, trying to gloss over their extraordinary,
suspicious presence at one of our missions. "And then, I suppose you provided the guide and they left the next day. But
what of the battle?"

"I'm coming to that," Jacobo said. "Those Dutchmen spent
three hours closeted with Father Poncelli and his secretary
before they retired for the night. The next day, when they
left, I saw that their pack animals were loaded with the oil.
They hadn't gone very far when an Apache raiding party attacked them. The youngest Dutchman, slightly wounded,
raced his horse back here to get reinforcements. It seems they
holed up in a draw and defended themselves. I gathered that
they had the latest firearms and plenty of ammunition."

"The vice-provincial and his escort were still here, then?"

"Yes, Ygnacio. Father Poncelli and Captain Cuevas con-
sulted briefly, and the Captain sent Lieutenant Salinas with
four men out as reinforcements for the Dutch. Unfortunately,
doña Beatriz, they were ambushed by a part of the Apache
group, which turned out to be much larger than anyone
thought. They never had a chance. They fought desperately
but the warriors circled them, picked them off one by one
with arrows and finally finished them with their lances. Late
that afternoon, after the raid was over, we recovered the bodies of your husband and three soldiers. We scouted the area,
searching for Corporal Ayala, and decided that the Apaches
must have taken him captive.

"Next morning, the captain and the other soldiers left with Father Poncelli after the funeral was over. We were doubly amazed when Ayala appeared soon after his companions had left—walked all the way here with a lance wound to give us an eye-witness account. When I asked him where he'd been, he said he'd begun to feel faint on his way back, crawled into some bushes and lost consciousness. Our expert in herbal medicine tended his wound."

Beatriz' voice was tremulous but cold. "And he got well, though it took him weeks."

Jacobo inclined his head. "I'm glad to hear that."

"Yes, and somehow he got back to Durango and found me. Tell me, though, what happened to the Dutch merchants?"

"There was plenty of evidence of battle, but no more bodies. We found splashes of blood where the Apaches would have been. The Indians must have carried off their dead and wounded, and the Dutchmen got clean away, maybe with minor wounds. They must have scared the Apaches off with their superior firepower. But the mission was not so lucky."

I interrupted. "You mean the raiders came here after a long battle with the Dutch? It must have been a huge war party!"

"It was. A milling, screaming mob of warriors besieged us for an hour and shot flaming arrows at our buildings and at anyone who ventured out. Four people were wounded, but not killed outright, although one of the women died the next day."

Beatriz, who had been following every word, asked a sharp question. "And where was Father Poncelli?"

"The vice-provincial and his secretary were safe inside the College. Some of our smaller sheds with thatched roofs burned, but most of the mission is adobe and tile. Our mission militia helped Captain Cuevas and the rest of the soldiers keep the attackers off. All at once, the Apache chief gave a signal and they all left. The attack was a diversion, I believe.

Their main goal was the theft of fifty horses—a grievous loss."

"And the next morning, you held a solemn Requiem Mass for my husband and his men, and for the dead Indian woman."

"That's right. Father Poncelli concluded his inspection, and he and the remaining soldiers rode back to Durango."

"You have no idea, Father Jacobo, what the Dutchmen and Father Poncelli were conferring about for three hours on the night before the attack?"

Our host hesitated for two heartbeats before replying. "No idea at all, doña Beatriz."

I could tell he was hiding something he didn't want her to know—probably on orders from Poncelli. What sinister affair was our Society involved in? What was in those bottles? How guilty was Jacobo Sedelmeyer?

Chapter VI
Return to Ures

Father Jacobo Sedelmeyer thinks that he can give me all this information about the Dutch merchants, Captain Cuevas and the vice-provincial, and I will do nothing with my knowledge. Does he have such a low opinion of this woman's intelligence? Or does he think I'm too blinded by grief to care?

I suspect that the entire Society of Jesus is involved in a trading scheme with the Dutch, those enemies of Spain. Cuevas was not acting on his own but was under Poncelli's direction. The vice-provincial might have been—almost certainly was—under orders from someone higher up in the Society. Those goods were transferred for resale at the gold mines in Soyopa. The Dutch never do anything unprofitable, so whatever they sell will go for a king's ransom. It had to be worth a fortune for them to come this far overland. It's all clear to me. After all, I am my father's daughter.

Whatever the business arrangement was, my beloved Mateo must have found out about it—by accident, I'm sure. To keep him from revealing what he knew, Luca Poncelli had Captain Cuevas send him out with an inadequate force to confront a large Apache band. The young merchant who asked for help surely told them what the men would have to confront.

Corporal Ayala told me the captain deliberately sacrificed my husband and his men, and Sedelmeyer's version of the incident confirms his story. That order was given as a death sentence, and four innocent lives were forfeited in the name of greed. What atrocious crimes these 'holy men' are involved in!

Jacobo Sedelmeyer has guessed something of the truth, but he's protecting his superior from me. Or maybe he thinks he's protecting me from the knowledge that my husband died for such an ignoble cause. Does he know the details of the deal? Why the order was given? I doubt it. I can't believe a man like him would be a party to murder.

What am I to think of Ygnacio Pfefferkorn? He lied when he told me there was no trade between the missions and the Dutch or other foreigners. How sad! I'd taken a liking to him. He seemed so naïve, so straightforward—with a great deal of warmth and generosity. Or could it be that he is ignorant of his own Company's shady activities?

℘℘

Father Sedelmeyer found us rooms in the College's dormitory. Doña Beatriz was accommodated in a separate wing, away from the students and priests. Would she, isolated like that, be sleepless and frightened? Restless noises from adjoining rooms told me no one slept much. But outside, I could hear nothing.

Despite the apparent quiet, there was an attack in the night. Alarm bells and running feet woke me at dawn. I heard a rap on my door.

"Father Ygnacio! The Apaches killed a guard and stole our horses!"

I opened the door and saw Sebastián knock on the next door and the next, repeating his message. We gathered in the courtyard before the church. Jacobo joined us shortly afterward.

A chorus of voices greeted him. "Father! What happened?"

"The Apaches are cleverer than we thought. They must have known from previous experience they couldn't take the whole mission, so they crept up and slit the throat of the guard who was watching the west side of the horse corral."

Beatriz' voice rang out. "Did no one hear or see anything?"

Antonio replied, "There was no moon. The Apaches killed Fernando, then took down a section of fence without making a noise. There were twenty horses in the corral. They took them all."

Jacobo smashed his fist into his palm. "Cayetano heard nothing? He was on guard only a hundred yards away!"

"No, Father," Antonio continued, "They must have led the horses out one by one, like ghosts."

Jacobo bowed his head. "Lord have mercy! What will we do without our means of transportation?"

Pedro, the cattle herder and guard, stepped forward. "That isn't all, Father."

"What next?"

"It was truly dark last night, Father. About three by the stars, I heard the cattle milling around. They soon quieted, so I didn't go down to investigate—I'm alone out there, you know. Twenty head of cattle were gone when it got light."

I spoke to Beatriz in a low voice. "That shows how desperate the Apaches are. They eat only horsemeat and scorn beef—if they have a choice. They must have lost a few battles with the Seris."

"We'll gather in the chapel for an hour of quiet prayer," Father Jacobo said, "and then celebrate a Requiem Mass for Fernando. We'll bury him right afterward."

℘☙

Beatriz and I followed the coffin to the graveyard. She stayed after the burial to visit her husband's grave and those of the three soldiers who had died with him. The lieutenant's grave had been seeded with grass that barely hid the raw earth with a sparse coverlet of green. The remnants of a mummified floral wreath leaned against the grave marker. She knelt beside the grave and for the first time since I'd known her, sobbed most bitterly, her shoulders shaking. Her body sagged forward until she was almost prone, digging her fingers into the earth. She remained there until she had exhausted all her tears.

I walked some distance away, not wanting to intrude, but stayed within calling distance in case she might need someone. Her pain tore at me, and for the first time in months no words of consolation—those well-rehearsed, often-repeated platitudes—came to me. I found myself biting my left index finger to the point of cutting the skin, leaving purple tooth marks on the knuckle. At last, she raised herself from the grave and came toward me, brushing herself off, her face puffy and streaked with dirt and tears.

I went to meet her. "I-I'm so desperately sorry, doña Beatriz. Your husband, Mateo, must surely be watching over you, loving you all the more for the extraordinary pilgrimage you've made for his sake."

She raised reddened eyes to mine for only a second. "You're very kind, Father Ygnacio. Sometimes I feel him near me, and other times he seems totally lost, cut off, forever gone. I'm waiting for a sign, Father. If only he'd contact me!"

I longed to comfort her but could think of nothing more to say.

She took a deep, shuddering breath and wiped her hands and face on her lace-edged handkerchief. When she spoke again, her voice trembled only a little. "Come, let's ask Father Jacobo where Mateo was killed."

The battleground was a mile from the mission, on a level plateau of table rock, where scant grasses and a few cacti had found a foothold. The soldiers had been crossing the open area when the Apaches surrounded them. We could see how it must have played out, just as we'd been told. Arrows came from all directions, so their horses' bodies gave them no cover. They stood back to back until they were all cut down.

Doña Beatriz dismounted while the guides and I waited for her on one side of the open area. I began a rosary for the sacrificed men. She walked every inch of the plateau, examining a prickly pear crushed and trampled in the fight, pausing over white gouges on the rocky surface made by horseshoes, boots, spurs or stray bullets. A few times, she knelt to touch a raw scar with her fingertips. I watched as she found dark stains on the rocks and pressed them with her open palms. Was she weeping again? Her lips were moving, perhaps in prayer or maybe asking her dead husband to touch her somehow.

She walked back towards us, her face drawn and white. She made a quick hand gesture, letting me know she could use a boost to get back on her horse. I lifted her, as I had that first time.

"Doña Beatriz, I'd be honored, ah,… it might help a little… if we prayed together back at the church."

She glanced down at me and quickly looked away, nodded and squeezed my shoulder. Her wordlessness told me she couldn't trust herself to speak. We walked our horses back to the mission, as silent as the taciturn guides.

We knelt amid the faint perfume of incense in the cool, shadowy interior. Beside the gilded wooden tabernacle, the vigil candle glowed through its red globe under an impressive crucifix, imported from México or Spain. The converts had dressed Christ's loins in a drape of real cloth, caked on one hip by the blood and water that had run down his side. The blood looked—and probably was—real. They had also covered the sculptor's carved hair and beard with real human hair. The glassy eyes, half closed in agony, seemed fixed upon us.

We prayed and recited a rosary together. She rose then with a long sigh.

"Thank you, Father Ygnacio, for your understanding and your desire to help. I just wish life were not so complicated."

We left the church together, and as we headed towards Father Sedelmeyer's house, I thought of the ride back to Ures, wondering if doña Beatriz would come that way.

"I'll look for a young priest or a scholastic among the instructors here to be my assistant for a while up at Cucurpe. And maybe I could find someone to escort you back to Durango. Would you like that? I'll be going back to Ures, then on up north to my mission. You could either head straight for Durango from here, or come back to Ures with me and then return—though that doesn't make much sense. Which would you prefer? Coming back with me would add unnecessary leagues to your trip."

She stopped and raised her eyes, her face bleak. "Yes… I guess my pilgrimage is done. I must go back. I had a purpose, a goal, but now that I'm here, it all seems so hollow. My soul was groping toward a man who's dead, who'll never return, who'll never know about my efforts anyhow. I thought I might feel his presence, that he might cross the void and touch my hand, my cheek, perhaps at his graveside, or maybe on the battlefield. But I felt nothing, only the abyss, a black, aching emptiness. I've achieved nothing, after all that struggle and exertion. And now I feel so empty. My heart has withered, dry as dust."

I put my arm around her shoulders. "Beatriz," I said, forgetting her title, "you mustn't think like that! Of course he knows about your sacrifice in coming all this way! He's here—somewhere near—watching you, loving you. You must believe that! You can't force him to answer you—it's like prayer— God answers us in ways we never expect. And so will Mateo. He'll help you, touch you somehow, maybe today or tonight, maybe a month from now. But he will. You *must believe.*"

I released her and she glanced at me sidewise with a faint smile. "I'll try, Ygnacio." She stood still, thinking. "About returning, I'd rather come back to Ures with you. That way, we'll both be able watch the novices, if we find one or two to escort me, and judge whether they can be trusted. I'm still young enough that 'the temptations of the flesh,' as you'd call them, might take hold of them. That's what I've been dealing with during this whole trip. You should thank God you're a man, Father Ygnacio. It's something you'd never have to worry, or even think about."

"Yes, I've given that problem some thought. We'll see what Father Jacobo recommends." We had reached the door of his house. As I raised my fist to knock, Father Sedelmeyer pulled it open. "You two are getting along famously, I see. Spent quite a time in the church." He fixed me again with narrowed eyes. "I hope you've been of some genuine help to doña Beatriz in her grief."

She nodded without speaking. We entered the house and I noticed that the largest window faced the church. "Yes, doña Beatriz and I prayed together. Perhaps that helped a bit." I hastened to change the subject. "Father Jacobo, I need someone to help me out at Cucurpe and Opodepe for a week or so. I have a special project, and doña Beatriz needs someone trustworthy to escort her back to Durango. Can you spare three good novices or scholastics for a little over two weeks?"

"What's the special project?"

"I'll need to talk to you about that in private for a moment, if you have time." I glanced at doña Beatriz.

"Yes, fine; we'll discuss it right now. Maybe I can think of three people who would fill your needs. Would you excuse us for a moment, doña Beatriz?"

Her dark eyes shifted between Jacobo and me with a shadow of a frown, but she agreed with grace. "Of course, Fathers Jacobo, Ygnacio. I haven't packed my things, so I'll go do that. Call me when you're ready, please."

"Excellent idea, Señora, just relax over there and we'll call you." We waited until the noise of Beatriz's boots on the hard ground had faded.

Jacobo faced me. "Well?"

I handed him the note from Andrés and waited while he broke the seal and read the contents. "Hmmm. So you're supposed to make contact with an Apache tribe in hopes of a peace pact. He says here he's made some headway with them, but with the murder and the uncertain situation, he can't pursue the matter himself, so he's sending you… into the Mababi Mountains, no less! What else can you tell me about this expedition?"

"Not much more. Father Andrés forbade me to reveal details. Of course I agree with him that even the faintest hope of a peace pact is worth pursuing. But since this tribe's ranchería is in the Mababi Mountains, I need any help or advice you could give me. I know you've explored there yourself."

Father Jacobo was silent as he rose from the table and took a few paces, swinging around to face me. "It strikes me as almost insane—if you're his only hope for a solution to this murder—that he'd send you out into the wild country to make a peace pact. There's more behind this than you're telling me." He shook his head, muttering to himself. When he spoke aloud again, he seemed ready to accept Andrés' request at face value.

"Rough country, rougher Apaches. All right, since you can't give me the details, I'll just have to assume he knows what he's doing and you'll be risking your life in a worthy cause. As soon as I've lined up some help for you, I'll pull together what information I have."

He continued pacing, his footsteps punctuating the silence. I waited motionless until he spoke again. "As for people to escort doña Beatriz, I think I have two youngsters for you: Enrique Ortuña, a fine young teacher, a scholastic up here from México, and a friend of his, Bendito Ortiz, still a novice. I'll take Enrique's place in the classroom until he gets back. Father Ramón Bernardo Zapata would make a good assistant for you, Ygnacio. He's teaching part-time and acting as my secretary. I can spare him, too, for a short while."

He opened the front door and leaned out. "Sebastián! Run and find Enrique, Bendito, and Father Ramón for me, please!"

Jacobo's chosen trio looked trim, eager and earnest. I'd soon see if they were also capable. They were keen to help and anxious for a break in their daily routine. While I explained what I needed, I could hear Jacobo rummaging in his room. He returned with a rolled and tied document, an inkpot, a quill, and a scrap of paper. I gave my last instructions to the young men, and they left, whispering excitedly, to gather their gear and prepare for a long ride.

Jacobo sat at the kitchen table. "I'll list some things you must take with you. I know you're an experienced traveler in these parts, but they're small items you might forget that could make the difference between life and death. Above all, be sure you take enough horses and pack animals."

"I'd counted on two mules and two horses. I'll need to switch horses every day so as not to overwork either one, and with the load of food and water I'd have to pack, two mules would be a minimum. What do you think?"

"That'll mean you'll be leading three animals, all you could manage in those rough hills. You'll have to carry at least a day's supply of water for you and the animals. You know how far apart streams or springs are, once you get away from the rivers. You'll need extra fodder for the horses and mules when you camp for the night, not to mention your own food. Take plenty of jerky and pinole, since they don't spoil. And take trade goods, of course, especially tobacco. Also piloncillo—brown sugar cakes. And take basic medical supplies…"

He dipped his quill and wrote down each item. After half an hour, he scratched his head with the hand that held the quill, smudging his hair with ink. "That's all I can think of now. Oh, yes, I almost forgot this document. It was Father Kino's map and a page or two of his notes on the Mababis. I've tested it, and found it accurate. Anything Father Kino did is reliable." He handed roll and list to me, and I nodded my thanks.

"Don't do anything foolish, Ygnacio. And that's not just a commonplace, my friend." After a pause, he blurted out, "For God's sake, be careful! It's more dangerous than ever up there."

⁝⁞

The way back to Ures looked different seen from the opposite direction. I understood why horses react to something they'd noticed going one way as if it were new and frightening on the way back. Beatriz was different, too: sad and silent. We stopped for lunch when the sun had reached its peak, and I asked Enrique to help her out of the saddle. He did so gingerly, shrinking from the unavoidable close contact. Once she was safely on the ground, he turned his back and crossed himself, praying for help in resisting the Devil, no doubt. Bendito stood to one side, grinning, scanning the horizon as if he'd seen nothing. I kept a straight face, opened the food basket and handed out tortillas and jerky, then passed the water gourd around. This would keep us until sundown.

We reached Ures by late afternoon on the second day. Our mounts pricked their ears and lengthened their stride when they smelled the river water. One of Father Andrés' Pima sentinels must have told him of our arrival before we came in sight, since he and Hernán were waiting outside the church to welcome us. Hernán took our horses, and we followed Andrés into his house.

A beef roast sizzled in a clay casserole in the oven, wafting an irresistible aroma, while Andrés pan-fried sliced *nopalitos* and ripe tomatoes over the fire, spiced with a chopped jalapeño and flavored with salt, sage and rosemary. A freshly baked loaf of crusty bread steamed as I sliced it. He poured us each a cup of wine, and I brought extra chairs, so we could crowd around the table. We took turns telling about the two Apache scouts and the sneak attack under cover of darkness, the death of the sentinel and theft of the mission's animals.

We did not discuss Lieutenant Salinas' death, nor did I want doña Beatriz to hear my speculations. Andrés, though he kept glancing at Father Ramón, was too discreet to ask about his future duties at Cucurpe. As our host rose to fetch a second serving of nopalitos, I joined him and spoke quietly while the others chatted around the table. "I need to consult you after they've gone to bed." He met my eyes and nodded.

We helped him wash the dishes, and then the young men and doña Beatriz headed for the rooms at either end of the stables. We were exhausted from the heat and the ride.

I held Beatriz back long enough to let the men get a few yards ahead, then walked with her part way. "What do you think? Will Enrique and Bendito do as escorts?"

"Yes, yes, I think so. Enrique's so afraid I'll drag him to Hell, he'll do anything to avoid touching me. He'll be all right—with his friend Bendito along as chaperone. They're nice young men who'll do their duty."

"I had the same impression."

"Did you see how Enrique turned his back and crossed himself after his first contact with me? You'd think I was the Devil's bride!"

We chuckled together, and I said goodnight. I called to the young men that I would see them at Mass in the morning, then returned to the priest's house and Andrés.

"Very disturbing information about the death of doña Beatriz' husband, Andrés."

"*Komm, Ignaz, setz Dich. Mehr Wein?* Sit down Ygnacio. More wine?"

We continued speaking our native language. "A bit, thanks."

"Well?"

"This is hard for me, Andrés—the implications are devastating. But I'll give you a bare recital of the facts as Father Jacobo told them. It began with that inspection tour of Mátape College by Father Poncelli and his secretary after they'd come through here, inspected your books and found them clean."

Andrés pursed his lips. "I wondered at the time why they brought those loaded pack animals and so many soldiers. But you're about to explain. Go on!"

"That same afternoon, a group of Dutch merchants arrived, also with a train of pack mules. They claimed to be on their way to the gold mines at Soyopa, but had taken a wrong turn."

"That's a pretty serious wrong turn, don't you think?"

"I thought so. Poncelli went about inspecting the College, but that evening he spent three hours with the Dutchmen. Jacobo said the Dutch left the next morning with their mules loaded with the 'bottles of oil' Poncelli had brought."

Andrés covered his lips with his fingertips, shaking his head. If looks were to be trusted, he was not involved in these dealings. He shifted his gaze from midair to me. "What do *you* make of that?"

"A trade took place, something to do with Soyopa gold. Father Poncelli may have been ordered to carry it out. But, if he'd thought it wrong, he could have refused to obey. After all, Saint Ignatius' *Letter on Obedience* clearly states, 'In all things *except sin* I ought to do the will of my superior and not my own.'"

"He might have thought it wrong, but not a sin, Ygnacio."

"True. There's much latitude for personal interpretation—despite all our rules and regulations on sin."

"So far, this story leads me to think the worst. But what of the death of the lieutenant?"

"A band of Apaches attacked the Dutch party before they'd gone far from the college. One of them came back for reinforcements, and Captain Cuevas, far from riding out in force, sent the lieutenant and five men—*five men*, mind you—to cope with the situation. They were ambushed, surrounded, overwhelmed and slaughtered, with the exception of one wounded man who returned to tell the tale."

"Did he tell it to Father Jacobo?"

"No, he may have been too badly wounded. But after he recovered, he found doña Beatriz, his lieutenant's widow, in Durango and told her about that battle. I suspect he told her they'd been set up."

"Possibly—if a common soldier is capable of working out things like that."

"Andrés, common soldiers, as you put it, have the same powers of deduction as the rest of us. I have no doubt he could see they'd been sent out for some reason other than defeating those Apaches!"

"You may be right. But what concerns me even more is this business with the Dutch. That's just the sort of thing our Society is suspected of doing. Up to now, I thought it was without foundation. You bring terrible news for us all and for me in particular. The accusations and reprisals against the Society in Europe are increasing. That's why King Carlos—or more likely his prime minister, the Conde de Aranda—sent this new Visitor General, José de Gálvez. He's violently against the Jesuits, and a scandal like this would be grist for his mill. I hear that in the king's new hierarchy, he outranks Viceroy de Croix, an anti-Jesuit himself. A wild wind is rising, Ignaz, that threatens to sweep us all away. It's painful to see any of us contributing to the storm."

I nodded, sharing his anxiety and impressed with his rhetoric. "I know. If the vice-provincial is involved in nefarious practices, who'll believe him even if he does exonerate you? Who'll believe any of us? I think it's our duty to write to the provincial in México and our father general in Rome. We must expose these covert dealings before they destroy us. I'll write as soon as I get back to Cucurpe and have some time to think this through. But first, I intend to take action on your behalf, as you know."

He stood and began to pace. "I'll write our provincial and father general right away. I need to explain my own situation as well as report that business with the Dutch and our vice-provincial's apparent collusion in sending Lieutenant Salinas and his men to their deaths. A sad duty, and as it regards my own case, perhaps a desperate one."

I remembered Father Jacobo's recommendations, and interrupted our train of thought. "By the way, I'll need trade goods to treat with Denzhoné. Do you have any tobacco or sugar cakes—piloncillo?"

"So happens I do. I'll get it for you to take in the morning."

I laid a hand on his shoulder. "It's late. We'd better sleep while we can."

He smiled up at me grimly. "Yes, while we can, Ignaz."

Chapter VII
Separation

The sun had just cleared the horizon. Beatriz and I stood together while Enrique held her chestnut mare, who nickered to her. I had just given the young man Andrés' letters, now tucked in his saddlebag like state secrets. Bendito was already on his mule. Our shadows stretched in grotesque caricatures towards the church door, where Beatriz and the scholastics had just said goodbye to Father Andrés.

She gazed up at me, her dark eyes grave, almost sad. "I'm sorry we can't go on riding together, Father, all the way to Durango. I've enjoyed your company. You gave me strength with your goodness and understanding when I was failing."

"If I've been of any help to you, doña Beatriz, I thank God for that. You'll do fine on the return journey. Enrique and Bendito will keep you safe. They take their duties seriously, since Father Andrés is also using them as messengers."

"I'll miss our conversations. I hope we'll meet again."

"Only heaven knows. I hope we may, and you'll be happier—in less pain and grief. Meanwhile, *vaya con Dios* and with my blessings."

She smiled, but her lips trembled as she stretched both hands towards me. I took them in mine. With a quick movement, she freed her hands and threw her arms around me, pressing her cheek against my chest. I was startled, but returned the embrace for a moment before stepping back.

She apologized. "Forgive me, Ygnacio. It's just that I feel safe with you. Leaving you is… is like leaving a protector. You are *Father* Ygnacio, after all." With that, she gave my arms a final squeeze and walked to her horse, asking Enrique to give her a leg up. Once she was settled in the saddle, he unhitched and mounted his mule, and the little trio turned their animals towards the southern trail. Enrique waved once, Bendito gave us a last look, and Beatriz called out, *"Adios! Adios, Ygnacio! Vaya con Dios!"* the same farewell I had just bid her.

ౠ

Enrique, Bendito and I are bedded down for the night near a rocky bluff. Enrique built a fire that should keep predators at bay for half the night. He seemed to discount the possibility that Apaches might see it and slaughter us in our sleep. I think he fears me more than threats from the outside. He's rolled in his blanket, using his mule's saddle pad as a mattress, his back to me. Bendito is quite indifferent to his brother's qualms, already snoring. I am propped against my saddle, thinking over the past three weeks. The firelight casts wavering, lurid patterns on the rocky wall behind us, confusing me as to what is reality, what illusion, perhaps giving me a foretaste of the fires of Hell.

I try to plan my future moves, but out here with the wind blowing sparks in my direction and wafting a distant coyote chorus to my ears, it's hard to imagine myself back in the city. Durango awaits, and so does Luca Poncelli. I know his residence is somewhere in the city, no doubt in the most luxurious quarter. Somehow, I must find out what game—murderous game—he's playing. Perhaps I can confess to him, maybe get to know his secretary. At any rate, I must become trusted enough to discover the truth, though I might be murdered in the attempt. He seems to have no qualms about such crimes.

I worry about Father Andrés. He might be arrested and found guilty of the captain's murder. He'd be hanged, I suppose, but where would he be taken first? Horcasitas? If it's Durango, I might be able to persuade the lieutenant governor to help him. Right now, out here, I can't imagine how.

Despite my grandiose designs, I find that I'm a silly, weak woman, after all. During most of my quest I've remained as cold and calculating as a chess player. But in the midst of my grief, my anger and suspicions, I found someone who touched my heart. The Jesuit priest Ygnacio has intrigued me and I can't stop thinking of him. He's an enigma. He appears pure and innocent, and yet he lied to me about the Dutch. Or did he? He looked both shocked and embarrassed when Father Jacobo told us about them at the table.

I've never met a man who showed more compassion for my sorrow. His words when I confided my utter desolation to him were gentle, wise and consoling. I fear I'm beginning to love him, while my love for my poor, dead husband continues undiminished, and I'm determined to avenge his death, even should it cost my life. Could this new feeling be a different emotion from the love I feel for Mateo? Should there be a different word, a new word, for it?

My confusion is due, I suspect, to the intense pressure I've been under, the uncertainty and the danger. If I'm honest, it was to be with Ygnacio that I rode back to Ures. It would have been smarter to ride straight south from Mátape. But it was such a relief to ride with him and to know I was safe from the leers and wicked thoughts of those soldiers. Yet, I hoped pure, innocent Ygnacio would have just a few of those wicked thoughts. How would I have reacted if he'd thought them and acted accordingly? Like a singed cat, I'm sure, or I would have coldly scorned him. How absurdly contradictory we are! How very weak and foolish!

℠℞

I left Andrés before dawn with feelings of dread: anxiety for myself and foreboding for him. A premonition told me I'd not get back in time to save him from arrest and imprisonment, if I got back at all.

I rode the stallion Corporal González had brought me when he found me at Nacameri, and a sturdy mule carried the trade goods. Instead of Beatriz, Father Ramón Bernardo Zapata rode at my side on a roan gelding. He was good company, but I missed her.

We stopped by Nacameri to check on my former patient, who seemed quite recovered, and to pick up Trina, my mare. We led her as far as Opodepe Mission, where we arrived the next day. She'd get proper care there. I introduced Ramón to the native officers, the gobernador and alguacil. The following morning, I presented him to the congregation at Mass. They had not expected my regular pastoral visit for another week, and the bell summoning them to the church surprised and intrigued them. Consequently, a full congregation heard Mass and met their temporary pastor. I explained what had happened at Ures, and that I would be away for a couple of weeks. They gave Ramón a warm welcome, and I could see they hoped he would become their full-time missionary.

We rode on at noon and arrived at Cucurpe after dark, when the mission Indians—except for the lookouts—had long been asleep. The two of us were worn out. We collapsed on our cots and slept like the rest. Diego, my *gobernador*, saw our horses in the corral the next morning, and woke me in time to say Mass.

It took only a day to familiarize Ramón with most aspects of life at Cucurpe, such as my 'angelic' choir that sang responses at Mass. He considered those crystalline voices to be a special, divine blessing. While I'd been gone, Diego had continued the harvest. I suggested that Ramón oversee the next project, to extend the cultivated area by another acre so that, come spring, we could plant corn together with squash plants to grow between the tall stalks. Soon we could sow the wheat I'd bought in Chihuahua last spring. Winter at Cucurpe was mild enough that it would grow if we had enough water.

I left the mission, confident that Ramón would meet the spiritual needs of my flock. I hadn't written the Provincial. My conscience pricked me, but quick action to save Andrés was more pressing than a letter that would take many days to arrive in México. Even after it arrived, weeks, maybe months, would elapse before any sort of decision would be made known in Sonora.

My old friend, Conejo the mule, trotted along behind me. Our brisk pace was necessary but tiring, and when dusk came I decided to camp by a dripping spring. The trail followed the convoluted canyon around a bend, where a bright green cottonwood sapling grew from a niche, with a tiny lawn of lush grass. The life-saving water dripped down a granite boulder, nourishing a narrow band of slimy green moss before pooling in a shallow basin. About a yard across, the basin allowed only two horses to drink at one time. I drank last, the cool spring water reviving both my body and my spirit. The hobbled animals grazed the succulent grass while I made my blanket-bed at the base of the cliff.

A vivid dream woke me at dawn. Doña Beatriz slipped as she mounted and fell. As before, I caught her, but this time lifted her into a passionate embrace. Her lips met mine for a long moment before I placed her on her horse. I started awake. My face burned at the sinful fantasy, and I said a quick prayer to banish all further thought of her. But once on the trail again, she haunted me. Her presence was so real, so powerful, that I almost spoke aloud to her when I fell into a half-doze. Her graceful form and gestures, her facial expressions and mocking smile constantly invaded my mind. Her husky laugh seemed all but audible, and once again I felt her touch with a shudder of delight that surprised and frightened me. God, give me strength! This Beatriz—unlike Dante's Beatrice, who had guided the poet to the Empyrean heights and contemplation of God himself—was opening the gates of Hell before me. The Devil's wiles extend far beyond immediate temptation, it would seem. Were there not enough dangers ahead without carnal distractions?

I threaded my way through the tortuous canyons and tumbled heaps of boulders, sometimes dismounting to lead my train of animals, skirting sheer drops onto rocky spikes below, struggling up grades so steep I almost had to crawl. We reached an abandoned ranch at nightfall. The buildings were partially burned, the ranchers driven out by the Apaches, perhaps killed. The corral fence was still intact, and I found edible hay in one end of the half-blackened barn. I unloaded my animals, watered them from the undamaged well, and fed them hay. I bedded down in the barn, since the house, badly damaged, exuded an atmosphere of horror and violence that would have produced nightmares.

I awoke late and hurried to load the pack mules, only to discover a strap on the pack saddle that had worn through and was ready to break. It was noon before I found materials to repair it. We reached the Sonora River by late afternoon, and dusk was deepening into night when we came in sight of the sheer cliffs that overhung Sinoquipe Village on the opposite river bank.

No activity could be seen around the mud-and-stick huts or in the tiny adobe chapel, no naughty children defying their mothers' calls. A pair of dogs yapped at my approach, and then a chorus joined in, but not a human in sight. Then my eye caught a movement at the door of a large hut. A black-robed figure, arms akimbo, thrust its head forward to identify the newcomer.

"Wolfgang!" I called, "Is that you? What are you doing here of all places?"

He answered in German, in the insulting tone I remembered well, as if he'd rather see anyone else at all. "*Um Gotteswillen! Da bist* <u>Du</u> *wieder, Ignaz! Woher kommst Du?* For the love of God, it's *you* again, Ygnacio! Where did *you* come from?"

"I'm on a mission to save a fellow priest. I have to find one of the Apache chiefs to seal a peace pact with his tribe."

I saw no harm in telling Wolfgang that much about my quest. Once dismounted, I began unloading my animals. "It's your turn, Wolfgang. Why are you here?"

He raised his arms in a wild, desperate gesture. "Measles, Ygnacio. We've given them measles, and they're dying of it. I've never seen such severe cases. High fevers, terrible rashes even inside the mouth, throat, and nose. Come on, then! What're you waiting for? I need help here!"

"I'll tend to the animals first." I led the mules and horses to the river in the increasing dark, unpacked four batches of hay, hobbled the group and turned them loose. Wolfgang issued an order as I climbed the bank.

"Bring me fresh water! Have to bathe this woman's forehead. That bucket there." He pointed.

I followed orders, felt my way to the river, filled the bucket and carried it into the smelly one-room hut. The tiny flame from a single candle revealed a middle-aged woman on a blanket-covered bed of branches.

"How many people are sick, Wolf?"

"It's about the end of the epidemic. The healthy ones fled the village, left the sick behind. We've lost seventeen people, saved eight."

"Those aren't good odds. Who lived?"

"Mainly the children, plus one tough old man and two women."

"You said the epidemic is about over?"

"Yes. No one has shown new symptoms for three days. But I'm used up. Haven't slept much this whole time. Why couldn't you get here sooner?" His dark eyes raked me with an accusatory glare.

"If I'd known…." I held out the bucket, and he pointed to a tightly woven *cora* with a scum of water in the bottom. I poured the bucket's contents into the basket, marveling at the Indians' expertise. Their baskets were so tightly woven that some could even serve as boats.

He passed me the rag he was using to sponge the fevered woman's forehead. "Go on with this—it might cool the fever enough to make a difference." He picked up a cora full of waste.

"Where are you going with that?" My nose wrinkled.

"I'll empty her slops and bury them outside the village."

"Why so careful, Wolf?"

"It's my theory that coming in contact with them spreads the disease. I've been digging a trench and burying slops as deep as possible. Exhausting work in the heat and with the soil as hard as it is."

I shot him an admiring glance. This was a different Wolfgang—peremptory and insulting as before, but jarred out of his earlier near-madness by these people's need. I pressed the dripping rag to the woman's hot forehead and sponged yellow crusts from the corners of her mouth. She moaned and opened her lips, so I squeezed a cool, thin stream onto her pustule-covered tongue,. I shuddered.

Wolfgang pushed aside the skin flap over the door. "Are you sure it isn't smallpox?" I asked over my shoulder.

"Can't be sure of anything, but the youngsters have a typical case of measles, as I remember them from my own childhood. It's the grownups who get this sick. Pray, Ygnacio, pray! Only a miracle will save this woman now. It's time for you to prove your faith, my brother; our works will not move God's pity."

I took him literally and knelt, praying aloud and with great fervor for God's mercy to return this village to good health. He returned after burying the waste, and we worked side by side with this woman and five other cases, every one as bad, in other huts. As dawn broke, he led me to an isolated hut where he'd taken the unburied dead.

"We must bury these people before the heat of the day."

"Do we have something to dig with?"

"I found a pick and a shovel a prospector left behind when he died digging holes in the mountains hereabouts." He pointed to the tools leaning against the charnel hut wall.

"So… you've been burying the dead all along?"

"As many as I could. My arms are worn out from swinging that pick—so you use it."

"Fine. Here's the shovel. We'd best get to work right away. It'll be hot as soon as the sun comes up."

"I've already baptized them. Did it before they died—I think. Hard to tell when they're unconscious. I didn't take time for the last rites. Couldn't afford to."

We said the prayers together. "The Lord Jesus Christ will change our mortal bodies to be like his in glory, for he is risen, the first-born from the dead…. "

Then we carried all seven adults, wrapped in their blankets, to a sloping graveyard on the north side of the village. Wolfgang had already dug ten graves—an amazing amount of work—and had marked each one with a crude wooden cross.

This time, we would bury the dead in a trench. Once below the hard topsoil, digging went easier, but the sun was up and the temperature rising fast before we finished. I worked in my under drawers, torso bare. Dirt clung to my body, and now rivulets of sweat trickled down, turning the dirt to mud and then making tracks through it, dripping off my back and chest.

"I hope four feet deep is good enough. I expect it will be. The bodies will mummify, anyway, before summer rains come again."

Wolfgang nodded as he wiped blinding sweat from his eyebrows. "Stay where you are. I'll drag the bodies to you."

I caught the corpses as he laid them at the lip of the grave and pulled them into the trench, tipping them to take up less room and placing them head-to-foot. When we finished the somber task with its increasing stench of decay, we scooped and shoveled the dirt into the pit. Only when the trench was filled did we pause for final prayers.

"Come, Ygnacio. Let's go down to the river for a good bath. I suppose you've had measles already. Forgot to ask."

I led the way to the streamside, holding my robe at arm's length, and waded in. "I had all those childhood diseases, I think. But I can't remember one from another by now. Mumps, chicken pox, measles—I hope—whooping cough—"

A deliciously cool shock wave from a bucketful of water struck my chest and splattered my face, interrupting my litany. As I stooped to wash my hands and arms, another bucketful sluiced over my back. I doused Wolfgang in his turn. We washed our robes in the flowing water, wrung them out and donned them. They would dry within minutes.

"I hope you brought some food. I've been out for a day, existed on water. I'm getting weak."

By now, the sun was hot on my baskets and bundles. We placed them in the shady guest hut he had appropriated as his temporary quarters. I opened the food *cora*, and shared out pinole, jerky, and tortillas. I kept back the dozen chopped beef tamales for lunch or dinner. Eugenia, one of my favorite Eudebe matrons, had made them. Wolfgang devoured his food with shaking hands.

"Get some sleep," I told him, "I'll make the rounds among the sick, and watch to see if others come down with it, God forbid! Then I'll rest, too."

He nodded. "I'll sleep here. You're welcome to this same cot; just see that the dogs don't get in. They're hungry too."

I left him and returned to the first woman, only to find that she had died while we were burying the seven. I prayed over her, wrapped her in her blanket, and carried her to the charnel hut where the other bodies had lain. As I trudged along I begged the Blessed Virgin to intercede for God's mercy on these poor sufferers.

The other five people were still alive, although some seemed lethargic. I gave them water, and for those who could tolerate food, mixed pinole with the water. I cleaned and washed patients who had soiled themselves, carried away slops and made them as comfortable as I could under miserable circumstances. Three hours later, Wolfgang reappeared.

"You sleep, now. It's still fairly cool inside."

I gave him an account of the patients' conditions and headed for the guest hut where I threw myself on his pallet, asleep before I hit the blanket.

Chapter VIII
Toward Apache Country

Four days passed at Sinoquipe, until we were sure the patients were out of danger, and the villagers were returning to normal activities. We buried the woman, Mitsha María, with due ceremony. Eight more crosses of mesquite wood bound with rawhide marked the graves.

The night before I left, I told Wolfgang what had happened at Ures. His comments, delivered in a matter-of-fact tone, gave me the eerie feeling he was half mad after all.

"I knew Andrés Michel would soon be in mortal danger. I told him so, and that only a miracle could save him—but I was not the one to perform it."

"How did you know he'd be in danger?"

"It was revealed to me."

I waited, but he added nothing further. To extract more information, I added details. "The captain was bludgeoned with the statuette of the Virgin Mary, strangled with Andrés' rosary, and there was a stab wound in the heart, inflicted after death."

He remained silent, eyes unfocused, staring into the candle flame. I tried again.

"Did you know beforehand that Captain Cuevas would be murdered, and Andrés blamed for it?"

He replied, but with another cryptic statement. "The captain deserved to die, but by the hand of God, not of man."

"What did you know of the captain?" Again, I got no answer. He rose in silence and began preparations for sleep, leaving me to do the same. I gave up and rolled myself in my blanket. Wolfgang did not seem to be setting out to mystify me, but he surely had some otherworldly source of knowledge. After puzzling for half an hour over his uncanny abilities, I slept.

The next day, he assured me he could now care for the villagers by himself and would soon follow me to Arizpe for food and rest. I continued my journey on that fifth morning, counting on reaching Arizpe Mission by mid afternoon.

☜☞

The trail north of Sinoquipe followed the Sonora River, crossing and re-crossing as it snaked down the valley. Willow shrubs and cottonwood sprouts grew along the stream, and farther up the bank huge cottonwoods, hoary with age, dropped white, decaying branches. I passed palisade-like cliffs that resembled fortified castles with sheer walls two hundred feet high. Above the line of hills bordering the river, a granite formation came in view known as *La Mano de Dios*—The Hand of God. I stopped to contemplate it. What would Beatriz think of this? I longed to share my impressions with her. The fully open hand must rise four hundred feet above the surrounding hills, palm toward me, thumb separate, fingers extended and together like someone ordering a halt. I'd seen it before, but this time it struck me as a warning and an omen. Was God telling me I was riding to my death?

The village of Arizpe came in sight, perched on a hill above the river. We climbed the steep road from the river bank and arrived in the cobblestone plaza, a patch of green grass in the center. I dismounted, squinting at the splendid church, dazzling white in the sun's glare. A massive bell tower rose on the left side. Here and there, where plaster had peeled away, I could see it was built of pink limestone blocks the size of bricks. The façade was adorned with five niches for saints' statues, the topmost holding an image of Nuestra Señora de la Asunción, patroness of the church, flanked by low-relief images of the moon and the sun. As the ascending Queen of Heaven, she soared between them on her way aloft. Over the arched entranceway, a plaque bore Father Carlos Rojas' name and the date the church was completed, 1756. Construction had begun in 1646 when the first Jesuit, Padre Jerónimo de la Canal, arrived at the site. Above the plaque, the sculptor had carved an imposing IHS, the H transfixed by a cross, the whole surrounded by carved sun's rays—the Company's symbol.

A hitching rail under a tree offered shade for my animals while I entered the church, anxious to find refuge from the August heat and glare. Penumbra and cool air caressed my face and hands. My sigh of relief echoed in the silent interior. I stood still, possessed by the memory of a forest pool near Mannheim where I swam underwater in sun-streaked coolness until my lungs nearly burst, then broke the surface among lily pads and blooming lotus—pink, lavender, yellow and white. Tree limbs met overhead like Gothic arches. I was in a cathedral there, just as here. I raised my eyes. Far above my head, heavy, dark mesquite beams spanned the nave, carved corbels supporting them on either side.

I moved through the church, the clack of my footsteps the only disturbance in the reverent silence. The painted retablos in the transepts amazed me with their complexity and beauty: on the eastern side, scenes from the life of St. Ignatius, on the west, of the Blessed Virgin. I reached the high altar and knelt at the rail.

"My Lord and Savior, if it is your will, please heal all sick villagers and help all priests in the missions who serve them. Keep me safe, O Lord, and bless my quest to save my friend Andrés. Blessed Mother, here in your temple, intercede for me. Lord Jesus, guide me; help me find Denzhoné and solve that dreadful murder. And please, guide our Company of Jesus, and let it not fall into tempta—"

A large, heavy hand grasped my shoulder. "Ygnacio Phapheserkorn! I could have sworn you were at Cucurpe or Opodepe. What brings you here?"

Ignoring the comic butchery of my name, I stood and turned to greet Father Carlos Rojas, S.J., Visitor General of Sonora and the Pimería.

"It's a long story, Father Carlos. I'm just up from Sinoquipe where there's been an outbreak of measles. Father Wegner had been nursing the whole village when I arrived five nights ago."

"Measles on the march again!"

"Yes, and I did what I could to help—little enough, since the epidemic was almost over. But I need to warn you. The plague is no doubt on its way up here. I may even be a carrier. I shouldn't have embraced you."

He snorted and beckoned me to follow. "I've survived about every disease the Devil invented."

He bustled off, his broad beam wagging under the black robe. I almost trod on his heels to catch the words that trailed behind him. "Another plague, eh, Ygnacio? There've been too many lately, and too many of you Padres sick with one thing and another. What with the Seris and the Apaches attacking and the Presidios doing precious little to stop it, we're under siege from man and nature. And what in God's name was Pío Wegner doing in Sinoquipe?"

"Lucky he was there, Father Carlos. Eighteen people died anyway, and half the village would have gone without him. Isn't he supposed to be at Cuquiárachi with Bartolomé Saenz? He didn't tell me so, but he may be on his way back."

"He's coming through here, is he?"

"Definitely. He was out of food when I got to Sinoquipe, so I left what I had with him. Slim pickings, though. He'll need to recuperate here with you."

"Good. Then I can tell him to get back to Cuquiárachi. Bartolomé Saenz is still there. That's a long story, too. I'll tell you in a minute."

We left the church by the side entrance and now stood on the rectory's veranda. He stopped and swung around, taking an awkward extra step to balance himself. Rojas had always been heavy-set, but now with lack of exercise and age— somewhere near eighty, I guessed—he had become obese. His size did not detract from his aura of authority. He tipped his head back and narrowed his eyes, examining me, his expression both shrewd and kindly. Sunlight behind him made a halo around his full head of silver hair. He would extract every scrap of information I possessed by offering tidbits of his own and inviting an exchange. I'd seen his *modus operandi* before.

"At least, you're not one of the sick ones," he said. "You probably heard that Father Joseph Och nearly died a while back. He even called in Juan Nentwig to give him the Last Rites—but he survived. They took him on a litter partway to Chihuahua, then in a carriage. He's nearly paralyzed, you know, in constant pain."

I bowed my head. "I heard."

Of course I'd heard. In addition to Father Loaiza's death, Joseph's illness also put tremendous strain on the mission system in Sonora. My eyes went out of focus as I remembered the Joseph I knew, his eyes sparkling with joy as he prepared to celebrate his first Mass at the Jesuit College of Würzburg. I heard again his boyish laugh when he discovered that Michael Gerstner, Bernard Middendorf and I—the four of us, newly ordained—would travel together as missionaries bound for the New World. He led the way as we marched together to Augsburg, and there he found the coach that took us through Austria, the Venetian Republic and across Italy to Genoa. It was he who spoke enough of the language to confess a dying soldier on a French ship docked next to ours in Genoa harbor. His charm and wit made our travels bearable and even joyful: around Gibraltar to Cadiz, across the Atlantic on the *Victorioso*, and then by mule-back from Veracruz, four hundred leagues through New Spain to Sonora. We forged an unbreakable friendship, and all these years we four kept in contact, sending letters that sometimes took months to cross the distances between our missions, carried by muleteers, arriving out of date, dirty and torn, but precious nonetheless.

"Who else is sick, Father Carlos?"

"Our former visitor, Manuel Aguirre, was. He started out with a bad cold, then his hands and arms became partially paralyzed. But he got better."

"Sounds the same as my good friend Joseph's early symptoms."

"Yes, and no one knows where it comes from. The Indians don't have it."

"It's something they're immune to and we're not. Well, we've brought them plenty of diseases that kill them but hardly faze us."

He turned toward the rectory. "Why are we standing here in the heat? You must be hungry."

I followed him inside. We passed several closed doors along a shadowy corridor brightened with floor tiles glowing in a blue, yellow and white floral pattern. The last door opened into the sitting room. Its windows looked out on a patio garden surrounded by a colonnade draped with flowering vines. He clapped his hands, and an elderly servant appeared.

"Lorenzo, set the table for two. This man is famished."

The setting was simple, the cooking unpretentious but abundant and delicious. I'd not realized how ravenous I was until I reached for my third helping of *cabrito asado*, grilled kid. The succulent meat was accompanied by tortillas, baked camote—yam—and a heap of wilted and buttered spinach fresh from the garden, all washed down with high-grade pulque. My appetite at last sated, I sipped my pulque, watching Carlos finish the cabrito.

He sat back with a satisfied sigh. "I expect you don't know I named Bartolomé Saenz to be Vice Rector at Opodepe Mission in Father Loaiza's place—may he rest in peace. Bartolomé would have moved from Cuquiárachi to Opodepe to relieve you of that burden. I know you've been doing a good job, caring for it in addition to Cucurpe, but I couldn't allow that to go on any longer. Pío Wegner would have come along as his secretary and assistant. But we had another blow."

I set my glass down and leaned forward. "What was that?"

"Apaches again. You remember from our yearly reunions that I've been requesting more priests from our Provincial, Francisco Zevallos, at least since '62. That's just four years, so I've probably been after him longer than that. He sent men repeatedly, and each time they got waylaid in Sinaloa, in Tarahumara country—priests are desperately needed everywhere. Three men finally made it all the way up here. On my instructions, our former Father Visitor, Manuel Aguirre, placed one of the new priests, Father Albarrán, at Cuquiárachi to relieve Bartolomé. He got to Cuquiárachi and was learning his duties, assisting Bartolomé. He was about to take over the mission and release Bartolomé to come relieve you."

"So how did the Apaches—"

"I'm coming to that. Bartolomé sent him to Fronteras Presidio to see the Captain who was sick. While he was there, the Apaches appeared on a hill near the fort and began to yell and shake their weapons at the presidio. Father Albarrán wanted to go back to the mission, but the Captain knew there was danger. He said if he felt better, he'd escort our man that afternoon."

"Was he? Did he?"

"No, he sent some soldiers, and as they passed a bush near the hill, a warrior jumped out and killed a soldier with several lance thrusts. Then the Apaches began to shoot arrows at the other soldiers."

"Was Father Albarrán hit?"

"No, he ran his horse back to the presidio, and arrived in such a state of terror that he couldn't speak, hear, or see. He became feverish and then fell into a coma. No one could revive him. He died in six days."

I crossed myself. "*Requiescat in pace*. Terrible news. It must have been his heart, poor man. That means Bartolomé is stuck at Cuquiárachi until Father Zevallos sends another priest, and I'm stuck with two missions."

"That's about it, unless he wants to trust Pío Wegner to run Opodepe. What do you think? You seem to admire his work at Sinoquipe. If I recommend Pío, the Provincial will follow my advice."

"You knew he left Cuquiárachi without permission and has been wandering from one mission to the next preaching Luther, didn't you?"

"Yes, Bartolomé told me the young fellow is unbalanced. But if you think he could handle a mission… I'm that desperate."

"He's a hard worker. You could place him at Opodepe and I'll supervise for a while. He could still wander off at any moment."

"Good idea." He clapped his hands. "Lorenzo, bring those *tunas*, please."

A crystal bowl filled with peeled prickly pear fruits appeared, pomegranate red, their ruby juices trickling down their sides. We began our dessert.

"Father Carlos, I know you're still making the rounds of the missions every year for your inspection report to the Provincial. How do you manage?"

His belly jiggled as he chuckled. "Good question, Ygnacio. I'm too fat to mount a horse without help, though once I'm up there, I can ride with the best of them." He shot me a sharp glance as if expecting me to challenge him. "I've got a horse big enough to carry me, but I only use him when the river's high or in flood. Otherwise, I use my two-wheel carriage. I can get everywhere with that in dry weather." He paused long enough to take a huge bite of *tuna* and continued talking, his mouth half full of seeds. "Changing the subject, though, with all the responsibilities you have, what on earth are you doing traveling up the Sonora River Valley?"

"As I said, it's a long story."

He swallowed the seeds. "Tell me. Tell me."

I began with Andrés Michel's request for help, relayed my observations about the murder, and explained the reason why the Captain and his men had come there in the first place: the suspicion—no doubt emanating from the viceroy's office or from the royal visitor—that Andrés, and maybe all of us, were carrying on illicit trade and hoarding the proceeds.

"Captain Cuevas examined Andrés' books but was murdered before he could tell his men what he found."

"You're sure Andrés didn't do it? It was his rosary, and he knew where to find the Virgin's little statue at a moment's notice."

"You know Andrés better than I do, Father Carlos. Do *you* think him capable of such a thing?"

"No-o-o, but it's obvious he's in terrible danger. I still don't see why you're here and not there."

"Andrés fully expects the governor to arrest him for the murder, since he had both the means and an apparent motive. He was negotiating a peace treaty with an Apache chief, Denzhoné. If he's detained, there'll be no chance of sealing that pact. I'm his proxy. He tells me Denzhoné has his ranchería in the Mababi Mountains north of here."

"So, who's minding your missions?"

"Father Jacobo Sedelmeyer lent me a young priest, Ramón Bernardo Zapata, who's teaching for him at Mátape. Said he could spare him for a week or two. I introduced him at both missions before I left."

"If Jacobo recommended him, he'll probably do well for a week or two, if he doesn't have to cope with some crisis. Meanwhile, you're risking your life, Ygnacio. There's more than one Apache chief in those mountains. I can't afford to lose another priest."

He held my gaze in silence, the pupils of his large brown eyes slowly dilating. "I'm about to command you to go home."

"Wait, Father Carlos! I didn't tell you everything. Andrés ordered me not to reveal…. There's a compelling reason—"

Carlos' imperious wave cut me short. "Tell me under the seal of confession, then, Ygnacio. I must know in order to make an informed decision." He clapped again. "Lorenzo! Bring me the stole I use for confessions!"

When he draped the stole around his neck, I knelt beside his chair and not only confessed my sins, my fears and doubts, but also told him that Denzhoné had been at the mission that night, and that I suspected him of the murder. I was seeking him not to bring him in, since he would certainly be executed, guilty or not, but to gather enough evidence to convince any court, whether ecclesiastical or secular, of Andrés' innocence. And incidentally, I would, if possible, seal the peace pact.

Father Carlos absolved me and as a penance I said the *Anima Christi* prayer, which he joined. Afterward, he leaned both elbows on the table, his head in his hands.

"It's a hard choice, Ygnacio. I may lose you in this attempt to clear Andrés, but if I send you home now, I'll more than likely lose Andrés. And I haven't even considered the consequences for the Company. What a scandal! I can see it now: a Jesuit priest and missionary executed for committing a murder to hide a scheme to swindle His Majesty. Our enemies would rejoice to have such a weapon!"

He paused for many minutes and finally spoke. "I understand why you're traveling alone. An army escort would make your mission seem like a hostile move. The Apaches would ambush and kill all of you…. All right, you have my permission. May the Blessed Virgin intercede for you, Our Savior protect and aid you—and may God forgive me if I'm sending you to your death."

At dawn, the discomfort of the tangled and damp bedclothes woke me after a night spent battling unremembered demons. Since there was time before the early Mass, I pulled out Father Kino's map and notes on the Mababi Mountains that Jacobo Sedelmeyer had so kindly given me. My finger traced the trail up the Sonora River Valley and through the Mababi Pass as Father Kino had drawn it half a century ago. The pass at first followed a tributary of the river that branched off to the east and then it continued roughly east and west. Two trails intersected it at roughly right angles, leading southward. Kino had marked both with dotted lines and the notation 'Indian trails.' Neither line continued far into the blank area labeled 'Mababi Mountains,' meaning he'd not penetrated deep into that wilderness. What a shame! I'd hoped for better guidance. I turned to Kino's notes, pleased to see a lengthy entry:

> *Indian trails* (he wrote) *intersect the pass through the Mababis at intervals. I have marked only the two that seem to be main pathways. These are used by the Seri and Pima tribes, although the warlike Apaches have begun to infiltrate the area as well. The westernmost of these trails is the easiest, although it will require the traveler to dismount at times and lead his animals. The trail at first follows a deep and narrow arroyo with sheer or overhanging sides, then it climbs through a region of tumbled boulders, many as big as a house. Progress is only*

possible on the single track. A spring of moderate size rises roughly in the center of the sea of boulders. The traveler must continue climbing for two leagues before he is clear of that rocky desert, and he must constantly watch for scorpions and snakes. He will then find himself in a typical mid-level mountain landscape, populated with live oaks, junipers, ocotillo and other cacti, which give way to pines at higher elevations.

Kino's information eased the residual anxiety from my early morning nightmares. Together, the map and the notes told me what I needed to know, the physical obstacles and their location. It was still obvious that I had no way of finding Denzhoné other than blundering into his territory alone and unarmed. As Father Carlos had said, I was risking falling into the hands of other Apache tribes, but I placed my faith in the trade goods. With them I could surely negotiate and find a guide to the right tribe.

At Mass, I avoided direct contact with members of Carlos' congregation, in case I might still be carrying the measles contagion. Breakfast afterwards was abundant, even opulent, given the usual fare of a frontier missionary. Eggs, frijol beans and fried potatoes spiced with a red chile salsa strengthened me, washed down with cups of hot imported tea. I had almost finished loading my animals when Carlos joined me, handing me a bundle of food for the trail.

"Lorenzo fixed this for you. It should keep you for three days, maybe more if you're careful. I don't have to tell you to be careful, but… Do be careful, my son!" His voice shook a little on those last words, and I gripped his arm in gratitude.

He placed his hands on my head and blessed me. "Our Lady of Guadalupe, Blessed Virgin and Queen of Heaven, you who sit beside the Holy Trinity, spread your mantle of protection over this son of yours. Saint Ignatius, guide him. Direct him to discern the right choices, to follow the right paths. Lord Jesus, be his inspiration and give him strength in time of trouble and danger. Never leave his side. This I pray in the name of the Father, the Son and the Holy Spirit." He embraced me. "Come back safely, Ygnacio."

"A thousand thanks for your hospitality and concern. May God and the Blessed Virgin remain with you too, Father Carlos."

I turned to wave as my little cavalcade rounded the corner of the church. Carlos stood still as stone, his hands tightly clasped, perhaps in prayer. He could have been a statue except for the breeze rippling the robe around his legs.

ೞೞ

Bacoachi, where I'd found hospitality the following night, was far behind me. A glance at the sun told me it was two hours beyond noon, and we were already into the Mababi Pass. A well-traveled branch trail came in sight, leading southward into the high mountains. The hoof prints at its mouth were made by unshod horses, therefore the path mainly— perhaps exclusively—served Indians. Apaches.

We turned to follow those bare hoof prints, my spare horse and pack mules trailing behind. My heart thumped against my ribs and my handkerchief soon became wet from mopping my face. Sweat tickled its way down my backbone. Maybe it was not too late to turn back. Carlos was right; I would most likely lose my life before my quest had half begun.

The trail led into the mouth of an arroyo that became a cleft in the mountain, so narrow there was no way to turn around, no way to flee. I was committed to this foolish enterprise by the landscape itself. Footing presented no problem on the gentle upward slope where water had ground the stones to gravel. The towering walls darkened the floor to dim twilight, cool enough that I shivered in my sweat-damp robe.

The sky was an irregular blue crack high above me, where a few minutes of sunshine might have penetrated at high noon. Too late for that. The walls closed in enough to bruise a knee, proving Kino's notes to be accurate. I must dismount and lead the horses. I backed our cavalcade down the trail until there was room to re-balance the loads so the pack mules could squeeze through.

We slipped and clattered our way upward, and the cut became shallower until the walls fell away entirely. Before us stretched a vast field of tumbled boulders. Huge, rounded blocks of granite ranged from the size of a wagon to the dimensions of a small mission church. They piled on top of each other, some teetering on what looked to be a mere inch of surface. Beatriz would have been amazed and delighted at their gravity-defying balance. I could almost hear her question and comment, *"What giant child toyed with this land? The slightest push would send them crashing and bounding down the slope."*

Again, the Kino notes were correct. Nowhere could one move among those rounded stone sides, slippery slopes and crevices except on the single pathway. Perhaps centuries of flowing water had formed it. Unshod hoof-prints became visible again. If a group of Apaches or Seris came this way today, my animals and I would have nowhere to hide. Our fate was in God's hands, and I prayed that by His grace we would find Denzhoné.

I poured water out of the skins into the cora-basket for my beasts. Each one drank nearly a gallon in a single draft. I scratched their foreheads and fondled their ears as they slurped, hoping their labor and mine was not in vain. My gourd held enough tepid water to slake my thirst with a pint left for next time. Kino's spring had better appear by nightfall or we'd be in serious trouble. The animals' feet seemed fine except for one loose shoe. I'd tighten it when we stopped for the night. The loads on the mules were lighter with so much water gone, and I made sure nothing was galling or irritating their backs and sides.

As the sun reached the western horizon, my lead horse threw up his head and whinnied. Were the Apaches near, or was he reacting to the scent of moisture? Around a bend, a wide spot appeared where bright green grasses made a startling contrast with the dusty boulders. God be praised! A basin four yards across glittered with pure water that reflected the glory of the sky, painted by the setting sun. We rushed to it, arranged ourselves around the basin as best we could, and all drank at once.

My saddle pad, damp and salty as it was, provided a cushion where I knelt and thanked God for bringing us safely this far. I unwrapped the food Father Rojas had provided: tortillas, pinole, jerky, and a little dried fruit, and ate voraciously. Then I rolled up in my blanket in my usual way, lapped it over my feet and lower legs to keep out insects and snakes and wrapped one side over the other. The cold made me shiver after darkness fell. My animals hovered close by, and we all dozed through the dark but starry night, uneasily aware of the weird surroundings and the rustling and clicking noises from the inhabitants of the boulder field.

₧₨

We passed beyond the tumbled rocks by midmorning, and the ascent into the Mababi Mountains began in earnest. A spectacular canyon came into view, boxed in by sheer rock walls at its apex. Here, junipers were eight feet tall, joined by a few tender green aspens in sheltered canyon nooks. I paused at two springs to drink, water the animals, and enjoy the view of the Sonora River Valley below us to the west. A trail of dust snaked toward the pass, made by a party of riders, no telling whether friendly or hostile. We toiled upward until sunset and came upon a stony but grassy meadow among piñón pines. I hobbled the horses after unloading them, ate and stretched my tired legs, listening to the silence unbroken except for an occasional whisper of the breeze through pine needles. *You'd better enjoy this,* I told myself, *it may be your last peaceful resting place.*

Chapter IX
Perilous Quests

I still think of Ygnacio Pfefferkorn. He seemed so intense in his desire to return to Cucurpe. What could his real purpose have been? He may intend to place himself in danger to help his friend Andrés Michel. I hope he does nothing to harm himself. But why should I care? He belongs to the Society just as surely as Andrés Michel and the vice-provincial. And yet, I would help him if I could.

Enrique and Bendito brought me safely back to my home in Durango, so empty now without Mateo. They bade me a ceremonious adieu, and hurried off to the vice-provincial's headquarters to deliver Father Andrés' sealed messages to be forwarded unopened to the provincial and the father general in Rome. I almost asked Enrique to take me with him—foolish impulse. It came of my wish to know whether the entire Society of Jesus in New Spain is embroiled in illicit trade with the Dutch and if so, what they are trading. If this business reaches further up the hierarchy, I'm determined to find a way to use it against them, for that would make them more responsible for Mateo's death than the army. I'm sure His Majesty would be interested in hearing about Jesuit trade with the enemy. I am only a woman and therefore a powerless toy for the men who run our society, but I *will* have my revenge. I must use indirect means to reach my goal, find a way to meet this vice-provincial socially, to gain his confidence and his confidences.

Lieutenant Governor Antonio de Figueroa came for tea this afternoon and we sat in the cool beauty of the grape arbor that surrounds my marble fountain. Red and white grapes, fully mature, hung over our heads, giving a most charming effect. I gave him a complete account of the trip—except for that mysterious exchange with the Dutch.

"And so at last I was able to pray at Mateo's grave and visit the battleground. There were still splashes of blood on the rocks where he was killed."

"They shouldn't have allowed you, a lady unused to violence, to see a thing like that."

"They're frontier missionaries, don Antonio. I wonder if they know what a lady should or should not see. At any rate, if I'd hoped to feel my husband's presence there, I was sorely disappointed."

"How did you get back here?"

"Father Sedelmeyer, Rector of Mátape College, lent me a couple of novices to escort me."

His forehead creased. "I assume they behaved themselves on the journey."

"Oh yes, don Antonio, they were quite proper."

He did not join in my laughter. "About Captain Cuevas' murder, I don't suppose you heard or saw anything that night?"

"As far as I could tell, no one saw or heard anything. He wasn't discovered until the next day, when Father Andrés and I nearly stepped on his body."

"It's beyond me why a man of the cloth would commit murder in the first place, and in such a foolish and blatant way."

"Perhaps it's for lack of practice. Seriously, though, I don't think he did it, even though there's no other obvious suspect."

He shook his head. "Perhaps the good Father suffered a moment's insanity. The captain must have found something incriminating in those books of his."

"The soldiers made the same remark. I fear all the authorities are thinking the same thing, and Andrés Michel is bound for the hangman's noose."

"Most likely." He waved his hand, dismissing Father Andrés and his problem. "Enough of that. There's a ball next Friday night, Beatriz. It... it's a birthday celebration."

"Whose birthday?"

"Uh... mine. Would you honor me with your presence?"

"Why thank you! I'm the one honored. Is this an intimate affair or a large one? I probably shouldn't attend parties quite yet. I'm newly widowed, you know."

"The guests—the women—should know that birthday celebrations are quite innocent. Your reputation should be safe. It's a big celebration. I owe *hoi aristoi*—all the society celebrities in town. They've invited me everywhere, and now's the time to repay them."

I smiled at his attempt to impress me with his Greek. "Still, don Antonio, I feel uneasy about appearing in public like that. I know it sounds rude, but could you give me an idea of your guest list?"

"Hmmm. Let me think.... Don Pascuale Domenico, the Italian businessman and his wife Carlotta, don Ernesto Borraquín and his Señora—the usual crowd that you see at the governor's parties. Besides that, a few church officials."

"Who?"

"The Archbishop—he's a Franciscan, you remember, and the Jesuit vice-provincial. Father... uh, What's-his-name."

"Do you mean Father Luca Poncelli?"

"Right, right. He's the one."

"I see. It is the usual crowd—the top echelon of Durango society. I'm flattered that you invite me."

"Well, will you come, Beatriz?"

I smiled and fluttered my eyelashes at him. "Thank you, I think I will." Perhaps I accepted too readily. What would Father Ygnacio think? Don Antonio probably considers me a 'Merry Widow,' and might take advantage of that thought. Perhaps that, too, is to my advantage if I can keep matters under my control.

ॐ

A horse screamed! My eyes wide, pulse pounding, I sat up, ready to leap to my feet but a lance blade pressed against my throat immobilized me. Five Apache warriors in the meadow unhobbled the horses and mules by simply slashing their ropes. Enough words were intelligible for me to gather that they'd come into the pass from the west and climbed the Indian trail marked by Father Kino. It must have been their dust I'd seen the day before. Their voices rose in excitement as they discovered the tobacco and piloncillo, my food supply, the water skins and the useful *coras*, but they became snappish soon enough. They'd surely been hoping for guns.

An older warrior spoke more slowly, in words I could understand.

"It's a Black Robe. They don't carry guns."

He loomed over me, shoving aside the lance held by the younger man who'd been threatening my windpipe.

"Stand up!"

As I obeyed, the younger Apache snatched my blanket. They'd find that useful, too.

"I seek Denzhoné," I said in my scanty Apache. "A friend, Father Andrés at Ures, sent me."

The gray-haired warrior stared, expressionless. "Denzhoné is not our concern. We take you to Itza-chu, our chief."

He nodded toward me and made a sign, and the young man seized and held me, while another went through my pockets. They left me my dirty rag handkerchief, but took my folding knife, held up in triumph. It was a gift from my dear friend Joseph Och. As it disappeared into the young man's pouch, a pang of regret stabbed me like a shard of glass—for the knife's sentimental worth more than for its quality and utility. *Ygnacio, Ygnacio! It's only a worldly object like all the rest, unimportant in the eternal scheme of things.* The thought failed to console me.

The warrior who took my knife spied the chain around my neck and with a tug he pulled out the silver crucifix my mother had given me on her deathbed. He prepared to tear it and the chain off me when the older Apache spoke.

"No!" he shouted in an alarmed voice. "Don't touch his medicine bundle! That has powerful medicine. Too dangerous!"

The younger man dropped the crucifix as if it burned him. At least they left me that small consolation.

My hands were tied cruelly tight behind my back, while one of the young warriors held the rope's other end. The blade of a lance prodded my back, forcing me to walk ahead of the cavalcade as it mounted the steep trail towards the higher hills. The pace was grueling and the trail rough, soon rising high enough to pass into a thin pine forest. When I slowed my pace or stumbled, the ever-present lance blade gouged me, cutting through my robe and penetrating my skin, shooting flashes of pain through my body. The tickling wetness must be blood mingling with sweat down my back.

Panting—half to catch my breath, half out of fear. A rock teetered. I stumbled, tried to balance but couldn't with my arms tied behind me. Fell again, this time bruising my thigh and hip. A painful jerk on my arms. No feeling in my hands. Laughter and jeering behind me. A whistle and crack of a whip on my back. On my feet again, climbing. Tree root. My foot didn't clear it. Down on my knees, gouging them, skinning them deeper, bruising a shin, blending new injury with old: whip, lance jab, a jerk on the arms, a cacophony of pain. Stumbling forward. *Oh my Jesus, hear me; in your wounds hide me. Never let me be separated from you.*

The party stopped at noon and shared my provisions, but I received neither food nor water, nor did the horses and mules, who looked at me as if wondering why I didn't tend to their needs. The Apaches were no kinder to their own animals. Their high spirits and banter told me they were counting on feasting on one of my horses that night—a tribal celebration. But what did they intend for me?

The afternoon's journey was a blur except for the endless trail that never ceased its upward climb. Falls became more frequent. My back must have resembled chopped meat with all the wounds. I slipped sidewise, struck my face against a tree trunk. More laughter from behind. Warm flow from my nose. I twisted my neck to wipe the blood on my shoulder. New problem—the soles of my shoes wore through, thin enough after that boulder field—now no protection against rocks and thorns. Agony.

Thanks be to God! The ranchería at last! Eight or ten teepees occupied a clearing with many Apaches, mostly women, busy with evening chores. Smoke from several fires rose as they prepared their food. All normal activity stopped and the group crowded around the returning warriors, exclaiming over the horses and especially over the proudly exhibited tobacco and sugar.

In all this excitement, I was not neglected. Children clustered around me, staring and making rude remarks. I must have been a sorry sight. One of them poked me with a stick, much to their general delight. They were training to be imps that inhabit Satan's realm, shouting with delight at my involuntary cringes.

Come now, Ygnacio, stand still and expressionless if you want them to respect you. If you don't react, maybe they'll get bored and leave you alone.

At least I had not cried out.

But the bear-baiting continued until a hand flung aside the deerskin flap over the largest teepee door, and a warrior stepped into the leaping firelight. He was taller than the other men, with a deep chest, broad, heavy shoulders and muscular arms. He donned a war bonnet decorated with eagle feathers as soon as he cleared the teepee's door. Chin raised, he peered down his nose through small, deep set eyes set in a narrow face, too rugged to be handsome. A long scar disfigured his left cheek. He surveyed the scene with a slow, deliberate sweep of his head, no other movement visible.

The mature warrior in our group approached him. "Itza-chu, Chief, I have captured this Black Robe and his stores. He claims to have been sent by Father Andrés of Ures, with a message to Denzhoné." At least, this was the gist of his speech, as I understood it.

Itza-chu first examined the goods, nodding and grunting in pleasure over the tobacco. It and the sugar would be his to distribute as he wished, and the rest would be shared among my captors. He chose my spare horse to be butchered and eaten that night. It seemed that the older man, the leader of the raiding party, would take my favorite mount as his own. At least he'd survive for a time, but after the Apache custom, he'd be ridden to exhaustion, then eaten in his turn.

Itza-chu, whose name, I knew, meant Great Hawk, now approached me last of all. He faced me, leaving a pace between us. My nose wrinkled at the odor of the grease he used to oil his skin and he could surely smell my sweat and blood as well. We locked eyes, and I maintained a steady gaze. A sneer lifted his lip.

"What message do you have for us?"

I'd considered what to say to a hostile chief if I were taken by someone other than Denzhoné. I drew myself up with as much dignity as possible, covered with dirt and blood, my hands still bound behind my back. My face must have been smeared from the nosebleed. At least I was as tall as he, for my eyes met his on a level.

"Father Andrés Michel offers a peace pact between you and the Spanish soldiers. He also wants you to come to his mission at Ures. There he will teach you about the true God, the God of the universe and of all there is. But first you must stop raiding our missions."

My language was pidgin Apache, with Spanish words inserted where I lacked an Apache term. Itza-chu's lip curled during my speech, sneering at its content or at the delivery, probably both.

"There will be no peace between our nation and the Spanish. Your missions are of no interest to me, other than as sources of horses and supplies." The chief folded his arms and intoned the last sentence like an incantation:

"We will kill you to the last man, woman, and child."

He turned to the young warriors who had captured me. "Take him to the spare teepee," he said, nodding at the one next to his own. "Tie his feet. He should entertain us well tomorrow."

They dragged me backwards into the teepee, where a warrior tore the robe off my back and flung it against the wall. Another man kicked me in the hamstrings, my knees buckled, and I convulsed with pain when I landed. He tied my hands and feet together and left after kicking me again. My bladder was about to explode and I urinated with a groan of relief. My under drawers were soaked, but I writhed backwards, away from the steaming pool. The burning wetness of the cloth prickled my skin.

I lay still, resting despite pain from uncounted injuries, listening and getting my bearings in the dark and foul-smelling teepee. My martyrdom would come tomorrow. *Dear Lord and Savior, give me the strength to endure!*

Some of my brothers had been captured and tortured to death by the Iroquois. They cut out chunks of living flesh and ate them in front of the victim or forced him to eat pieces of his own body, cutting off hands, noses, penis and testicles, avoiding the vital organs in order to kill him slowly, using firebrands to sear the shrinking flesh and stop the bleeding so the agony could last longer. The Apaches invented exquisite tortures, too. They'd once captured and raped a mestizo girl. They fattened her over several weeks, then hung her by her wrists above a moderate fire, enjoying her writhing and screams until she roasted to death. Had there been cannibalism? My own fate would be a variation on such a torture.

I writhed, too, sweating in the cold mountain air, my heart thumping, my mouth sticky, dry as ashes.

Control yourself, Ygnacio. Think of the sufferings of Jesus on the Cross. Tomorrow you will die a martyr's death—through him, with him, in him, but most of all, for him.

But my uncontrollable fear focused on the agony of that Cross rather than upon the glory of Jesus' triumph over death. Would I be able to say, with him, "Father forgive them, for they know not what they do"? Or would I howl for mercy, as they hoped and anticipated? One thing was certain. There would be no mercy.

My quest had failed. Now, Andrés Michel would surely be executed for the murder of Captain Cuevas. Nothing could stop that, unless the murderer confessed—a dim prospect!

Pain fragmented my thoughts, back to self. My side ached; my back was afire with bruises and cuts and my legs began to cramp. The ropes, drawn too tight, caused a numbed tingling in my feet, and I no longer felt my hands.

My horse's death scream shocked me, and I jerked against my bonds. Excited voices gabbled as the tribe flayed and butchered the victim. Before long the odor of roasting flesh filtered through chinks in the teepee wall. They must be cooking the heart, lungs, and liver, perhaps the kidneys. These would go to Chief Itza-chu and his family; the tribe would feast on the haunches and shoulders. Chunks of meat spitted on poles would rotate over a bed of live coals. My stomach surprised me with a loud rumble. I must be hungry, but the thought of eating a friend, my horse, revolted me. My sticky tongue almost rustled as I licked my cracked lips. As a dead man, thirst was a minor concern.

Hours dragged past. The tribe gorged itself to much laughter and some chanting. The familiar odor of tobacco smoke penetrated the teepee wall. They should be grateful to me for the good things I had brought them, but to them my torture and sacrifice tomorrow would count as one more 'good thing,' a spectacle like the ones the Romans once enjoyed.

Silence fell at last. The darkest hour of the night had come along with the dark night of my soul. Thoughts of San Juan de la Cruz and of Fray Luís de León invaded me; both, like me, cruelly treated as prisoners. I began to recite *"En una noche oscura,…"* but was interrupted when the flap of my tent opened slowly, noiselessly.

A shadow stepped inside. Stillness. He must be waiting for his eyes to adjust to the darkness. I shrank away when he crossed to me, avoiding the muddy spot my urine had made. A small hand covered my lips, but gently. This was surely a woman.

The hand withdrew and began to feel the rope that bound me. She must have known how the knots were made, because after running her hands over my bonds, she began to undo the first knot. With an abrupt tug she released the length of rope that tied my feet to my hands. A surge of relief washed over me. I could stretch my spine into a normal posture. She gently grasped my wrists. Untying them would be more challenging, since my flesh had swollen around the rope. Her light fingertips passed over swollen flesh, ropes and knot. When she found the knot, she began working on it. The first tug did not undo it, but the second one did, and the ropes unwound. Knife-sharp pains flashed through my wrists and up my arms as the flesh came back to life. She turned without pausing to the bonds on my feet. It took minutes for feeling to return enough for me to control foot movements.

She thrust the robe at me, and I pulled the tattered garment, reeking with sweat and stiff with blood, over my head. She again placed her hand over my mouth and led me outside. Everyone had gorged and drunk themselves insensible on pulque, and snores came from several teepees. She took my hand and led me into the forest. We became darker shadows among shadows, silent and quick, driven by fear of discovery. She paused only because I limped. My soleless shoes gave no protection from rocks and pinecones. She crouched, felt my feet, then cut the hem of my robe and severed two square pieces from the skirt. She stuffed the bottoms of my shoes with the folded cloths.

A vertical cliff face barred our way in the black night. My guide led me to a faint trail at the cliff's base, a pale white streak in the darkness. The forest reared up on our right, black against the slightly paler sky, and as we climbed along the cliff, the trail became a narrow ledge less than a foot wide, sloping to a precipitous drop on the outside, the rocky wall of the cliff on my left. As we rose, the forest seemed to sink, showing only the black conical tops of pine trees, and then nothing at all, only vacant darkness. We came to a fissure in the cliff, its base choked with brush. The woman removed the thorny bush blocking the entrance and helped me climb into the rift, replacing the bush behind us. I followed her, scrambling painfully over gravel and boulders, following the cleft in its twists and turns, until we came to a sheer rock face where I could barely see toe and handholds. At last she spoke.

"Take off shoes. Climb with bare feet. Take off robe. Robe make you fall." She was speaking Spanish—broken but clear. "Follow me now."

She climbed rapidly, and I followed, my robe draped over my back, its sleeves along with my shoelaces tied at my throat. My weakened wrists might fail at any moment, and my bruised feet shrank from the pressure of the climb. One hand slipped as a tendon twisted and went numb. I hung on with the other hand and thrust my feet further into the holes. After a moment, I continued to climb, enduring with clenched teeth. Twenty feet or more, and, despite the surge of excited energy that had buoyed me until now, exhaustion buzzed loud in my ears, dizzying me. My legs and arms began uncontrollable shaking, their failure and a plunge to the boulders below a near certainty. I glanced up to guess, in this inky night, the distance still to climb. The woman had disappeared. I reached above my head for the next handhold and found a flat surface instead. A shelf! Now I could see a wide ledge abutting another cliff that continued upward, pierced by narrow caves. She grasped my arms and helped drag my body onto the stone platform. I lay still, panting, and saw to my amazement that she made the sign of the Cross.

"These sacred burial caves. No one dare come here. Spirits take revenge. I come here. I know spirits love Christian woman."

My voice came in a hoarse whisper. "Who are you? Why did you save me and bring me here?"

"You servant of most high God. I bring you where they come not. Here. Food. And here. Water gourd. You stay here till next night. I come back. Bring blanket, more food. I look for Denzhoné."

"Thank you! God bless you! But who are you?"

"Here, I called Qumara, wife of Itza-chu. I go now. Must be asleep beside mate before he wake up." And with that, she was gone.

Chapter X
Hunters and Their Quarry

I've just returned from Lieutenant Governor Antonio Figueroa's birthday ball. I went prim and proper, dressed in black, but since my husband was killed a mere seven months ago, there were plenty of venomous whispers behind fluttering fans. I arrived on the arm of Lieutenant Echegaray, the man don Antonio chose to be my escort for the evening.

I pretended to notice nothing and spoke modestly to those people I knew—quite a number. When I came near, they all became polite and even cordial. I caught up on their news, concentrating on the successful business people at the ball, asking discreetly about recent lucrative transactions. Most of the men were delighted to boast of their achievements, especially if they'd outwitted a buyer, selling for more than their goods were worth or else buying for less. None of their tales seemed the least bit suspicious, though they were flattered that I took such an interest in affairs their own wives considered the ultimate in boredom.

As I worked my way around the room (never dancing, since that would have seemed too scandalous), I noticed don Antonio keeping me in view. Once, he smiled in my direction and I nodded back, but since he was escorting María Magdalena, Governor Pineda's niece, he did not approach me. A Franciscan prelate chatted with a man robed in black, probably the Jesuit vice-provincial, standing near the refreshment table, wineglass in hand.

Like many Jesuits of higher rank, he was quite at ease in this social situation, dressed in a lustrous black robe with gold buttons, his shoes highly polished. His short, wavy mane of iron gray hair glimmered in the light of the chandeliers, his biretta tucked under his arm. A man of medium height, heavy set, he would run to fat if he were not making arduous mule-back journeys to trade with the Dutch. His features were heavy but handsome—resembling portrait busts I'd seen of ancient Roman senators. I approached him indirectly, speaking to people—mainly men—along the way. I've always had more difficulty attracting women friends than men, and the women were avoiding me because of my scandalous behavior.

Once the Franciscan archbishop had moved on and the Jesuit was left alone to watch the dancing couples, I broke off my latest conversation and joined him near the table. He turned his back to the dance floor and began helping himself to several of the tiny slices of bread heaped with pâté of duck. As the servant dished up a small helping of fruit for me, I spoke.

"Good evening, Father Poncelli."

I had just learned that his fondest ambition was to return to Rome to further his career, even though I'd also heard that career building was strictly against Jesuit principles. He turned to me abruptly, eyes wide, apparently surprised that an unknown woman should address him by name. I smiled.

"I don't believe we've met, Father. I am Beatriz Urrutia, widow of Lieutenant Salinas, who was an acquaintance of yours, I believe."

His reply came without hesitation in a mellifluous baritone. "Ah yes, of course! I keenly felt the loss of the good lieutenant, your husband, and have included him in my prayers."

"I thank you for that, Father. You are best placed to know what happened out there at Mátape, and I'd love to hear about those sad events from your point of view. I miss my beloved husband and think about him constantly. It would help me achieve some peace of mind, however temporary, if I could find out more about his final battle."

Father Poncelli did exactly as I had hoped. He laid a beefy hand on my arm and invited me to follow him to a quiet corner, where we could talk undisturbed. We found two chairs in a nook behind a pair of potted palms.

"Your husband was a young man after my own heart, Señora. He was vigilant and rigorous in his duty. He was a pleasant travel companion during those times when we had a moment to converse, but a man of sterling principle. If I were disposing military ranks—none of my business, of course—it would have been he, not Captain Cuevas, who would have headed our little expedition to Mátape."

I was struck by the terms he used to describe my husband: 'vigilant and rigorous,' 'sterling principle.' He confirmed my suspicion that Mateo had caught him at something underhanded and confronted him with it, heedless of the consequences to himself. That would have been typical of my Mateo.

"You speak of an *expedition*, Father. What do you mean by that?" I produced my sweetest, most innocent smile.

"Oh, merely an inspection tour, Señora. Sometimes we higher officials are called upon to investigate where there might be irregularities."

"Oh, yes, Father, I understand. But it struck me odd at the time that you took so many men along. So I thought perhaps, since you just called it an 'expedition,' that my husband helped you with a special mission. That's all."

"Ah! I see! No, it really wasn't that much out of the ordinary. We often take a larger military escort along if there's a threat of Apache or Seri attack. But I assure you, your husband was entirely conscientious in his service and he was a courageous fighter."

More adjectives: 'conscientious' and 'courageous.'

Father Poncelli continued, now asking me a question with a suspicious gleam in his eye. "I am informed, Señora, that you have just returned from a grueling horseback trip to that very mission you ask me about. Why did you go there? And since you were there, do you really need to hear my account of things? I can hardly conceive of it—a woman riding all that way! You are most remarkable!"

I nodded in acknowledgement. "Thank you, Father!" His network of spies was efficient—although it was possible that Enrique or Bendito had reported my doings to him. "Yes, I went to Mátape to visit my husband's grave, to pray there and see the site where he was killed. I know it sounds foolish, but it somehow helped. It put a final seal on our lives together, Mateo's and mine. I don't know if you can understand what I mean, Father Poncelli, but I'd still be most grateful if you'd tell me how things were that day. Your perspective will be unique, since you are an eyewitness."

He obliged, giving his own version of the events at Mátape, which differed from Father Sedelmeyer's only in small details. That is, except in the matter of the traveling merchants. Not a word about Dutch traders. I decided not to press him further or he would become suspicious (or I should say more suspicious than he must be already) and would avoid my company in the future.

"Thank you, Father Poncelli, you've been most helpful. I'm so happy that my dear husband served you well on his final... expedition." Poncelli flashed me a guarded look, then seemed reassured. "I do hope we can talk again soon," I concluded.

"I hope so indeed, Señora, your gracious company has given me much pleasure."

He took my hand and bent over it with practiced gallantry, and we parted. As I drifted away from him, I evaluated what the conversation had told me. If I had only his account to go on, my husband would have died defending the mission, not in rushing out to reinforce the traders who were already fighting the Apaches. Poncelli was too smooth, too oily. He seemed the type who'd never spurn a lucrative transaction. That he was involved in some nefarious business was clear from his total avoidance of any reference to the Dutch. If he'd exclaimed over the bizarre arrival of their mule train, I might have considered his innocence a possibility, something I now knew to be impossible. Father Poncelli had betrayed himself. His guilt had caused a misstep that revealed him as less than the clever judge of character I'd thought all Jesuits to be. Contrary to my first impression upon leaving him, I realized that I had learned quite a lot from that apparently trivial conversation.

My best coup of the evening came in a fragment of another conversation I overheard between two of the less wealthy and prestigious businessmen at the ball. I was looking for the lieutenant in order to ask him to escort me home when I noticed the two men standing behind potted palms in the nook opposite the one where I'd just chatted with Poncelli.

"We'll be receiving another shipment of those new German muskets in a few days. They're an amazing improvement over the Spanish guns. We have a reliable buyer for ours—a solid, steady customer, you know. Only problem is delivering them to him thoroughly disguised as something else. Can't imagine what he does with them, in his position. But he's probably making a huge profit."

The two men laughed, and the other replied, "Well, we're also making a huge profit, so he's welcome to his." He glanced up and saw me lingering nearby, and gave his companion a sharp nudge. I glided by without a glance at them, looking anxiously in other directions as if seeking the lieutenant. I hoped the two men believed my actions were innocent and trivial. At that moment, I did see the lieutenant and swept across the floor to take him by his arm.

"By the way, Lieutenant Echegaray, do you know who those two gentlemen are—the ones standing in the nook over there?" I asked as we made our way through the crowd to the spot where the lieutenant governor was standing. He glanced at the men as we passed on the other side.

"Oh, yes—that's García the dry goods merchant and his partner Pacheco. Their firm's here in the central part of the city—Pacheco y García. No, the other way around. García y Pacheco. Not the wealthiest merchants in the city, but definitely up and coming. Why do you ask?"

"Just curious. They had their heads together in such a conspiratorial way that I wondered who they might be. They looked as if they were planning a revolution." I laughed, and at that moment we succeeded in breaking through the crowd around Lieutenant Governor Antonio Figueroa.

After I'd properly thanked him for a most entertaining evening and again congratulated him on his birthday, I parted with friendly thanks from the lieutenant after he had escorted me home where I now sit, thinking. Perhaps I begin to have an idea just what that heavily escorted 'expedition' was all about.

‖

Qumara was gone. I slumped on the shelf, exhausted and limp, hearing forest whispers beyond the fissure, amplified by the narrow, vertical walls. Gusts of wind whistled uncannily among the caves in the cliff, like a giant playing his flute. The piney air refreshed me, and I thanked God for his mercy in saving my life through his servant, Qumara. For a moment, joy straightened and lifted me. Free! Alive! Then reality clutched at my heart along with the cold that set me shivering, teeth chattering in the wind. The tattered and filthy robe gave me scant protection, but the gourd Qumara had given me helped slake my thirst. I drank only a little, holding each swallow in my mouth to dampen my cheeks and tongue. There would be no more water until tomorrow night. Once the drawstring on the leather food pouch gave in to my impatient tugs, chopped fruit, nuts, and dried meat tumbled into my hand. I limited myself to one handful. Yes, hunger gnawed at my stomach, but my condition could not be serious. I'd gone without food and water for only twenty-four hours, and had drunk plenty of water from the springs along the trail the day before.

The insistent burning sensation on my back reminded me of the jabs from the warrior's lance. My fingers explored the wounds as far as they could reach. Some cuts lay flat, but others were puffy and painful, probably infected. My wrists were also swollen, cut and bruised. Examination of my knees and ankles could wait until daylight.

Faint light told me that two of the five caves were barely big enough to serve as tombs, two more were useless holes. The largest cave offered the only chance of shelter. I crept inside and felt rather than saw two corpses wrapped in cloth. There was no odor of decay; the bodies must be mummified. The night was chilly, so sleep would be possible only here where the bodies of the dead provided a windbreak. I lay down, tried to avoid pressure on my knees and other bruised parts, worried briefly about infection from the filthy robe, but placed everything in God's lap. With my knees drawn to my chest to preserve warmth, I fell into an exhausted sleep.

The chill pre-dawn wind woke me, rustling the leaves of nearby aspen trees and rubbing branches together with a creaking sound. I sat up, disoriented, then the horror of the previous day flooded my mind. Light filtered in. The mummies were carefully wrapped head-to-foot in beautifully woven, once-bright cotton blankets, the colors muted and mellowed by time. I said a brief prayer for the peace of their souls, and struggled to my feet.

Every joint and muscle protested, making the simple act of rising a painful chore. I moved out onto the platform. The cleft we had followed last night continued past the ledge, snaking into the heart of the mountain, where it narrowed to a crack and disappeared. The sheer rock sides of the mountain rose vertically behind and before me. Ledges on both sides of the nearly sheer cliffs had caves similar to the ones to my back. Ladders of holes dug for hands and feet led up to them. My refuge was a complex, vertical graveyard. To my left, pale blue sky shimmered in the distance. Aspen trees clung here and there in crevices and on tiny outcrops, dwarfed by their inability to find adequate root space. The sun was up but hidden by the mountain, so my ledge remained deep in shadow. Would Beatriz believe any of this if I ever had the good fortune to describe it to her? Surely, she'd take it for a wild fantasy. Strange how, in my imagination, I shared every remarkable thing I saw with her.

I sat on the cold stone, ate another handful of food and drank a few swallows of water, then looked at my injuries in daylight. None were serious, barring infection. The day passed in prayer, nibbling, sipping water, alternately dozing and worrying, then praying for peace of mind and a clear head to deal with whatever came next. I lay naked while the sun passed above me, hot and bright on my ledge, its healing rays bathing me front and back. Sunlight cures various ailments, including colds. It might heal my back as well. As soon as it passed beyond the mountain and chill air returned, I donned my filthy robe again.

Long after dark, probably after midnight, faint sounds came to me of someone climbing my wall. Surely, it was Qumara, but I readied myself to push an intruder, a warrior, off the ledge. My rescuer reassured me in a low voice when she came within a foot or two of the top. She unwrapped a bundle she'd balanced on her head and handed me pozole and strips of roasted horsemeat—flesh of my spare horse, my friend— along with another gourd of water.

"Eat! You need strength. It go well with you?"

"I'm better, but my back is infected. Jabs from a warrior's lance."

"Let me see."

She turned me so the faint light from the moon struck my back. I pulled the robe off my shoulders, and she ran her hands over the wounds.

"What happened when they found me gone?" I asked, "Did they blame you?"

"No. I brush out footprints. In morning young boy go in to taunt Black Robe. He come out shouting, 'Black Robe gone! Escape!' Then everybody come see. I drop rope in teepee when we leave last night. They think you undo knots. Itza-chu punish young warrior, one who tie you. Beat him. He say he tie you tight. They say not tight enough."

I tried to feel pity for the fellow, but somehow could not.

She finished examining my back and pulled the top of the robe over it. "Yes. Infected. I bring medicine tomorrow. I already send young son today find Denzhoné. I tell Itza-chu boy go find coneflower root. Coneflower strong medicine for wounds. When son come back tomorrow with Denzhoné, I bring."

How could she be so bold as to bring a rival chief to see me openly? "Then you know Denzhoné! Do you mean to come in daylight? But what about Itza-chu?"

"I know Denzhoné from tribal powwows. Itza-chu and band of best warriors gone on deer hunt. Begin preparations for winter. Bring in meat and hides. I command when they gone. I meet Denzhoné outside village. They not see." Qumara lifted her face to me and I regretted the darkness, curious to see this woman who had saved my life and perhaps Andrés' too.

"Here." She handed me the short, shawl-like blanket she wore around her shoulders, "Wear this, not robe. Robe dirty. This soft, clean. Better for back. Tomorrow I bring Indian clothes. Moccasins." She was preparing to go.

I blessed her with the sign of the Cross. "May God keep you safe in all your ways."

"God bless you, man of God," she replied, letting herself down over the lip of the ledge, her sure feet finding the first footholds. "I back tomorrow when sun shines."

In my dreams that night, someone led me by the hand through another dark forest. Pain racked my body, and the shadowy figure stopped to stroke my face. Her sweet voice told me to be patient, for soon my sufferings would be over.

She embraced me and laid her head against my chest, and the moonlight revealed Beatriz in my arms, not an Indian woman. My sleeping self thrilled, and I held her closer, kissing her up-turned face, forehead, eyes, and ripe mouth, my body reacting in a most unseemly manner. I awoke to find that the reaction was not only a dream. I scolded myself, praying for guidance. Should I recite the Act of Contrition? After all, none of this misbehavior was willed. In the end, I did pray, "Oh my God, I am heartily sorry for having offended thee…." After all, the flesh is weak, and I did not intend to give my conscious consent to its waywardness.

Next day, I sat on the blanket Qumara had brought. My face must still be smeared and dirty, and I hoped to be minimally presentable when speaking to Denzhoné. I rubbed my face with saliva and a fragment torn from my robe, smoothed my hair, running my fingers through it, then basked naked in the sun to dry the sores on my back. My skin turned a pale gold, an improvement on the sickly white I began with. At intervals, I rose and paced back and forth like a caged bear. The confinement was irksome, though my body needed rest. I mourned the loss of my breviary to carry out my devotions.

By mid-afternoon when the sun had left the ledge, slight noises came to me from below. I leaned out and saw a woman who could only be Qumara climbing with a sizeable bundle on her head, while an impressive-looking man, certainly a chief, squatted on his haunches at the cliff base. Qumara placed her bundle on the ledge first, then nimbly stepped upon it. I saw her in daylight for the first time. Slender and lithe, she must still be in her thirties, with a heart-shaped face and lustrous black hair in two thick braids over each shoulder, tied with red cloth. Her eyes were large, luminous, and very dark. Smiling, she glanced up at me, knowing I appreciated her beauty.

"I give you new clothes, man of God. Then Chief Denzhoné come up." She stooped to untie the bundle.

"Gracias, Qumara!"

She held the clothes out to me, piece by piece. There was a breechclout, which I put on, turning my back to her, discarding my soiled under drawers, tucking them under the robe that lay folded near the middle cave. She next gave me a pair of leggings and a doeskin vest, beautifully tanned, serviceable but plain. I put on the leggings first.

"I doctor back, knees and feet," she said, removing a cork of wood from a squat jar containing a dark mixture. "This mescal jelly and coneflower. It heal infection." She rubbed my sore back, then worked the jelly into my knees and feet, wrapping each foot in lengths of clean rag. While she pulled moccasins on my feet, I put on the vest, a sleeveless garment that reached to the waist with no fasteners in front, leaving the chest exposed. Now, I could be identified as a Christian only by my complexion, blond hair and blue eyes, and the precious silver crucifix on its chain around my neck.

"Now you ready to see chief," she pronounced, and stepped to the cliff's edge, gesturing to the man below.

Denzhoné climbed to the ledge in seconds. He swept me with an appraising look, then, glancing around the ledge, he noted the black robe folded near the central cave's entrance. Face to face he was more imposing than I'd thought when looking down at him.

He tapped his bare chest. "Denzhoné."

"Father Ygnacio."

"You come see me?" His Spanish, though better than my Apache, was too primitive for complete communication. Nonetheless, I began to deliver my message. I told about the murder of Captain Cuevas, and that all the evidence pointed to his friend Father Andrés as murderer. I described the wounds I'd found on the captain's body and the moccasin tracks I'd discovered.

"Father Andrés told me about you, Chief Denzhoné, and his hopes for forging a peace pact with your tribe."

My information came out haltingly, often with Qumara's help, who supplied an Apache word or expression when I was stymied. Her passive knowledge of Spanish outstripped her ability to speak it. She and Denzhoné understood why I had come, while we learned each other's languages.

"Father Andrés is in the gravest danger. Our people will almost certainly kill him if we do not find the real murderer. I'll not accuse you, Chief Denzhoné, or betray you to our people if you are the man who killed the captain, but I need to know the truth. Did you kill that soldier?"

The chief's face remained impassive throughout my recital. He spoke briefly with Qumara, requesting a full translation of my last words into Apache before he answered. When she had finished repeating the last sentences in his language, he spoke again briefly to her. I understood him, but waited while she relayed his words to me. "He say you may lie. You must swear you not betray him before he speak."

I held up the crucifix on its chain around my neck. "I swear by my living Savior that I have told you the truth and will never betray you, Denzhoné."

Qumara nodded at the chief, who trusted me enough to speak. "I come one night to talk with Father Andrés. I go into church and not find. I wait but he come not. I go into garden. See soldier lying there. Walk around him, see he killed with holy statue and choked too."

I held up my hand, and Qumara translated 'garden' and 'holy statue' into Spanish. I nodded and Denzhoné continued.

"I think my friend kill him. Soldier my enemy, maybe enemy to Father Andrés too. If yes, then soldier doubly my enemy. I stab him to show I stand together with Father Andrés. Then I hear noise, see more soldiers. I leave."

"You didn't see Father Andrés that night?"

"No, I not find him. I go. I leave knife in soldier's chest so my friend Andrés not blamed."

My heart sank. The chief told the truth. His demeanor and the simplicity of his words convinced me. Primitive people the world over have acted in similar ways. Hadn't the Greeks mistreated Hector's body after Achilles' victory? But where was the knife? Who had taken it? Why? Where was it now? Its absence threw the blame directly upon Andrés. Who would wish him harm?

I thanked the chief for troubling to come see me. "Your friend, Father Andrés, spoke of a peace pact. He sent me in his place to seal it. Can you do that for his sake?"

The chief turned away and strode back and forth on the ledge, brows drawn together. Qumara squatted with an expression of quiet waiting. I stood in silence with bowed head, praying he would accept the pact.

He stopped and faced me again. "I not make pact with you, only with Father Andrés. So much I promise, though. My tribe never attack Ures mission again."

"But will you and your tribe come there to learn how to be Christian?"

The corners of his mouth crinkled. "I tell my people. If anyone want to be Christian, they come."

I understood his polite refusal and admired his skill. "You are a wise man, Denzhoné, and a cautious one. I pray that you will bring your tribe to Ures one day soon."

After all this effort, my hopes were dashed. Denzhoné's innocence meant I must review the facts, begin again. Some little thing, overlooked so far, would surely point to the real killer. There were, beside Andrés himself, two other suspects

     Florence Byham Weinberg

that I knew of: the marrano corporal… what was his name? Ayala? and… Wolfgang! He'd been there the day the captain was murdered. Andrés told him he could sleep in the hayloft. He could have murdered the captain that night. His enigmatic comments at Sinoquipe indicated that he knew more than he was telling. Motive was lacking, but perhaps he truly was mad, as he'd seemed in the beginning. A sharp pang of regret, almost guilt, clogged my throat, for I liked the eccentric young priest. I'd go to Cuquiárachi where he must have arrived by now, and drag the truth from him.

I raised my head. My two companions stood politely waiting, watching me in the Indian way. Long silences were not considered 'awkward,' to be filled with chatter.

"There were two others at Ures that night, beside the soldiers," I said. "I must find them. Either one could have killed the captain. I must question them and do everything I can to save my friend Andrés."

Denzhoné's voice vibrated with sympathy. "You willing to suffer much and maybe give your life for him."

"He is innocent. I'll do what I can."

I turned to Qumara whose Christianity had puzzled me from the start. "You've risked your life to save me and bring Chief Denzhoné to me. You told me you are a Christian. Please tell me your story."

"This take long. We sit."

"Aren't you afraid the tribe will miss you?"

"No, they used to me. I bring them healing herbs. Gone for long times."

Still stiff and sore, I sat with a suppressed groan while the two of them squatted on their heels. Qumara spoke in torturous, broken Spanish interlaced with Apache words that either Denzhoné or I understood and translated.

"Ten year ago, I fourteen year old. My tribe, called Upper Pima by missionary, live north of place with name Tucson.

Long dry years make us hungry, thirsty. We go south, maybe find water. Come to mission, San Xavier del Bac. Find water, work for priest if he give us some. He give food too. I go with other young people, hear priest teach doc… doct…"

"Doctrina, Qumara."

"Yes. That right word. Black Robe kind. Mass beautiful. Church smell good. Pretty pictures look real, people made of wood too, painted."

"Saints' statues, I think."

"Yes. Priest say that. I leave field work to hear of Jesus. I learn. I go to priest, ask for baptize. He cry and thank God."

"And were you baptized?"

"Yes and three others."

She paused and I prompted her. "What happened then?"

"Apache raid. I walk with Black Robe when they come. He stand between me and them. They strike him with lance. Maybe dead, don't know."

Who preceded Antonio Castro, the priest I knew at San Xavier? Whoever it was, he'd not been martyred. Wounded, perhaps, but not martyred.

"Chief of raiding party young warrior Itza-chu. He take me by hair, put me on horse. I slave and mate. Have his sons, two. One learn from me, other only from him. Itza-chu treat me good, make me first wife."

"But you remained Christian?"

"Yes, man of God. Never forget. It teach me better way. I pray to Lady of Guadalupe and Jesus and Black Robe."

"You think the priest was killed?"

"I think so. When boys grown, I come to mission."

"You are in constant danger, then."

"Yes, but sometime like now I do good thing."

"Bless you, Qumara! May God repay you!"

Chapter XI
Cuquiárachi

Denzhoné moved to the rim of the ledge. "I sorry we lose friend Andrés, you and me. Your tribe will kill him. He a brave man."

He must still believe Andrés had killed the captain, and the murder had been a noble deed.

He raised his hand and said goodbye in Apache, then vanished over the lip of the ledge. His sudden absence depressed me as if it were an omen of Andrés' disappearance.

Qumara doctored and wrapped my feet again to prepare me for the coming journey. She showed me an extra pair of moccasins.

"You wear out one pair. Get to mission with worse holes in feet. So I give you two. I give you jar of ointment, too. Back healing now. Let sun dry back for short time every day. That help."

She packed my things in her travel pouch, settled it on her back and swung off the ledge. "You follow, climb down now." She smiled, encouraging me.

I looked around the stony platform for the last time, making sure I'd left no sign of my presence that might betray my rescuer. Then I followed her down the cliff face. The descent seemed to take an hour as I groped for the next foot or handhold, stiff, awkward and shaking with fear now that daylight showed me what a single slip would do. I joined her at the base, sweating and trembling, where she stood grinning, mocking me, yet understanding.

"You like child climb down first time." She handed me the pouch. "Here food, moccasins and salve and black robe and old shoes. Wear only Apache clothes. Robe make you target."

"Thank you! You've saved my life and sanity in so many ways! From here I must go to Cuquiárachi. Is there a good trail?"

Wolfgang had said he'd follow me to Arizpe Mission after making sure life was back to normal in Sinoquipe, and Father Carlos was going to order him to return to his mission and to Bartolomé Saenz.

Qumara answered, "Yes, Ygnacio, Man of God. I know Cuquiárachi. It toward sunrise. I show you how to go. Come, we go back to forest."

She led the way to the mouth of the cleft and into the forest, stopping in a patch of sunlight. There, she scratched a quick map in the dirt. It showed the cleft we'd just left, the trail we were on, and an intersecting trail that wound down the mountain to join the pass on the eastern side. She marked a spring where I could rest and drink.

"Trail not much used. Too narrow for horse or mule. Dangerous. Run along edge of cliff. Follow ledge under overhang. No room for slip. You take care."

"I'll try."

She brushed out the map, sprinkled pine needles over the scar, and I followed her deeper into the dense forest that more than matched the *Schwarzwald* of my homeland. These pines, perhaps hundreds of years old, awed me and dwarfed us as if we were insects. No axe had ever been heard here. Her voice startled me in the whispering hush around us. She pointed.

"Trail start there to sunrise side of pass."

"God will reward you for your goodness. Please be careful! Come to my mission when you can. I'm at Cucurpe." I made the sign of the Cross over her and blessed her.

"Yes. Cucurpe. I come if I can." She took both my hands in hers. "God speed, man of God." Her black eyes seemed huge in her heart-shaped face, beautiful as she turned away.

I called after her, "God bless you!"

She glanced over her shoulder and raised her hand, then vanished in the shadows of the virgin pines. I moved as rapidly as my injuries allowed in the opposite direction, following the steep descent. My heart brimmed with gratitude but I feared for her safety. I prayed that she had not sacrificed her life for me.

Father Kino had not mapped this route; there had been no dotted line on the map that marked a trail intersecting the eastern side of the pass. What fate had his map and notes suffered? Perhaps they had kindled the fire that roasted my slaughtered horse. I moved through a dark tunnel of shrubs with pine boughs arching and intertwining overhead. I'd not be seen here. Even on the cliff edges and ledges, I would be less visible, traveling alone on foot in Apache disguise, my faithful animals left behind to their fate.

The day wore on from dawn to mid-afternoon. For a breathtaking half-hour the trail hugged a sheer rock face with a 400-foot drop below. Qumara was right: any slip would be fatal. I prayed to Our Lady of Guadalupe with each step, not daring to watch the hawks that soared so close they almost brushed me. One dropped past me like a stone, and my eyes followed it down, down. It seized a mourning dove in flight and rose with heavy wing beats, a few of the dove's gray feathers drifting slowly earthward. Beatriz would cry out in pity at the sight. As it passed me, the dove, clutched in those deadly talons, stared at me with wild eyes, its beak agape. I knew that terror.

I continued along the ledge, at one point leaping a three-foot gap with nothing to hold on to, landing on the other side and teetering with arms outstretched until I regained my balance. Once on solid ground again, I sent up a fervent prayer of thanks to God, Saint Ignatius, and Our Lady, who guided my steps. I'd seen no humans, only a lone coyote and a small herd of deer.

By now, foothills surrounded me with rocky ledges thick with mesquite, ocotillo, and organ pipe cactus. The main road through the pass should be near. The path ducked into a narrow, stony canyon, and the trickle and splash of water echoed ahead. I licked cracked lips. The spring poured from a crack in the cliff and dropped ten feet into a pool below, the margins adorned with blown-in leaves. I lay prone for a long drink, enjoying the spray from the waterfall. Brilliant green ferns clung to crevices, their graceful fans swaying when the water struck them or a breeze passed.

Here, a miniature tropical forest recreated a flawed Garden of Eden, including a palm and a grove of fig trees, their snaky white roots exposed where they rambled over boulders to reach the soil. A few hideous trees the Indians call 'torote' stood about, their trunks and branches thickly armored with squat but exquisitely sharp brown thorns. Poison tipped, no doubt. In the distance where the trail breasted a knoll, an ancient, lightning-blasted sycamore raised a half-blackened trunk, still white in patches, above a maple and a few sweet gums.

I climbed the knoll. At last, the main trail lay below. Cuquiárachi was still six leagues distant and the afternoon was well advanced. Fading twilight glimmered on a rocky outcrop near the trail that promised shelter for the night and a good hiding place, at least for a man lying down. A smooth, level area behind the rocks would serve me—as it had served the Indians—as an observation post to watch the trail without being seen.

At daybreak I limped on sore feet until midmorning when I reached a roadside spring with a marshy pool. Here was enough water to bathe, rest my feet, and wash the tattered and filthy robe. I would wear it when I came near the mission. It would never do to be shot by a nervous guard who could mistake me for an Apache. The sun had warmed the pool to bath temperature. I unfolded the black robe and submerged it and the foot bandages at the water's edge to soak, held down by rocks. I hid my travel pouch and Indian clothing, waded in and floated for half an hour among the reeds. I rubbed myself all over, beginning to feel human for the first time since my capture. Without soap or yucca root, my hair would still be greasy, but my face would be clean, though adorned with a week's unshaven blond beard.

A clatter of hooves in the distance set my heart pounding. A party of Indians approached the spring to water their mounts. Among the horses and mules, I recognized my old friend Conejo and knew this to be part of Itza-chu's tribe. At least my mule was still alive. A stand of reeds screened me from the spring, and I submerged without a ripple until only the side of my head, one eye and my nose remained above water. I could stay underwater only by clutching the reed stems close to the oozy bottom. If the party came to the pool, they would surely see my robe and bandages, but they remained near the fresh water at the spring's source. After they had drunk and loitered there for what seemed an eternity but was probably only minutes, they rode eastward toward the mission.

I waited for many minutes before wading through oozing mud to find my laundry. My skin, brown from exposure to the sun, was puckered by its long bath. It was past noon, and I must hurry. Eyes and ears alert, I finished washing my foot bandages, scrubbed the remnants of dried blood and sweat from the black robe and spread my laundry on a sun-heated boulder to dry while I finished the food. I salved my feet and replaced the almost-dry bandages, pulling on the second pair of moccasins.

Twilight deepened into night as the mission came in sight, built with a heavy gate in solid eight-foot adobe walls, topped with fiercely armored nopales, prickly pears. I pulled the tattered black robe over my Indian clothing and yelled to the guard.

"Father Ygnacio Pfefferkorn to see Father Bartolomé Saenz. Will you admit me?"

"Wait where you are."

After a moment the gate opened a crack, and a torch held high illuminated a small circle outside. I stepped into the pool of light, and the guard could see, despite my darkly tanned skin, that I was blond and wore a black robe.

"Yes, it's a missionary, all right," he called over his shoulder.

The gate opened wider, and Father Saenz himself raised the torch. "Ygnacio! How?... Come in, man! Where's your horse? Your pack mule? Come in! Come in! You look like you've been mauled by a mountain lion!" The torch behind him transformed him into a black rectangle, unrecognizable except for his gesture. He vigorously scrubbed the end of his nose with his right forefinger, a nervous habit I'd noticed at our meetings in Mátape.

I almost fell into his arms. "Long story, Bartolomé. Captured by Apaches, Itza-chu's tribe. Escaped—with help. Exhausted. Have to sleep. Tell you everything in the morning."

His eyes lingering on my tattered robe, beard and swollen feet. "You've been through hell, that's obvious. You can sleep to your heart's content in the extra room. Nobody will disturb you, I'll see to that."

He led me to a room just large enough for a cot and a washstand.

I sat on the cot and looked up. "How is Wolfgang?"

"Wolfgang? You missed him by twelve days. He hardly took time to say hello, let alone ask my permission for his wandering. Why?"

"I'm here to find him. Carlos Rojas told me days ago he'd command him to get back here. I'd hoped he was here ahead of me."

"No such luck. We'll talk in the morning. Get your rest. Good night and God bless." He set down the candle and closed the door behind him. Before it had snapped shut, my clothes had fallen in a heap on the floor. I collapsed on the cot, pulled up the blanket, and drifted at once into a deep sleep.

Beatriz came to me, there in the tiny cell. She sat on the cot and leaned down, her flowing hair brushing my face. I reached for her, drew her close, kissed her lips.

Her throaty voice, so well remembered, pleaded, "Ygnacio, Andrés will die if we don't help, and I need you, Ygnacio… Ignaz…"

She faded into filmy dimness, and I groped for her in the black night. "Beatriz!"

The sound of my voice echoed as I sat up. I cried out again, "Beatriz!"

My head pounded and my fingers closed on my temples. Was this a true message? It tallied with my own fears for Andrés. That must be it; I'd embodied my fears in the wraith of Beatriz. Did I love her? What did that really mean? All I knew for certain was that she obsessed me, waking and dreaming. I began to recite a Rosary for her and for Andrés, and reached the fifth decade when I fell asleep again.

I slept long in comfort, lulled by a deep sense of security for the first time in many days. Full daylight through the small, high window woke me. A sunbeam lit the washstand, where a straight razor and a bar of soap lay next to the clay pitcher and basin. I bathed quickly, the cold water washing away the last wisps of sleep, and used a chip of mirror to shave off my beard. I put on the Indian breechclout, the tattered robe and the moccasins and went in search of my fellow priest.

He sat near a window in his great room that combined kitchen and living area, writing something, probably a letter. The bright light shone with pitiless clarity on the smallpox scars that disfigured his otherwise handsome face. "Ah! There you are, Ygnacio. I let you sleep as long as you could. How about something to eat? There's food on the shelf in the back of the fireplace-oven over there." He punctuated his remarks with a vigorous nose-rubbing.

"Thank you! I needed that rest. The shaving equipment came in handy, too."

"Good, good. Now, eat." He rose, wound a rag around his hand, reached into the oven and lifted a clay plate off the shelf. "Sit down, man, sit down."

I obeyed and sat, elbows on the table. He handed me knife and spoon, and poured me a brew that resembled chamomile tea. I pointed at the mug. "What's this?"

"Oh, a little plant that grows around here. Looks like chamomile, but isn't—maybe a New World cousin. Same yellow color, flowery aroma, but a different flavor, not unpleasant, and hasn't killed anyone yet. Now, eat while it's hot!"

His cooking was simple and efficient. He had broken four eggs on the clay plate, scrambled them with a pinch of salt and a sprinkle of crushed fresh thyme leaves, along with chunks of bacon. He'd added a dollop of fresh salsa combining chopped onion, tomatoes and red chiles. The mixture had cooked slowly on the shelf in the back of the oven, absorbing flavor while he tended to other tasks, such as writing his letter. He pushed corn bread and a knife toward me on a breadboard. "Here's the staff of life."

I began to devour my meal, moaning with pleasure at the first bite.

He set aside the letter and quill pen, corking the ink bottle. "I see you've been starved, too. Now tell me what happened. It should make a good story."

"It's a *long* story…." I told him the saga beginning with Andrés Michel's summons. I got as far as my departure from Carlos Rojas and Arizpe Mission when Bartolomé raised a hand.

"I expect the authorities have arrested Andrés by now, with that much evidence against him."

"I'm afraid you may be right. I had a dream last night…"

"Humph!" He tilted his head and his piercing brown eyes bored accusingly into mine. "So tell me, how did leaving him and going off on a wild goose chase after an Apache chief and a peace pact help matters? Achieving that is about as likely as me growing wings today and flying to heaven."

I withstood his gaze. "Andrés thought the pact would save many lives. Both of us wanted to save lives!"

His gaze remained steady as he shook his head. "You risked your life, and from the look of you, you almost lost it. Something you're not telling me made that worthwhile. What was it?"

I hesitated, but by now the information was no longer worth concealing. "I suspected that Apache of killing the captain. I wanted to prove it to save Andrés—and to seal the peace pact."

"And did you?"

"No. Neither the one nor the other. Instead, I was captured by Itza-chu's tribe, tied hand and foot and tossed into a teepee to wait overnight for my sacrifice the next day."

"And?"

"And the chief's wife, a converted Upper Pima Indian kidnapped at age fourteen, rescued me and set me free."

"God works in mysterious ways. So you never found that Apache, the possible murderer?"

"Itza-chu's wife brought him to me. He didn't do it."

"And the peace pact?"

"Rejected. At least he promised that his tribe wouldn't attack Ures Mission. That's all."

"Ah. So who *did* kill the captain? Anyone else at Ures that night who might have had motive and opportunity?"

"Two. A corporal, Saúl Ayala, and… Wolfgang. Either one might have had the opportunity. I don't know about motive."

He nodded. "Ah, yes, Wolfgang, that rascal. Well, that explains why you're here."

Chapter XII
Wolfgang

I shook my finger. "Now, Bartolomé! Wolfgang can be trying at times, but hardly a rascal."

He gave his nose another vigorous rubbing, allowing himself room to think before replying. "You haven't had to live with that man for months at a time! I thanked God when he took off on his 'pilgrimage' to the other missions. He hoped to enlighten all of you, since he made no headway with me."

I nodded. "He made the rounds. He was at Mátape, showed up at Cucurpe some time later, and went from there to Ures. You say he came back here?"

"Yes, for a lightning visit, maybe to pick up something he needed. In his usual enigmatic way, he didn't say."

"And then I discovered him at Sinoquipe. He'd found the whole village dying of measles."

"Did he stay to help or run?"

"He stayed. Without him the whole village would have died. I got there when the plague was in its final stages. Seventeen died, but a lot more lived, thanks to him. He's a brave man, but mysterious."

"Hmm, yes," Bartolomé nodded slowly. "He's been a great help to me from time to time—when he's in the mood. But mostly he's been a distraction and a hindrance. I complained to Carlos about him, but so far, nothing's been done. At least, I didn't call him a heretic, though he comes mighty close."

"He's been reading too much Luther. The man seems *loco de remate* sometimes, and at others downright clairvoyant. He told me things he couldn't possibly know by any natural means. He prophesied to Jacob at Mátape and to Andrés about the murder—if it was a prophecy. I left him at Sinoquipe when I was sure he could handle the final stages of the villagers' illness. He said he'd go from there to Arizpe, get food and a good bed from Carlos. When I alerted Carlos, he said he'd order him to come back here to help you, Bartolomé."

"I'm sure Carlos told you about Father Joseph Albarrán's death," he said. "I was supposed to be transferred to Opodepe to assume the duties of father rector and relieve you of double duty."

"Yes. I was heartsick to hear about that. We've lost three priests counting Joseph Och's illness and Father Rector Loaiza's death from heart failure at Opodepe. Now you're stuck here until our provincial can send someone to replace Father Albarrán."

"What about Wolfgang? Did Carlos Rojas share any plans for him with you?"

I smiled. "He's considering a temporary appointment as missionary to Opodepe under my supervision—as if Wolfgang would pay any attention to my advice—leaving you here. He hadn't made that decision as yet. He's waiting to see if he loses Andrés to the civil authorities and me to the Apaches."

Bartolomé stared at me. "Carlos took quite a risk, letting you go into the Mababi Mountains after that Apache."

"He knew that. He hesitated for a long time between losing me and losing Andrés. As you see, he didn't quite lose me—yet." After a silence, I added, "By the way, I'd like your permission to go through Wolfgang's things."

"What? Why? There isn't much there."

"Because I think he may know more about the death of Captain Cuevas than he's been letting on. He was there when it happened. Andrés told me he invited him to sleep in the barn loft that night. I checked, and the loft has a direct view of Father Andrés' garden. That's where Captain Cuevas was found the next morning—bludgeoned to death with a statuette of the Virgin."

"Was there a moon that night?"

"There had to be, because I looked out the window of the guest room in Andres' house two nights later, and clearly saw in the moonlight…" I let my sentence drop. I didn't want to tell him I had seen an unearthly sight, a vision of angelic beauty: Beatriz, her hair long and undulating in the silvery light, praying before the church.

"Well, maybe he did see something. But why would Wolfgang have anything in his room that would help you find the murderer?"

"Look, Bartolomé, I *like* Wolfgang. I worked four days side-by-side with him in Sinoquipe, fighting the measles. We washed vomit and feces from the bodies of the dying. We buried people together. He's a powerful source of energy and, I think, integrity. But the captain was murdered. I know Andrés didn't do it, despite all the evidence against him, and I know the Apache didn't either, so—"

"So you think *Wolfgang* did it?"

"He was there. He had the opportunity, even if I haven't found a motive as yet. A mission Indian could have done it, but none of them had a motive, and they're in bed by the time of night he was killed anyway. I don't believe Wolfgang did it; I hope he didn't, but I need to look through his things. He might have left something behind that would connect him with the murder."

"What sort of thing?"

"Anything. A diary notation, a biblical quotation, a scrap of the captain's uniform, the knife that made that wound… anything."

"Humph!" Bartolomé folded his arms. His troubled face told me he was far fonder of Wolfgang than he let on and felt protective of his 'assistant.' "Oh, very well. Go ahead, go through his things. I'm giving you permission only because

Andrés' life is in immediate danger. But I want to be there to see it, if you find something incriminating."

He led me past the guest room and opened the door to a cell containing a bed with its washstand, a closet, a large chest, and a desk.

"Here's his room. Search it all you like. I'll be staying, of course. I'm just as curious as you are."

I began with the disordered bed, checking under the mattress, shaking out the blanket. Nothing. Next, I went to the closet where a couple of worn robes hung, with handkerchiefs and a rosary in their pockets, nothing more. Then, the desk. On top a Psalter, a Bible, a copy of *De civitate Dei* by Saint Augustine, a copy of the *Exercises* of Saint Ignatius, sheets of paper, some covered with Wolfgang's slanting, hasty handwriting, a quill pen, a dry inkwell, and a dish of sand for blotting wet ink. I scanned the writing. Wolf had jotted down his thoughts on Augustine's theology, interesting but irrelevant at the moment. In the single desk drawer, more paper, another quill pen, a rosary, a dirty handkerchief.

I moved over to the chest, my last chance. As I raised the lid of the chest, Bartolomé peering over my shoulder, an Indian boy came to the door.

"Father Saenz! My mother! She's in labor—has been for hours. She wants you to give her the last rites, Father! Come quick, please!"

I straightened and turned towards Bartolomé. "Shall I wait? Do you need help?"

He shook his head. "No, no… I can't stay; this is an emergency, but…. All right, go ahead, but be sure to show me anything you find. I'll be back as soon as I can."

"Of course, Bartolomé. Call me if you need me."

The top shelf of the trunk contained a stack of books. Below the shelf lay civilian clothes and a pair of black dress shoes with bright buckles, keepsakes from his early days. As I replaced the shelf, a shadow fell across me from the window. I glanced up, but saw nothing—a passing cloud, perhaps. I bent over the chest. Under the books in the top layer, an edge of cloth protruded, another handkerchief, maybe. I pulled and it raised the books. The handkerchief unwound to reveal a large, horn-handled knife. I held it to the light and saw inlaid decorations in the handle—Indian, probably Apache designs. There were traces of blood on the blade. I sniffed it. Yes, blood.

A pair of hands like pincers gripped my shoulders, yanked me back, and I cried out. A voice hoarse with fury spoke next to my ear as I rose to my feet, off balance.

"*Sohn einer Hure! Bastard!* You son of a whore! Bastard!" he screamed in German, "I thought you were my friend! What in Hell do you think you're doing, going through my things?"

His last words echoed what I'd said to him on our first encounter, and the irony struck me even as I twisted to see Wolfgang's face, distorted in rage. His grip was powerful, more so because of his anger. He slipped his right arm under my armpit. I had to break his hold to prevent him from getting a lock on the back of my neck. Now! Before he could place the other arm, I ducked and twisted to the left, and threw my entire weight against him. It worked. I spun and faced him, dodging. A flurry of fists came at me, and I parried, although his knuckle grazed the side of my jaw, peeling off skin.

"Wolfgang! Get a grip on yourself! Stop! Let me explain!"

I danced away from him on sore feet, hamstrings butting against the bed. I did a backward somersault across it, landed on my feet and stood with that barrier between us.

He panted, more from anger than exertion. "Nothing's private—hasn't been since I joined the Society, of course…. Odd—nothing's sacred, either! What irony!"

"No, Wolf, I can explain—"

"And what are *you*, Ignaz? A spy for the vice-provincial, that Luca Poncelli? Am I to be drummed out of the Society for my Augustinian views? Are you collecting evidence to have me excommunicated?"

He whirled and ran out of the room. I vaulted the bed and ran after him, catching him as he paced the plaza in font of the church with long strides. He pounded his thigh with his fist.

"Calm down, Wolf!" I gulped air. "No! I'm not trying to have you excommunicated… just… trying to save Andrés Michel's life. He told me you… were at Ures the night of the murder. *You*, Wolfgang." I paused to breathe and let my heart slow down. "I know Andrés didn't kill Captain Cuevas, and you did have the opportunity, even though I think it unlikely. But I had to make sure. You weren't here, so I got permission to go through your things. I'm sorry, Wolf. I know it violates your privacy in the worst way."

He glared for a long moment and I feared he might strike me again. Finally, the rigidity left him; his fists uncurled. He opened and closed his hand, looking at the skinned knuckle that had grazed my jaw. He wrapped his handkerchief around it and stood, heaving a great sigh, staring at me for a minute or more. At last, he took another lungful of air and exhaled.

"All right, all right, Ygnacio. Let's talk about Father Andrés. Maybe pool what we know. I don't think he killed the captain, either. But since you all but accuse me of murder, let me tell you what I know."

The trickle of blood from my skinned jaw began to run down my neck, and instead of my handkerchief, I felt the Apache knife in my pocket where I had thrust it when he first attacked me. I raised a shoulder and wiped the blood against it. Before I could ask him about the knife, Wolf gripped my arm, locking eyes with me.

"You were right, Ygnacio, when you said that day in your kitchen that I must be in spiritual crisis. That was true, though I didn't want to admit it."

Now I stood still and waited.

"I had begun to question the entire Jesuit enterprise— predicated on salvation through works, mainly. It became obvious to me through my readings that really *everything* depends on God's grace."

What was he getting at? He'd just been trying to break my neck and now, instead of discussing the murder and my suspicions, he was giving me a theological lecture.

"First of all," he continued, "I read it in Saint Augustine— and I did get hold of some of Luther's essays, too—but most impressive was a book you may have seen in my trunk. It's by a man named Jansenius. The title is *Augustinus.*"

"Yes, I know the book. It's on the Index." My comment didn't seem to register. Wolf plowed on.

"You see, Jansenius was impressed with Saint Augustine just as I am. He also says that without God's grace, we can work ourselves to death and still not be saved. We've got to work within his *grace*, Ygnacio, with His *GRACE!*" His voice trembled and he stretched his hand toward me and I, unsettled by his intensity, saw tears about to spill.

He must be insane after all. I would humor him. "Of course, that's right. We know that the efficacy of our works depends on God's grace, but we Jesuits only *seem* to ignore it in practice. Really, it's a matter of emphasis." I paused to see if he was listening and raised my voice. My message was important. "Wolf, you've got to be careful! You're playing with fire. I mean that literally. Luther is heresy, and Father Rojas sent all of us a new directive from the Holy Office—the Inquisition—that warned us against Jansenism. That, too, has been declared heretical. Surely, you read the document too."

He stared at me glassy eyed, then abruptly walked on, towing me by the arm he still held in his grip. "I got so emotional—I'm still worked up over this—that I went out on a mission of my own, to convert all of you to my point of view. I've done a poor job of that. My passions get in the way, you see, and I become very unpersuasive."

Obviously, none of my words had reached him. I decided to let him talk this through, uninterrupted.

"On my travels, I visited not just our missions, but the ranches of settlers and the hovels of miners. I talked to all of them. I found out that someone in the Society is very busy trading with those seculars, especially with the miners. It's one thing to trade farm produce and cattle to the ranchers—that's legitimate when the proceeds are used to feed and clothe converts at the missions and to buy books—but it's something else entirely to sell guns to the miners!"

I took a step backward. Maybe he wasn't mad after all. "Guns? Who's selling guns? You say *we're* involved?"

"Yes. Especially with the miners at Soyopa. The ranchers around Ures said they traded a lot with the mission for farm goods. I began to think Father Andrés was guilty of illegitimate trade along with the legitimate. He has the reputation of being a hard driving, productive farmer and rancher himself, so I thought maybe his hard driving had extended to gunrunning."

My heart was heavy with this confirmation of something I had suspected ever since I'd heard Father Sedelmeyer's story about the events surrounding Lieutenant Salinas's death at Mátape. Something surely was traded to the Dutch on that occasion. Probably guns—and four men had died. But Andrés Michel was not the culprit; the corruption went much higher. I needed time to think what to do. For now, I'd not interrupt Wolf with a question about the knife. I scanned the plaza. A trellis occupied the center, draped with a healthy trumpet vine still loaded with blossoms. The shady bench offered a good place to rest my abused feet. But Wolf was striding the length of the plaza and back, and I kept up as best I could.

"So you investigated for yourself?"

"Yes—although it was an annoying distraction from my main purpose, to save your souls and our real enterprise here. I came to Ures the day four soldiers and a woman got there. I'd come in from one of the ranches, hot from walking in the sun, so I stepped into the open door of the tack room, to cool off in the shade, you see. I was sitting on a stool, resting in a dark corner when I saw them ride in. As he dismounted, the captain spoke to the sergeant. He said, 'I'll examine Father Andrés Michel's books today. I'll bet he's serving himself instead of God, like another Jesuit I know.' He gave a nasty snicker, and I resented that, even though I feared he might be right."

"Did you go out and speak to them?"

"No. I stayed where I was and watched. When the captain went to help the lady down from her horse, he grabbed her ankle and ran his hand up her leg. I was shocked."

"And what was her reaction?"

"She struck at him with her whip, but he dodged and laughed. Then she said, 'I'll have you decommissioned if you ever try that again.' He laughed some more, then took her around the waist and set her on the ground. You could see he wanted to do much more than that, even with the men looking on. A corporal with black, curly hair challenged him. He said, 'You touch her again like that and I'll kill you.' He seemed furious, and he meant what he said."

"How did the captain react?"

"He said, 'I'll have you court marshaled for insubordination!' but the corporal stood up to him and said, 'You wouldn't dare, knowing what I know.'"

"And then?"

"The captain got very quiet. The other two soldiers, a sergeant and another corporal, were watching with their mouths open. Then Father Andrés came out of the church, greeted everybody and showed the soldiers and the lady where their rooms would be."

I cast a longing eye at the trumpet vine arbor, but Wolf strode on. "I know where those rooms were, but go ahead, tell me what you saw."

"There were three rooms, two small ones at the end of the stable building closest to the church and a large one at the other end. The lady was to sleep nearest the church, the corporal who'd protected her in the room next to hers. The captain and the other two were shown to the big room. They were passing the tack room where I was hidden when the captain told Father Andrés he'd examine his books that afternoon."

"And what did you do then?"

"The soldiers and the lady disappeared into their rooms. Father Andrés had returned to the church and I followed him. He'd gone into the sacristy and left the door open. I rapped on the doorframe and went in."

"Did you ask him about illicit trade?"

"No, not really. I thought I'd wait to go into detail until the soldiers had left. We talked for a while and he apologized for not putting me up better, since the guestrooms were already occupied, but told me I could sleep in the hayloft. The captain passed me on his way in as I left the church. I think he was about to examine the books."

"I suppose it was during your conversation with Andrés that you told him he would need a miracle to save him, but that you were not the man?"

"How did you know that? Those were my parting words. I thought he was guilty of trading with the local ranchers and the miners, and the captain was hard on his heels. He must have remembered what I said and told you."

"That's right. Look, Wolf, let's go under that arbor and sit on the bench. This story is too long to be told standing in the hot sun. Besides, my feet are sore. Did anything more happen that afternoon?"

"Not until after dinner. I decided to investigate on my own and went to talk to some of the Indian officials. I talked to the alguacil first. The only trading he knew of was between the mission and the locals, the normal sale of surplus produce to earn money for mission needs. He told me to see Hernán, the gobernador, who'd be able to tell me about anything strange going on."

We brushed leaves and twigs off the bench and sat in the shade, a light breeze fanning our faces.

"It was dark by then," he continued, "and it took me a long time to locate Hernán. To put him at ease, I asked him about his daily duties. Then I asked about illegitimate trade. He was outraged. 'Never has Father Andrés done anything under-handed,' he said. 'There's been absolutely no clandestine trade out of this mission!' I was amazed at his command of Span-ish—despite his thick accent."

I nodded. "Hernán's a capable man. But you told me it was dark by then. Why was that important?"

"Because both of us heard a commotion in the direction of the church. Yelling, then the fainter noise of a door slamming. Then quiet. We waited—couldn't *see* anything, of course—but nothing more could be heard. I couldn't tell whose voices we had heard. I would have recognized Father Andrés' voice, and his wasn't one of them. We went on talking. I asked Hernán if he knew about trading from any of the other missions, and he knew nothing directly, although he'd heard about ranchers getting supplies and cattle from other local sources. He con-firmed that at least one of the other missions was trading, but not necessarily involved in criminal activity. I left him about half an hour later."

"Did you go see what had caused the ruckus?"

"No. It hadn't continued, so I thought it was trivial. I was tired, so I climbed into the hayloft. I tried to read my breviary after the moon cleared the mountain, but gave up after a bit. I looked out. The moon had climbed higher, shining nearly as bright as day. Something caught my eye over in Father Andrés' garden, just beyond the brush fence. It looked like a man lying on his back, spread-eagled."

I leaned forward, tense. "Was he moving? How much time had passed since you heard the noise while you were talking to Hernán?"

"Maybe an hour, maybe more. The man was very still. Too still. When I started down from the loft to help him, give the last rites or pray over him, I saw movement. It was an Indian—an Apache, maybe—standing over the body. He bent over it, walked around it twice as if deciding what to do, then he took something off his waistband and struck at the body on the ground."

"What did you do?"

"I froze where I was. What could I do at that distance, anyway? I could see no reaction from the man on the ground. He seemed beyond help. Just then the sergeant and one of the corporals walked out of the stable door below me, talking in loud voices and pointing toward the church. The corporal wanted to go find the captain and the sergeant was shushing him. If I heard the corporal right, the captain had gone out saying he needed a second look at Andrés' books and hadn't returned yet. He found that strange. The sergeant said they shouldn't worry about the captain; he was probably with the lady. He laughed, but the corporal didn't."

"Where was the Apache?"

"He ran when he heard the voices. He kept low, crouching and running until he got to the adobe wall in back of the garden. He vaulted the wall and disappeared. The two soldiers never saw him."

"So then what did you do?"

"I waited until the soldiers went inside, slipped down from the hayloft and over to the church, figuring I wouldn't be seen so easily if I went through to the garden from there."

"Why did you think it necessary to sneak around? After all, you were doing your duty as a priest."

Wolfgang leaned forward, resting his chin on his cupped hands. He straightened and stared into the distance, eyes unfocused as if trying to reconstruct the scene and the mood. "The whole situation seemed uncanny to me. I was scared there was a killer on the loose and I was in danger."

"Yes… that's understandable. So, you say you went to the church. Then what?"

"I went out the side door and found the body. It was the captain, just as I'd thought. Dead long enough for all that blood to clot, but still faintly warm. I could make out a knife sticking in his chest. I leaned closer. It was an Apache knife, from the decorations on the hilt. The warrior left it behind when he ran."

I fished the knife out of my pocket. At last, I would find out why Wolfgang had hidden the knife in his trunk. "Was this the knife?"

Wolf leaped to his feet. "*Verdammt nochmal!* You *are* an efficient sneak!"

"Sorry, Wolf. It's a matter of life or death for Andrés, you know."

He glared, stalked a few paces away, strode back and forth and finally exhaled a gust of air through pursed lips. He turned back to me. "All right, all right, I know… now. Yes. I pulled the knife out of the wound, wrapped it in my handkerchief, and put it in my pocket."

"Why? If you'd left it, the soldiers would have blamed an Apache, not Andres."

"But I had no idea who killed the man, and I didn't stop long enough to see how he'd been killed. I knew it wasn't the Apache, so I didn't want him blamed. That's how I saw things at the time."

"And why did you keep the knife? You could have hidden it in a thousand places. Why hide it in your trunk?"

"Because something kept telling me it would be important one day—at least to save the Apache's life. I had no way of knowing what happened to Andrés afterward. What I did back then was more based on emotion, on fear, than on reason. I came back here twelve days ago to put that knife where it would be safe."

"And a few moments ago, you found me snooping through your things. No wonder you attacked me. But I still don't understand. Why didn't you tell Andrés what you'd seen? I know he didn't see you again, and the soldiers and doña Beatriz never noticed you were there."

"I left the mission at once. I was confused and horrified at what had happened and just wanted to get away, to put distance between me and all that blood. It never occurred to me that Andrés would be blamed for the killing. I thought the captain had died during that fracas Hernán and I had overheard, and Andrés wasn't a party to that, or if he was, he kept totally silent during it. So, I walked through the dark hours to the nearest ranch and slept till dawn in their barn."

"I think we'd better put heads together with Bartolomé to figure out what to do next. It's getting late. We'd better see what's happened to him. A woman in labor was asking for the last rites. She couldn't have died, or we'd be hearing the death wail."

We found Bartolomé at the entrance to the church, reaching for the bell rope to ring Vespers. The woman had not died. He had saved both her and her child, turning and delivering the baby, who had been in breech position. He was drunk with joy over God's mercy, and invited us to sing responses at Vespers. Our story could wait.

The church was a simple adobe rectangle, its walls an arm's length thick. The bell hung in an arch over the entrance door. Before long, converts filled the little church to capacity. It was a 'hall church' much like my own only smaller. Heavy mesquite beams spanned the ceiling, roughly carved corbels supporting them at the sides. Simple as it was, it seemed an island of sanctity in the midst of chaos and struggle, where I breathed an atmosphere of peace in the flickering candle light.

Over supper, back in Bartolomé's comfortable great room, Wolfgang told his story, and I told mine. We sat around the table, piecing our information together.

Wolfgang shook his head. "You risked your life to find information I already had. I could have let you know nearly everything you learned in the Mababi Mountains. I knew the man was dead when the chief knifed him. What a waste of your time, effort, blood, and your life, almost! When you left me at Sinoquipe, you'd only said you had to find an Apache chief to seal a peace pact. I didn't connect that to the Apache I saw circling the captain's body, and I had no idea Father Andrés was in mortal danger. I'm truly sorry!"

"The killer was not Father Andrés," I said, "nor was it Denzhoné, and obviously, Wolf, you didn't do it."

He waved the idea away. "Of course not! And two of the soldiers didn't do it, either, since they were in their room talking and laughing when the murder took place."

Bartolomé gave his nose a vigorous rubbing, tipped his chair back and stared at the ceiling. "Hmmm. Perhaps someone connected with the illegitimate trade slipped into that garden and killed the captain because he was coming too close. Or maybe the captain himself was mixed up in the gun running and the murderer was eliminating him for one reason or another."

"I think we should go back to Ures and question the Indians," Wolfgang said, "If we're lucky, we'll find someone who saw something unusual that night, however trivial it might seem to them."

"I agree," I said. "That's the logical next step." Suddenly, I sat forward. The solution to the murder was so obvious! "Wolf, you spoke of another corporal who challenged the captain when they arrived at Ures. He seemed to have a grudge against him. I remember his name, Saúl Ayala. Corporal Miguel González thought he, not Andrés, had killed his captain. We know Ayala didn't stay in the same room with the others, and he left at daybreak on the morning after the murder. González told me."

We stared at each other. Where was Saúl Ayala now?

Chapter XIII
Dilemmas

September weather in Durango continued mild, and I spent as much time pacing the paths in my spacious patio garden as walking the floor in the house. My elegant salon and library couldn't contain me, and my rose garden, full of late blooming and fragrant blossoms, couldn't distract me. Instead, my inner struggle became far worse. Despite my best efforts, I'd made little progress in gathering incriminating information against Luca Poncelli.

The letter to him from Father Andrés pleading his case, the one the soldiers carried back here, obviously had no effect, since he has done nothing to defend his missionary. It wouldn't surprise me if he burned the letter without showing it to anyone. Come to think of it, the letters Enrique and Bendito were carrying to be forwarded to the provincial in México and the father general in Rome may have suffered the same fate.

Why such dire suspicions? I was nearly certain Poncelli was buying guns from those merchants, García and Pacheco. If so, he'd have destroyed anything that would betray him to his superiors. But try as I might, I hadn't found any real evidence against him. Don Antonio, the lieutenant governor, was very discreet on that score. I had to think up some other way of uncovering the truth. Certainly, Luca Poncelli wouldn't tell me: I spoke with him at a couple of social functions since the ball, and he was always very oily, but he revealed nothing further. I'm sure he suspected I was trying to find out more about Mateo's death; his conscience must have told him that much. He might have suspected I knew something about his trade with the Dutch. After all, he couldn't be sure what I learned when I was at Mátape. I'd get nothing more from him. Perhaps I should have someone spy on him. My butler, Roberto Durán, would be willing to help, I'm sure. I need to give that more thought.

They brought Father Andrés Michel in chains into the city about a week ago from Horcasitas in Sonora. The court session had just concluded, and I needed to know if it convicted him of murdering Captain Cuevas. If so, he'd be executed after the Church and civil government settled formalities. The lieutenant governor told me so.

The creaking garden gate made me jump. Remedios, my maid, hurried along the path between rose bushes, clutching her black shawl around her narrow shoulders. She'd gone to find out about the trial from her friend, a servant in the judge's household. She began to speak before she reached me, brushing back a lock of graying hair, a little out of breath, a crease forming between her finely arched brows.

"Señora, it was a mockery of a trial. They rushed the poor priest through without allowing him to say a word in his own defense."

My voice betrayed my distress. "A conviction so quickly? Why were they in such a hurry ?"

"We're under a new sort of government here in New Spain, doña Beatriz. Even the new viceroy doesn't have the final say in certain important matters of state—it's that royal visitor, José de Gálvez y Gallardo. He's our real ruler."

"What does that have to do with Father Andrés' case?"

"Señora, it has everything to do with the case. A special envoy brought a directive—an official document—from this Gálvez, setting aside normal court procedures. That's how my friend put it."

"What was in that 'directive'?"

"Judge Fernández read it aloud to the court. It said here was proof of Jesuit corruption. King Carlos III has been advised for some time that the Jesuits are carrying on illicit commerce to enrich themselves and accumulate power. In this case, when the unfortunate captain found direct evidence of illicit trade in the Jesuit Andrés Michel 's financial records, the priest murdered him."

A cry of anger escaped me. "Ay, Remedios! What a travesty! An underhanded political game! They're undermining justice, and poor Father Andrés will pay with his life. I was at his mission, and know the man is innocent, completely innocent! What else did José de Gálvez say?"

"That the priest would be hanged for his crime. But the judge ordered that the execution be delayed for ten days in case extenuating evidence should come to light. He seemed to think Father Andrés might not be guilty and was being used as a scapegoat."

"Ten days... and how many have passed since he was sentenced?"

"This is the second day, Señora."

"Thank you, Remedios. Leave me now and let me think."

I watched her slender, black-clad figure disappear into the library through the French doors and returned to my pacing among the roses. The only influential person I knew was don Antonio. I would appeal to him most urgently. He'd surely heard all about the trial.

Once in my upstairs bedroom, I put on my best widow's weeds, a black silk dress with lace panels over the skirt, lace sleeves and upper bodice arranged to give enticing glimpses of cleavage through the complex weave of the lace. I wore my black kid gloves and highly polished high-heeled shoes. I finished the ensemble with a heavy gold necklace—one of Mateo's last gifts to me—and my gold hoop earrings, dabbing a touch of lilac perfume on my wrists, my throat and behind each ear. I made sure my hair was sleekly combed and knotted. The governmental offices are not far from my house, so I took a black parasol and walked. The day was balmy, and I swept into the lieutenant governor's office still cool and wafting fragrance.

I could see from his secretary's face that I'd created the proper effect. He leaped to his feet, bowed and eyed me appreciatively.

"Good day, madam, may I help you?"

I smiled. "I've come to consult with Lieutenant Governor Antonio Figueroa. Is he free? I need his advice on an urgent matter."

"Very good, madam, I'll see."

Don Antonio came out immediately. His greeting was formal, but the smile was genuine. "Good day, doña Beatriz, A pleasant surprise, indeed! I'm informed that you need to consult me urgently. Please come into my office and tell me what the matter in question is." He turned to the secretary. "Ernesto, see that we are not disturbed by other visitors."

The secretary bowed. "Very good, sir."

I hadn't seen his office before. Oriental rugs adorned the shining tile floors; landscapes of the Sierra Madre and oil portraits of past governors hung on the white walls. The furniture was Louis XIV, handsomely upholstered in flowered silk brocade. Don Antonio's pride was his delicate desk, with its finely carved legs and carefully applied gold leaf. I admired everything, including the matching floral drapes at the mullioned, ornamentally barred windows. A graceful chandelier hung from the middle of the high ceiling, bearing at least two dozen candles. The crystals sparkled; it was as scrupulously clean as the rest of the room.

He invited me to sit before the desk, then tugged the maroon damask bell pull on the wall. The door opened and Ernesto appeared once again. "Could you instruct the kitchen, please? I need refreshments for the lady." Turning to me, he asked, "Hot chocolate or tea?"

"Tea would be lovely."

He nodded to the secretary, and added, "Bring the appropriate sweets, please." He turned back. "To what do I owe this honor?"

Like Ernesto, he had already eyed me, noticing, I'm sure, how carefully I had prepared myself for this interview.

I opened my fan and fluttered it in time with my accelerating heart. "I've come to appeal to you in the matter of Father Andrés Michel's execution." My voice seemed higher than normal, my words stiff and formal. "I have certain knowledge that the man is innocent. I cannot reveal how I know this, but it's true. I'm asking you—beseeching you—to stay his execution." I could have delayed my request until after a few more pleasantries, but with only eight days left before Father Andrés' execution, it was extremely urgent, and I thought it best to be as forthright as possible.

He leaned back in his chair. "Ah! Then you learned something more important during your travels than the location of your husband's grave." He paused, his head on one side. "I suppose it would be useless to press you on how you know this priest is innocent. You must know—or think you know—who killed our captain. Just whom are you protecting?"

"Quite right, don Antonio, useless. My lips are sealed on that question, but I swear to you Andrés Michel is innocent—on my honor, on the salvation of my soul." The words echoed in my ears, almost comically stilted.

He seemed surprised by my intensity. The rap on the door caused us both to start. A valet entered, carrying a silver tray with a china tea service and a plate full of honey cakes. He poured two cups while we sat in silence. As the valet excused himself, closing the door softly behind him, don Antonio sugared his tea and sipped slowly, staring at me over the rim of his cup.

"This is obviously important to you."

I nodded, pretending my attention was on my tea and honey cake. "Yes it is, very. I don't want to see injustice done. In this case, grave injustice. The waste of a good man's life."

He bit his honey cake in half and chewed, his eyes narrowed. "Officially, I don't have jurisdiction in this matter, but

I can pull the right strings to stay the execution. What you propose is a business transaction, my dear. I will expect payment for using my power and influence in such an unofficial and unorthodox way."

I feared what was coming and nearly choked on a crumb of cake. "Payment, don Antonio? You know I'm not a wealthy woman."

"Oh but you are, Beatriz," he said, dropping my title. "You possess wealth beyond compare: your beauty. I would merely ask that you share a few moments of that beauty with me."

I knew it all along. My pulse beat in my throat. Could he see it? Of course I understood him. Of course I'd dressed so carefully to entice him, since, after all, I am an experienced woman. And yet, giving myself, prostituting myself in a business transaction, revolted me, but I was willing to do almost anything to save Andrés Michel. I looked up and saw him watching me with fixed attention. He was more than casually interested, since he leaned forward, his breathing matching mine, quick and shallow.

I forced a smile. "Don Antonio, you have me at a severe disadvantage. In a normal transaction, the work is done first; payment comes later. If I 'pay' you now, what guarantee have I that you will honor your half of the bargain?"

He smiled back. "My dear, I am a man of my word, a man of honor. If I make a contract, I will keep it. And I pledge to you, Beatriz, that I will honor my commitment. Father Michel will not die."

I hesitated, my hot face and strained voice reflecting my fears and doubts. "But, Antonio, there is pressure from Royal Visitor Gálvez to have Father Michel executed. You surely must know that. How can I be certain that you, a mere lieutenant governor of a faraway province, can—or even want to—save his life?"

His expression became serious. "We are lucky to be far from México, Beatriz. They'll use the information, true or false, about Father Andrés' corruption to attack all Jesuits. That's what is important to them; his execution is a minor matter by comparison. It's the local officials I have to deal with. Look, my dear, if it would help you trust me, I'll give you this ring." He twisted a heavy golden ring off his little finger.

"What is it, don Antonio?"

"A family heirloom. You see, our crest is still visible. I've worn it since I was a boy. It identifies me and my heritage. It would be a severe blow if you were to lose it. Receive it as a token that I will keep my word. Use it against me if I don't."

I held the ring in my palm, feeling the heft of it and knowing the weightiness of the occasion for us both. I slipped the ring on my right index finger, where it was still loose. "I will take care of the ring," I said.

He rose and stretched his arm toward me. "Now come, give me your arm. Let me show you something."

I stood, feeling suddenly chilled, trapped by my own machinations. He lifted my cold, inert hand, kissed it, kissed the ring, then led me through a door into an inner sanctum, a room that clearly served a double purpose. Smaller than his office, it contained a large oval table with twelve chairs around it for confidential meetings among Sonoran officials or businessmen. High windows in the opposite wall lit a comfortable sofa in an alcove that could be concealed by a set of heavy green velvet curtains, now drawn back. On the wall behind the sofa hung a large painting of a reclining lady in white silk, her curves clearly visible through the thin cloth, abundant curly black hair framing her face, and her glowing black eyes fixing the spectator with a direct stare.

"Come, stand by the table where you can see better," Antonio said, "and I'll tell you about the painting. But first, what do you think of it?"

"It's very lifelike. The painter knows female anatomy very well. See how the silk clings to her body, just as it would in real life. Who is the painter? Where did you find such a fine work?" I was relieved his attention was focused on something beside me.

"When I was in Madrid last year, I attended an exhibition of paintings by young artists—apprentice painters, if you will. This one caught my eye—it was finer than any other work in the show." His tone was quietly conversational, and I knew he was trying to calm my obvious agitation. He continued, "An intense young fellow somewhere around eighteen with a mop of curly brown hair told me he had painted his ideal of beauty. He said he was striving to find the perfect portrayal of her—this was merely one of many. His name is... Francisco Garo... no, Goya. That's it. I brought it home in triumph and hung it in this room. Do you like it? You said it is lifelike, and it is. But you didn't say you liked it."

I glanced at him and saw he was serious. "Yes, yes, I do. She's very pretty."

"But not nearly as beautiful as you, Beatriz. Now," and he took me gently by the elbow, "I'll help you get ready. I was a married man, you know, and am well aware how carefully one must treat a dress as lovely as this one." He bent to give me a gentle kiss on the mouth—almost a chaste kiss—then began to unbutton the dress at the back. He carefully lifted the skirt, and helped me get it over my head without mussing my hair. He held me by the shoulders and admired my arms, then took off my corset, my petticoat, shoes, silk stockings, at every step pausing to admire new revelations of beauty, as he put it. A couple of times he groaned and muttered my name under his breath.

I stood trembling, enduring his kiss and his touch, trying to control my feelings, reminding myself that I was there to save Andrés Michel. Had I actually snared myself in this situation? Was I dreaming? The sound of his gentle voice was all too real.

"My dear, I'm so sorry we have to come together this way. I had dreamt that we might have quite a different sort of under-standing. You see, I've been longing for this moment for years, since you first came here, in fact."

I felt a hot tide of blood rush to my face. Glancing down, I could see my shoulders and breast glowing pink. I'd known all along he was attracted to me. I had used him already to force the army to give me permission to go to Mátape, to provide an escort and the right horse that would carry me safely. Now he was using me, and it was too late to back out now—that is, if I wanted to save an innocent life.

"Well, Antonio," I answered at last, omitting the 'don,' "here I am. Enjoy what you've bargained for. Who can foretell what the future will bring?"

He removed his brocade waistcoat, puffy-sleeved white shirt, satin breeches, silk stockings and buckled shoes—everything down to his under drawers. As if from a distance, I saw a man in middle age, probably around forty-five, still with a handsome enough body, a flat stomach and muscular chest and upper arms. He embraced me, burying his face between my neck and shoulder, just breathing on me for a moment. Then he began licking the hollow of my neck. He ran his hands very gently down my back, then up again, lightly, barely touching my skin, just skimming along, giving the sensation of butterfly wings.

He led me to the couch. Throughout the lovemaking, I thought of my Mateo, my beloved whom I was betraying, pretending it was his embrace I felt, his groans I heard. Flashes came to me of another man: tall, blond, in a black robe. His arms had cradled me, too.

Antonio then led me to a small side room where I found a flowered china basin with matching pitcher filled with water, a sponge, soap and a towel. He was fully dressed when I reappeared, still shaking like a violated virgin. He held my trembling hands for a moment and then patiently helped me into my clothing, adjusting everything I could not see in the mirror so it seemed not to have been disturbed at all. He even helped me tuck in stray wisps of my hair.

He conducted me back through his office and out into the reception area. "Good day, doña Beatriz," he said, bowing. "I hope we shall see each other again soon. Rest assured that I will heed your petition and do everything in my power to comply with your wishes."

I glanced at the secretary, who was watching the two of us, his lips curved with the merest suggestion of a smile.

Once back home again, I was bemused by the speed of our 'transaction,' but at the same time admitted that the man showed good breeding as well as abundant experience with women. I was grateful for his delicacy, and yet I had besmirched myself, lost respect for myself, and I was sure I'd lost much of Antonio's as well. But I feared I must go back to him. I'd forgotten to question him about illicit trade going on between the Jesuits and the Dutch. He surely knew of it. And now, I'd have to worry about becoming pregnant. Mateo and I had no children, but perhaps with this man.... What would I do if I was with child?

I became increasingly agitated, my conscience bothering me more and more. Even though I'd given my body to a man I didn't love, committing this sin to save the life of an innocent priest, I could neither rest nor forgive myself. After all, I loved Mateo, and my fondest desire was to remain true to him until death. At the same time, a quiet little voice spoke to me, reminding me of a tall, powerfully built, blond man. He was a man with an excellent background, well read, agreeable. But he was a priest—a Jesuit!—a man who could lift me in his arms as lightly as I could lift a broom, and place me gently on my horse's back; a man who seemed naively aware of my attractions, and yet who resisted me, apparently without effort; a man with the absurd name of Ygnacio Pfefferkorn.

It was nearly dark when I decided to see the prisoner, Father Andrés. If nothing else, he would welcome the sight of a person he knew. Still dressed in my lacy finery, I threw a crocheted black shawl over my shoulders. I would go to the prison and demand to see him.

Roberto, my butler, called a carriage for me, and I instructed the driver to take me to the prison building. He gave me a strange look, but obeyed my orders. He handed me out of the coach and I tipped him well, told him to wait, and entered the prison. There was no one at the desk behind the grille when I arrived, but the clerk was not long delayed. When he returned, I demanded to see Father Andrés Michel. He hesitated for a moment, but must have decided that a priest would neither do me harm nor try to escape. He beckoned me to follow him.

We walked down a flight of stairs and along a dusky corridor, lit here and there by guttering candles. At last, he stopped and rattled a batch of keys on a chain. When he found the right one, he opened the door. Then, seeing no light in the interior of the cell, he took one of the hall candles off its holder and stuck it to the window sill. The guard told me to bang on the door four times and shout "¡Pronto!" when I was ready to leave.

Father Andrés and I stared at each other. He had lost weight, his gray hair straggling in greasy mats over his forehead. He had a two-week, unkempt beard and he looked ten years older, stooped with the weight of ill fortune.

He spoke first. "Doña Beatriz! Is it really you? Thank God someone I know has come to see me at last!" He moved forward to take me by both hands, and I saw he was dragging chains on his feet. He glanced at the ring on my pointer finger but made no comment.

"Father Andrés, I can't tell you how sorry I am that all this has happened. Come, let's sit on that bench and talk for a moment. I have good news for you, Father." Without letting go of his hands, I moved to the stone bench, where we sat side by side. "Father, I have reason to believe your sentence of death will be commuted."

"Oh? How can that be?" He blinked at me in the wavering candlelight. "I knew from the beginning I'd be executed for Captain Cuevas' murder. All the time, while I was keeping vigil, when Ygnacio was looking at the body, searching out footprints, going after my Apache friend—I knew I would hang for the murder. God has his mysterious purposes. You see, I believe there are purposes beyond anything our poor human understanding can grasp. I'm resigned to them. His will be done."

I still held his hands, wondering about footprints and an Apache. No matter. I spoke to encourage him. "Father, my poor

Father Andrés, I'm here to tell you that you'll not die. Not now. I've seen to that. Your execution will be commuted, because I know you're innocent, you see."

He was startled but merely clutched my hands tighter, evidently gaining strength from the contact. "What do you mean, doña Beatriz? You're not making sense. You wouldn't try to deceive an old man, would you? You say my execution will be commuted. But what are you *really* saying?"

At last, I disengaged my hands, hesitated, then dropped to my knees before him, tearing the lace on my skirt. I hid my face in my hands and spoke the words of the Sacrament of Confession, "Bless me, Father, for I have sinned."

Chapter XIV
Hot Pursuit

"*Ignaz! Du lebst, Gott sei Dank!* You're alive, thank God! And Pío Wegner! What are you doing here?"

Father Jacobo Sedelmeyer of Mátape greeted us when Wolf and I arrived at Ures shortly after nightfall, dusty and grimy, exhausted and hungry. Hernán heard us coming, and we found him before the church, ready to help. He held our horses when we dismounted, then handed their reins to Juanito, the boy who shadowed him, to water and feed them.

Jacobo gave each of us a quick embrace. For days, I'd feared we would be too late, that Andrés would have been arrested and jailed while I was away chasing Denzhoné. Jacob's words confirmed my fears.

"I'm sorry it isn't Andrés standing here to greet you. He was arrested for murder—"

I sagged with despair. The worst had happened, after all my struggle. My voice shook. "Oh, NO! When? What have they done to him? Any news?"

Jacobo laid a hand on my shoulder. "They came for him about five days after you left Mátape. Since then, we know they took him in chains to Durango, but I have reason to hope they haven't executed him yet. We haven't heard one way or the other."

"What reason do you have for hope, Father Jacobo?" I asked, "and how did you come to be here?"

Hernán interrupted. "Father Jacobo is here because I sent a messenger to Mátape when Father Andrés was arrested. One of the scholastics came to say Mass and hear confessions and that worked for a while, but Father Jacobo knew a major mission like Ures needed more attention. So, he took his subordinate's place for a week, to make sure everything is running smoothly."

"It's running smoothly in large part because of you, Hernán," Jacobo said. He spread his arms wide. "We really know little for certain, only that I think Andrés is still alive. But I'll tell what little I know at supper. For now, we need to get you two settled for the night." He walked around me, squinting at me in the moonlight. "You look a little worse for wear. Why don't you go down to the river and bathe?"

"What will we wear afterwards?" Wolfgang asked, brushing his dust-laden sleeves.

"I'll bring you a couple of Andrés' spare robes, if I can find them. They may not fit, but they'll cover your nakedness until Marta or somebody can wash yours. I'll have her repair your robe, Ygnacio; that'll give her quite a challenge. Wait here and I'll get some soap, and while you're down there, I'll see to supper." He strode toward the rectory.

"They *can't* execute Andrés… can they?" Wolfgang sounded subdued.

"I'm afraid they can. I pray God they haven't already done it, and Jacobo is right, that there's still hope."

He was back with the soap and passed it to me. Wolf and I walked to the river's edge in a dark mood. In obedience to the Society's precepts on modesty, we undressed separately, using willow shrubs as private undressing rooms. Wolfgang turned his back so as not to glimpse me naked when I crossed the sandy bank to the water.

The half moon lit the scene with a benevolent glow, turning the river into an ever-changing flow of diamonds. The cold shock became a cool caress as I moved deeper. I found a place where I could swim five or six strokes before grounding myself on a gravel bar. I sat on the bottom, water up to my neck, the current tugging at me. The quicksilver water rippled and sparkled all around me; the air smelled sweet, tangy with a hint of mesquite smoke from cooking fires. The beauty of the night and the river's gentle flow calmed and consoled me. Tomorrow, we would continue doing all we could to save Andrés.

"Wolf! Come on in, I won't look."

I submerged my head, came up blowing and blinking water out of my eyes, then washed my body and hair with the gray mission soap. My back was still scabby in places, and I soaped it as far as my hands could reach. Wolf was submerged at the other end of our swimming hole. When he came up, I tossed him the precious bar of soap, making sure my toss was true.

Jacobo materialized out of the shadows on the bank, looping two clean robes over a willow shrub. I waited till he'd gone, then waded to shore and slipped Andrés' robe over my head. It was too short and too narrow in the shoulders and chest. I left the top row of buttons open, sure that Jacobo would not object to the temporary breach of decorum. Wolf had better luck with his robe. We walked up the slope to the rectory, breathing in the fragrance of meat smoking over mesquite coals.

We devoured Jacobo's hearty meal and then, over cups of red wine, told him what had happened since I had left Mátape with Beatriz and the young Jesuits.

He finally interrupted. "So what are you doing back here? Tell me that first; then I'll tell what I know about Andrés."

Wolf answered, "We decided to interrogate all the Pimas in the mission to find out what they saw on the night of the murder."

"That's a lot of work, my friends."

"Yes," I said, "but there are two of us, and we'll begin right after Mass tomorrow morning. We're at a dead end, you see. Denzhoné was here the night Captain Cuevas died, but he didn't kill him. Wolf was also here, but *he* didn't kill the captain. That leaves us with one other suspect—"

Jacobo held up a hand. "Here's the bit of news I have for you. Two soldiers came through here five days ago, asking if I'd seen a lone soldier by the name of Saúl Ayala. It seems Ayala was here the night of the murder, too."

I set down my cup of wine with a clack and leaned forward. "Amazing! He's our one suspect. Who were the soldiers?"

"A Sergeant Morelos, if I remember right, and Corporal Miguel Something-or-Other."

"Miguel González?"

"Yes, yes, that's right."

"Did they say why they were looking for Ayala?"

"Yes, they got talkative after I treated them to a good meal and three cups of wine. Seems they went to Horcasitas and reported Captain Cuevas' death to Governor Pineda, how it was done and the other details."

"So, did Pineda issue an arrest order for Andrés?" I asked.

"Yes, he sent soldiers to bring him in, while the sergeant and the corporal stayed there. By the time the soldiers returned with Andrés, Pineda had decided he'd have to send him to Durango because of complications with us Jesuits and the Church. He also sent a messenger to the royal visitor, José de Gálvez, describing the case."

"If the execution must wait for the Church and the Jesuits to come to some conclusion, it might be delayed indefinitely," I said.

"I bet the governor was glad he wouldn't have to hang Andrés himself," Wolf said, "I'm sure the two know each other from 'way back."

"Yes, but he clapped chains on our poor brother to make sure he wouldn't make a desperate break for it." Jacobo snorted. "They treated him like a common outlaw because, I think, they're afraid of that royal visitor, Gálvez. That man wants to hang us all, evidence or no."

I nodded. "So I hear. When did Corporal Ayala show up?"

"They said Andrés and his guards had left Horcasitas for Durango a day and a half before Ayala got there. His horse stepped on a rattlesnake and bucked him off. The horse was bit and Ayala was hurt. Anyway, he was delayed by several days getting to Horcasitas."

"What business did he have with the governor?"

"Morelos and González said he'd claimed from the beginning that he had a message for the governor, but instead of delivering that, he made a formal statement about the murder. He told them what he'd written."

"Did they tell *you?*"

"Yes. He formally stated that Father Andrés Michel had nothing to do with the killing and was completely innocent. He further said that he was turning himself in and would stand trial for the murder."

"So why were Morelos and González here looking for him?"

"Because he delivered the statement to the governor's secretary folded and sealed with wax, and before the governor could open it, Ayala excused himself, walked out and disappeared. Governor Pineda was furious and sent men to inform all the presidios to be on the lookout for Ayala. There seems to be some suspicion that Ayala made a false confession. They have to find him to make sure. Pineda sent the sergeant and corporal back here."

I caught Wolf's glance. "What did I tell you, Wolf? Now we need to find Corporal Ayala and settle the matter once and for all. Even if he isn't the murderer, he knows something important that might clear Andrés' name."

Wolf looked doubtful. "Should we go on with our plan of questioning the converts?"

"It's even more urgent. We might find out from them if Ayala is the murderer, or they might have seen something that would implicate someone else. Whatever we do, we must hurry."

He nodded. "If the Church has done its typical dithering, Andrés is still alive."

I lifted my cup. "Here's a toast to hope, the slow grinding of the Jesuit and Church bureaucracies and, of course, to the mercy and *grace* of God."

Wolf gave me a sharp look, then a hesitant grin.

›‹

The sun had not yet risen, and we had already begun questioning our first Pimas. We had announced at Mass what we intended to do, asking the members of the congregation to cast their minds back to the night of the murder to recall, as best they could, anything helpful. Father Andrés' life was in danger, we told them, and anything they remembered might help us learn the truth.

Hernán and the alguacil made sure we spoke to everyone. They brought groups of people to wait in the back pews in the church. The people came up, one by one, to sit in front of Wolf or me. When we had finished one group, the next one entered and sat in the pews, awaiting their turn. As we interviewed, we recorded name, sex and age of each person along with a summary of each statement, in case we needed to recall someone.

A few were too eager to help and invented imaginary things seen or heard, some with plausible stories. But when we compared their testimony with others', we eliminated the 'helpful' lies. At dusk on the first day, we had discovered nothing new that we considered accurate.

By afternoon of the second day, Wolfgang and I were beginning to despair. I had recorded a number of new leads, only to draw a line through them when further interrogation proved them false.

Wolf was luckier. A boy of about nine named Felipe had been interested in Captain Cuevas' doings. He admired the man's guns and his uniform. He ignored his mother's calls to come to bed and continued to follow the captain at a distance, even after dark, and it had been quite dark before the moon rose that night. When Felipe got to this point, Wolf called me over to hear his story:

"I was watching behind a low wall across from the tack shed and saw the captain go into the room at the end with two other soldiers. I was about to mind mama and go to bed, when the captain came to the door. He turned toward the church, but I didn't see what he saw. He looked all around but didn't see me, and then he went into the church. After a little while I heard voices and some sort of fight, then a door slammed—somewhere inside, I think. I waited, but didn't hear any more and nobody came out, so I went home to bed."

"How close to the church were you?" Wolf asked.

"I stayed across from the tack shed. You can see how far that is."

"Hmmm, about thirty paces."

"And at that distance you could hear the voices?" I asked, "That's pretty far off."

"They were loud enough. But after the door slammed, I couldn't hear any more. So, I went home."

"But before you went, could you tell whose voices they were?"

"One was the captain. I didn't know the other voice. But I saw something the next morning."

"Oh?" We both leaned forward, and our chairs creaked their own exclamations.

Felipe's face became a smug mask, now that he had the full attention of two priests. "Yes." He lifted his chin with drooping eyelids, looking down his nose at Wolf. "A soldier was staying in the room next to the lady's."

"That's right, it was Corporal Ayala," Wolf said, "What did you see?"

"I got up early, when the first gray light showed, because I wanted to see the captain when he got up and watch what all of them were going to do. When I reached my spot across from the tack room, I saw the corporal come out of his room next to the lady's and knock on her door."

"Yes, and what happened then?"

"She came to the door, and they stood there talking for several minutes."

"Could you hear anything?"

"No, they talked low."

"And then?"

"The corporal saddled his horse and packed his mule and rode away. That's all. I never saw Captain Cuevas again until the funeral Mass. I'm sorry he got killed. He looked good in his uniform. I want to be a soldier like him some day."

I ruffled the boy's hair. "Who knows, maybe you will be. Thank you, Felipe, you've been helpful. Please tell your mama we're glad you didn't go to bed right away that time. But don't make a habit of disobeying your mother!"

When the church pews were empty at last, we sat down together. "Well, Wolf, did Felipe add anything you didn't see from the hayloft?"

"Not much…. Not really. Captain Cuevas saw something or somebody in the church and went to investigate, was attacked, ran out into the garden and received the death blow."

"No, Wolf, I think he got into a fight like Felipe said. There may have been a discussion behind that closed door—the one that slammed—and it turned out badly. *Then* he ran out into the garden and received the death blow."

"Your reconstruction makes me think Andrés did it," Wolf said. "We know the captain told Sergeant Morelos and Corporal González that he wanted to take another look at those books. He may have seen Andrés in the church and went to confront him."

"Yes, but nobody, at least not Hernán and the boy, recognized the second voice. You told me back at Cuquiárachi that Hernán knew it wasn't Andrés."

"So who…? Ayala?"

We shook our heads and went to dinner.

⁎⁎

At last! I avenged my husband's death, even though it cost me much inner struggle. It deeply scarred my self respect, and my conscience continued to trouble me, despite the absolution I'd received from Father Andrés.

Rather than go back to Antonio to pry out information on the illicit trade in his province, I called in my butler, Roberto Durán. I had thought of a plan. Berto had served my family for decades—since boyhood—and had come with me when Mateo and I left Toledo. He was devoted to me, did anything I asked, and he knew this city in all its aspects, including its seamier side.

"*Sí, doña Beatriz ¿en qué puedo servirle*?" How can I serve you?

"Berto, on my trip to Mátape to visit Mateo's grave, I learned that he'd been ordered to defend a mule train of Dutch Merchants when they were attacked by a band of Apaches. Mateo and four other men. They were all killed but one."

"Yes, Remedios heard what Corporal Ayala told you, so I know all that. The corporal blamed the captain, but you think it was the Jesuit who gave the orders. Is that right?"

I shook my head in mock disapproval. "Remedios shouldn't be gossiping to you! Ah, well, it saves me long explanations. That Jesuit is their vice-provincial, Luca Poncelli."

"Ah. I know of him, doña Beatriz."

"At Lieutenant Governor Antonio Figueroa's birthday ball, I overheard two merchants, Señores García and Pacheco, whose business is downtown here, talking about the fancy German muskets they've imported. It seems they sell them disguised as something else to an important someone in the city." I summarized the events at Mátape and concluded, "My Mateo was not so well armed."

"What do you want me to do, Señora?"

"I need proof that Poncelli is the one receiving the merchants' guns. If you have friends, you can set up a round-the-clock vigil to watch their place as well as the vice-provincial's. But I only have money enough to pay for two, maybe three men at the most."

"Lieutenant Mateo Salinas, your beloved husband, was my master, doña Beatriz. I want to find his murderer as much as you do. I'll work for nothing and will find three others—maybe Jaime and 'Nando, and one more."

"I'll find some way to make it worth your while, Berto. I won't let you work for nothing, though I truly appreciate your kind offer. Those merchants must deliver when no one can see them. The logical time would be after the cantinas close around midnight. That's when you need to be especially alert."

On the sixth day, Remedios woke me at three-thirty in the morning by the cathedral clock. Berto was waiting to tell me something important, she said. I tied my hair back and threw on a dressing gown, then met him in the salon. I was wide awake, tense with excitement.

"*Señora, creo que tengo la prueba de todo lo que hemos platicado*. I have proof of everything we talked about."

"Tell me, Berto! What proof?"

"Yesterday at noon, a heavy wagon drawn by two teams of oxen pulled up in front of García y Pacheco's place, and unloading began."

"*Two* teams of oxen? That wagon must have held tons! A fortune!"

"They all acted like it. No one left to go eat. They all scrambled to unload the wagon and carry some canvas bundles inside the warehouse. They were greasy-looking as if they were soaked with oil. Not a one was left on the loading dock as usual."

"So how did you know what was in them?"

"As careful as they were, still there was one little accident. One *Indio* lifted a bundle and snagged the one underneath. It partly unwrapped, and some of the contents slipped out. They were shiny new muskets with fancy finished wooden stocks. He grabbed up the guns, looked all around like a guilty man, re-wrapped them and carried them away. After that, around one o'clock, half of the men left for their meal, the other half stayed until the others came back, and then they went to eat."

"And you stayed on watch all that time?"

"Yes, I was too excited to think of anything else. By late afternoon, they came out on the loading dock, with different-looking bundles. They were heavy canvas, fixed to fit on a mule's back, each one divided in two halves. They were half as long as the originals, and, sticking out of each side of every bundle was the neck of a big bottle with a cork in it. How could that be?"

"That's how the guns were disguised the time they went to Mátape, Berto. That's what the missionary, Father Sedelmeyer, told me. The bundles looked like bottles of some kind of oil."

"They loaded a wagon with those bundles and late that night they hitched up two teams of mules and drove off. I followed the wagon at a distance by the sounds it made, but they stopped."

I leaned forward, my hands like claws on the arms of my chair. "But you found them again?"

"Yes. They were in the most elegant district of the city. When I came around the corner, I saw a glimmer of torchlight just before a gate closed. I could hear them pushing a bar across it. I knew the house: it belongs to the Jesuits. It's where that Father Luca Poncelli stays."

"Ah. Good work, Berto!" I felt a surge of fierce joy. "Could you see who received the shipment?"

"I wanted to make sure, so I slipped along the fence, keeping in the shadows in case they'd posted a lookout. There was an oak tree growing against the wall. I could hear clanking noises from inside. I climbed the tree, enough to peek over the top even though it was eight feet high. There stood Luca Poncelli himself, directing the unloading with two servants—valets, not priests—with torches to help the workers. They stacked the goods in a shed next to the house, and got ready to leave."

"Did they see you on their way out?"

"No, I slipped down and ran along the wall, in the shadow. I was around a corner by the time they came out."

"So what do *you* think those bottles are for?"

"They're decoys, doña Beatriz, just as you said. There were too many bundles to take with any one mule train, so Father Poncelli must mean to make two or more trips to several mines."

"You've done an amazing job, Berto. Wait here a moment." I returned to the bedroom, opened my jewel box and took out my gold necklace, worth far more than needed to pay all the men. Mateo would approve—after all, I have uncovered the conspiracy that killed him, and my vengeance is sure.

My main task was done, but the second one, equally important, was to see Father Andrés released. Conditions in that cell were inhuman, and it would not take long for them to kill the priest. My purpose was to save his life, after all. I decided to pay another visit to Antonio Figueroa. I dressed as before, this time in a different but equally alluring black gown, and presented myself to his secretary, who lost no time in informing his master. My heart pounded just as before, and I dabbed perspiration from my brow with a lace handkerchief, but at least I knew what to expect. Don Antonio seemed overjoyed to see me, and immediately conducted me into his office.

"Beatriz! Good of you to call on me. It's been far too long since your last visit."

"Ah, Antonio, I did write you a warm note of thanks for your previous kindness. I've had other business to attend to, and I'll tell you about that, but I'm still troubled. Our act of mercy is still unfinished."

His eyes opened wide. "What? What do you mean, Beatriz? Still troubled? Why?"

"Before I can sleep at night, I must know that Father Michel is truly out of danger. I must do everything in my power to have him released. He's an innocent man condemned to life in prison, where he'll soon die. I've seen his cell and I know."

His face drooped. I think he'd hoped I'd returned for his sake. He pondered the question for a moment. "Release.... I don't have that kind of power, my dear. But I pledge that I'll use every contact, appeal to every friend."

His ready consent made me think he believed without question that I knew the killer, and it was not the priest. Such faith in me, such restraint in not demanding that I reveal the real murderer, indicated the depth of his love. I was deeply touched.

I smiled to relieve the tension that filled the room, threatening to smother us both. I tried to think of something light, inconsequential, and unconnected with Father Andrés. I blurted, "I don't imagine you've acquired any new paintings in such a short time, Antonio."

He matched my slightly ironic tone, but with a serious note underlying the banter. "No, but I have a new engraving, Beatriz."

"Oh? What is it?"

"Your name, etched on my heart."

We laughed together at his sentimentality, and then, becoming serious and holding myself upright, my hands folded in my lap, I made my plea.

"Antonio, please don't think me ungrateful or greedy. You and I" (and here I lowered my eyes out of shame) "have done only part of our task. Ah... you see... as I just said, our good Father Andrés is still in terrible danger. Antonio, you're my only link to power. A link that... that is precious to me."

My voice faltered into silence. My emotion was genuine, as was my shame, since I had dropped all pride to beseech him. Antonio was a true friend, generous and steady, if a bit too eager. Yes, I truly was fond of him. "Antonio, for the sake of our affection that was... consummated last week, let's... cooperate to get that innocent man entirely free of their clutches." I felt the heat of my blush warm my cheeks and my bosom.

He sat looking at me for a long moment, until I became uneasy. His eyes, locked on mine, searched my soul, as I pleaded for the freedom of a man who was of little importance to him, except to secure my affection.

"My dear Beatriz," he said at last, without dropping his gaze, "I'll leave no stone unturned, and I won't ask why the life and liberty of this one sad priest should mean so much to you."

Could this man truly be in love with me? His faith in me left me amazed and deeply moved. It might be a dereliction of his duty to accept my word without pressing me further. If the royal visitor was informed of his activity, it might cost him his position.

Far more had transpired between us than that earlier "business transaction." One injustice, at least, might still be reversed. I held out my hand, which he grasped with great warmth. "Thank you! I thank you with all my heart, Antonio! You restore my faith in humanity!"

"You can rely on me, Beatriz. Please come visit us at home, my dear. My children and I would enjoy your presence."

ଛଡଃ

After two days of trial and error I was satisfied with my formal, detailed and logical letter to the viceroy in México, denouncing the criminal activity of the vice-provincial, Luca Poncelli of the Society of Jesus. I sent copies of the same letter to the Society's provincial, also in the same city, and to their visitor general in Arizpe—although I had no idea whether the whole Society was involved in illicit trade. I did not write to the royal visitor, since I had no idea where to send the letter. The viceroy would surely inform him. The three letters went off by mail carriers not connected to Poncelli's office. May the sword of my vengeance strike him!

Chapter XV
The Vice-Provincial Comes to Ures

"Come get it while it's hot!" Jacobo waved when he saw us. "Leg of mutton tonight."

I scanned the fireplace-oven and the table. Our places were laid. The savory meat, browned and topped with crisped rosemary leaves and garlic cloves, graced the center of the table. Beside it sat a bowl of rice, another of gravy, and a plate piled with grilled nopal pads. The aroma was irresistible. Jacobo, his hands wrapped in rags, carried a bubbling pot of frijoles from the oven.

"One second while I get the wine." He brought a jug of red Parral wine and poured us each a glassful. "So, what did you discover today?"

We sat and said grace, then filled our plates. "Wolf, you go first," I said, and turning to Jacobo, "He was here when the murder happened and saw a lot himself."

Wolfgang nodded. "A boy, Felipe, saw Cuevas go into the church. The captain apparently saw someone in there."

"Did Felipe see who it was?"

"We're not that lucky. There was a quarrel, a door slammed, then nothing for a while. The boy went home to bed."

Jacobo shook his head. "That's not much. You already told me that much, Pío."

"Call me Wolfgang, please, Father Jacobo."

"Alright, fine, Pío… Wolfgang. Anything else?"

"The next morning Felilpe saw Corporal Ayala knock on doña Beatriz' door. They talked for a while, then he saddled up and left with his pack animal."

Jacobo raised his eyebrows. "Interesting. Did Felipe hear anything?"

"Not a word," I said. "It's possible that Captain Cuevas saw Ayala in the church that night and went to settle a score with him. Ayala had already threatened him over his unwelcome advances to doña Beatriz. You'd witnessed that, Wolf. Cuevas might have tried to discipline his subordinate or maybe he threatened him. They quarreled, Cuevas left the church by the side door, Ayala followed and killed him with the statuette of the Blessed Virgin."

Jacobo nodded slowly. "It's possible, even likely, Ygnacio."

"Either that, or Andrés really did kill the captain," Wolfgang said, one eyebrow raised.

₧

Morning Mass and breakfast over, I paced the plaza before the church in the cool morning air. I'd go after Ayala. Maybe he'd gone back to Durango and not into the wilds as the governor seemed to think.

Wolf appeared out of nowhere, pointing south. "D'you hear that?"

"*Yeee-haaaaa!*" Then the crack of a whip, braying, whinnying, the chink of bridles and spurs, and the beat of hooves. Father Jacobo ran outside, joining us in the plaza as the cavalcade appeared. In the lead came the military escort: a captain, a lieutenant and, guarding the rear, ten men—the same type of unit that had escorted that 'visit' to Mátape almost eight months ago. Following them rode Father Luca Poncelli on a handsome mule, a pacer. Then, on a gray mare rode a vaguely familiar Jesuit, slumped in the saddle, his head drooping forward so that his broad-brimmed hat covered his face and upper chest. He lifted his haggard face. Andrés! We rushed toward him. I grumbled under my breath that protocol decreed we greet the vice-provincial first.

While we stiffly welcomed Father Poncelli, we glanced in Andrés' direction, making signs that we would be with him soon. Jacobo helped Poncelli down from his mule and formally invited him to enjoy the mission's hospitality.

I paid my respects. "Good morning, Father Poncelli. Where are you headed with this impressive escort and such abundant supplies?" At least eight mules bore heavy bundles with the necks of bottles protruding here and there.

"Father Ygnacio—isn't it?—we're on our way to Misión Banámichi with goods for several villages that have suffered for months from a lack of essentials."

"I'm surprised Visitor General Carlos Rojas hasn't taken care of that. After all, he's only a few leagues upstream. Which villages could these be, Father?" I smiled disarmingly, I hoped.

Poncelli narrowed his eyes, but seemed flustered. "Oh, ah… Banámichi, San Felipe de Jesús, and the little villages round about."

"Ah."

I excused myself and moved to greet Father Andrés. "Ygnacio!" He gave a shadow of his old hearty smile, "Give me a hand here! I'm worn out from riding this jolting old nag. Need to see how much you've improved this place since I got dragged away!" I reached up to assist him, and he virtually fell into my arms. "Thirteen days' ride is too much for an old man like me."

"You're not that old, Andrés." I made sure he was steady on his feet. "We thought you were condemned to die for Captain Cuevas' murder. We heard you were in prison."

Wolfgang joined us, and supported Andrés on the other side. "The sentence must have been commuted. How did you get out?"

Andrés' face betrayed a mixture of emotions. "Yes, the sentence of death was commuted. I'll tell you what I can later. For now, let's attend to the vice-provincial."

Hernán had hung back at first and now joined our little group. He was concerned, but he spoke as if Father Andrés were returning from a casual trip. "Welcome back, Father Andrés! I expect you will want Marta and the other women to prepare a meal for everyone. Do I have your permission to butcher a steer? That should provision everyone adequately."

Andrés smiled, as we all did, at his gobernador's stilted Spanish. "Thank you, Hernán. By all means, butcher a steer and start those grills and ovens going—I wouldn't mind a juicy steak. I'll leave the rest of the meal up to Marta's imagination. Let me know if you want anything special from the stores. And take care of the mules and horses." With this, he turned to Poncelli and Jacobo.

"Let's go inside and sit on chairs for a change. Ygnacio, you or Wolfgang must be familiar with my kitchen by now. One of you can make us something good to drink. Chocolate, maybe."

I searched the kitchen shelves for the chocolate and the precious wheat flour, finding both in metal containers to keep out insects. In the end, my concoction needed more chocolate, sugar, and a pinch of salt to brighten the flavor. It could have used a vanilla bean, but such luxuries are rare on the frontier. We sipped the brew, listening to Luca Poncelli's uninterrupted monologue about directives from the provincial in México, Francisco Zevallos.

When Poncelli paused to sip his drink, Andrés beckoned to me. Would I help him to his room? He needed rest before the noon meal. "Father Poncelli, I beg your pardon. I think I'll retire for a few minutes if you don't mind. Ygnacio, here, will help me."

The vice-provincial replied in his mellifluous voice, "Of course, Father Andrés. You need to recuperate from your recent ordeal." He nodded to me, giving tacit permission to withdraw. I glanced at Wolf, and could see by his burning eyes that he would dearly love to debate with the vice-provincial about grace versus works, no doubt. I shook my head at him. He gave me a slight lift of the shoulders in reply, taking another sip of hot chocolate.

I helped Andrés to his feet. His halting gait told me he was in pain. He sank on his bed with a sigh, lifting his feet upon it. "Have a look at my ankles, Ygnacio. They need speedy attention. Indian medicine, not ours. Rita will know what to do."

His high-topped shoes were soiled and encrusted on the inside, stuck to his ankles in places. I was shocked at what I saw and smelled. The skin was broken and scraped away around the swollen ankles, the flesh weeping infected matter.

I gasped. "What caused this? The shackles?"

"They put those iron bands on my legs before they took me from here and chained me to the saddle like the murderer they thought I was. I wore them at Horcasitas; I still wore them in Durango. Find Rita and tell her to hurry. If something isn't done soon, I might die of blood poisoning."

"I'll find her!"

An aged white-haired woman, her sun-baked and weathered face creased in a network of wrinkles, flipped a tortilla as I approached. She glanced up and greeted me by name, speaking Pima. "Hello, Father Ygnacio. How is Father Andrés?"

"He wore chains for weeks, Rita, and his ankles are infected. He needs your medicine, quick, or he might die of blood poisoning."

She set aside her tortillas, and spoke to a boy standing by. "Get a pick and shovel from the shed, and the iron rod. Find two more boys to help you dig up a mescal on the slopes over yonder. Get a big root, wash it well. Go now, and hurry!" She turned to me. "Wash his ankles with warm fresh water and clean cloths. Put pads of clean linen under them, and wait for me."

In twenty minutes, she knocked on the rectory door. Wolfgang sprang up, answered it, and asked Poncelli. "Is she allowed in here? The rules say a woman isn't allowed into a priest's house."

I poked my head through the door between Andres' bedroom and the living quarters. "It's Rita, who knows all about herbal remedies, Father Poncelli. Do I have your permission to let her in? She must be in her seventies."

He grunted, nodded, and, ignoring the commotion, continued lecturing Jacobo. I was thankful he was able to keep Poncelli busy.

Rita placed a jar of liquid on Andrés' bedside table. "This is juice of the mescal root. It has strong powers to cure old and new wounds." She soaked two clean rags in the mescal juice and wound them around the puffy, infected ankles. Andrés cringed at the sting.

"Good you feel the sting, Father Andrés," she said, "That means your flesh is still alive. If it feels, it will heal." To me she said, "Leave the juice on the legs until it begins to dry. Then burn the rags and wrap his ankles with clean cloths. Tie them on so he can walk. Find shoes that do not rub, so he can move around. Then give him food. He needs food to strengthen him. I will tend him again later."

I had full confidence in her powers. I'd seen Jevho, the medicine man at Guevavi, use similar cures. Andrés had begun to relax during her treatment and now lay with closed eyes, his breathing slow and regular. I covered him with an Indian blanket and tiptoed out to join the captive audience in the salon.

Savory odors of roasting beef wafted into the open window, and my mouth watered. Two hours later, we were seated at long trestle tables that Hernán had set up in the plaza, feasting on succulent steaks accompanied by the inevitable frijol beans, a squash concoction from the mission gardens, tortillas and hot sauce. Cool watermelon, crisp and sweet, arrived for dessert.

We were surprised that Andrés had the strength to join us. His color was better even after so short a rest. He had found slippers that would not rub his wounds, and Wolf and I made sure he took a serving of everything. He ate with moderate appetite, then returned to bed.

Later, after Poncelli retired to his room and Jacobo was writing a report, we again looked in on Andrés.

"Tell us how you were released—if it isn't confidential," I said.

"It was through the lieutenant governor's influence—don Arturo Figueroa—on my own recognizance. I learned the reasons why he was concerned with my case, first to have my sentence commuted, and then to gain my freedom—but I learned them in the confessional." He paused, and we knew nothing more could be said on the subject. He raised himself on one elbow. "But what happened to you, Ygnacio? You were about to risk your life in Apache territory, tracking down Denzhoné."

"Yes, and I did." I told him how I had set out to find the Apache chief, stopping along the way at Sinoquipe to help Wolfgang cope with the measles epidemic. After reporting on the visit with Carlos Rojas, I told of my capture by Itza-chu's people and my rescue by his Christian wife, who had also brought Denzhoné to me.

Andrés' face tensed. "Well? And what did he have to say? We know he was here on the night Captain Cuevas died."

"He circled the body twice, just as I saw when I examined his tracks. He thought you had killed the Captain, so he stabbed him—he says to show his solidarity with you. Wolfgang actually saw him do it."

Andrés turned to Wolf. "You saw him? How was that?"

"It was just as Ygnacio tells it, Father Andrés. The moon had risen, and I saw Denzhoné from the hayloft when he circled the body. He stabbed the captain and when he heard the soldiers' voices, he dropped the knife and ran. And I still have it." He extracted the knife from his pocket. "See?"

Andrés took it and turned it over, a crease of concentration between his brows. "Yes, I think I know this knife. I've seen him use it to cut food. I'm glad you eliminated my friend from your list of suspects. And the peace pact?"

"He promises that his tribe will never attack Ures. That's as far as it goes. I'm sorry I didn't do better, Andrés."

"It's a start, Ygnacio. Now that you've eliminated Denzhoné and Wolf as suspects, and—I hope—me, who's left?"

"Corporal Saúl Ayala. Governor Pineda is searching the province for him. After you left Horcasitas under guard, Ayala turned up. He'd intended to stop them from taking you to Durango, but he was delayed by an accident."

"So why is he being sought?"

"He wrote a deposition stating that he would stand trial for the murder. As Jacobo tells it, he didn't quite confess to killing the captain, but he left very little doubt."

"Do you think he did it, Ygnacio?"

"Very likely. He'd had angry words with the captain over his unwelcome advances to doña Beatriz. He had joined the other soldiers and the lady on their way up here to examine your books. I suspect they had a fight over her and Ayala murdered Cuevas."

"What do you think, Wolfgang?"

Wolf turned his face to the window, only his sharp profile visible. "He is in love with the lady. I heard that in his voice when he challenged the captain. A man in love is capable of anything."

His words brought a flash of jealousy. Ayala and Beatriz had been together on the trail to Ures. The boy Felipe had seen them in intense conversation at dawn, the morning after the murder. Were they in love? My hands clenched, but then my conscience stabbed me, bringing gloom in the wake of my jealous musing. I, too, seemed to be "in love." Would I be capable of anything?

I heard the strain in my voice. "I'll go after Ayala, Andrés. We still need to clear your name." I was not sure whether I spoke out of jealousy or concern for my brother.

"You'll do nothing of the sort, Ygnacio. Let the civil authorities take care of themselves; they are no concern of the Church. I command you both to return to your missions, where your neophytes need your services."

Wolf and I exchanged glances, then spoke, almost in unison, "Yes, Father." We bowed our heads in submission.

I narrowed my eyes. "I now remember a conversation with doña Beatriz here, at your table. She told us she and the lieutenant governor were great friends, and he had asked the governor to give her the horse she was riding. Do you recall that, Andrés?"

"Yes… and you asked her to put in a good word on our behalf with the lieutenant governor. I remember that too."

"Well, she must have done exactly that, thank God! And he has given you back——."

Wolfgang laid a hand on my arm and turned to our superior. "Father Andrés, I'm afraid there's more bad news. In my travels I discovered some disturbing things, and they, very deeply, concern the Church."

Andrés twisted to face Wolf. "What things? Does this have something to do with illicit trade?"

"Yes. You know about that business in Mátape, of course, where Lieutenant Salinas was slaughtered."

"Yes, I remember everything I've been told."

"Briefly, this is what I found during my travels. Ranchers and miners, especially up and down the river valleys and in the mountains themselves, tell consistent tales of commerce between Jesuits and themselves. Of course, a certain amount of trade in cattle, horses, and food is legitimate if conducted for the right purposes—but then there are the miners' stories. They've bought muskets, German-made guns of the latest model. They paid five times their worth in gold and were glad to have them. But the merchants who sold them—Dutch merchants—reported they'd bought the guns from the Jesuits. Their reports tally with the events at Mátape."

Andrés' face turned to stone. "The reports to the Provincial and father general that I sent with Enrique when he and Bendito escorted doña Beatriz back to Durango must have been 'mislaid,' and not by Enrique. Did you write the report you intended to send, Ygnacio?"

"I'm so sorry, Andrés, I didn't take time to do that in my rush to find Denzhoné."

I waited, but Andrés remained silent, mulling things over. "Ygnacio," he said at last, "I just commanded you to return to your mission at Cucurpe."

"Yes, Father."

"Across the mountains east of Banámichi are gold and silver mines. Work has restarted on a number of them despite Apache raids. Nacozari, Cumpas, Chunerobabi, El Barrigón…. Any one of them could use 'supplies' to fight off the Apache. So… instead of returning to your mission, I'm ordering you to put yourself in grave danger—the same danger Lieutenant Salinas was in over eight months ago. You'll escort the vice-provincial, and if you can, find out for sure what's in those heavy bundles on the mules."

I gasped in surprise, and Andrés continued as if he hadn't noticed.

"Banámichi isn't far from the trail across the mountains to Cucurpe, so tell Poncelli you'd like company on your way home. I'm sorry to risk you this way, but we must know. If we prove the worst—what we suspect—we'll report to the provincial and directly to the father general in Rome, and this time see that our messages get through."

I'd already been thinking of accompanying Poncelli to get a look at those bundles. But the reality and Andrés' command sent ice water through my veins.

Chapter XVI
Ygnacio, Assistant to Luca Poncelli

Wolf and I attended Luca Poncelli's Mass the next morning. His booming baritone filled the church, and a glance at the Pimas told me they were impressed. The vapid homily was filled with threadbare platitudes:

> Dearly beloved, we are all children of God,
> who loves all of us equally. Although we may
> suffer hardships in this life, our Lord Jesus has
> reserved a glorious reward for us in heaven. Have
> patience therefore, and shoulder your burdens.
> Pick up His cross and follow him…

We rolled our eyes at each other a couple of times when we knew we were not being watched. After Poncelli intoned *Ite, missa est* and we responded *Deo gratias*, we went to see if Andrés was awake, since he'd not attended the service. Rita had lectured us the night before on his need for rest, and told us that, although moderate exercise was in order, he was not to be dragged out of bed early in the morning on a day when he was just beginning to heal.

We found him eating a breakfast of soft-boiled eggs, hot sauce, tortillas, and slices of the mesquite-smoked ham he had cured himself.

"Rita just re-wrapped my legs. Gave me another treatment with that dratted mescal juice. Burns like Hades, but the ankles feel clean afterwards. Thank God for her. Knows her stuff. Our own doctors should take lessons from her."

Wolf and I exchanged glances. Judging by his appetite, our vigorous Father Andrés would soon be back. I spoke to him first. "Have you said anything to Father Poncelli about my accompanying him to Banámichi, or should I broach the subject myself?"

He beckoned me closer to his side, glancing toward the door. "Where is Luca right now?"

I shrugged and Wolfgang answered. "He's out in the stable, looking over those bundles with the bottles in them."

"Good. Quickly now, before he comes. I'm certain he knows that I think he's involved in trade with the Dutch. In those letters I wrote to the provincial and the father general, I also said I suspected he was implicated in the death of Lieutenant Salinas and three of the four men sent with him to fight the Apaches at Mátape. You gave Enrique and Bendito those sealed documents, Ygnacio, to deliver to the mail carrier in Durango. I never dreamed they'd fall into Poncelli's hands, but they must have."

"But surely, he wouldn't break the seal on letters addressed to his superiors."

He looked grim. "From his attitude towards me on this ride from Durango, I'm convinced he read my letters and probably destroyed them. I believe he would have found a means to do away with me, too, if the lieutenant governor were not involved. He certainly gave me no consideration for my weakened state or my injuries on the trip up here."

Wolf snarled, his brows a single black line.

"What I mean to say is this," Andrés continued, "It would not be wise for me to suggest that you accompany him to Banámichi. He'd immediately think you were spying for me. He'll probably think so anyway. You need to approach him yourself and offer your services. Act innocent. He knows very little about you—the less the better. All he knows for sure is that you helped me yesterday, tending to my wounded ankles. So, go with God, Ygnacio, ride with him to Banámichi, and I'll pray for you."

I embraced him, blessed him and asked the Blessed Virgin and Saint Ignatius, who knew about such matters, to guide Rita in healing his wounds and restoring him to good health. As Wolf and I walked outside into bright morning sunshine, Poncelli strode toward us, obviously anxious for his breakfast. His question carried an acid overtone.

"Am I to suppose you two young men have already broken your fast?"

"No, Father Poncelli, we were just coming to see where you were. We were hoping to break it with you." I felt like a hypocrite.

"Capital! What does Ures have to offer a hungry vice-provincial after he's said Mass and needs to prepare for a strenuous day's riding?"

"Well, Father," I replied, "We have a choice. You can have pinole, sugar and milk, and I think there's some honey, too, or you can have eggs as you like them, fresh bread or tortillas and ham. Or all of that. What may I offer you, Father?"

He chose eggs and ham, scrambled in the battered frying pan. I served him slices of the bread still warm from the oven, dipped honey into a shallow dish and set that beside him. Finally, I brewed hot chocolate to accompany his breakfast. He complimented me on my culinary skill.

I gave him a demure, blue-eyed smile. "Thank you, Father. I'll be leaving for Cucurpe this morning, and would truly enjoy some educated and informed conversation. I wonder if you'd object if I accompanied you to Banámichi?"

He stared, a spoon full of scrambled eggs halfway to his mouth. "Come along if you like, Father Ygnacio. But I'll expect you to make yourself useful if we need you."

"Father Poncelli, that goes without saying." I punctuated my reply by snapping the chocolate tin shut.

Hernán had served breakfast to the soldiers after they attended Mass. I heard him tell Juanito that they insisted on loading the mules themselves, since the vice-provincial had given strict orders that none but they were to touch those bundles. The same number of people made up the departing cavalcade as before its arrival, only I would take Father Andrés' place. I hoped I wouldn't fall under the same pall of suspicion.

Wolf made a fuss at our parting. He drew me to one side, speaking rapidly in a low, urgent voice.

"I don't like this at all, Ygnacio. I have to obey Andrés' command and so do you, but the whole thing smells. It scares me. I'd trade places with you if I could. Be careful, Ygnacio! This man Poncelli's dangerous, a renegade, a minion of the Devil. His greed has driven him mad. Don't be his next victim! You're moderately intelligent, Ygnacio, so use your brains and stay out of trouble. And furthermore—"

I gripped his arm, interrupting his tirade. "Wolfgang! You know I'll do my best to carry out my orders and stay out of trouble. Use that faith of yours to pray for me. Remember," and I squeezed his arm, "Faith and God's grace *together with works* will save us. And if I should die in the course of this trip, well, what then? We all do that sooner or later." I blessed him, commending him and all his *works* to God. He watched me with a long face as I turned back to the cavalcade in its final preparations for departure. To 'make myself useful,' I held Father Poncelli's stirrup for him when he mounted.

The trail to Banámichi began on an easy slope, following the Sonora River upstream and rising only gradually. Then the way became steep as it climbed the pass through the mountain range, clinging to the side of the river gorge where millennia of floodwaters had carved a deep, ruggedly scenic canyon. The river's silver ribbon hundreds of feet below snaked from one side of the gorge to the other, split by miniature islands, bordered by greenery, shrubs, willows and a dozen other tree varieties I could not identify. What joy it would bring to ride this gorge with Beatriz! We'd share our reactions to the beauties of the landscape, laugh and chat together.

The trail leveled off and widened once we were beyond the pass, and I watched Luca as he paced along at his ease on his gray mule while the rest of us trotted. I was careful not to be obvious, but could see out of the corner of my eye that he was watching me, sizing me up. He struck up a conversation.

"How are you doing at Cucurpe? Conditions are rather primitive, aren't they? Have you thought of moving up in the world? Getting a position as secretary to a prelate in the city, for example?"

I digested that for a moment. One of the solemn promises we make before ordination states that we shall not procure any office for ourselves either inside or outside the Society. In other words, no Jesuit should seek personal advancement. Unfortunately, this seems to be one of the hardest vows to keep.

"Dedicated missionaries on the frontier are hard to find, Father. I feel privileged to serve at Cucurpe, especially since my people there hear and understand. They learn. The Eudebe and Opata tribes give me great joy. They are good and willing converts. As for the conditions, yes, they're Spartan, but I didn't come here to live a life of luxury. The city wouldn't suit me at all. In a clerical job I'd be out of touch with our real purpose."

He gave me a dark look, probably interpreting my words as a rebuke. He could either be testing me to determine whether I was a devoted missionary or fishing to see if I might serve him as a useful flunky back in Durango. He changed the subject. "Has any gold been discovered in the neighborhood of Cucurpe?"

"Nothing active in the immediate vicinity, Father. The best mine I know of is Saracachi, half a day's ride northeast of my mission in the San Antonio Mountains, where they mine both gold and silver. I've never been there. Then there's Buena Vista—rumors have it they've found silver, but I've seen only farms and ranches, no mining. It's a day's ride due north. Father Nentwig tells me that while he was visitor, he knew of gold and silver mines near Opodepe Mission. He saw a seven-ounce gold nugget from there."

"Yes, I know about those and that the best one is Saracachi. From the maps I've seen, it's quite close to Cucurpe."

"Close as the crow flies, but the terrain is rough, and I hear the Apaches have attacked it recently."

Poncelli nodded and lapsed into silence.

He must be planning his next sale of muskets and was considering Cucurpe as his base of operations. I could picture a mule train of 'lost' merchants arriving at my mission, mysteriously coinciding with an inspection tour by the vice-provincial.

We paused at noon to refresh ourselves and our animals, finding an opening in the tangled brush where we could ride to the river. There, under the umbrellas of ancient sycamores, we dismounted on a gravelly beach, stretched our legs, and pulled provisions from our saddlebags for a meal. The soldiers led the pack mules to the water, supervising them as they drank greedily. Poor beasts, their burdens were heavy and hard. The men tending the mules needed to take care that their backs were not galled. My fingers twitched with the desire to lay hands on one of those bundles. If an animal got into trouble, I could leap to its assistance before a soldier got there and, if I were lucky, get a close look at the load.

We left the riverside about an hour later, refreshed and rested. The pack mules, most important for the success of Father Poncelli's illicit trade, were the least fortunate, since they were not unloaded during mealtime, and were kept under strict supervision, not allowed to graze on the river grasses.

They did get plenty of water. After leaving the gorge behind, we followed the river bed, fording several times as the stream snaked its way along the valley.

Late that afternoon, one of the mules collapsed. I was riding stirrup to stirrup with Poncelli, but was closer than any of the soldiers to the animal in distress. I reined my horse around to its side and dismounted. The wretched mule was struggling to rise under his impossible load, but I could see that one hind leg was shattered. He had broken the cannon bone stepping in a snake hole near the side of the road. I began working at the buckles that fastened the bundle to his back, and noticed a three-cornered tear where the canvas had snagged on a rock when the mule fell. I inserted my fingers and opened the tear wide enough for a quick look at the contents. I glimpsed the bluish sheen of metal—a polished gun barrel—before I was roughly shoved aside.

"No one's to touch these animals but us. Vice-provincial's orders," the sergeant fairly shouted. "Get back! You're in my way!" He pointed his pistol at the unfortunate mule and fired one shot into the center of its forehead. The mule's struggles ceased and its forelegs slowly slid forward; its head fell upon them, tongue lolling out. The sergeant shoved me farther away without heed for my status or my person. The soldiers finished the job I had tried to begin, unloading the heavy bundle of muskets from the mule's back.

"What do you think you're doing, Ygnacio?" An angry baritone voice grated in my ear. "You knew only the soldiers were to tend these animals." Poncelli's eyes were mere slits, looking at me with a sly, knowing expression. Had he seen me find that rip in the bundle? If so, my life was in danger.

"Just obeying your command to make myself useful, Father Poncelli," I said, doing my best to disarm him. "I know mules well. These have been too heavily loaded from the beginning, and I could tell from the way this one fell he was badly hurt. I was trying to remove that load to see if he could be saved. It was second nature for me, Father. I'm sorry if I intruded where I wasn't wanted."

"Did no one tell you that you were not to go near those pack mules?"

"Not until the sergeant pushed me out of his way and shot this one, Father." I was telling him the truth. No one had actually told me, although I had known.

"Get back on your horse, and stay out of our way." He turned to the captain and snapped out a command. "Captain, see that the bundle is loaded on one of the extra horses. Have that dead mule dragged off the trail and let's get going."

I obeyed Poncelli with all speed and now sat my horse, watching the flurry of activity. We got underway again and I rode in silence, fearing to make another false step. After we had covered a few more leagues, Poncelli resumed his conversation with me. "Do you know Italy, Ygnacio?" I noticed he had dropped my title.

"Only Genoa, I fear, Father, though one day I hope to see Rome."

"Yes, indeed. Rome is the queen of cities, the center of the civilized world, and has always been so, even before the advent of Christianity. But now that our holy and apostolic Church has made it our center, Rome is without equal anywhere in the universe. It is the heart from which radiate truth and salvation for all mankind."

This rolled off his tongue in his honeyed voice as if he were preaching to a vast congregation.

I turned away to hide my amusement, then spoke in a meek and naïve tone. "Were you born in Rome, Father?"

"Yes, indeed, a Roman born. I trust that I shall be returning there in the near future. Ah! You should see Rome from the Palatine, or from atop the Castel Sant'Angelo. From there you can see the papal residence and gardens, the dome and part of the façade of San Pietro, the great basilica. Do you enjoy art works, Ygnacio?"

"Oh, yes, Father Poncelli. And I know that Italy is full of the most wonderful religious art—painting and sculpture, mosaics…. There are beautiful examples in Genoa. The cathedral, the churches, are very rich."

Such neutral chitchat filled the time, keeping me from asking embarrassing questions as we passed through four missions with their Indian villages with only a halloo and a wave. One thought never left me. Had Poncelli seen me peek into the rip in the canvas cover?

We were welcomed in Banámichi at nightfall by Father Francisco Villaroya, a younger man who hadn't been in Sonora long. He'd been posted to Bavispe, another mission, but was back temporarily. I'd met him at our Juntas, and admired his vigor and enthusiasm. He cut an imposing figure standing before the church in the twilight, tall for a Spaniard, with blue eyes and light brown hair. He greeted the vice-provincial with perfect etiquette, ushering him into the priest's house for refreshment before dinner, but he returned to walk with me like an old friend, his arm looped over my shoulder. "We're planning a splendid dinner in honor of this visit," he told me. "We've butchered a cow and a sheep, and we'll have mixed meats with every fancy vegetable our cooks can think up. Panes dulces for dessert with fruit."

He guided me into an isolated nook and spoke in a near-whisper. "How are you getting on with the vice-provincial? Beware of that one. He's a sly old dog. Can bite you when you least expect it."

I thanked him, and later at dinner was relieved not to be seated next to Poncelli, although, while mainly addressing Father Francisco, he sent a few darts my way.

"For someone who claims not to be interested in gold and silver mining hereabouts, your colleague from Cucurpe, Father Francisco, seems to know the scene quite well."

I had opened my mouth to deflect the innuendo when I caught sight of Victor, the gobernador who had supervised the table service. He made a sign as if he wanted to speak to me in private. What could he want? There was no way I could leave the table now.

"I only know what wandering miners have told me, Father Poncelli," I said.

"Ah, Ygnacio," he said, still deleting my title, "You seem far better informed than that. Perhaps you've set up some lively trade with those wandering miners?"

I shook my head. What amazing audacity!

After the meal, I looked for Victor, and saw him vanish into the kitchen. Father Francisco showed us our sleeping quarters, and tired from the day's journey, we all withdrew to rest. My room was in an adobe guesthouse at the end of the corridor closest to the uncultivated side of the mission away from the river. I noticed that the door had no lock and that the large window had no bars or other closure. Winds from the east could sweep through that window with no hindrance at all.

Still wondering about Victor, I went out to take care of nature and noticed an old Eudebe man loitering in the patio. On my way back, he took me by the arm and drew me into the shadow.

"Do not sleep soundly tonight, Padre Ygnacio," he said in his own language, calling me by name. "I am the Victor's father, and my daughter lives at your mission at Cucurpe. She tells me you are a good man and a true Christian. My son has overheard plans from one who is not Christian. Two soldiers will enter your room tonight: one to hold you, one to smother you to death. They will release a rattlesnake in the room—

after they make it bite your hand. All will believe you died from that."

The cold efficiency of the plan made me shudder. These soldiers must be well paid. How could Poncelli be sure they would not some day betray him? Surely, he didn't intend to murder them, too.

I thanked the old man for my life. "Who is your daughter at Cucurpe, my father? If I can be of help to her, I will. That way, the good you do me will be passed on."

"Her name is Lupe—for Our Lady of Guadalupe that you teach about. I will have my son saddle your horse. He will tell you how best to ride to Cucurpe, by a trail only we know."

"Oh, yes! I know Lupe. She's the best of the best."

He smiled. "I must go now. May Our Lady watch over you." He melted into deeper shadow.

I moved into the moonlight and strode up and down for a few minutes as if meditating, seemingly unmindful of the doom hanging over me, my hands clasped behind my back. Any watchers would see me there and follow my movements as I entered the guesthouse, walking down to my room with noisy footfalls, shutting my door behind me with a definitive, loud click.

I began immediate preparations for escape. There was only one blanket on the bed, so I folded the thin mattress, creating an irregular bulge in the middle, and covered that with the rumpled blanket. I arranged the pillow to make it appear that I had wrapped it around my head to shut out noise and cold air from outside. If someone glanced in at the window or the door, it should look enough like a person to reassure him I was fast asleep in the bed, although at the first touch, my little hoax would collapse.

In silence, I collected my belongings, leaned out the window, placed my bag at the foot of the wall, then climbed out. Instead of heading directly to the corral, I made a beeline for the oleanders that marked the limit of mission property. On the other side, wild country began. Behind the oleander screen, bending low, I moved in a wide arc until I came to the stables. At the corner where the stable wall ended and the corral fence began, Victor, the gobernador, met me, holding my horse by the reins.

"Come, this way, Father. Keep pace with me outside the corral fence. You'll be partly shielded from sight by your horse and me."

We came to a small gate that faced the mountains. It was farthest from the mission and rectory. Victor opened it and continued to lead the horse with me walking on his off side. At last, we reached the river trail and the dark shadows of trees. Like his father, he spoke to me in Eudebe, knowing that Jesuit missionaries would understand the language of their converts, while Spanish soldiers would not.

"Mount your horse here where they can't see you. Follow the river north until you see a white rock the size of your horse's rump on the right side of the trail. There, turn toward the river. You won't be able to see an opening, but there is a trail there among the bushes. Urge your horse forward, and he'll find it."

I nodded, concentrating all my powers on his directions, knowing that my life depended on them.

"Cross the river and the bushes on the other side. There are tall standing rocks there. They look like a solid wall, but ride to your left and you'll see a cleft in the rocks. Go through and you'll find a faint trail. There will be a moon until late tonight. Follow the trail until you come into a narrow canyon. Continue even in the dark, because there is no other way to go. At the top of the canyon, a rocky ledge seems to close the trail."

"But how can I get past that in the dark?"

"If you travel at a steady pace, you'll be there before the moon sets."

"But, you said that the canyon would be dark?"

"Yes, because it's deep. When you get to the rocky ledge, get off your horse and lead him to it. A set of rough steps begins behind a boulder. Lead your horse up those and you'll be at the top of the pass. On the other side, the trail is plain and the slope gradual. You'll spend another day following the trail through a winding valley that runs roughly north-by-northwest. There's water there—springs and a small stream. After another ridge of hills, your trail joins the main road to Cucurpe from Sinoquipe and the burned-out ranch. Give the horse his head and he will take you home."

"God bless you, Victor! With His help and yours, I'll get home." I glanced toward Banámichi. "You'd better go; they'll be looking for you by now. I'll greet your sister Lupe for you." I made the sign of the cross over him and vaulted on my horse. Victor gripped my ankle for a second and then blended with the black shadows along the trail.

I urged my horse along the shadowy trail until the round white boulder came in sight, where I reined him to the left. I whispered in his ear, *I'll call you Pegaso, like the flying white horse in Greek myth. My escape depends on you!* Once across the river, I found the gap in the standing rocks and followed the faint trail that led steeply upward.

Often enough I lost sight of the trail, but Pegaso continued as if it were plain as day. The moon was high and small when I saw that the trail plunged into a narrow crack, a black pit where moonlight did not penetrate. The canyon. I paused at its mouth and listened. Perhaps I'd been followed. I heard only "safe" sounds: a stamp of Pegaso's hoof and a jingle of his bit, the faint rustling of nocturnal creatures, calls of night birds, and the distant yapping and wavering howls of a pack of coyotes.

The passage through the echoing canyon became a torture. It seemed as if we were traveling along a narrow stone trestle over an abyss, an endless plunge through blackness waiting for a single misstep. Unreasoning dread stifled my breath, and I prayed that Our Lady of Guadalupe deliver us from this mouth of Hell, but it was Beatriz, her face and voice that calmed me. She rode at my side, and I was no longer afraid. At last, the canyon walls became shallower until all at once I could breathe again. We were bathed in moonlight, but found our way barred by a rocky ledge.

I dismounted and found the crevice in the ledge. I felt with my hands, finding steps of a sort shrouded in deep shadow. Pegaso followed dubiously, but heaved himself up the steep incline with only a couple of slips. We stood at the top of the ridge, a bold, moonlit silhouette for any watcher to see. I prayed there were no Apaches. The moon also revealed the narrow valley beneath us. My eyes followed the trail that descended a sloping hogback until, a few hundred yards below, it ducked under a grove of trees.

We sheltered there for the night, where a spring-fed trickle began. I drank but otherwise fasted while Pegaso found plenty of succulent grass and cool water. At dawn, we were on our way again. The second night, we breasted a ridge of hills and saw beyond them the San Miguel River Valley. At last! A white streak marked the Sinoquipe-Cucurpe trail.

But return was not that simple. Pegaso threw up his head and his nostrils began to quiver. I clamped my hand on his nose. He must not announce our presence. Echoes of hooves striking rocks came to me before I saw riders on the main trail, descending at unsafe speed. Who were they? I squinted in the moonlight, blinked and rubbed my eyes. Eight riders… eight soldiers. Poncelli had kept two as guards and sent the rest to capture me.

Chapter XVII
Unfulfilled Desires

No matter what I do, I cannot achieve peace of mind. Instead, matters grow steadily worse. Those letters I wrote to the two highest Jesuit officials in México have received no reply. I fear they have been ignored, since their author is a mere woman, therefore suspected of lightheadedness, duplicity, or even of the Devil's wiles—or all at once. Or, as I feared from the beginning, the provincial and the visitor general are also involved in criminal trade. As for the viceroy, he wrote me one line—aside from all the correct and empty opening and closing courtesies. "In the name of his Majesty, King Carlos III, I thank you for your informative letter, Madam, and will take all necessary measures to see that its contents are conveyed to the proper authorities." Perhaps he actually will forward its contents to someone who can take prompt action—the royal visitor, for example—but I fear I'll be the last to know.

I've seen the lieutenant governor, but only on social occasions. On one of them, when the Marqués de Fonseca invited me to a dinner party, Antonio also attended. He found a few moments to speak to me on the balcony of the hacienda, to tell me how lovely I looked and how he longed to see me for another chat—alone. He begged me to come by his office the next afternoon: "Only for tea, I give you my word." He impressed on me how much he wanted my company. I hesitated but then accepted, because I was still curious whether he knew about the gun running.

The following afternoon, I arrived at 4:00 by the cathedral clock as he had asked. He met me as I entered and led me into his office, telling his secretary to alert the kitchen, as before, that we wanted tea and the best sweets of the day. As soon as we were out of earshot, Antonio began to speak.

"Beatriz, you surely must know that I love you. I'm miserable without you—I lie awake all night, and if I drop off for a moment, I dream of holding you in my arms."

"But Antonio, I am a woman of honor. My reputation…"

"I would never besmirch your honor, my dear, my beloved. I want you near me… under any circumstances you should wish to specify."

I was dumbfounded by his intensity. The servant with the tea service arrived in time to allow me to collect my thoughts. I made a little speech.

"Antonio, you've been kind and helpful beyond measure, and I like you very much but I don't love you. If I were to accept your offer, our liaison would be that of a lover and his mistress, and I can't tolerate that. I'm glad to keep you company socially, perhaps even to meet you from time to time like this for tea—although even that damages my reputation. But you must know that I still love my husband—whose death only took place eight months ago—and if I should love someone else..."

My verbal flow was running away with me, and I began a different tack. "I'm delighted to have you as my good friend. Is that so impossible? Must every relationship between man and woman become an intimate one?"

He sat in silence for a moment, then poured the tea. "You spoke oddly a moment ago. You said, 'If I should love someone else.' *Are* you in love with someone else, Beatriz?"

Now it was my turn to sit silently, while I sipped my tea.

"Yes and no, Antonio. The man is not available... and neither are you, in any way that would make it possible to consider your plea. But I really need to speak to you about something else entirely, far from these questions of feelings for each other. Forgive me if I speak boldly, but you should be used to the way I plunge into things. I believe Mateo was killed because he discovered that the Jesuit vice-provincial, Luca Poncelli, was selling guns to the miners of Soyopa Gold Mine through Dutch middlemen. Were you aware of this trade? Or did Poncelli manage to keep it hidden within the Society?"

Antonio straightened with a jerk that nearly upset his teacup. "How do you know all this, Beatriz?"

"My question is, what do *you* know? Our friendship depends upon your answer."

His face became grave. When he spoke, his hesitant tone told me it was against his strongest inclination to reveal such things to me.

"I knew it was happening. My informants told me cargoes of German muskets of the latest, most exquisite design have been unloaded at Veracruz and brought overland by ox train to Durango. They were delivered here to a local firm and—"

"Yes, García y Pacheco," I interrupted. "I know the firm."

"How, Beatriz, in God's name?" He stared as if he suspected I'd prostituted myself to gain that information. Tea and sweet morsels were forgotten. "Yes, I knew that much," he resumed, "but didn't know where they went from there. Only that they were showing up at the mines some weeks later. So tell me, *please*, how you come to know more!"

I told Antonio about my trip to Mátape, the first real account of it I'd given him.

"We were at Father Jacobo Sedelmeyer's dinner table, Ignaz and I. Father Jacobo told us that Poncelli's mule train was unusually large and heavily loaded, guarded by ten men and two officers: Captain Cuevas and my husband Mateo. Father Jacobo was shocked that the heavy load was transferred next day to the pack train of a party of Dutch traders who just happened to arrive at Mátape, 'lost,' and seeking the Soyopa mine.

"I think Mateo must have discovered what those mules carried. Then, when the Apaches attacked the Dutch train on its way to Soyopa, Poncelli and Cuevas colluded and sent Mateo and four men to their deaths, knowing they were too few to stand up to the Apaches."

"But, Beatriz, so far this is only speculation. You don't really know what the mules were carrying and you haven't concretely connected the vice-provincial to the gun running."

"Just wait, Antonio, I'm getting to that. At your birthday ball, Poncelli, in conversation with me about my trip to Mátape, completely 'forgot' to mention the Dutch traders who played such an important role during his visitation, although he was very unctuous about my husband. The way he described Mateo's character and behavior, overstating his 'rigor' and 'dutifulness' and so on, led me to suspect my husband had learned what Poncelli was taking to Mátape, and confronted him with the knowledge. I concluded that Mateo's death and that of three of the four men was the result of his discovery and his honesty."

"Aha! Then the captain was also responsible for your husband's death, since you say he and Poncelli made a joint decision to send him and his men out. He was paid off to keep his mouth shut, I'm sure. Poncelli must have been delighted, not regretful, to hear of his murder—"

"And was also delighted when Father Andrés was wrongfully accused and arrested for the killing."

"Yes... And yet, if you knew Poncelli was responsible, why didn't you denounce him? ...Don't answer that, Beatriz. I can see how dangerous the man is. But how did you prove to your own satisfaction that he was gun running?" He leaned forward, eyes wide and lips parted, excited to find answers to problems that had nagged at him, grateful to me for supplying the missing links.

He hitched his chair closer to the table and leaned on his forearms. His hands lay next to mine; I could feel their heat. But he'd given his word that this would be a simple afternoon tea. I ignored his imploring hands.

"Ruthless as he is," I said, "Poncelli is not ruthless enough. He left the lone survivor of the massacre alive. From Father Jacobo's account, he didn't find out right away, and he may not know even now that a corporal, Saúl Ayala, lived. The man was wounded, but as soon as he could, he came to me here in Durango and told me the whole story from his point of view. That's when my revenge took shape and when I asked your permission to go to Mátape. Ayala knew they'd been sacrificed. He wanted his own revenge.

"Once I knew Father Andrés Michel was safe, thanks to you, I asked my butler, Roberto Durán, to spy on García y Pacheco. He was there when the latest shipment of guns was delivered, and he followed the wagon when they were transferred to the vice-provincial's residence. He climbed a tree and watched as Poncelli himself directed the offloading and storage."

"And have the new guns gone out?"

"Yes, a heavily loaded pack train left a week ago."

"And how do you know this, Beatriz?" His voice was now full of admiration, replacing his earlier skepticism.

"He took Father Andrés with him. They left with an army escort and a loaded pack train. My man Roberto was watching for me."

"I knew that once he was released, Father Andrés would be escorted back to Ures by the next visitor. So Poncelli killed two birds with one stone. I only hope our bird Andrés is still alive."

He paused for two heartbeats, then said, "You mentioned someone named Ignaz who had something to do with your trip to Mátape. *Ignaz.* I know a little German, and that's a German version of Ignacio. And it's the name of the Jesuits' founding saint, Ignatius. So... just who is this Ignaz?"

I was surprised and caught off balance. I didn't remember naming Ignaz, and the sudden question startled me. I must have blushed, though I tried to answer casually.

"Ignaz... is just one of the missionaries. He was at Mátape too."

Antonio wouldn't allow me to escape so easily. "And how do you come to know him so well that you name him without a title?"

My heart began to pound, my breath coming short. "Oh, if you must know, he escorted me from Ures to Mátape."

"Alone?"

"Yes."

"Why? Where were the soldiers?"

"Captain Cuevas was murdered at Ures. They had to go on to Horcasitas and report to Governor Pineda. My goal was trivial by comparison. I was left stranded, and Ignaz... Father Ygnacio... offered to escort me instead."

"Ah, I see. And he approached you... as a man approaches a woman?" He restrained his anger, but barely. His tone was icy.

"No! No, you don't see at all, Antonio. And you have no right to question me, and in such a tone of voice! Nothing improper—absolutely nothing—happened on that trip. Father Ygnacio was the soul of propriety. It's just that... that we were alone together."

"Something more must have happened, else why would you fall in love with a—of all people—a Jesuit priest?" Antonio's face was red; he was truly angry by now.

I told him the truth. "When we left Ures, I was mounting my horse from a block of stone, the beautiful chestnut Arabian-Andalusian that Governor Pineda gave me thanks to you, Antonio. My foot slipped. Ignaz, Father Ygnacio, was nearby. He caught me in his arms, stepped up on the stone and placed me on the saddle. And he helped me dismount and mount a couple of times after that. But never familiarly."

Although I was destroying my relationship with Antonio, I felt relieved, even exhilarated, to be talking openly at last about Ygnacio.

Antonio's face was stony. "And what is this German priest like, physically? This Jesuit, this minion of Poncelli's?"

"He's not Poncelli's minion," I retorted, "When I left Ures, I felt sure he was planning to find out who really murdered Captain Cuevas."

"Has he found out?"

"I have no way of knowing."

"You haven't been in contact with this Jesuit?"

I blushed again, my cheeks burning. "No, no contact."

"I want to know what he looks like, this... this priest."

I twisted my hands in my lap. "Tall. Straight blond hair, cut short. Swept back from his forehead—high forehead. Slender but well knit. Very strong. Blue eyes, hawk nose, high cheekbones. Is that enough?"

"I know the type. A pious prig, I suppose."

"No. Pious enough, but personable and well educated, from a good background. But, surely, this is enough, Antonio."

He drummed his fingers on the tea table, his whole body tense. "And his reaction to you?"

"He was aware of me, of my physical attractions, if you will, but simply turned his back on them. When we parted, he left me as easily as... as if he were a eunuch or another woman. He has no feeling for *me*, rest assured. And now, you know my secret, and there's nothing I can do about it, nothing to change it or to undo it. I wish it had never happened."

"And what is this paragon of virtue's full name?"

"Ignaz Pfefferkorn," I replied, stiffly.

He laughed a little, for the first time that afternoon. "A ridiculous name! Ygnacio *Pimienta*, Ignatius Peppercorn indeed. Well, well. And you say you haven't been in touch with Father Peppercorn since that time?"

"No, I've already said as much."

"I've noticed you haven't been wearing my ring the last few times I've seen you. I asked you to keep it safe, remember?"

"It's in my jewel box, Antonio. It was too big and threatened to slide off. It's safe there, but I'll be happy to give it back." I rose to my feet. "Now, if there's nothing further to talk about, I'll be on my way. I assume I'll see you again one of these days at some social function. Thank you for the tea."

He continued sitting, staring up at me, his face unreadable.

"You always give me much to think about, Beatriz. Your company is never dull. Sit down again for a moment, my dear. There's more to be said. Oh, don't look so cross. I won't hound you any further about the ring or your Father Peppercorn. As you say, there's nothing to be done about that. But about your Father Poncelli, I need to know this: what action, if any, have you taken, based upon your knowledge?"

I remained standing, but answered his question. "I wrote to the viceroy, the Jesuit father provincial and visitor general."

"And did they reply?"

"Only the viceroy. A one-line note saying he would forward my information to the proper authorities."

Antonio hummed to himself, drumming his fingers again. "Yes. Well, they may not have taken you seriously. But they will when I write seconding your denunciation. I'll do that immediately." He rose and took my arm. "I'm sorry I subjected you to such an interrogation, Beatriz. But you must understand that I'm a man in love. Men in my position tend to be jealous, as I still am of your handsome priest. Just remember, my dear, he is 'unavailable,' just as you said. But I am not."

As we moved towards the door, I contradicted him. "Oh, but you *are* unavailable for any relationship other than one most damaging to my status and self respect. Yes, we've had a 'business transaction,' the price I paid to save Father Andrés and see him released. But I refuse to go any further. I have no desire to become a 'kept woman.' Anyway, I'm sure you'd never marry a woman recently widowed and beneath your social class. I shall remain independent until I find someone legitimately available."

He looked thoughtful. Before I was out of earshot, I heard him call his secretary. "Come into my office, Manuel, I have letters to write!"

As for Ygnacio, it was balm to my soul to talk about him with someone, even though that someone considers himself his deadly rival. If I were not so confused by my emotions, I would think the situation funny. I confessed my attraction to Ygnacio to Father Andrés, and received a stern, admonitory lecture about my sinfulness in feeling anything but gratitude and the love of Christian charity. He admitted that he'd made a grave error in allowing what amounted to a breach in current Jesuit practice—that a lone priest should escort a woman. A situation created by the Devil to achieve the Devil's ends, he said.

Afterward, rather than thinking less about Ygnacio, I have thought more often about him, dreaming of him too, reliving the moments when we were together, when he held me in his arms—something he should never have done. And yet, he did it out of caring and Christian love, to save me from injury.

I remember Father Sedelmeyer's speculative look when Ygnacio helped me off my horse, and again when he saw us come out of the church together, Ygnacio with his arm around my shoulders. My nerves tingle yet with the feel of his body next to mine, the weight of his arm. Now that I've spoken openly about him to Antonio, my tortures have become even worse. And yet, I'm no half-grown girl to have such fantasies. God help me!

₧⁖

The soldiers hadn't seen me. I watched the cavalcade until they rode out of sight. What should I do? How did Poncelli dare to use them as his private army? Were they to shoot me on sight, or escort me back to Banámichi? Probably the latter.

He must have made up some story to make it seem legitimate to hunt me down.

My options were simple: to find a hidden nook and wait until daylight or continue toward Cucurpe now. If I holed up, I'd have to wait for the men to return to Banámichi, else they'd meet me on the trail. That might mean a full day's delay. They might even take a different trail. Maybe they were returning to Horcasitas and I'd be waiting days in vain. No, I'd follow them now and hide on the hill above the mission where their movements could be watched. I mounted and began descending the trail.

Pegaso maintained a steady pace without stumbling even after the moon had set. But my exhaustion and hunger brought dizziness and a feeling of total unreality. We were swimming through a sea lit by clouds of crystalline motes of brilliance. They shone the way for my horse but not for me. I clung to the saddle horn, feeling that I would be swept into that sea at any moment. Staring at the ebony silhouette of the mountainous horizon helped restore my sense of balance and gave solidity and direction to our movement.

Cucurpe came in sight as the sky began to pale toward dawn. I headed first to the river, knelt upstream from Pegaso, and both of us eagerly drank the cool water. There was no visible movement from the village. It must be an hour before Mass. I scanned the hillside above the mission church and the converts' village. Yes, the mesquite grove I remembered was dense enough to hide my horse and me. I mounted and trotted across the cultivated bottom-land and up the hill. We passed the village at two hundred yards. The soldiers' horses were penned in the corral, still picking at wisps of hay left from the armloads they'd been given last night.

I dismounted and led Pegaso to the center of the grove, where lush grass grew. I tethered him, hoping he'd graze rather than call to the horses below. I pulled my blanket from the saddlebag and looked for the least uncomfortable spot among the rocks. A boulder the size of a washtub, split into halves, shielded me from sight and gave me a view of the valley through the crack. I cleared away thorns and settled down to watch.

Sleep overcame me despite rocks, pebbles, and a few overlooked thorns under my blanket—not surprising, since I hadn't closed my eyes for more than twenty-four hours. The sun, already far above the mountains, woke me when it began to roast me in my black robe. An anthill of activity at the mission below brought me to full consciousness. The soldiers, busy saddling their horses, called out, swearing or giving orders. I couldn't quite hear their words, but at least I'd see which way they'd go from Cucurpe. Father Ramón came outside to watch them leave. His stiff spine and nervous gestures told me the visit had not been pleasant. The men mounted without a wave and set off at a trot toward Banámichi. It must indeed have been an expedition ordered by Poncelli to capture and bring back one Ygnacio Pfefferkorn.

My bones protested when I stood and stretched, my stomach rumbling, my mind fuzzy. If those soldiers turned back, they'd just have to find me coming off the hill. I led Pegaso, staggering into the village on foot.

My *topil*—the Eudebe in charge of guests—saw me first and raised a shout.

"Padre Ygnacio is back! He escaped the soldiers! He's here!"

My beloved converts crowded around me, touching, embracing, patting me, some with tears in their eyes. They bombarded me with questions, all coming at me at once, deafening and confusing me:

"We thought you were dead."

"The soldiers came to take you away."

"They searched the village. They beat us."

"We thought they'd kill you if they found you."

"Where have you been?"

"What happened to you?"

"Tell us!"

I held up my hands, and by some miracle, they quieted. Though reeling from exhaustion, I had to tell them something.

"A soldier, a captain, was murdered at Ures. Father Andrés, the missionary there, was blamed for it. I tried to find out who killed the captain. I haven't found him yet, but I think I know who did it. I just escaped from someone who was planning to kill me. He sent the soldiers."

Father Ramón bounded out of the priest's house and stood at the back of the crowd. I waved to him and saw Lupe, too, near the back.

"Lupe! Your father and your brother Victor saved my life. Your father warned me two nights ago that I'd be killed if I didn't leave Banámichi, and Victor told me where to find the secret trail across the mountains. That's why the soldiers didn't catch me. I owe my life to your family, Lupe. I'll always be grateful."

Her broad smile rewarded me, but my brief explanation had not satisfied the others.

"But you've been gone for weeks! There's more to your story, so tell us, please!"

Ramón pushed his way through the converts, took me by the shoulders and peered at my face. "You look terrible, Father Ygnacio. Thin. Dark circles under your eyes. Your robe is more patches and stitches than original cloth."

"The robe's story can wait. More important, I haven't slept in a day and two nights, and I'm starving." I turned to the crowd. "I'll tell you everything tomorrow at Mass."

The crowd parted to let us through, and I followed Ramón into our house, feeling the touch of many hands as I passed.

"I've got a leg of grilled rabbit, Ygnacio, and part of a baked yucca root. That's about all. And there's pulque."

"Good. That'll keep me alive."

"Here's some pinole, honey and salt. Go ahead and use the honey to flavor it, we'll get more eventually. It'll help fill you up and give you strength."

The food vanished in seconds, washed down with gulps of pulque, almost before I could thank God and Ramón. He poured a second cup. "I'm as eager as the neophytes to hear your story, Ygnacio, but I'll wait with the others till morning. Now, you need rest."

I lurched to bed, dizzy from exhaustion and tipsy from two brimming cups of pulque.

Twenty hours later, just before morning Mass, I finally opened my eyes. I took out my violin that I hadn't touched in weeks, and during the Mass, played shaky versions of the *Kyrie eleison* and *Gloria* with the choir, then, more assured, played an additional *Gloria* by Handel. The music restored me as if I'd stepped into another world where danger, pain and exhaustion did not exist. Music is the language of God.

My homily satisfied everyone's curiosity, but I skirted issues too delicate for general knowledge. After such a long absence, celebrating the Eucharist moved me to the core, and my voice shook as I raised the wafer and the chalice.

A week passed while I ate well and tried to catch up on my rest. But rest was shallow and intermittent. Every minute spent sleeping seemed a minute closer to Andrés' murder or mine. On the second day back, I forced myself to begin writing the long-delayed letters, bitterly regretting that I hadn't taken the time before I left to search for Denzhoné. If I'd done so, Poncelli's misdeeds might have been halted by now.

Three letters contained the same information, those to Father Provincial Zevallos, to Visitor General Carlos Rojas, and to Father General Lorenzo Ricci in Rome.

✝

"My Beloved Father Provincial Francisco
Zevallos:

P.C.&c.

I deeply regret to inform you that I have witnessed our vice-provincial, Luca Poncelli, on his
way to commit a crime, one he has committed at
least once before, and perhaps many times before
that. He sells German muskets of the latest model
to middlemen who in turn sell them to the miners who exploit the gold and/or silver mines in
Sonora Province. He makes "inspection tours" to
missions near the mines…."

I gave the details of his dealings with the Dutch at Mátape
and the death of the soldiers, then of the trip to Banámichi,
my discovery of the muskets through a rip in a container, the
subsequent threat against my life and my escape. I added my
belief that both Father Andrés and I were in danger, since
Luca Poncelli now knew we had discovered his clandestine
gun-running.

The heaviest blow to my superiors would be confirmation
of such a breach of the Company's Constitution and purpose,
and the fearful damage to us that illicit trade of any kind—especially gun-running—could do if it became generally known.
I prayed my letters might stop the fatal process, but feared
they might already be too late. Detailing those accusations,
those admissions of grave scandal within the Society, grieved
me so much that at times I had to wait until my hand stopped
shaking before I could write legibly.

I added a more personal letter to Father Carlos, giving him
a close account of my search for Denzhoné, my capture by
Itza-chu and my rescue by his Christian wife, Qumara. I told

him about my visit to Cuquiárachi and what I had learned from Wolfgang. That part of the story might raise his opinion of his eccentric subordinate, who was about to take charge of Opodepe Mission.

My letter to Andrés reported my trip to Banámichi and my brush with death. I reminded him that Poncelli could be planning an attempt on his life, and to be on the alert. I also asked him to send Wolfgang to take over Opodepe Mission, which Father Ramón had not visited for over a week. Ramón could then return to his normal duties at Mátape, and mission life in Sonora could resume its quiet routine.

I strolled through the mission village, talking with my people, answering questions about my dangerous journey, and listening to their stories of hardships or achievements.

"Father, could I speak with you, please?"

The voice came from behind. I turned and saw Lupe. "Of course! Here?"

"No, Father, in the church, please."

I followed her inside. She began as soon as we were out of earshot of the others. "A boy came from Banámichi yesterday with messages for me and you too."

My breathing quickened with alarm. "Not bad news, I hope?"

"No, no one's hurt, not badly anyway. Victor was accused of hiding you, since you and your horse were gone. That big Father, the one who came there with all those mules, had him caned to find out what he had done with you."

"Victor beaten? That's intolerable! Go on! What else did you learn? What happened to Victor?"

"He merely told them you took your horse during the night and left, going north. He didn't know where. Maybe to Arizpe. But the big Father didn't believe him. He sent soldiers here to catch you."

"Yes, I know. And they mistreated all of you. I'm sorry about that."

She nodded. "Victor's message said another mule train came to Banámichi while the soldiers were away. The mules were driven by white faces that were not priests and not Spanish."

"Aha! And then the bundles were transferred from the big Father's mules to theirs."

"Yes, Father. How did you know?"

"I know of another time when the same thing happened. Where did they go, those white faces and their mules?"

"North, Father. That's all we know."

I digested what she'd said. The best mines were north of Banámichi. "Thank you for telling me. How is Victor?"

"Bruised, but he will heal. He is young. The boy said Father Villaroya was furious and quarreled with the big Father."

"He'd better be careful. Tell me, though, has the boy, the messenger, gone back already?"

"No, he stayed to play with my son. But he'll go soon."

"I have letters for Father Carlos Rojas in Arizpe. He can take them partway."

"I will tell him, Father. He is trustworthy."

"I don't doubt it. You know, of course, Lupe, that your brother and your father saved my life, and... and I have something I'd like to give you. It's a small gift, but better than nothing. Come with me, please."

She watched while I lit the sealing wax candle with a live coal, dripped wax on the flap of the folded letter to Carlos Rojas, and imprinted the hot wax with my IHS seal. I penned his name and Arizpe Mission on the outside. She blew on the wax till it hardened, then tucked the letters in her belt and followed me into my house. I opened the heavy leather chest, hoping the insects had not bored through and spoiled the stored cloth inside. Luckily, the four yards of sturdy blue cotton material were intact.

"Here, Lupe. There's enough to make clothes for your children and perhaps a skirt for you, too."

She received it in both arms and laid her cheek against the cloth, smiling with glowing eyes as she walked away. That was enough thanks for me. I promised myself I would watch for chances to do more for her in the future.

ಹಿⳐ

I pulled another corncob off its stalk, my arms nearly full. My converts surrounded me, harvesting the last of an abundant crop of corn. A shout reached me from the hill.

"Ygnacio-o-o-o-o! You're alive! You survived after all!" It was Wolfgang's voice. I dumped my armload of corn in the nearest basket and ran up the hill, arriving out of breath.

He gave me a rough embrace. "You must have at least nine lives."

"And I've used… at least three… of them during this trip. How's Andrés?"

"Active. Back on his feet. He's got anklets of scabs, but Rita saved him from gangrene. He'll be mostly recovered soon—he'll have a permanent limp, though. His left Achilles tendon was damaged, but he gets around. I helped out by saying Mass every other day and assisting as much as possible on Sundays."

We walked to the rectory. "How about some of that mesquite tea I tried to tempt you with months ago?"

His grin was a bit sheepish. "I'll give it an honest try this time, my friend."

I poured the tea and sat facing him. "What other news from Ures?"

"Poncelli came back. He was in a hurry and refused to say Mass. Just ate Andrés out of house and home and left at dawn the next day."

"I hope you kept Andrés well guarded the whole time."

"I've had a twenty-four hour watch on the rectory and on his bedroom ever since you left, especially while that devil was right there."

"But where did Poncelli sleep? The priest's guestroom is just across the hall from Andrés' bedroom."

His grin was triumphant. "He slept there allright. But Juanito slept across Andrés' door, Hernán's brother slept under his window, and Hernán himself slept on the floor of his room, armed with a knife. Nobody could move without them knowing it."

"Thank God! Thank *you*, Wolf. And during the day?"

"Someone is always with him. Hernán or his brother. They go armed and everyone knows it."

I gave a sigh of relief, nodding in satisfaction. "Have you heard anything about Corporal Saúl Ayala? Did the governor's soldiers bring him in?"

"I don't think so. My friends out there, the ranchers, the miners, and even some of the soldiers know where to find me. They'd report to me if Ayala had been seen or captured. But not a whisper. He can't be in Sonora."

"He's in Sinaloa or back in Durango. Maybe all the way to México. They'll never catch him, and Andrés will always be under suspicion of murder. They'll always think the Jesuits had the influence and the connections to save a guilty man's life. I find that intolerable. I'm taking this personally. I *must* clear his name!"

Wolf took a long sip of mesquite tea and cocked his head on one side. "You've already spent three of your nine lives trying to do just that. Don't you think you've done enough?"

"No, Wolf, no. I've invested too much sweat and blood—literally, Wolf—in this quest. I can't, I *won't*, give up now. I'm going after Ayala.

Chapter XVIII
Gathering Storm

Wolfgang shook his head. "You're forgetting your vow of obedience, Ignaz. Andrés commanded you to go about your proper business here at your mission."

He was right. After I calmed down enough to use my God-given powers of reason, I conceded that Saúl Ayala would escape my pursuit for now, thanks to the Vow of Obedience. My proper tasks were converting, evangelizing and teaching. I suppressed my anxiety, eagerness and keen hunting instinct, sent Wolf on his way to Opodepe Mission, and turned back to normal duties.

Once reconciled to my routine, I was content to teach my people about Jesus Christ and His way of coping with a cruel and uncaring world. My Eudebes and Opatas, much more than the Pimas I'd worked with at Atí and Guevavi, were eager students of everything I taught, including the Spanish language, reading, basic mathematics, and learning about the wider world. They would soon fulfill the ideal I had for them and become productive citizens of New Spain, able to compete for a livelihood with Europeans, able to defend themselves against predators who would try to trick them into working in the mines or on ranches, where they would be exploited as slaves. There was little I could do to defend them against outright kidnapping by mine owners. Up to now, they'd been protected by distance and rugged country between me and the nearest mine at Saracachi.

For days, then weeks, then months, nothing disturbed my daily tasks of saying Mass, finishing the harvest, teaching, practicing new songs, and preparing the fields for spring planting. During the quiet winter months, we added new branches to the acequia system that watered the fields. The major project, building a new granary that would be proof against vermin—both insect and four-legged—lasted until mid-June.

But what had become of doña Beatriz? Her image, her husky voice and teasing laugh sometimes took on startling reality. Would the ache ever fade? It was as if I'd been wounded by an arrow tipped by a long, slow-acting poison. The idea made me smile. The ancients invented Cupid with his bow and arrows to describe this very thing. How could I, a committed priest and missionary, be the victim of such a thing?

Would I ever see her again?

„‮

I had written a report to Visitor General Carlos Rojas the last day of July—my birthday—but did not expect a reply before late August at the earliest, and today was only the seventeenth, just over a year since Corporal Miguel González had summoned me to investigate his captain's murder. I felt isolated, hearing no recent news. That evening, after a full day's labor, I strolled, eased by a cool breeze, to the hillside where I could get the best view of the sunset. Cumulus clouds had passed overhead all day, and the setting sun reflected off their many layers with nuanced variations of color, beginning with the most brilliant gold, then a layer of bright orange, tapering off to shades of pink and lavender. As the sun dipped behind the hills to the west, it sent up a flash of blinding rays shining in several directions like a monstrance that set the horizon ablaze just before the darkness came. I worshipped God through the beauty of his creation and praised him for his goodness in allowing me to occupy this post, in placing me in this blessed mission.

The next morning, I rejoiced again, stooping along the rows of pungent-scented tomato vines, my hands green with their juices, pulling off the brilliant red globes. A few were to be eaten at once; most would be cut and laid on tiles to dry in the sun for use all winter. My people worked beside me, some of them in a neighboring field digging yams. Abruptly, we all straightened and peered in one direction. My lookout on the north side had given a whistle to warn of strangers approaching.

The two men who stood side by side on the ridge near the church were both Jesuits. Squinting, I could make out Fathers Alfonso Espinosa from San Xavier del Bac and Tucson and Rafael Díez from Guevavi, both north of Cucurpe.

I'm waving, but getting no reaction from either one. Where are their horses? What could be wrong?

I focused on the captain who rode toward me across the fields. He was no stranger. I recognized Juan Bautista de Anza, whose father, the former governor, was an honorary Jesuit. I placed the tomatoes I was holding in a basket and went to meet him.

"Juan! Good to see you! What news?" His face told the tale. Far from his usual broad smile, he wore a mask of misery. "It must be grim, judging from your expression."

"I'm so terribly sorry, Padre Ygnacio. The news couldn't be worse. But didn't you get the circular letter from Father Visitor Juan Salgado? He summoned all of you to Mátape for a special meeting."

"No, I haven't had news of any kind for weeks, now. What sort of meeting?"

"It seems that none of you Padres up here in the north received the letter. That's why Father Alonso and Father Rafael are with me now. This is what I know. Governor Pineda, under orders from King Carlos' Royal Visitor, José de Gálvez, commands me to arrest all of you and to escort you to Mátape. Fathers Espinoza and Díez are in my custody."

I stared up at him, eyes wide, open-mouthed.

"A-arrest? Mátape? B-bu-but why?" The words sounded alien and high-pitched. My mind raced, churning out possible answers. Could this arrest, this summons, be the result of Andrés' and my letters? Had Poncelli's corruption reached so far? Did the viceroy believe the rumors—the ones accusing us of cruelty and enslaving the Indians, whispered about since the Pima Revolt of 1751? Or was this the result of European politics and the freethinking that Andrés and I discussed a year ago?

"Forgive me, Father, I don't know why," Juan hesitated, then continued, his brows knit in distress, "only that my orders are to take you in. They say it will be explained once all of you are gathered at Mátape."

I managed a question. "*All* of us?"

"I'm afraid so. Make your arrangements to come with me, Father."

"What, now?... *Now?*"

"Yes."

"Wait while I decide what to take."

"You aren't allowed to take anything, Father. Just the clothes you're wearing, your crucifix and your breviary. All your property—everything in the mission—belongs to His Majesty King Carlos III."

"Is that why my brothers Espinosa and Díez are on foot? Did you confiscate their horses and mules, too?"

"I'm afraid so. This whole thing makes me sick, Father Ygnacio, but those are my orders. I'll have to put chains on you before we get to Mátape. Actually, I'm supposed to chain you now, but I can't endure the thought."

"My violin? Can't I take along a single consolation? It's a family heirloom. It's—"

"Property of the king, Father Ygnacio."

"What about my research? All my notes on the tribes of this area, the plants, animals, insects—its geology and climate? And—"

"All property of His Majesty, Father."

"Property of the rats and insects, more likely. Property of the wind."

"You can take your breviary. Maybe a few notes, if you can conceal them well…"

"I hear you. But… how long will this last?"

"I really can't say. As I told you, all will be explained once you gather at Mátape."

"Can I at least gather my people and tell them?"

"I have no instructions about that, Father Ygnacio, so I say yes."

"Captain de Anza, I'll see that you and my two brothers are fed before we have to leave. Is that allowed?"

"Strictly speaking, no. But who's to know? Yes, we could all use some nourishment."

Summoned by the bell, my people crowded into the church, curious to learn why they were being called in the middle of the day. I seated the captain and my two brothers to one side of the altar, then mounted to the pulpit. Would it be for the last time? My gaze swept over my Eudebes and Opatas, trying to memorize their faces, to recall all at once what we had accomplished together over the years. I began in a husky voice:

> "My dear little sheep, my people, your shepherd is being taken from you by force. Don José de Gálvez y Gallardo, Marqués de Sonora, has ordered my arrest and removal along with all the Jesuit missionaries in all our provinces in Sonora. No one knows why as yet, nor how long we will be

gone. All our property has been seized in the name of the king, His Majesty Carlos III. I leave here on foot with only the crucifix my mother gave me and my breviary. Diego and Pacheco will take care of you until my return. At least, I hope I will return. If I do not come back to you, it will be that I am a prisoner, my freedom taken away. For now, God be with you. Trust in his goodness, pray to him often, pray for me, and that our clement, loving Lady of Guadalupe will have mercy on us all."

My words raised a universal howl of grief, and my fantasy transported me back to my departure from Guevavi years before. As I descended from the pulpit, my people rushed to embrace me. They surrounded me as if to protect me, while the young men threatened Captain de Anza, backing him against the wall. His face showed shock, then paled and stiffened in fear.

"Stop! Stop! Calm yourselves!" I shouted again and again until my voice was finally heard over the weeping and the protests. "This is not the captain's doing. He's carrying out orders from His Majesty, King Carlos, and I must obey. Now, don't forget the lessons I've taught you. Study, work and grow your crops. Tend the animals. And pray for yourselves first and then for all of us Jesuits. Goodbye, my lambs. I'll return if I can."

I nodded to the captain and we three prisoners followed him to the hitching post where his saddled horse waited. We walked ahead of him southward down the river trail.

⁝⁞

I'd known that Lieutenant Governor Antonio Figueroa had been married, had children, and was now a widower, but I'd never met the children. His wife, María Angélica, died in childbirth, but the midwives were able to save the baby. The boy, Balthazar, is now four years old. Antonio proudly introduced him and his older sister Alicia to me at the garden party he gave a week ago. They are beautiful children, and the little girl idolizes her father.

I've seen Antonio at other gatherings. He tells me each time that his feelings for me have not changed. I am fond of him and tell him so, but a warm friendship is no basis for becoming a man's mistress, and I tell him that, too. During one conversation, he reported that the Jesuits had quietly replaced Luca Poncelli as vice-provincial. He said Poncelli made a desperate attempt to escape, but was caught on the road to México. He had put on civilian clothes and had credentials "proving" that he was a wealthy merchant trading in tea, rice and wheat. Antonio knew little more, but I'm anxious to hear the whole story. His residence has become a dormitory for scholastics teaching at the local Jesuit College. Antonio didn't know if they had named anyone to replace him, and no one seems to know where he has gone.

I'm pleased to see that the Society disciplines and corrects itself—although not soon enough. From my visits to Ures and Mátape, and from my acquaintance with various levels of priests and scholastics, I learned that the great majority of the men in the Society are performing their proper work, living lives beyond reproach. Despite their best efforts, though, it seems to me that their missions have failed to reach their goal of integrating the Indians into mainstream Spanish culture. The natives I saw at Ures and Mátape would not be able to survive in our world without special help from the Fathers. Ignaz told me his Eudebes and Opatas are more advanced, but could they survive on their own? Or would they become dupes and slaves of the Spanish overlords, the owners of huge ranches and plantations?

⁎⁎⁎

A terrible calamity has struck us here in Durango. A few nights ago, around the tenth of July, all Jesuit holdings in this city were seized by royal troops, and the Jesuits—priests, brothers, and novices—have been taken prisoner. I am told this is a universal move against the Society, decreed by His Majesty, Carlos III. They are to be expelled immediately from Spain and all its dependencies, sparing no one.

Antonio and I denounced Luca Poncelli's misdeeds at a moment when every infraction must have been carefully compiled into a massive dossier of evidence against the Society. Our true testimony might have been combined with the collection of lies and calumnies being spewed out against them. Ours may have added the spark that set off the fire. It is true that I wanted retribution against the Jesuits for the death of Mateo, true that I labored to find a means to discredit them, because, in my anger, I held them all responsible for the deeds of one man. But I learned as I came to know Ygnacio and Father Andrés, not to mention Father Jacobo Sedelmeyer, Enrique and Bendito, that the good, the holy, devout, dutiful, frank and open outweighed the bad.

I cannot sleep at night thinking what horrors those men on the northern frontier must be suffering. My beautiful and innocent Ignaz will be destroyed, along with all he has worked so hard to accomplish. I weep for him as a paradigm of all those missionaries. If I could do anything to save him I would—but my appeal would be to the lieutenant governor, just as much bound by orders from José de Gálvez, and, as I understand it, from His Majesty King Carlos III, as is the Society of Jesus.

Our Jesuits were quietly marched to the outskirts of the city from their house where they had been held captive and loaded into coaches. The moneyed gentry provided horses and coaches (and Antonio secretly contributed two of his own) so the exiles could at least ride to Veracruz. That is where they will be loaded on ships and deported back to Spain. Only God knows what fate awaits them there.

The people found out where they were gathering and turned out *en masse*. I'm sure most of the city was there. They covered the coaches with flowers and watered them with their tears. We all waved handkerchiefs and anything else we could lay hold of until the coaches were out of sight. What a terrible loss for New Spain! For Spain herself!

What angers me most is the attitude of the regular clergy, quick to take advantage of the prevailing wind. Our new Bishop, Ernesto Hidalgo, replaced our former beloved bishop who resigned his post because of the expulsion of the Jesuits. Out of curiosity, I went to Bishop Hidalgo's mid-morning Mass on Sunday. He preached a fiery sermon, claiming that the Jesuits had hoarded pearls from oyster beds off California, had buried gold from the Sonora mines, that they were hypocrites, abusers of the Indians in their missions, thieves and traitors to the Church and to the Crown. I walked out in anger and hurt at his slanders and half the congregation walked out with me, making as much noise as we could. Our act made me feel better, but didn't help the situation.

One remark by the bishop angered me more than the others. He claimed that the Jesuits, by their subtle wiles, had bewitched the people. That explained the expressions of profound love and grief that accompanied our poor priests on their way. If his homily is printed and published, posterity may believe it. But we, the citizens of Durango, know better.

Worst of all is our powerlessness to do anything about it.

༄ ༄

Wolfgang, arrested At Opodepe Mission, was as astonished and unprepared as I'd been. His clairvoyance did not extend to state politics, it seemed. We arrived at Mátape tired, dusty and hungry, our spirits low. No activity was visible around the college. The students and novices had been ordered home. We were confined to the refectory where there were tables and benches, but little comfort, physical or spiritual. Crucial information was missing. We were arrested and dispossessed, but why? What would become of us? We huddled in small groups speculating on possible reasons for the arrests, and none could imagine an adequate explanation.

We were allowed a drink of water when we arrived, then waited until nightfall for food. The group from the east was still missing: Bartolomé Saenz, Carlos Rojas, Alejandro Rapicani, Juan Nentwig and Nicolás Perera among others.

A week passed before we saw them. Captain de Anza had gone after them, and to our surprise he came with a group on foot but bringing in Nentwig and Perera on stretchers. I could only imagine the bone-crushing jolts they had endured while lying on their backs being pulled by mules over the rough trails. The captain had tried to persuade Father Perera, well along in years, to stay behind, but he had insisted on coming into exile with his brothers. Another week went by before all thirty-one of us had been arrested and collected. They then marched us into the church. At last! Our speculation would finally end and we'd be told the reason for our disgrace and destruction.

The soldiers closed the doors after all of us had entered the sanctuary, and the windows that had begun to glow with the last light of the sunset were darkened by the silhouettes of sentries standing outside each one. Someone tried the main door, and found it locked. I made my way to a side door, with the same result. All of us were talking and whispering when there was a sudden hush. Carlos Rojas appeared from the sacristy, a soldier at each elbow. He held up a paper, cleared his throat twice, and began in a quavering baritone. His emotion, so foreign to his usual demeanor, froze us even before he had read a full sentence.

> *"Por motivos reservados en su real ánimo, y siguiendo los impulsos de su real benignidad, y usando de la suprema potestad económica que el Todopoderoso le había concedido para la protección de sus vasallos…."*

> "For reasons reserved in his royal soul, and following the impulses of his royal beneficence, and using the supreme economic power that the All Powerful had conceded to him for the protection of his vassals…"

Carlos, stumbling over the words, his body trembling, continued reading the royal decree, followed by the decree from His Majesty's Royal Visitor, José Gálvez:

> "His Royal Highness, King Carlos III, orders the immediate seizure of all Jesuit houses, colleges, and universities, the seizure of all persons, who are to be sent as prisoners within twenty-four hours to Veracruz to be deported. All archives are to be sealed; all personal papers and other possessions seized. The prisoners are allowed to take only their prayer books and the

clothing necessary for the trip. If any Jesuit, even though ill or dying, be left remaining in his house of residence, the person responsible for failing to carry out the royal order will be summarily executed".[2]

His voice died away, swallowed by profound silence. We stood pale as death, unmoving, our breath stopped in our lungs.

---

[2] The king's orders excluded those Jesuits who were old and infirm—they were to be left behind to die. However, the orders were altered by the Royal Visitor, José de Gálvez, Marquis of Sonora, who, like the new Viceroy de Croix, hated the Jesuits, and acted as mouthpiece for the king with greater authority than his nominal superior, the viceroy. No mercy was shown those unfortunate men of the Company of Jesus who were expelled under his jurisdiction. Despite these orders, however, sixteen aged or ill Jesuits were left behind—although none in Sonora. Gerard Decorme, S.J., provides this information in: *La obra de los Jesuitas Mexicanos durante la Época Colonial, 1572-1767* (México: Antigua Librería Robredo de José Porrúa e Hijos, 1941) I. 457.

Chapter XIX
The Hurricane Strikes

The extent of the disaster became clearer as we awoke from the initial shock. Widened eyes sought and found each other, voices spoke, but in a whisper, for we were surely at a funeral. Wolfgang stood by my elbow and I sensed his whole body vibrating, taut as a bowstring.

"Wolf, why do they lock us in and surround us with armed men? This monstrous decree comes from His Majesty himself, our secular lord. We are bound by our vows to obey him, since he can dispose of us and our bodies like corpses of the dead."

"Which is exactly what we'll be before long," he answered with typical caustic precision. "How do they propose to get us to Veracruz within twenty-four hours? They have no idea of the size of this New World! You see, Ignaz, this is what comes of our blind reliance on ourselves and our works, while we neglected our faith in God's Grace, our spirituality."

"True of some, certainly true of Poncelli. As always, the many reap the whirlwind where the few have sown—"

"Look!" Wolf interrupted, "Who is that man sitting slumped in the pew over on the left? It's Poncelli himself, isn't it?"

We stood halfway to the altar, and I followed Wolf's pointing finger towards the left rear of the nave. There sat a huddled figure, big-boned, tending toward fat but not quite—a contrast with our leanness. His head was bowed, and I could see a shock of iron gray hair.

"If it isn't Luca, it's his twin brother. Why—how—is he here? I didn't see him in the refectory. Did he just get here? He keeps a residence in Durango and only travels up here to do his so-called inspection tours. Father Zevallos must have demoted him to assistant at a mission."

Wolf's chin came up. "Divine justice."

Next morning, 25 August 1767, Captain José Bergosa took charge of the march to San José de Los Pimas, roughly half-way to Guaymas on the coast. He made sure we ate our beans and pinole and drank as much water as we could safely hold. With sorrowful face and muttering under his breath, he formed us into rows of five men each, the weakest in the middle. The third row was structured like a bookshelf with three thin, elderly priests in the middle, Carlos Rojas on one end, Luca Poncelli on the other. Similar in bodily conformation, the two could not be farther apart in moral values, negative on one side, positive on the other. Carlos spoke gentle, encouraging words to the men nearby, but Poncelli spoke to no one and avoided eye contact.

Bergosa gave the order to march along the Mátape River. As we left the mission and college grounds, the Indians mourned our departure with long ululations and howls, weeping as for the dead. We reacted by holding our heads high, hoping to leave them with the principle engraved in their minds that we had so insistently taught them: obedience—especially to the King of Spain.

Father Sedelmeyer called out, "Farewell, farewell, my children. Our hearts will remain here with you until death. Do not mourn for us. We have been found worthy of suffering exile for Christ."

Muttered words of agreement that sounded like a collective groan reminded me that many of the Jesuits here were criollos, Spaniards born in New Spain, sons of patrician families now to be exiled from their homeland by a foreign king.

Our older brothers suffered during the march from heat exhaustion and excessive exertion. Captain Bergosa halted the group to move them into any shade he could find, where he handed out precious water from skins filled at Mátape and carried on pack mules. Our progress was slow, since Fathers Perera and Nentwig were still following on their mule-drawn stretchers. We spent two nights in the open air, under guard and by the light of watch fires. We were unable to keep warm except by huddling together, since our traveling gear and sleeping blankets had been confiscated. By noon on the third day, we staggered into San José de Los Pimas, received by the sorrowful villagers.

As soon as they could, they set up makeshift accommodations in the central plaza: trestle tables and benches under shelters made of poles, roofed with sparse thatch. Wolf and I sagged forward on benches, facing each other, our elbows on the table. I was chewing a mammoth bite of beans folded in a tortilla, when a large hand gripped my shoulder. It belonged to Captain Bergosa.

"Father Ygnacio, your colleague Father Nentwig wants to speak to you. The trip has been hard for him. He says he needs to tell you something before he dies."

I racked my brain to guess what that might be, found nothing, but rose and followed the captain.

"Over here, Father. The village women are caring for him and Father Perera in the rectory."

I crossed the threshold into the rectory's cool interior. An Indian woman in a shapeless dress, her black hair braided and wound around her head, beckoned to me. "The sick one is here; the old one is there."

I nodded and entered the room where she stood. Father Juan Nentwig, whom I remembered as robust, ruddy and agile, lay with his eyes closed, his brown hair lying in sweaty strands across his gray forehead. He opened his eyes when he heard my footstep.

"Good. You came, thank you, Ygnacio. I won't confess to you, but I want to apologize."

"What ever for?"

"I did you an injustice at Guevavi Mission, before you were transferred to Cucurpe."

I inclined my head and waited.

"I denounced you to the provincial for insubordination. I'd ordered you to stay clear of that medicine man, Jevho, and his dangerous ideas. You disobeyed. I understand by now what you were doing…. You were trying to understand better…."

He was running out of breath. "Yes. The better I understood him and his ideas, the more persuasive I could be in teaching him our doctrine. But he was too smart for me. He figured out what I was trying to do and left with his people and half of mine."

"And you were removed from your post. I'm so sorry, Ygnacio. I surely caused you much grief."

"It wasn't your word alone, Juan. Others reported the same thing. I was young and blind in those days, willfully blind. I didn't *want* to see the threat to the mission Jevho posed. But it all ended well in Cucurpe, in a far more rewarding mission. Thank you for apologizing, Father, but there was no need. I was hurt back then, but I also understood your concern. You were father visitor, after all, carrying out your duties."

"Maybe so, but I had to clear my conscience." He reached for my hand and gave it as hard a squeeze as he could manage.

Thanks to the compassion of the officers escorting us into exile, we remained in San Juan for two days to allow the weakest among us to recuperate, and the villagers found blankets for us. We slept in the church, on holy ground. At first light on the third morning, young Captain José Antonio de Vildósola organized our group to continue our march down the sandy trails toward Guaymas. We arrived on 2 September about noon. A few desolate adobe huts remained there, along with the ruins of an abandoned church and priest's house. On a rise, a musket shot from the shore, stood a new barracks. The hastily-built structure of adobe with a thatched roof would house soldiers due to arrive from México, but since they'd not yet come, we were herded inside. Horses and mules occupied part of it. This would be our temporary prison.

Within the first week, twenty colleagues from Sinaloa joined us, including my close friend Bernardo Middendorf. They had reached Guaymas in two large canoes, paddled by their faithful Indians. One elderly priest, Ignacio González, had been left behind. His colleague, José Palomino, a veteran of over thirty years' service in his mission at Huiribis, walked in unaided but was close to collapse. We now numbered fifty-one men in one rough building meant for half that many.

Weeks passed while we waited for the soldiers to arrive with the ship that would take us south, but none came. We scanned the sea in vain. Our sentries allowed us out on the dunes, but most men kept to the barracks where there was shelter from the sun. We ate wormy pozole, rice, and a few beans, not sufficient to nourish fifty-one men for long. Those of us strong and clear-minded enough divided our poor rations—in case the soldiers and the ship were long delayed. And they did not come. The well water stank like a fetid marsh, was brackish, warm, and disgusting. We began to suffer from scurvy and loose teeth. Our gums became inflamed—bloody sometimes—and we knew we would lose our teeth and with them our means of staying alive.

We were plagued by heat and vermin. The horses and mules attracted hordes of flies and mosquitoes that flew through the open windows and drank our blood. We huddled on the bare earthen floor, visited by scorpions, centipedes and tarantulas. Many fell ill with contagious diseases that quickly swept us all, weakened as we were by poor nourishment and black depression. Those of us who tried to comfort the others were often the ones most in need of help.

One small consolation during those dark days was the company of friends. Wolfgang was as happy as I to sit on the dunes with Miguel Gerstner and Bernardo Middendorf. We shared memories of our joy and anticipation as we left Puerto de Santa María on the ship Victorioso, bound for New Spain. We spoke our native German, and no one reprimanded us or ordered us to speak 'cristiano.' The fourth member of our original group, Joseph Och, had been sent to Mexico City for medical treatment weeks before the order of expulsion arrived. By all accounts, he was virtually paralyzed. Had he been expelled from there, or had he been left behind to die?

⁎⁋

Time stands still when one has nothing to do, but human flesh decays all the faster. Every day was like every other, and we strove to say our Masses and our prayers, read our breviaries, and keep track of the liturgical year. But, since we knew, deep down, that time was standing still, we became irritable, angry, sullen, withdrawn, some with hallucinations, some with spells of outright madness. And we decayed. Surely, all those identical days were just an illusion, and we had just arrived yesterday? Yet one look at gaunt, gray or yellow faces, loose teeth, bleeding gums, and spreading brown spots on our skin told us that time, like the surrounding sand, had slipped through our fingers; our lives slipped through our awareness with as much significance as a handful of that same sand.

I stood on the rise outside the barracks, shaded my eyes and looked seaward. Not a sail in sight. The waters of the bay were a sheet of glass, the barren little islands like miniature black volcanoes. The strip of beach below lay deserted, where receding wavelets left a glittering border along the strand. No, not deserted: gulls, plovers and sandpipers strutted along that strip, dipping their beaks into the shining surface. They must be finding food. My body trembled with hunger and weakness. Perhaps I, too, could find something edible on that shimmering beach. Our kindly officers were long gone, but the sentries might be persuaded to let me go down and look. I approached the closest man.

"Good morning, Private."

"What is it, Father? What do you want? You're not allowed to wander around out here."

"You know we're not getting enough food in there, don't you?"

"What do you expect me to do about that, Father? We aren't faring much better."

"Here's what you can do. Let me go down to the beach and see if I can find something we can all eat. You can guard me. Point that musket at my heart. Shoot me if I make a move to escape."

"You're being silly, Father. I'd never shoot you."

"And I'd never try to escape. Where would I go? But tell me, are there any rules against going down to the beach?"

He rubbed his forehead and ran his fingers through his hair. "I can't think of any... not specifically... if you're guarded." His voice trailed away.

I took quick advantage. "Then let me go down to the beach. If I don't find anything, nothing is lost, nothing gained. If I find something, then there is gain for all of us."

He hesitated, then called to his companion, "Hermano, I'm taking this man down to the beach. Watch the others."

The announcement was greeted with a yawn. "Fine, hermano. Enjoy the stroll."

I led the way through the dunes and down to the beach where the waves hardly rippled on the shore, protected as it was by the islands and rocky promontory. In their eternal rhythm, the swells heaved themselves landward, wet a narrow strip of beach, then receded. As the water drained away, holes appeared in the sand and iridescent bubbles rose above each hole before they burst. Living creatures must be breathing under there. What could they be? Were they edible? I searched and found a driftwood stick and dug. God was with me. Between six and eight inches deep, I found a brown and shiny clam as wide as my hand was long. I seized it and rinsed wet sand from it, looking around for a rock. Higher up, close to the dunes, I found one, returned to the beach where the sand was still packed by the water and smashed the shell. I scooped out the tough, still-moving body and ate it raw, ignoring the clinging grains of sand, savoring the salt-bitter taste and the sensation of fresh, clean moisture. I had barely chewed, but already felt life-giving power flowing from it into my starved body. I dug for more and found eleven, although many dug faster than I did and escaped me. I ate three and decided to take the rest back to my starving brothers.

Seaweed had washed up on the beach, long ribbons of dull, blackish green interspersed with translucent bladders the size of my thumb. I carried a tangle of weed to the water, rinsed off the sand and tore loose a piece of ribbon with my teeth. It was chewy, fishy, tough, with little flavor, but not fibrous. I ate more. The bladders were tougher, so I left them alone. I'd take this back to the barracks, too.

I walked up the hill with eight clams in the bag made by the skirts of my robe, the seaweed in my right hand.

"Wolf! Try this. It's good—or at least, it's food. Clams are some sort of meat. They'll keep your strength up."

Wolf hunched his shoulder against me. "You'll get sick from eating that offal, Ygnacio. Mark my words. It'll poison you."

I cleaned and boiled the clams along with pieces of seaweed. Wolf would not allow even the soup to pass his lips. I had better luck with the elderly priests who were weakest, especially with the men who had lived close to the sea. As the days crept by, I could see that those who ate the clam and seaweed soup kept their teeth, became thinner but not emaciated, were the last to succumb to contagious diseases, and remained in better spirits than those living off the stale beans and rice. I added a few tiny crabs to the soup whenever I could catch them. They were too small to crack for their meat, but they added their juices.

The pinole was gone by now, worms and all. The skins of the weakest began to bloom with yellow and brown spots like fungus infections. I recruited Jacobo Sedelmeyer to help me harvest clams, but the area of the beach where we were allowed to scavenge was soon almost empty of them except at very low tide, when we would bring in dozens. When the clams ran low, Private Atanacio allowed us to explore further, and we found abundant oyster beds among the rocks at the mouth of the Yaqui River. Larger crabs scuttled among those rocks, meatier and easier to catch. Even Wolf began to share those meals. I learned by trial and error which seaweed was edible, which not. Some of it made me violently sick, which I could not afford, as weakened as I was already, but Jacobo and I were still strong enough to nurse many sick brothers, dosing them with oyster, clam and crab soup.

∞∞

Yes, it was Luca Poncelli we'd seen that day in Mátape Chapel, slumped in a pew. He'd gotten wind somehow that he was about to be stripped of his office and sent to Oposura Mission to assist Father Joseph Garrucho. Being a man of foresight as well as ruthless and resourceful, he had already laid plans for his escape in case he were caught or denounced for gun-running. His change of clothing hung in his closet: He would exchange his black robe and biretta for a merchant's silk suit and brocade vest. He had ordered a powdered wig from México, made to measure. His friends García and Pacheco lent him a fine coach and a team of four and a driver, to take him to Veracruz. Leaving the religious life behind, he would pose as a wealthy merchant, trading in tea, rice and wheat. He'd no doubt planned a series of further disguises that he would assume one after another, until his trail was lost. He carried an iron-bound chest with him, full of his ill-gotten gains. Sad for him, though, Pacheco had a crisis of conscience and denounced Poncelli to the Jesuit father visitor who had come to depose him and escort him to Oposura. He was overtaken in San Luís Potosí, his treasure confiscated.

The life of relative ease and abundance he'd led to that point laid the foundation for his collapse at Guaymas. He was in no condition to bear the hardships that tried the fittest of us almost beyond endurance. Father Garrucho had been next to Poncelli on the march from San Juan de Los Pimas, and steadied him a few times when he staggered. He'd gasped something to Joseph about a pain running down his left arm, and that he couldn't catch his breath.

When we arrived at Guaymas, he was physically sick, throwing up before we entered the barracks. He curled up in a corner and slept for forty-eight hours. Wolf and I checked on him during a sleep that seemed more like death, and found his chest still rising. Although he awoke, he never recovered from the strain of the march. He lasted four months, then came to me, his robe hanging loose on his big frame. The flesh on his face sagged in drooping gray folds, and he spoke through colorless lips. His demeanor was humble, the old autocratic style gone.

"Father Ygnacio, I need to talk to you and then confess, if I may."

"Why me, Father Poncelli?"

"Because the load of guilt I bear toward you is greater than toward any other man here. But I'll tell you my story before I make a formal confession."

"Very well, Father. I'm listening." I knelt beside him as his words tumbled out. His story was long. He described his pride and ambition and the invincible urge to mount the dangerous and 'romantic' adventure—gun running—that had made him rich. He admitted to the deliberate murder of Lieutenant Mateo Salinas and his men, and his exploitation of the 'weak vessel,' as he called Captain Nicolás Xavier Cuevas, to carry out his orders. Then he looked at me.

"I'd seen you at a meeting in Mátape several years ago, and was struck by your beauty."

"M-my *what?*"

"We Italians admire the blonde refinement of the northern tribes. You embody the Greek ideal better than the Greeks themselves. Perhaps that is one reason why the Goths captured Rome so easily—the Romans found them beautiful."

I stared at him but said nothing.

"When I came through Ures with my load of guns that last time and saw you there, the old attraction was rekindled. You asked if you could ride with me to Banámichi and you cooked my breakfast. You served me, and although both your utensils and your raw materials were primitive, you were deft. The meal was delicious."

"Thank you, Father Poncelli."

"I offered you—indirectly, mind you—a post as my secretary back in Durango, but you countered that with blather about being happy in your isolated mission with those savages at Cucurpe."

I waited.

"Then you betrayed me. You contrived a way to spy on the goods I was carrying. I knew you'd seen the muskets through a hole in the canvas."

"And *you* contrived a way to murder me that night."

"Yes. I'd known all along you were Andrés Michel's catspaw." He shot a dark look at Andrés, seven yards away. "You destroyed all my rosy plans for you—for us. I felt I had to kill you. Then you gave me the slip and I sent the soldiers after you. But you were too clever. You avoided them."

I could see he was reliving that ride, those emotions, that anger and urge to kill. "And how do you feel about all that now, Father Poncelli?"

"Ah… I'm most bitterly sorry, Ygnacio… Father."

"Then you are in the right state of mind to make your confession?"

"Yes, Father," he said meekly, "Bless me, Father, for I have sinned."

He finished the confession with the prescribed words, "Oh my God, I am heartily sorry for having offended thee…"

I absolved him in the name of the Father, of the Son, and of the Holy Spirit. His shoulders began to shake with ragged sobbing, and he took my hand and pressed it to his lips. "Please give me the Last Rites now, Father Ygnacio."

"But surely, this is premature?"

"No, I feel myself failing. My time is very near. I must prepare myself for eternity, whatever that might bring, God help me!"

I administered Extreme Unction. He thanked me and drifted off to sleep with a tiny smile on his lips. He died in his sleep a week later.

ໝ

Despite our best efforts, we also lost Father José Palomino of Sinaloa, who had lasted over seven months in those miserable conditions. Word of his death got out, probably through the soldiers, and the Yaqui Indians came for his body, which they bore away for burial in his mission cemetery at Huiribis. He had been loved.

Chapter XX
Death March

At last, May 1768, sails on the horizon! Ships in the harbor! They disgorged soldiers, troops sent by Viceroy de Croix to put down Indian uprisings, and—as we later found out—to scout the land for gold. It was this expedition, these ships, we had waited for during more than nine months to take us down the coast to San Blas.

One small ship accepted us on board, and we traded misery on land for greater hardship at sea. We were becalmed while our water soured and our food spoiled. Crammed together, our space was so low that, kneeling, we could not hold our heads upright. We slept three to a bunk. The average coffin had more space. The bunks became our dining tables, our sitting rooms and the 'park' where we strolled and meditated. In our weakened condition, more of us became victims of scurvy.

The captain finally put in at Puerto Escondido on the lower Californian peninsula for fresh supplies, but for fear of reprisal from Royal Visitor José de Gálvez, he put to sea again before we could begin to recover. A fierce storm struck the ship and nearly sank us—we were overloaded and leaky. We commended ourselves to God and awaited our death, but we received no such mercy. We limped into port at San Blas on August ninth. The trip that should have taken six days had lasted three months.

Once the rowboats delivered us near the shore, we staggered out of the shallows and onto dry land where Governor Manuel Rivero met us, nearly weeping at our condition. He served the best meal we had eaten in many months, but some, like Wolfgang, could not hold down the rich food. Fresh soldiers were waiting impatiently to deliver us to Veracruz. These were newly imported troops under José Gálvez' command, who had little connection with the people and culture of New Spain and no sympathy for us and our condition.

We began our march at dawn on the third day after our landing. It had been raining, and the road often disappeared into overflowing swamps and salt marshes where we waded in water up to our waists. Those of us who were stronger supported and even carried the weak and elderly through the morass. I carried my friend and former neighbor from Aconchi Mission, Father Nicolás Perera, who had been brought by stretcher to Guaymas, but was now expected to walk or to manage a horse. He had risked his life hundreds of times in his ministry to the Seris. I carried him on my back like a child, and he rested his chin on top my head.

His rusty voice buzzed in my ear. "Are you sure you can do this, Ygnacio? You're not much better off than the rest of us."

"I'll manage, Father Nicolás. Especially for you." My foot skidded on the muddy bottom just then, and I staggered but—thank God!—didn't fall.

"You see, my son, you only have two legs. That soldier's horse has four. If he slips, he has less chance of falling."

The explosion of a musket shot jolted us. Several of us cried out.

A soldier on the far right shouted, "Alligators! Beware of alligators! One just attacked my horse."

We searched the murky water, our hearts beating hard. I saw none, but a monster could surface among us at any moment.

"I made a terrible mistake insisting that I be exiled with the rest of you," Nicolás said, ignoring the present danger, "I've been nothing but a burden for you—just one more mouth to feed when there was far too little to eat."

"We're glad you came with us. You honor us with your presence."

But our clothing, our blankets and even our breviaries were soaked before we came to the end of the series of swamps.

ⅎ⏣

We stumbled into Tepic, where we were received by the people with pity and kindness. A generous rancher, don Francisco Posadas, took us to his hacienda where he gave us good horses. There we rested, drank cool, clean water, and ate what we could tolerate of the abundant and delicious meal he served us. Many were so starved that they could only eat a small portion. But hardly had we finished the meal when our guards lashed us onwards, oblivious of our moribund state.

From then on, our progress became a death march. After we passed through Tetitlán, many of my brothers could no longer hold the reins and were tied on their horses. In Ahuacatlán, three died, Enrique Kürtzel among them. Two more fell on the road from there to Ixtlán, one of them Pío Laguna from Besaraca, the other my poor young colleague Pedro Díaz, last to serve at my first mission, Atí. In Ixtlán, ten died, among them Francisco Villaroya, who had received me along with Poncelli's mule train in Banámichi; my beloved elder friend Nicolás Perera, whom I had earlier carried on my back; Juan Nentwig, who had felt such scruples about his treatment of me while I was at Guevavi Mission when he was father visitor, and Alejandro Rapicani, with whom I had laughed and chatted whenever I visited Mission Batuco.

The rest of us struggled onward to Magdalena de Jalisco. There, two Fathers collapsed, one of them our good Father Visitor Manuel Aguirre, dead on 25 September. In Tequila, Wolfgang lovingly administered the last rites to his superior, Bartolomé Saenz, who forgave him for his errant ways and for his jansenism.

"Pío, Wolfgang, if you live, try to be a good Jesuit, not a disciple of Luther! Peace be with you, my son." He squeezed my friend's hand and turned his face away, taking a few agonized breaths before eternal stillness silenced him forever.

Sick and miserable though I was, I was concerned about Wolf. He was reduced to skin and bone, had developed a constant cough, and his dark eyes burned like coals as he looked at me out of his pasty-skinned, skull-like face. The soldiers had allowed us to drink from the public fountain in the central marketplace and to rest for a few moments in the shade. Wolf had been muttering in delirium at intervals since we had left Ixtlán. Now, as we sat or lay on the stones around the fountain, I felt his forehead, and found it burning hot. He was running a high fever. He pushed my hand away.

"Let me be, Ygnacio. Your hand's just adding to the heat. These stones feel good—they're cooling. Give me the last rites, my friend. I know I'll never have the strength to rise from here."

The words came in panting gasps, interrupted by gurgling coughs, giving him scarcely time to breathe. I quickly administered the sacrament of Extreme Unction.

"I have committed the sin of anger toward these soldiers who have viciously abused my brothers. I have also hated those evil advisors who have so criminally misled our king and sovereign lord. May God forgive me." After completing his confession, he clutched my hand. "Live, Ignaz," he told me, "someone must bear witness to our story."

He lapsed into unconsciousness, and in about an hour, his breathing simply stopped. He had smothered to death.

Miguel Gerstner and Bernardo Middendorf tried to help me bear his body to the nearby parish church, but we were too weak and exhausted to lift him. I was on my knees beside him when a shadow fell across me. A soldier.

"I've been ordered out from Guadalajara to help get you the rest of the way to the city. You are the Jesuits from Sonora and Sinaloa, aren't you?"

I raised my eyes to his, too numb to reply. I nodded, and at last mumbled, "Yes, what's left of us."

"My name is Saúl Ayala. I know something of that country. I was at Ures…"

I found the strength to stand. "Saúl Ayala! Corporal Ayala! Then you're the man who killed Captain Nicolás Cuevas! This man here at our feet, Father Wolfgang Wegner, saw you quarrel with him right after you arrived at Ures."

"Wait! I—"

"That murder caused us untold suffering. Father Andrés Michel was falsely accused and imprisoned for committing it." I gestured toward Andrés, collapsed against a tree a few feet away.

Ayala tried again, holding up his hand. "I turned myself in at Horcasitas and confessed to that murder in writing to get Father Andrés released—and I see that my ruse succeeded; he was released. But I gave my jailors the slip and escaped because, you see, although I know who did kill the captain, I am innocent."

I locked eyes with him with all the energy I could muster. "Then tell me who *did* kill the captain! My whole purpose in staying alive has been to clear Andrés Michel's name."

He shook his head with a twitch of his lips. "I understand your intensity, Father… Father, uh…"

"Ygnacio Pfefferkorn."

"Father Pfefferkorn. You see, like you, my entire being is devoted to protecting the good name and person of the one who did the deed. In my eyes, the act was fully justified. Nothing can force me to reveal that person's name. Now, let me help you carry this poor priest to the church."

I stood staring but not seeing him, my grief blinding me, exhaustion fogging my mind. If Ayala was innocent, then who…? But I avoided the thought. My first duty now was to my beloved friend lying at my feet. "Andrés!" I called, "Come with us, we are carrying Wolfgang's body to the church."

"Wolfgang died?" His face showed shock and grief as he joined us, bending over the body, his lips moving as he made the sign of the cross.

The parish priest promised to give my friend a proper burial. All five of us, including Ayala, prayed over his body, and hot tears scalded my face as I wept for my courageous, truth-telling companion. We were not allowed to stay to see the grave dug or to hold a graveside service. I left Wolf lying alone before the altar, and after commending him to God's special care, I was marched away with the rest.

⁞⁞

Twenty-nine of the original fifty-one men staggered into Guadalajara. In the city, our condition evoked tears of pity and compassion. The Royal Agent must have been proud indeed to present twenty-nine skeletons to his superior and be forced to mention the twenty who had died on the march from San Blas.

Our new custodians carried the sickest—the majority—in coaches to the Hospital de Betlemitas. The rest of us were taken to the hacienda of Toluquilla, once a stately property in the country, but which was now surrounded by the bustle of the growing city. We were confined without access to visitors, but were allowed two weeks' rest and food.

Most of us in Toluquilla were housed in rooms whose doors opened out on a central patio, but Miguel Gerstner and I had a room with a barred window on the street. After a full day of good food and a night's rest, I was energetic enough to pull a bench to the window and climb on it, giving me a view of the people passing below.

A carriage drew up and the groom helped a woman of extraordinary beauty to alight. I held my breath as I recognized her. Doña Beatriz! I called her name, but the noise of passing carriages and street vendors was too great. I called several times, but she did not hear. For a moment, she turned her head my way as if she sensed something, but then she moved on, out of my line of sight. I was weak enough to weep. She was carrying a basket, the groom two more, and shortly afterward, the guards came to our rooms with gifts of fruit, bread, and cheese. I blessed my beloved benefactress for her charity.

We in the hacienda were ordered to move on to Veracruz first. I begged to stay, however, to travel with the nine priests who were being treated in the hospital, among them Andrés Michel and Bernardo Middendorf. I left with them on 14 February 1769. The New Year had come and gone twice since our arrest. When we moved on toward the port of Veracruz, we were placed in coaches and wagons. Although the roads were rutted and the carriages jolted us unmercifully, no more of us died during that last stretch.

Once again, we were jailed to await the arrival of a ship that would take us back across the sea. Two more died of *vómito negro*—yellow fever—while we waited in a filthy, dirt-floored, vermin-ridden inn. Veracruz was notorious for yellow-fever deaths, and the church cemetery was filled with new graves of Jesuits who had arrived before us, had waited, like us, for ships to take them further into Limbo, and who had contracted the disease and died while they were delayed.

Finally, on 8 April 1769, a French ship, the *Aventurier*, arrived. It had brought two mathematicians, one a Frenchman, the other Spanish, who were on their way to Baja California to witness a solar eclipse there. This would be the vessel that would sail to Spain with twenty-seven of the fifty-one missionaries who had embarked at Guaymas, subject to the king's decree. Those words, read to us that night in Mátape, will repeat themselves forever in my nightmares.

♋

I know from what I have seen for myself that my worst fears about the fate of the missionaries in Sonora were childish compared to what really happened to them. It is beyond comprehension that in our day and age, in a civilized, Christian nation, we can treat our fellow humans—our priests, even—in such a bestial way. No, not bestial—far worse: diabolical. The tortures of Hell could be no worse. Animals may hunt and eat members of another animal family, but they do not torture their own kind for months and years on end, delighting in inflicting the most degrading abuse on both minds and bodies.

Much has happened to me in these last two years. As I have already said, I met Antonio's children at a garden party at his hacienda, and the three of us took an immediate liking to each other. With Antonio's permission, I began to visit them almost daily and took them on outings, including an extended horseback trip into the mountains—with a competent escort, of course. Baltazar adored the entire trip; Alicia too, though she missed her father. It was a welcome escape for me, an opportunity to ride horseback once more, as I had done on that fateful trip to Mátape nearly three years ago.

Antonio noticed that the children came to depend upon me for affection, guidance, and, of course, recreation, although it took months for that to become clear to either of us. One afternoon he caught me as I was about to leave his mansion after spending another day with the children.

"Beatriz, please, come into the sitting room; we must talk."

I willingly followed him, wondering if he would propose something more than that I be his "woman."

"I see that the children love you as I still do, despite everything I've said. I know you have some affection for me—you've proven it over these past months through your concern and care for my children. You've spent many hours of your time."

"They're beautiful children. I had free time and once I knew them, what more natural thing than to help them when they seemed to need someone—a woman—to fill a void?"

He took my hand. His face was serious, eyes pleading. "Could you fill my void as well, Beatriz? There is no impediment to our union. I am a widower, you a widow. Class differences mean nothing to me, as they didn't to your noble husband. I love you just as deeply as ever—perhaps more maturely, and I've seen abundant proof that my love has not been misplaced. Now, if you could only love me, just a little, perhaps you could consider marrying me, Beatriz."

I had anticipated the possibility that Antonio might ask me, and had thought long and hard about such a match. By now, I knew he was a good man with high moral principles, despite his wandering eye. But who was I to fault him for that? A pang plowed my throat and chest every time I thought of Ygnacio. Had he died of abuse? Where was he now? My love forever groped toward him, my secret love, but could never reach him. Perhaps he was as dead as my beloved Mateo.

I'd long ago understood that my feelings of grief for Mateo, like my love for Ygnacio, were parts of me that could not be denied, but that could be set aside. It was time to begin a new phase of my life, and I decided to accept, should Antonio propose marriage. Now I answered him with conviction.

"Yes!"

I wrapped my arms around him and he reciprocated with an embrace both fervent and tender. But we waited until the first week of this month to marry. We traveled south to the largest real city within a reasonable distance: Guadalajara. It was a quiet ceremony in the beautiful Jesuit church there. Even though the regular clergy had taken it over, I insisted on paying the Society that tribute.

While we honeymooned there, visiting the parks, going to the opera, I heard that a group of Jesuits were being brought through on their way to Veracruz for final deportation. So late? How could that cruel order of expulsion have been carried out in such a laggard and sloppy manner? Antonio enquired of the Archbishop, who, he reported, pointed his nose in the air with an expression of disgust.

"Yes, that riffraff is due to arrive here today or tomorrow. They'll be housed either in the hacienda de Toluquilla or in the hospital—depending on their condition. Then we'll hustle them out of here as quickly as possible. We can't have traitors to His Majesty loitering about in our city."

I did not see them brought in, but from what Antonio told me, they were mere skeletons in rags, the majority unable to walk on their own, being supported by their brothers who could themselves barely stand. The majority were hustled off to the hospital, since it was clear they would not live another day without immediate help. A few were taken to Toluquilla where they would be imprisoned until their departure.

I decided to take baskets of fruit, bread and cheese to Toluquilla, since bread is the staff of life, the other things full of life-giving essences. The hired groom and I got down from the coach on the street where Toluquilla's main gate opens and pulled out the baskets. As I started toward the gate, I thought I heard someone call my name. I turned, but there was no one other than wandering vendors in the street along with noisy passing carriages. I walked on and heard my name again, but decided it must be an echo of one of the merchants' calls. I firmly suppressed the idea that the voice was Ygnacio's. I was a married woman now.

We traveled from Guadalajara to Veracruz in Antonio's luxurious coach. We were due to embark on a handsome ship, the Santa Catalina, since Antonio intends to take me to his home in Santiago de Compostela to present me to his family.

My husband and I strolled down to the dock two days ago, to admire our ship and go aboard to see what our accommodations would be. As we approached the gangplank, we saw a group of chained men marching to a neighboring ship, a French one, the *Aventurier*. They were a miserable lot, about twenty-five of them, I guessed, wearing the remnants of clerical robes that were more grayish brown than black. As they approached, I realized they were Jesuits, a remnant of the large numbers deported at least a year ago.

I remembered the group brought into Guadalajara before we left there. I had taken them a small gift of food, but had no idea who they were or where they had come from. They'd been closely guarded, so I had not been able to find out, although I'd tried.

Perhaps this was the same group that had spent two weeks in Toluquilla or in the hospital in Guadalajara. I searched their faces to see if I could recognize anyone. It was difficult. Their jaws were covered with matted beards; their faces gray with ill health, starvation and dirt. And then I saw him, one of the tallest. He still carried himself well, although he showed clear signs of abuse. Ygnacio's hair was matted and long, like his beard, but still blond, dirty but blond. He had raked his hair back from his face with his fingers, and it lay in greasy strands at the back of his neck. His face was undamaged, though haggard and thin: the eyes and nose the same, the rest obscured by the beard. His left sleeve was torn off his shoulder, revealing a bony upper arm that showed several badly healed scars, perhaps the marks of whips.

"Antonio!" I whispered urgently, "Ygnacio is among these men! Can you stop the group for a moment so I can speak to him?"

My husband had examined the approaching men just as I had. He told me later that it came as no surprise that one of them was my former love, Father Ygnacio. He stepped into the path of the sergeant who was in charge of the prisoners. "Sergeant, I am Lieutenant Governor Antonio Figueroa of Sonora. These priests are from my province. I request that you halt this group for a moment; I wish to speak to one of them."

The sergeant was impressed by Antonio's demeanor, his clothing, and his rank. He halted the chained men. Antonio approached the only man among the twenty-seven—I had now counted them—who could be Ygnacio.

"I presume you are Father Ygnacio. I believe my wife would like to speak with you." He turned and moved away to a discrete distance.

"Father," I began, "I don't know if, after all you've obviously suffered, you remember me."

He looked at me with the only part of him I wholly recognized, his brilliantly blue eyes. In them I could see his essence, crystalline blue against a pure white background. They crinkled at the corners as he smiled. I cursed the ragged beard that hid his lips.

"Thank you for the delicious food you brought us in Toluquilla in Guadalajara, doña Beatriz," he said in the voice that had echoed so often in my dreams.

"How did you know?" I blurted, taken aback.

"I could see you from the window of my cell. I called you, but you couldn't hear me over the noises in the street. You are remarried, I see. Very well remarried. My congratulations!" He spoke to me as if we were chatting together at a garden party.

"What will become of you, Father?" I brought us back to reality.

"God only knows, Beatriz... doña Beatriz."

By that little slip, I knew he remembered our closeness.

"I will try to find out... help you if I can."

He smiled just a little, gently. "I doubt if you can prevail over the wishes of King Carlos, doña Beatriz. It is good to see you. Please forgive the state we're in—we must all look like scarecrows. May God bless you!" He made the sign of the cross as best he could with his manacled hands.

I reached out and took his hand. "I must confess to you, Father Ygnacio. Something—something monstrous—is weighing on my conscience." I turned to the sergeant. "I know this priest from long ago. There is something I must confess to him. Something only he and I know about, but that I must confess before he leaves New Spain. Please allow these other priests to rest for half an hour while I confer with my Father Confessor."

The sergeant's face puckered as he considered my request. He seemed to be at a loss. I beckoned Antonio. "My dear, I have something to confess to Father Ygnacio. Could you please give the sergeant instructions to allow the other priests to rest over there in the shade while I speak to him?" When Antonio's brows drew together, I reassured him. "We'll both stay in plain sight."

"Oh, very well, Beatriz. Maybe this will exorcize the last ghost that stands between you and me. Sergeant, do as the lady says. We cannot stand in the way of matters of conscience."

With great reluctance, the sergeant detached Ygnacio from the chained priests and issued an order to the rest, "Over there in the shade of that warehouse. You understand that there's a confession going on." His voice conveyed more than a touch of sarcasm, but the priests nodded solemnly and trooped over to collapse in the dust, cooled by the shade of the building.

I led the way to a tree, where a discarded crate offered a place to sit. We sat side by side, and I began to tell him my story, before beginning the formal confession.

"It's about Captain Cuevas, Father."

He nodded, piercing me with those intense blue eyes of his. "You killed him, of course."

"How did you know? When did you know?"

"I suspected you early on, but fought it to the point that I never mentioned your name in connection with the murder; refused to think it. I willed it not to be true. I eliminated every other possible suspect, hoping against hope I would exonerate you."

I wrung my hands. "Please don't think I'm evil, Father. Let me tell you how it happened."

"Go on, tell me, Beatriz."

"Captain Cuevas didn't want me along on that trip to Ures and Mátape. The lieutenant governor forced him. It was clear from the beginning he was uneasy to have his former lieutenant's wife added to his inspection team."

"His conscience bothered him, with you as a constant reminder."

"Yes, and besides that, he was a confirmed woman-hater. He considered women nothing but trouble, a hindrance, giddy, unable to stand the rigors of the trail, making unreasonable demands."

"And you proved him wrong."

I nodded. "When I proved to have as much endurance as his men, when I remained sensible and made no demands, his attitude improved in one way—but his disrespect simply showed itself in a different area: lust. He began making advances by touching me whenever he could and making suggestive remarks."

"He was trying to salve his conscience by turning you, in his imagination, into a loose woman"

"Apparently so, Father. The men under his direct command resented it but could do little to stop it. Thank God, Corporal Ayala joined the group shortly after we left Durango and acted as my chaperon."

"Did he quarrel with the captain right away?"

"No, he simply blocked Cuevas' access to me. I could see that the captain hated and feared the corporal. The first overt quarrel came when we arrived at Ures."

"I knew about that. Wolfgang Wegner overheard it."

"Ah, yes, 'Pío' Wegner. You told me about him on that ride to Mátape, and we discussed him at supper later. Shortly after nightfall on that first day at Ures, I went into the church to pray. The sanctuary was dark except for the votive candles and the vigil lamp, but I made my way to the altar rail and knelt."

Ygnacio leaned toward me, his face strained. "And then?"

"Then I heard footsteps behind me. I turned and saw the captain standing there. He didn't speak but simply grabbed my arms, stood me up and turned me around, as if I were a rag doll. I shouted, 'Get your hands off me! Leave me alone and at least give me the privacy to pray!' My voice came out hoarse and grating—I didn't recognize it. He laughed and I slapped him. He shouted an obscenity at me, then clamped his hand over my mouth and dragged me toward the sacristy. I struggled and resisted, but I'm not a large woman. He was twice my weight. He bundled me into the moonlit sacristy and slammed the door behind us. Then, Father... then..."

Ygnacio groaned. "You needn't go on. I can imagine the rest."

"Oh, but you must know, not merely imagine. Then you can judge the extent of my guilt and my sin."

"Only God judges, Beatriz."

I sat silently for a moment, breathing and gathering courage. "And then... he raped me. He tore at my widow's veil, left it dangling by its ribbon and kissed me, violently, crushing my lips against my teeth and cutting them. I continued to struggle, and he punched me in the stomach. He didn't want to mark my face, it seems."

"Tell me what happened afterward." Ygnacio's voice was gentle.

I exhaled a long breath in gratitude. The tension in my chest relaxed. He did not condemn me, not yet.

"Afterwards, Cuevas stood up without a word, leaving me there on the floor like a slab of meat. He walked out of the sacristy, still buttoning himself as he crossed before the altar. I was wild with shame and fury that he thought he could assault me, besmirch me, destroy my honor and walk away with impunity."

Ygnacio's face had become dark with rage, his fists clenched in his manacles, but he merely said, "Go on, Beatriz."

"I pulled my clothes into some semblance of decency and went through Father Andrés' desk. I hoped to find a knife but only found papers and a rosary. I clutched it to my bosom as I ran into the church. A votive candle burned under the beautiful little statue of the Blessed Virgin. I ran to ask for her help, but instead I saw that her image would fit my hand exactly. I begged her forgiveness and followed the captain clutching the heavy little statue."

"And you found him."

"He had left the side door open and stood in the twilit garden. He stretched and yawned, as if he had just accomplished a noble deed. I halted in the doorway, my fury mounting. He was about to turn when I made a sudden rush and struck a tremendous blow to the back of his head with the statue's base. He fell to his knees with a moan, his hands clutching at his head. It was atrocious."

Ygnacio stared at me, expressions of revulsion, admiration, concern and worry chasing themselves across his face. "Tell me the rest." Now his voice was constricted.

"The captain collapsed on his back, unconscious, but he was still breathing. It was an appalling sound, noisy, like snoring. I still had the rosary in my left hand. I looped it around his neck and twisted until that gurgling snore stopped. He would have died anyway with his head caved in, but I couldn't stand to have him suffer any longer. I waited three or four minutes and twisted one last time to make sure. The rosary broke and

I threw it into the darkness at the back corner of the garden. I stood up, stunned, unable to believe what had happened to me and what I'd done to him. It was all too monstrous. I went back through the church and out the front door to my room in the near side of the stable."

Ygnacio's head was bowed, one hand clutching his forehead. "My God, my God, Beatriz! I know you're a strong woman, but how have you borne the guilt all these months without going mad?"

"I didn't last all the way, Father. I confessed the whole thing to Father Andrés in the prison cell in Durango. He's the only one who knew, and of course he couldn't tell anyone. But my struggle with guilt has not lessened since that confession. I needed to confess to you, too."

"And I was leagues away, trying to find Cuevas' murderer and clear Andrés Michel's good name."

"I'm sorry, Ygnacio, I probably risked your life during that search. I had a quest, too, another purpose to fulfill: to prove that Luca Poncelli conspired with Captain Cuevas to send my husband and his men to certain death against a superior force of Apaches, and to bring Poncelli and anyone who conspired with him to justice."

"I can see that you had to pretend ignorance and innocence immediately after the rape and murder. But given the horror of the situation, how did you manage? You must be superhuman!"

"I had a full day to compose myself while the body was lying in state and while Father Andrés sent for you to investigate the crime—and the soldiers, especially the sergeant, were blaming the priest. By the time I spoke to you after the funeral, I was wearing a mask of blamelessness."

"A very convincing one, too."

"But it wasn't fully in place the first morning after I'd killed the captain. Father Andrés took me into his garden, poor soul, to show me his flowers. He stumbled over the body, and I had to pretend…. Actually, it was no pretext. I was horrified to see that man transformed into a livid corpse with flies all over his head—and I had done that! I screamed."

"But you had to go on to Mátape, to find out how the Jesuits were involved in your husband's death. At the time, you didn't know about Vice-Provincial Poncelli."

"Only that my husband had escorted him and his mule train."

"You should know, Beatriz, that Luca Poncelli has paid his debt. He died on our torturous way here, while we were delayed for nine months in Guaymas. He confessed to me. His soul, too, was in an agony of guilt. May he rest in peace. And now, my dear, I pray that the Lord will grant you his peace as well.

"I pray that he will. And now, Father Ygnacio, *I confess to Almighty God and to you, Father, that I have sinned….*"

I completed my confession, my quick analysis of the sins I had committed since my arrival at Ures, almost three years ago. "*For these sins and those of my past life, I am deeply sorry.*"

Ygnacio looked thoughtful, his head on one side. "You were looking at that ship, the Santa Catalina, weren't you?"

"Yes, Father. Antonio and I are sailing to Galicia. He wants to introduce me to his family."

"Then this is what I want you to do as penance. Make a pilgrimage across Spain to the sanctuary of Monserrat in Cataluña. That's where the Jesuits' patron saint, Ignatius, first went to dedicate himself to a life of abstinence and service. I'm named for him, since I was born on his feast day, 31 July. Pray there. Then visit the cave in Manresa where he did penance. Pray there, too, and ask God's forgiveness. I believe you will find peace if you do as I suggest."

I recited the Act of Contrition, and he absolved and blessed me. We made the sign of the Cross together.

"*Give thanks to the Lord for he is good,*" he said.

"*For his mercy endureth forever,*" I replied.

Then we rose and turned toward the others, Antonio waiting with them. I clutched Ygnacio's hands, torn, scarred, dirty and manacled as they were. "Vaya con Dios, Ygnacio. I shall never forget you."

"Nor I you."

He nodded in the sergeant's direction, to signal that our session was at an end. The sergeant, impatient with the delay, gave the order to continue the march. Ygnacio never turned his head, but boarded the *Aventurier* with the rest. He looked my way as they climbed the gangplank, stumbling as he stepped over the side to enter the ship. Then he was gone. Forever.

੩੦੦੪

We were marched to the dock in chains as if we were desperate criminals who would attempt to escape. We were a miserable sight, the twenty-seven that remained of us, the ragged remnant of the joyful troop who had come with such high purpose and spiritual enthusiasm to New Spain. It was good to be out in the open air after ten days in that filthy, vermin-infested inn on short and half-spoiled rations. But now we felt God's blessed sunshine on our faces and a fresh breeze from the Gulf. Our guard felt it too, and marched us along at a good clip, which some of my brothers were finding hard to match. I had weathered our hardships a little better than most, although I was a rack of bones. Still, I was swinging along, chafing only at the chains on my wrists that forced me to curtail my arm movements to match those of the men on either side.

Two tall ships stood in the harbor. I noticed a handsome couple strolling towards the nearest one. The smartly dressed gentleman was pointing at the ship and bending his head to talk to the elegant lady on his arm. And then my eyes focused entirely on her. I knew that gait, that lift of the head, that graceful movement of the arm. It was Beatriz. They had seen us and turned their heads in our direction. Then, I saw her stop her companion. She looked directly at me. Beneath the grime, behind the matted beard and long hair, despite the dirty and tattered robe barely covering my skeletal body, she knew me.

The gentleman walked purposefully toward us, Beatriz still on his arm. Then he confronted the sergeant and gave his name, requesting that he be allowed to speak to one of us. So this was Lieutenant Governor Antonio Figueroa, the man who had saved Andrés Michel's life! He came around to my row, and addressed me.

"I presume you are Father Ygnacio." I nodded confirmation. "I believe my wife would like to speak to you."

My heart skipped a beat with a crushed sensation. His wife! Then I rallied. Why, dear God, should I feel such an emotion, I, a Jesuit priest and missionary? I was glad for her; it was a wonderful solution for her troubles, an end to her grief.

She came to me as her husband, the lieutenant governor, moved away. Then she asked me if I remembered her. We chatted for a moment, and I congratulated her on her marriage. She offered me her help. Vain hope! And then she requested that I hear her confession. The sergeant was in a hurry to be rid of us, but the lieutenant governor's authority persuaded him, and he unchained me from my brothers.

Now I learned, at last, how the murder happened, how the captain attacked and robbed Beatriz of her dignity as a human being, tearing her from her prayers, manhandling and striking her, crushing her mouth with his lascivious lips, violating and abandoning her "like a slab of meat," as she put it. She was prevented from killing in self defense, but killed to save her honor, and I knew honor was supremely important to a Spaniard. We condone a murder committed in self-defense. Was not this a form of defense—of her dignity, her worth as a person equal to any other, including any man, in the eyes of God?

I absolved her and we parted with dignity. Our group was marched quickly to the gangplank of the *Aventurier*, where we turned to board the ship. I could see the two of them, Lieutenant Governor Antonio Figueroa and Beatriz—my Beatriz, God forgive me!—standing there, watching us climb. I kept her in sight as long as I could, tripping on the side of the ship as I stepped into the vessel.

They took us below to our 'quarters'—coffin-like cubicles where hammocks were strung close together, one above the other—and locked us in. I suspected this ship had been used for the slave trade. I lay down on my hammock, fighting to control the jumble of emotions that still overwhelmed me, thoughts of all we'd been through crowding my mind.

We sailed to Havana where the ship anchored for a few more weeks. Governor Bucareli did not allow us to come ashore, and only rarely were we permitted to stretch our legs on deck. At last, we weighed anchor and arrived at Cádiz on 12 July 1769, over three months after leaving Veracruz.

೮೦೦೮

I stare out the window of our former hospice, now our prison, in Puerto de Santa María. We are packed into this formerly beautiful building thirty, forty to a room. I think of Wolfgang and count him lucky to have been spared further indignities, further suffering. Our fate is uncertain, but we know that we German speakers who served in Sonora have been singled out as special traitors to His Majesty, Carlos III. It is unclear what our crimes are supposed to be—I am due for interrogation in an hour. Perhaps I will find out. But no matter what happens now, no matter how black the immediate future, with the help of my God and Savior, I will survive to serve him once again. I will live to bear witness to our story, honoring Wolfgang's last request. Yes, by His Grace I will live, Wolfgang, by His Grace.

About the author

After retiring from academic life in 1999, she was freed to devote herself to writing fiction, she produced eleven novels, ranging from fantasy to historical romance and mystery. Nine are currently in print: two historical novels about the French Renaissance, one, a romance, published in France in French translation, and the other, a life of the publisher Etienne Dolet. Books about the Southwest include three historical novels, one about the missions of San Antonio in 1731, the second about the expedition from Mexico up the Rio Grande in 1581, forty years after Coronado, and the third about the life of a young Tejana, born in 1814 in Bexar de San Antonio, who was twenty-two years old at the time of the Alamo Battle. In addition, four historical mysteries, featuring the eighteenth-century Jesuit missionary Fr. Ignaz (Ygnacio) Pfefferkorn, his activity in Sonora, his imprisonment in Spain, and his return home to Germany. Three of the Pfefferkorn novels are available in Spanish translation, the fourth in German translation.

A departure from her historical novels is the fantasy-thriller *Anselm, a Metamorphosis.* In this novel, she takes seriously the philosopher René Descartes' proposition that mind and body are completely separable, since he believed mind and soul to be synonymous and therefore immortal. *Anselm* works out the possible consequences of this theory in a novel that examines the psychological and theological implications, while remaining a heart-pounding page-turner.

Florence's favorite animals are horses—an intense love affair over many years—and cats, her constant companions. She enjoys music, travel, hiking, biking, gardening, riding, and swimming. Most of all, she enjoys the friendship of like souls and their lively conversation.

Glossary

Agave – the century plant, also known as the **maguey**. It was used by the Pimas for healing wounds and infections. It produces a valuable fiber and its juice is fermented to produce **pulque**.

Alguacil – constable, the chief law-enforcement officer among the natives at a mission.

Apache – Originally Plains Indians, this aggressive tribe moved into the areas now known as Texas, New Mexico, Arizona, and northern Mexico around the time Cortez invaded Mexico.

Cholla – a jointed cactus with many branches, no leaves and many spines that grows to a height of around four feet. Buds and tender joints are edible and good, roasted in pits lined with seepweed. Cholla is especially useful, since it can be gathered year-round, though naturally better when young and tender.

Cilantro – coriander leaves.

Conejo – rabbit

Eudebe – a tribe of Indians in north central Sonora that were particularly receptive to European religion and culture. The tribe is now extinct, having been decimated by white man's diseases.

Gobernador – literally, governor. The chief Indian officer in a mission, who had responsibility for his people. He was next in command after the missionary.

Maguey – See agave.

Marrano – The Spanish name for someone secretly practicing Judaism.

Mesquite – a woody plant that grows in the form of a low, wide-spreading bush, a low tree, or, in wetter climates, a tree reaching heights of eight to ten meters.

It belongs to the legume family and produces beans
that are edible in all stages. As tender young beans,
they are bundled and baked or roasted with meat; as
more mature beans but still green, they are crushed
in a mortar and cooked in a pot; as fully ripe and
dried beans they are soaked, boiled, and crushed to
extract their sweet juices, used for atole (a sweet
drink) or for syrup. Mesquite meal is made into
sweet rolls and round cakes. When burned, mesquite
wood lends a savory flavor to smoked meats.

Mestizo – a person of mixed Spanish and Indian heritage.

Nopales or nopalitos – the tender young pads of the prickly
pear. These are cleaned of their spines, sliced and
cooked either as part of a stew or breaded and fried
with tomatoes as a side dish similar to okra with
which they share a similar texture. The flavor is dis-
tinctive and slightly sour, indicating that they are a
good source of vitamin C.

Ocotillo – a cactus consisting of long, slender branches
all springing from its base. It is thorny and in dry
weather has no leaves. In wet weather and in spring
it sprouts tiny, narrow leaves and on the ends of
the stalks, bright, China-red, flame-like flowers. It is
known as candlewood and candle of the Lord.

Olla – a large clay jar or urn.

Opata – a tribe of Indians in north-central Sonora, occupying
roughly the same area as the Eudebe tribe. They, too,
were eager to learn Western religion and customs.
They also were decimated by European diseases and
are now extinct or intermarried with other tribes.

Organ pipe cactus - The second largest cactus next to the
Saguaro, growing as tall as 23 feet. Instead of having
a central stem, however, a cluster of 5 to 20 slender
branches grow from a point at ground level and

curve gracefully upward. These water-storing trunks
are about 6 inches in diameter with deep-green,
rounded ribs. Fruits lose their spines at maturity,
opening to display edible, red pulp. This fruit has
provided a food source to Native Americans for centuries. The pulp can be eaten as is, made into jelly or
fermented into a beverage.

Piloncillo – Piloncillo is made from pure, unrefined sugar
that is pressed into a cake or cone shape. It tastes
very similar to brown sugar with a molasses flavor
(even though it does not contain molasses) and it can
substitute for anything that calls for brown sugar. Its
name means "little pylon" because of its shape.

Pima – a tribe of Indians occupying much of Sinaloa and Sonora. They were hunter-gatherers, and consented to
come to the Jesuits' missions, although they were less
eager to accept European ways than the Eudebe and
Opata tribes. The "Pima Revolt" of 1751 was a local
uprising that took the lives of two Jesuits and many
settlers, and wounded many. It was put down by
Captain José Díaz del Carpio in March 1752.

Pinole – cornmeal mush or an aromatic chia powder sometimes mixed with chocolate, often used with fruit or
nuts—an ideal trail food, since it rarely spoils.

Piñon nuts – pine nuts.

Pulque - fermented juice of the maguey, varying in alcoholic
content, usually comparing roughly with Mexican
beer.

Saguaro – the giant cactus usually associated with Arizona
desert landscapes. It produces a large and delicious
fruit containing red pulp and black seeds that can be
eaten raw. The sweet pulp is useful to produce juice,
jam, jelly, and when fermented, wine. The seeds are
parched and ground to form a pasty meal that can

be formed into cakes and eaten at once or stored for later use. The meal can be mixed with other ingredients such as wheat flour, cornmeal, chia seed, etc., to make various highly nutritious treats.

Seri – a tribe of warlike Indians who occupied the same general area as the Pimas. They attacked other tribes, settlers and missions, and used deadly poison-tipped arrows.

Tilma – a poncho-shaped cape made of cactus fiber, usually yucca.

Topil – a native officer in charge of guest accommodations at a mission.

Torote – a tree native to Sonora, its slick, brown trunk and branches armored with hundreds of squat, black-tipped thorns. Only a worm could climb it unharmed.

Tortillas – unleavened bread made of wheat or corn flour and water. The finished tortilla resembles a French crêpe, with a very different flavor and texture.

Tunas – the ripe, sweet fruit of the nopal or prickly pear, of the cholla, the organ pipe, or of the saguaro. These are used as sources of sugar, as dessert fruit, or as sources of juice to make atole (a sweet drink). The juice can also be boiled down to make syrup or jelly; fermented, it makes an acceptable wine.

Historical Appendix

Ignaz (Ygnacio) Pfefferkorn, S.J., Life and Career

Father Ignaz, a real person, was born in Mannheim-am-Neckar, Germany, on July 31, 1725 (Saint Ignatius of Loyola's feast day). His father, a highly placed official in Mannheim, died when he was eleven, his mother when he was 14. At age 17, he entered the Jesuit novitiate in Trier. As a scholastic, he taught classical languages and rhetoric at the university in Koblenz, being ordained a priest early in 1755. He set out almost at once for the New World, traveling with three companions, Bernhard Middendorf, S.J., Michael Gerstner, S.J., and Joseph Och, S.J. They crossed Italy to Genoa, sailed around Gibraltar, and awaited a ship to take them to New Spain in the Puerto de Santa María, the port that serves Cádiz.

They were there when the huge earthquake and tidal wave of 1 November 1755 struck. Their hospice building, set back from the ocean, was damaged but not destroyed. The tidal wave did it relatively little harm, although many in Cádiz drowned. The group of young Jesuits bound for the New World forced a reluctant captain to set sail on Christmas Day, 1755. They landed first at Havana, Cuba, then at Veracruz, where they were met by the Governor of Sonora, José Tienda de Cuervo, and their Jesuit colleagues from the College there.

The four friends traveled by horse and mule-back, first to Mexico City, then with many adventures on to Sonora, where they were assigned to serve at four different missions. Ignaz was sent first to the farthest northwestern point in Sonora (northwestern Mexico), a mission called Sonóita. But the church and rectory had been destroyed in the Pima Revolt of 1751; its missionary, Father Enrique Ruhen, S.J., martyred. Ignaz and his escort of soldiers, fearing for their lives, withdrew to Atí (now Atil) Mission, where he served for five years with great success. He was transferred to Guevavi Mission in what is now Arizona because of ill health, but remained there only two years. He last served in Cucurpe Mission, where he had his greatest success with the native population.

His arrest came in August 1767, followed by the horrors narrated in this work. He and a remnant of his companions arrived at Puerto de Santa María in July, 1769. Ignaz was held prisoner there for six years, accused, along with the other non-Spanish Sonora Jesuits, of treason against His Majesty, Carlos III. The official reason given for their indefinite imprisonment was that they knew and would betray state secrets. But the only state secrets they knew were the locations and operations of their missions. The supposedly missing gold of the Sonora mines and pearls of California provided unofficial motives for their detention and interrogation.

Since the Jesuit prisoners at Puerto de Santa María had opportunities to talk among themselves, the Royal Council was persuaded that it would be prudent to separate the 'dangerous conspirators' by sending them to remote and isolated monasteries. Ignaz was moved in 1775, two years after the total suppression of the Society of Jesus by Pope Clement XIV, to Nuestra Señora de la Caridad Monastery near Ciudad Rodrigo, west of Salamanca. He remained there for two years.

Once his sister, Isabella Berntges, found out where he was, she persuaded the Elector of Cologne to begin negotiations for his release with King Carlos III and the Spanish Royal Council. Fr. Pfefferkorn was freed on Christmas Eve, 1777, taken by coach to Irún on the border between France and Spain, and dropped there. He made his way in the dead of winter on foot back to the Rhineland where he rejoined his sister and her family.

Ignaz was fifty-two when he was released from prison after eleven years as a missionary and more than ten in captivity. During the remaining twenty years, he wrote a massive three-volume work about the fauna, flora, geology and geography of Sonora. Two volumes remain to us, the third has been lost. Ignaz died at age 73 on June 16, 1798, and was buried in St. Servatius Church cemetery in Siegburg.

Truth and Fiction

The murder of Captain Nicolás Xavier Cuevas is fiction, as are the consequent actions. Doña Beatriz and Lieutenant Governor Antonio Figueroa are also figments of my imagination, as is the enigmatic but likeable Wolfgang Wegner and the young Jesuits from Mátape (Ramón Bernardo Zapata, Bendito Ortiz and Enrique Ortuña). The villainous vice-provincial, Luca Poncelli, who embodies everything a Jesuit is NOT supposed to be and do, is also my creation. The mission Indians, while fictional as individuals, are portrayed, along with their internal governance and living quarters, as Fathers Johann Nentwig, Joseph Och and Ignaz Pfefferkorn describe them in their works. Similarly, the Apaches are characterized very much as Nentwig and David Roberts depict them in their books. Nentwig in *Rudo Ensayo* calls them *the enemy*, and Roberts, although sympathetic to the Apaches, does not hide their considerable flaws in *Once They Moved Like the Wind.*

Otherwise, I depict the real world of two centuries ago, where only horses, mules and oxen provided transportation, a world without supermarkets or general stores, where all food came from field or garden, where all cooking was done over wood fires. I have described cooking methods, available foods, and likely menus at the missions. Material to make the clothing worn daily came from far-away cities or was woven from cotton or wool. In that world, household furniture was painstakingly brought overland by oxcart or made with whatever tools one had brought from the Old Country, from the nearest (400-mile distant) city, or had created in a blacksmith forge. Paper was a precious rarity and mail service consisted of occasional mule drivers who brought supplies from population centers or, perhaps it was carried by Indian runners or special couriers, maybe by the Jesuit Fathers themselves. Water, except along rivers and where wells had been dug, was a rare and precious commodity; daily bathing and shaving was done in a pan or basin of cold water or once a week in a wooden tub, with homemade soap made of lard and ashes. There was no plumbing, and oil lamps, although in limited use in cities, were not available at the missions, for lack of oil. Hence, candles provided lighting at night.

I describe the missions as I have seen them and as I reconstruct their likely appearance in the 18th century along with their settings. Sonora landscape varies from deserts with saguaro, cholla and prickly pear cacti, to higher elevations with high desert vegetation—mesquite and ocotillo, to the foothills and the mountains with their live oaks, junipers and virgin pines. In low lying areas near the rivers one may find mini-tropical jungles with vines, ferns, palm and fig trees; the rivers are lined with sycamores, cottonwoods and willow shrubs. The vertical graveyard in the Mababi Mountains is fictional, but it might just be up there somewhere—few people even now know every inch of that wilderness. The Mababi boulder field is modeled on the more northerly one in the Dragoon Mountains of today's Arizona.

All the missionaries are historical except those specified above. Incidents recounted in the plot not directly connected with the murder are also historical. For example, Father

Carlos Rojas describes himself in his unpublished letters to the Provincial, Francisco Zevallos (nowadays spelled Ceballos) just as I portrayed him. He explains to his superior how he gets around to inspect the missions, on horseback only during flood season and otherwise by two-wheeled buggy. The story of Father Albarrán's placement in Cuquiárachi and his death from the shock the Apaches gave him is also taken almost word for word from a letter by Rojas. And he really does spell Ignaz' name 'Phapheserkorn'!

I show the other missionaries in their proper settings—as far as I have been able to determine them—although there may have been last-minute shifts. Bartolomé Saenz served at Cuquiárachi, Andrés Michel at Ures, Jacobo Sedelmeyer at Mátape, etc. At the time, according to Rojas, Ignaz was maintaining two missions: Cucurpe and Opodepe, because of Father Rector Francisco Joseph Loaiza's sudden death.

Expulsion of the Jesuits

Most of all, I want the reader to know more about a traumatic episode that blots the history of the West, a stark example of man's basest inhumanity to man, emanating from ideas current during the 'Age of Reason.' The fate of the Sonora Jesuits dramatizes a single episode in the expulsion of all Jesuits from Spain and its colonies in 1767, followed by suppression of the entire Society of Jesus in 1773 by secular and religious forces, including the Church of Rome itself. As one of the most shocking events of the eighteenth century, it is also one of the least known and studied. Its story forms an important additional dimension of my book.

Therefore, the timing of the arrests in Sonora, the manner in which the priests were brought together at Mátape, held there, then marched to Guaymas, what happened at Guaymas, the ship voyage of three months down to San Blas and the Death March to Guadalajara are as factual as I could make those events. Exceptions are the presence of fictional Luca Poncelli and fictional Wolfgang Wegner, and their respective death scenes.

The three-volume work Ignaz Pfefferkorn wrote in his retirement—*A Description of the Province of Sonora*—covered his observations as a missionary and prisoner. Two volumes still exist and have been translated into English. A third volume containing his personal experience of expulsion and imprisonment as well as his difficult mid-winter trek across France and back to the Rhineland has been lost. In its absence I have pieced together events from Bernhard Middendorf's fragmented account, Joseph Och's report, from published treatises and archival records.

Documents at Tumacácori National Park, Arizona, in the Archivo Histórico de Hacienda in Mexico City, and in the Archive of Ethnohistory at the Arizona State Museum, University of Arizona, Tucson, attest that Governor Pineda forwarded orders from the Royal Visitor José de Gálvez regarding the arrest and expulsion of the Jesuits in his province on July 14, 1767. These were to be read to the assembled priests on July 24 and put into effect on July 25. However, due to distance and difficulty of travel, there were many delays. For example, Ignaz wrote to Carlos Rojas on July 31 with no mention (and probably no knowledge) of the expulsion. He was arrested on August 18, 1767 by Captain Juan Bautista de Anza, who also arrested Andrés Michel around that date.

The army personnel in Sonora ordered to carry out the Royal Visitor's orders did so with extreme reluctance and as mercifully as they could. Captain Bernardo de Urrea was a close friend of Fathers Nicolás Perera, Bartolomé Saenz, and Carlos Rojas, since the priests had performed baptisms,

    Florence Byham Weinberg

marriages and burials for him and his family. Whereas the governor's orders were to leave the sick and aged Jesuits behind to die, Captain Juan de Anza transported elderly Nicolás Perera and ailing Juan Nentwig at least as far as San José de los Pimas and perhaps all the way to Guaymas. The delay at Mátape was caused by Anza, who took as long as needed to transport the two men on stretchers without unduly stressing them. Captain José Bergosa, in command of the column of expelled Jesuits from Mátape to San José de los Pimas, was so distraught that he said he "had no stomach for deceit" and hoped he would never be called upon again for "so disgusting a task." The young Captain José Antonio de Vildósola was as disturbed as the others and almost as outspoken.

At Guaymas, Bernhard Middendorf describes the brackish, stinking, tepid well water, the spoiled, wormy rations and the plague of insects of all sorts. Ignaz' discovery of clams, oysters, crabs and seaweed and his efforts to help feed his starving brothers are fictional, but something of the sort must have happened, else those 51 men would surely have died of scurvy and other starvation-related diseases over a period of nine months. Middendorf also describes their three-month ordeal during the sea voyage from Guaymas to San Blas. Gerard Decorme brings together Middendorf's account and information from other sources in describing the Death March from San Blas to Guadalajara. The circumstances of the wait in Veracruz—the squalor and the deaths from yellow fever—are drawn from Joseph Och's eyewitness account.

The following Sonora Jesuits arrived on the *Aventurier* at Puerto de Santa María from Veracruz and Havana in July 1769. These are the original spellings in an unpublished document from the Archivo Histórico Nacional in Madrid (see bibliography):

Ultramarinos… <u>Misiones de Sonora</u>:
1. El P. Joseph Garrucho
2. P. Carlos de Rojas
3. P. Alonso Espinosa
4. P. Luis Vivas
5. P. Joseph Neve
6. P. Miguel Almela
7. P. Benito Romeo
8. P. Antonio de Castro
9. P. Jacobo Seddermeyr
10. P. Custodio Ximeno
11. P. Francisco Paver
12. P. Joseph Roldan
13. P. Miguel Gerstner
14. P. Xavier Gonzalez
15. P. Andres Michel
16. P. Diego Joseph Barreda
17. P. Bernardo Middendorff
18. P. Franco Yta
19. P. Vicente Ruvio
20. P. Ygnacio Pffercon
21. P. Joseph Juan Texedor.

Twenty-seven embarked; twenty-one landed to be counted by the purser or jailor. Six more of the 51 missionaries who were arrested in Sonora must have died in transit.

A brief history of the Jesuits and a summary of events leading up to their expulsion from Spain and its colonies might help the reader understand the process leading to the disaster.

Bare bones history of the Jesuits

A Spanish former military man, Ignatius of Loyola, later sainted, founded the Society in 1539, its main purpose to establish missions and reform European education. Pope Paul III confirmed the new Society in 1540. It increased rapidly in size and influence, establishing missions in Goa, Hindustan, China, and widely in both North and South America. Its schools and colleges were models of reformed educational methods. It came to wield great power and influence within the Church as well as in the secular realm, in politics and trade as well as in education. Its success as well as its excesses led to its expulsion from Portugal in 1759. In France, it was suppressed in 1764 and expelled in 1767. The Spanish King Carlos III followed suit, expelling the Society from Spain and all its dependencies in 1767. Pope Clement XIV suppressed the Society altogether in 1773. It was reinstated in 1814.

Events and attitudes leading up to the Expulsion

The eighteenth century was the period of the Enlightenment, when the French 'Philosophes,' the Encyclopedists Voltaire, Diderot, D'Alembert and Rousseau set out to correct what they considered to be centuries-old 'abuses and superstitions'—chief among them, the Christian religion. The main target was the Church of Rome, and within the Church, the order most active and visible in European society through its missions, schools, colleges and universities: the Society of Jesus.

Prime ministers and other secular administrators in the various European courts were partisans of the new theories and envious of the influence exercised by Jesuit confessors to royal persons. The Marqués de Pombal in Portugal, the Marquis de Choiseul in France and the Conde de Aranda in Spain, all prime ministers, were heavily influential in bringing about the expulsion of the Jesuits from their respective countries.

Portugal was the first to expel its Jesuits, due to the efforts of Pombal. He published libelous tracts alleging the fabulous wealth of the missions and their plotting against the royal person. Using an assassination attempt against King Joseph I as an excuse, he expelled the Society from Portugal and seized its property. The Jesuits were shipped in great misery to the Papal States and all their schools and universities closed.

In France, the Jesuits were suppressed by royal edict of King Louis XV as a consequence of the speculation and bankruptcy of Father Lavalette, Jesuit Superior in Martinique, who defaulted on a 2,400,000 franc loan. The father general in Rome, Lorenzo Ricci, refused to make good on the debt, which infuriated His Majesty. Also, Madame de Pompadour, the king's mistress, had been refused absolution by her Jesuit confessor, which hardened the king's attitude towards the Society. They were evicted from France in 1767.

In Spain, Aranda along with the Justice Minister Manuel de Roda and the Minister of Finance, Pedro Rodríguez de Campomanes, persuaded King Carlos III to form a secret tribunal. The conspirators drew up the famous Decree of 27 February 1767 that expelled and ultimately destroyed the Company of Jesus. The king was persuaded that the Jesuits had plotted to assassinate him and would continue to do so as long as they existed, that they were sworn enemies of the House of Bourbon, that they had committed untold crimes against the State and against Christianity itself, and that their *Constitutions* were contrary to all rights, both human and divine.

On the night of April 2, 1767, the king's order of expulsion was carried out simultaneously in all of Spain. Approximately 6,000 Jesuits were arrested, their houses, universities and colleges seized, rendering them propertyless, homeless, stateless exiles. They were launched on the Mediterranean Sea on any ship or boat that could float, bound for Civitavecchia, the port of Rome, but the Pope closed the port against them. Thousands of priests and brothers spent months on vessels wandering from closed port to closed port as they died of starvation and scurvy. Corsica received the survivors, but they continued to die there for want of food and medical treatment. Eventually, a remnant was allowed to cross through the less hostile states of Italy. A number of the surviving Spanish and Mexican Jesuits (about 397) remained in Italy near Bologna, while other nationalities returned to their homes in various European countries. They also took refuge in Frederick the Great's Lutheran Prussia and in Catherine the Great's Eastern Orthodox Russia, where they were put to work teaching in schools and universities.

In 1769, Pope Clement XIII died after trying to take the Jesuits' part. His successor, Clement XIV, tried to lessen the impact but bowed to ecclesiastical and secular political pressure. He suppressed the Society altogether in 1773. Before expulsion and suppression, The Society had 41 provinces, 22,589 members, of whom 11,295 were priests. Father General Ricci died in prison in Rome in the Castel Sant'Angelo under the pontificate of Pius VI.

The Society was reinstated in 1814, after which it resumed its missionary labors and founded new schools, colleges and universities, including some of the great universities in North America.

Final Speculations

From early on, opinions on the Society of Jesus were sharply divided. Partisans were enthusiastic, but enemies were virulent and in the end violent. Protestants hated the Jesuits, since Pope Paul III had instated the Society in order to stem the tide of the Reformation. Jesuit disciples of St. Ignatius were dominant figures at the Council of Trent that determined the direction of the Church of Rome for four centuries. The Roman Church, both the regular clergy and the older orders—Benedictines, Franciscans, and especially the Dominicans—viewed the Jesuits with suspicion because they were new, untried, enjoyed unusual privileges and immediate success. They were envied for their freedom to move about in society. All other orders were based in convents and monasteries and were obliged to sing the Hours and to wear peculiar clothing, something the Jesuits escaped doing. The Dominicans accused them of heresy and repeatedly tried to bring them before the Inquisition.

A mere seventy-two years after the Society's inception, a forgery was published in Krakow, the *Monita Secreta*, purporting to be official Jesuit advice to the Society's members. The treatise outlines stealthy ways of seizing power in both church and state by becoming confessors of wealthy families and of royalty, of creeping into households by ingratiating themselves with rich and foolish widows, etc., and whispering poison into willing ears. The entire tract reeks of ambition, craft, and unscrupulousness. It was widely published, widely believed. Its intent and effect were similar to the smear against the Jews called *The Protocols of the Elders of Zion*.

Secular power centers watched with growing apprehension as Ignatius' innovative Society appealed to wealthy and powerful families wanting to place their sons in ecclesiastical positions but who did not want them confined to monasteries. Their boys had been brought up taking their family's power politics or commercial success for granted, and they continued to exercise the skills they had learned, even though such behavior was strictly against Ignatian rules.

The Society was a source of continuous political agitation as well, for example in supporting the Wars of Religion in France until Henry IV promulgated the Edict of Nantes that guaranteed freedom of religion. They later influenced Louis XIV to revoke the Edict of Nantes, resulting in the expulsion of the Huguenots from France. They waged a fierce battle against Jansenism, which ended with the razing of Port Royal, Jansenism's center. In Queen Elizabeth I's England, many young Jesuits secretly entered the country from France to minister to the suppressed (and supposedly abolished) Catholic community. When these priests were discovered and arrested, most were executed in public spectacles by drawing and quartering, and their martyrdom contributed to continuing religious unrest in the kingdom.

In Martinique, Father Lavalette's commercial enterprise exemplified the sort of activity practiced by a few sons of powerful families. Misbehavior was limited to a small number, but those few occupied powerful and important positions, hence the reputation of all Jesuits was damaged, including that of the ones faithfully carrying out their ministries.

In New Spain, the Jesuits ran a remarkably clean operation, though King Carlos III was persuaded that corruption and skullduggery reigned supreme there as well. The Royal Visitor, José de Gálvez, was sent to root out such misdeeds. Inspection teams like the one dispatched to examine Father Andrés Michel's books might well have existed.

Because of their many beneficial activities, not only in missions and classrooms, but also in churches and hospitals, the Jesuits were well loved by the people, and the order of expulsion came as a total shock. The population of Durango reacted to the expulsion much as I report it in this novel. Such reactions occurred in many towns and cities. The people resisted the order and wept at the loss of their beloved priests and benefactors. Some, like the populace of San Luís Potosí, revolted against His Majesty's troops and were violently and cruelly put down by order of Gálvez. Many were executed.

No such prominent criminal figure as my fictitious Father Luca Poncelli ever existed among the Jesuits of New Spain. However, he typifies the sort of activity the new Viceroy de Croix and Royal Visitor Gálvez were sent to discover and root out.

The question remains: once they were arrested and dispossessed, why were the Jesuits so harshly treated? In looking back over history, a pattern of human behavior emerges. Any group singled out by race, religion, custom, or disease (such as the lepers of old), was isolated and abused. They were suspected of causing the ills of the moment (as the medieval Jews were accused of causing the Black Plague), confined to ghettos, expelled or even killed. Through the centuries, we see many examples: in the Middle Ages, the Jews were exiled or locked in their synagogues and burned; the Jesuits were exiled, starved, imprisoned and killed in the eighteenth century; in the twentieth, the Turks massacred the Armenians, and the Nazis slaughtered many millions of Jews, gypsies, homosexuals, and the mentally deficient or deformed. 'Ethnic cleansing,' a new term, was invented to whitewash mass murder of Albanians in Bosnia by Serbs. This massive atrocity took place recently enough that most of us remember it. Similar rapes, tortures and massacres have taken and are taking place in Africa at the present moment.

The worst abuses have been committed by people who believed most fervently that they were acting for the benefit of community, king, country, or God. Innocent American

Muslim families are, as I write this, enduring discrimination, abuse and death threats.

To quote a song from the era of the Viet Nam War with a slight variation: "When will we ever learn? *When will we ever learn?"*

Minor Supporting Characters

The following are persons whose roles in the story are minor, but who are worth mentioning. Those names preceded by an asterisk are historical:

Minor supporters:

*Juan Bautista de Anza, Captain;
*José Bergosa, Captain;
Enrique Borraquín, Businessman in Durango;
*Antonio María de Bucareli, Governor of Cuba;
*Carlos Francisco de Croix Viceroy of Mexico;
Pasquale and Carlotta Domenico, Businesspeople in Durango;
Lieutenant Arturo Echegaray, Beatriz' Escort to the Birthday Ball;
Mariano Fernández, Judge in Durango;
*José de Gálvez y Gallardo, Royal Visitor (Inspector) Appointed by King Carlos III;
García y Pacheco, Businessmen in Durango;
Fr. Ernesto Hidalgo, Bishop of Durango;
Patricia O'Meara, Rancher's Daughter, Guevavi;
Private Ernesto Parral, Guard at Guaymas;
*Juan Claudio de Pineda, Governor of Sonora;
*Francisco Posadas, Rancher near Tepic;
Private Atanacio Rivas, Guard at Guaymas;
*Manuel Rivero, Governor of Nayarit;
*José Antonio de Vildósola, Captain

Minor Supporters (Jesuit):

*Fr. Manuel Aguirre, S.J., Father Visitor and Missionary at Bacadeguatzi;
*Fr. Joseph Manuel Albarrán, S.J., Missionary at Cuquiárachi;
*Fr. Antonio Castro, S.J., Former Missionary at San Xavier del Bac;
*Fr. Pedro Díaz, S.J., Young Missionary at Atí;
*Fr. Rafael Díez, S.J., Missionary at Guevavi;
*Fr. Alfonso Espinosa, S.J., Missionary at San Xavier del Bac;
*Fr. Joseph Garrucho, S.J., Missionary at Oposura;
*Fr. Michael (Miguel) Gerstner, S.J., Friend of Fr. Ygnacio;
*Fr. Ignacio González, S.J., Missionary in Sinaloa;
*Eusebio Francisco Kino, S.J., Pioneer Jesuit Missionary in Sonora;
*Fr. Heinrich (Enrique) Kürtzel, S.J. Missionary at Movas;
*Fr. Pío Laguna, S.J., Missionary at Besaraca;
*Fr. Francisco Joseph Loaiza, S.J., Rector and Missionary at Opodepe;
* Fr. Bernhard (Bernardo) Middendorf, S.J., Friend of Fr. Ygnacio, Missionary at Movás;
*Fr. Johann (Juan) Nentwig, S.J., Missionary at Guasavas;
*Fr. Joseph Neve, S.J., Missionary assigned to San Xavier del Bac;
*Fr. Joseph Och, S.J., Friend of Fr. Ygnacio;
*Fr. José Palomino, S.J., Missionary in Huiribis, Sinaloa;
*Fr. Francisco Paris, S.J., Missionary at Ures;
*Fr. Francisco Xavier Pascua, S.J., Missionary at Bavispe;
*Fr. Nicolás Perera, S.J. Veteran Missionary of 42 years' service; Missionary at Aconchi;
*Fr. Alexander (Alejandro) Rapicani, S.J., Missionary at Batuco;

*Fr. Heinrich (Enrique) Ruhen, S.J., Martyred Missionary at Sonóita;
*Juan Lorenzo Salgado, S.J., Father Visitor;
*Fr. Philip (Felipe) Segessser, S.J., Former Missionary at Ures;
*Fr. Tomás Tello, S.J., Martyred Missionary at Caborca;
*Fr. Francisco Villaroya, S.J., Missionary at Banámichi;
*Fr. Francisco Zevallos. S.J., (modern spelling Ceballos), Provincial

Selected Bibliography

Primary sources:

Nentwig, Johann, S.J. *Rudo Ensayo: A Description of Sonora and Arizona in 1764,* Trans. Alberto Francisco Pradeau and Robert R. Rasmussen. Tucson: The University of Arizona Press, 1980.

Och, Joseph, S.J. *Missionary in Sonora: The Travel Reports of Joseph Och, S.J. 1755-1767,* Trans. Theodore E. Treutlein. San Francisco: California Historical Society, 1965.

Pfefferkorn, Ignaz, S.J. *Sonora: A Description of the Province,* Trans. Theodore E. Treutlein. Tucson: University of Arizona Press, 1989.

Unpublished letters on microfilm from Jesuit Fathers Carlos Rojas and Miguel Aguirre to the Provincial Francisco Zevallos (Ceballos) and from Governor Juan Claudio de Pineda to Padre Visitador Juan Lorenzo Salgado from the Archive of Ethnohistory of the Arizona State Museum, University of Arizona, Tucson, AZ.

Archivo Histórico Nacional, Madrid. Departamento: Clero, Legajo 777 #11. *Relación hecha, en virtud de Orden del Real y Supremo Consejo de Castilla en el Extraordinario; de todos los Regulares de la Compañía que han arribado ala Ciudad del Puerto de Santa María, procedentes de los Dominios Ultramarinos...* (List of surviving Jesuit missionaries arriving from Sonora in the Port of Santa María from Veracruz and Havana in late 1769.)

e-mail correspondence with Don Gárate at Tumacácori National Park.

Secondary Sources:

Burrus, Ernest J. and Zubillaga, Felix. *Noroeste de México: documentos sobre las misiones jesuíticas, 1600-1769.* México : Universidad Nacional Autónoma de México, 1986.

Clevenger, Ben. *The Far Side of the Sea: the Story of Kino and Manje in the Pimería.* Tucson, Jesuit Fathers of Southern Arizona, 2003.

Decorme, Gerard. *Obra de los jesuitas mexicanos durante la época colonial, 1572-1767.* México: Antigua Libraría Robredo de J. Porrúa e Hijos, 1941. 2 vol. (The first volume contains a detailed account of the expulsion from Sonora, including <u>excerpts from Bernhard Middendorf's and Joseph Och's chronicles</u>.)

Dunne, Peter Masten. *Pioneer Jesuits in Northern Mexico.* Westport, CT: Greenwood Press, 1979.

Mundwiler, J. B., "Deutsche Jesuiten in spanischen Gefängnissen im 18. Jahrhundert," *Zeitschrift für katholische Theologie,* XXVI: 4, 1902, pp. 623-672. (Contains excerpts from Bernhard Middendorf's chronicle.)

Naylor, Thomas H. and Charles W. Polzer. *Presidio and Militia on the Northern Frontier of New Spain: a Documentary History.* Tucson: University of Arizona Press, c1986-

Polzer, Charles W. *Rules and Precepts of the Jesuit Missions of Northwestern New Spain.* Tucson: University of Arizona Press, 1976.

Rico González, Victor. *Documentos sobre la Expulsión de los Jesuitas y Ocupación de sus Temporalidades en Nueva España (1772-1783).* México: Universidad

Nacional Autónoma de México, Instituto de
Historia, 1949.
Trueba, Alfonso. *Expulsión de los Jesuitas: o, El principio de
la revolución.* México: Ed. Campeador, 1954.

Notes

[1] Asterisks indicate that this person is historical.

[2] The first English version of his book, translated by Theodore E.
Treutlein, was published by the University of New Mexico Press
in 1949, and has been reprinted with a foreword by Bernard L.
Fontana in 1989. The original German edition came out in two
volumes: *Beschreibung der Landschaft Sonora*, (Köln: Langenscher
Buchhandlung, 1794-1795).

[3] The ruins of Los Santos Ángeles de Guevavi Mission are located
in what is now southern Arizona near Nogales, in Tumacácori
National Park.

[4] See Gerard Decorme, S.J., *La Obra de los Jesuitas Mexicanos
Durante la Época Colonial, 1572-1767* (México: Antigua Libraría
Robredo, 1941), pp. 272-275.

www.ingramcontent.com/pod-product-compliance
Lightning Source LLC
Chambersburg PA
CBHW071418200726
48294CB00002B/437